HIDDEN DANGER

She saw only shadows, nothing more—for another instant. A black mass—the evil ambiguity of that term disturbed her—the size of a man. Even men. Partly out of sight, round the bend at the end of the otherwise empty hallway . . .

Moving, Cheryl thought, into the faint illumination of the subdued ceiling fixtures—then *seeing* who it was, just at the second he headed toward her, *ran* toward her—

Rushed toward Cheryl, while she jabbed the key futiley at her front door lock; heard the pounding, masturbative pulse of rock music more with her half-stopped, tremblingly tensed body than with her sharp ears—

Realized then that she had selected the wrong key, just as he came racing up behind her, deadpan and dead-looking—and threw out his long, thin arms to grasp and embrace her . . .

Leisure Books by J. N. Williamson:

NOONSPELL
THE HOUNGAN
THE TULPA
THE LONGEST NIGHT
PREMONITION
PLAYMATES
WARDS OF ARMAGEDDON
BROTHERKIND
THE OFFSPRING
EVIL OFFSPRING
GHOST
THE RITUAL
QUEEN OF HELL

J.N. WILLIAMSON

LEISURE BOOKS NEW YORK CITY

For Mary
and with special affection for Gary A. Braunbeck,
adorable Alaina Marie Grisley, Dean R. Koontz,
Lori and Barbara, and David W. Taylor.

A LEISURE BOOK

Published by

Dorchester Publishing Co., Inc.
6 East 39th Street
New York, NY 10016

Printed in the United States of America

ACKNOWLEDGEMENTS

Appreciation for a variety of favors and helpful acts must be expressed to Jeannette M. Hopper and Cheryl Sayre and incredible *GAS Newsletter,* J.W. "Doc" Rogers, jovial editor John Littell, and the late Ray Peuchner.

Dead to the World

Part One

The Important Point

"Advertising is 85 percent confusion and 15 percent commission."

—Fred Allen, *Treadmill to Oblivion*

"You gotta get a gimmick if you want to get ahead."

—Veteran stripper in musical, *Gypsy*

"If you have an important point to make, don't try to be subtle. Use a pile driver."

—Sir Winston Churchill

"The more we identify with the abstractions of science . . . the more we detach ourselves from our own personal, concrete existence. Such an attitude . . . will eventually cancel us out altogether."

—Katherine Ramsland, Ph.D.
The Psychology of Horror and Fantasy Fiction

"Parents are the bones on which children cut their teeth."

—Peter Ustinov

"If evil has a meaning . . . it is insensitivity to the sufferings of others . . . the opposite of what we mean by civilization and evolution."

—Colin Wilson,
The Encyclopedia of Murder

1

Missing one hubcap and brazenly sporting another that had been hammered on, the seven-year-old Cadillac—cream colored in its distant youth, its room-width windshield now generously spackled with the corpses of slow-moving or suicidal bugs—sped lopsidedly toward the land of golden opportunity.

In more or less direct and characteristic rebuttal to the lusty wind and splotches of drab snow and ice stubbornly clinging to State Road 475, the driver dipped his right toe and coaxed a risky burst of further speed from the aging vehicle. His calendar had informed him it was spring now, and Wes Teagle had a fortune to make when they reached their destination.

The motley crew inside the Caddy—which had every conceivable right to the term, though each of them would have hotly denied it—comprised the following:

Two equal, boldly enterprising partners in a newly formed business of marginally honorable intent—one who was soon to turn forty and was unspokenly terrified by the prospect, and an ingenuously unabashed communist whom numerous ladies had imagined to resemble (depending upon their individual years) Clark Gable or Tom Selleck;

A petite brunette of gloriously Gallic extraction named Angelane Dubois O'Brien, whose frizzy hair was deemphasized and even turned fetching by wise eyes and the most improbable blue, the communist's live-in lover whom he worshiped even more than the memory of Karl Marx;

An ancient male with a basically collapsed torso and green eyes that could still sparkle or ignite on command, Wes's prodigal dad, so wispy after his long-delayed return home that the life-loving commie thought twice about inching the window down and thereby exposing the old fellow to the complementary late winter forces;

And a six-foot three, fair-haired former basketball star named Cheryl. Had Cheryl Conrad been a foot shorter, she might have been a cuddly blond version of Angelane O'Brien, but that would have rendered her fine hookshot of negligible value. Cheryl worshiped Wes, the non-communist and driver, but knew he hated tall women. Which meant, women taller than his own five-nine.

The entire crew looked forward avidly to the new phone room's first operation.

Far north of Indianapolis but just short of Carmel and far south of prosperous Zionsville, Stillwind Valley waited, supine between jeweled points of Hoosier richness, for just the sales exploitation it needed. Or so it seemed to the phone crew. Properly pitched and plundered, any diamond in the rough such as freshly reopened Stillwind Valley could become another many-faceted gem for its whole community to bask in. And all it would cost them, skimmed off the top by the Wesken Company, would be the customary ten percent.

Plus—it went without the saying of Weston Floyd Teagle or his laidback, oft-laid, and likeable partner Kenny Higgins—whatever wholly justified extras, bonuses, or inconspicuous ripoffs the boys and the rest of the phone room personnel might garner without inciting the suspicious natures of the town fathers. Wes generally called them "town daddies" because it made local authority figures seem less threatening or powerful. He also translated "suspicious natures" to "conservative ways," along with the other terms that were rather less complimentary.

Short-sighted and bespectacled, he glanced away from the residually rimey road into the backseat of the official Wesken Company car to where the father he scarcely knew was squeezed like an old Ipana tube between the disparate pair of women. "I never found nobody in Indiana who appreciated the last of us real entre-*pee*-noors," Wes said. He added, pointedly, "Acourse, I never been outta the state much or had your advantages. You find that t'be true in your world-wild travels, Ocie?"

The oldster paused. "People who lack a sales-minded disposition tend to *ob*-ject to the natural order of human life, Weston," he allowed. Ocie'd hesitated to determine just what his only acknowledged offspring had said. He'd come home to the south side of Indianapolis nearly twenty-five years after deserting wife and Wes for a free-wheeling selling career that had taken him to the forty-eight "*con*-tiguous United States plus Paris, France," and blunted Wes's resentment by being thinner, nicer and deafer than expected. "Folks don't *per*-ceive that their God-given obligation is t'buy what we salesmen sell."

"Salespersons," Cheryl Conrad said softly, glancing sideways at Ocie, and down.

"And they got t'be *per*-suaded at all costs, great or small," he continued as if the ex-basketball-playing blonde had not corrected his chauvinism. "Because that's what made our nation great and mighty in the eyes of the world, and that's *who* did it, too: the selfless and sacrificin' gents of the sales persuasion," Ocie blinked toward Cheryl. "Gents and ladies."

"It's 'entre*pre*neurs,'' Angelane said softly from the other side of the old man. She gave Wes Teagle a dynamite smile when he glanced sharply back at her, then almost shyly averted her gaze.

"Road, keep the peepers on the road, mate," the communist beside Wes also reproved him. He pronounced it *mite* and the word didn't seem incongruous when one sized up their Mutt and Jeff personas. He didn't mind Angelane smiling sweetly at Wes since they *were* mites—Kenny possessed an array of accents that he employed for the purpose of matching-up with the backgrounds of would-be customers, but he preferred doing an Aussie—and Wes knew how much he adored the gentle Angelane. "Or we're liable to wind up doin' business with blokes of the undertaking persuasion!" Ken's fluffy, tan brows formed a frown line. "Stillwind Valley sounds a bit too much like one bleedin' graveyard anyways!"

"We've done business with mortuaries before," Wes retorted, "and come away smellin' like roses." He hesitated to grin, but followed his friend's suggestion. "Remember, Ken? We was workin' at Levi Maxcraft's phone room, over to Jasper, and Levi's partner Oliver Orhne came up with a special—two plots on Glorious Sunset Hill for the price of one! You'n me led the whole room in setting up appointments for Doc and Purvis—once I thought up the idea of playin' a recording of funeral music right over the phone!"

"You didn't have the idea, you bleedin' capitalist," Kenny argued, faintly reddening. "I did."

"Like hell, you Christ-killin' red atheist!" Wes snapped back. Both Cheryl and Angelane giggled. "But why should anybody expect honesty from a man who thinks 'Thou shalt not lie' and all the rest of the Ten Commandments was specially put down for Charlton Heston?"

"Don't turn psalm-singer on me, Teagle," Kenny growled, shifting in his seat as if truly fed up but managing a wink in Angelane's direction. "You're no Cliff Macy. The last time you were inside a church, the minister decided he was in the wrong business and went into construction work—and the damn building burned down!"

"Boys, *boys*," Ocie Teagle murmured from behind them. He leaned forward with arthritic difficulty from between the smiling young women, cupped the backs of the boys' necks with fingers like flesh-colored wire. His fond, rasping chuckle was a pure echo of lifelong professional hype and the unfortunate whiny note in it was a reminder of Ocie's emphesyma. He'd confessed that serious illness to his son—which was why Ocie's skills were more suspect than their own business tactics—but Wes wondered what other ailments he hadn't bothered to cite. "It won't do for fellas just startin' out in partnership together to fall out over the past. The land of opportunity awaits us all, gents, just up the road apiece."

"Gents and ladies," Cheryl murmured, but

doubted Ocie heard her.

His father was both right and wrong, Wes ruminated, spotting a sign that read STILLWIND VALLEY 2 MILES. The wrong part involved the fact that Kenny Higgins and he had spent much of the past four years together expressing affections for one another by pretending to blow up, even call each other names. That was why the girls had grinned; they understood how close the partners were.

But Ocie had been gone too long to know it or even to understand the way midwestern folks—Hoosiers especially—formed lasting friendships, then kept 'em that way with an unspoken pledge to quarrel over nothing but the really unimportant things. And Ocie couldn't know that while he and Kenny would do almost anything for each other, it really bothered Wes that the lanky, handsome ex-Chicagoan believed that the world should turn communistic. Not the way it was in most places today, according to Kenny, but the way ol' Karl Marx—the unfunny Marx brother—had spelled it out. "I claim it wouldn't hurt the world to try either real communism or real Christianity once," Kenny said often. "The only bad thing about either one is the people who read just what they want to read and rush out to found a new cell or church!"

Nothing much made sense about their friendship or, for that matter, their beliefs, Wes thought for the thousandth time. He caught Kenny winking at him just then to make sure they'd both been bullshitting and smiled back with a shrug of dismissal. Each man was pushing forty hard. But Kenny hated having to stay in the midwest, because Angelane's family lived in Ohio, while Wes believed the sovereign State of Indiana and its absolute devotion to basketball was positive proof that God Himself existed. It was why he'd hired Cheryl Conrad to start with. Wes sighed. A man who refused to marry and father kids because he "wouldn't do that to anybody" and who had, in Nam, dutifully served a country he no longer loved, was both an avowed pinko and the most decent man Wes Teagle ever met. *He* postively *adored* America, but he'd pulled the strings of his life to avoid the draft! None of it made sense but sales.

Yet where ole Ocie-the-Unknown-Father was on target, on the money, was in imagining that Stillwind Valley—another mile ought to put them on the outskirts of town—was their main chance. It had to be, Wes told himself as he had repeatedly, nail-chewed fingers tightening on a steering wheel kept manageable with layers of tape. It fucking *had* to be.

Because this was the only time he or Kenny Higgins had had the nerve, the capital, and the mutual unemployment to set up their own phone operation. None of their other leads for a sales campaign to kick things off had come through, and a couple of independent clowns like Wes Teagle and his buddy might well have to look for another line of work if the good burgers—he had no idea an *h* belonged in the word because the salespeople he knew were obliged to view their prospects as underdone meat ready to be grilled and bagged by precisely the right pitch—couldn't be motivated to buy what the Wesken Company wanted to sell.

Wes turned forty this year; he felt it and feared it, and the remote possibility of having to get the hell out of the phone business left him literally constipated with images he couldn't evacuate. Kenny, he had two years of college to fall back on—or at least he *could* use 'em if he would stop introducing himself to everybody who wasn't a potential customer as "Ken Higgins, mate, I'm a card-carrying communist." Things weren't like that for Wes. When Ocie booked, years ago, Wes had seized upon his father's urgent need for income as a fantastic excuse for dropping out of school and going to work. He had only been pissed at Ocie for a week or two because he sensed that Mom wouldn't have permitted him to quit if the old man had stayed put. Since he'd really loved his father—Jesus, it was hard as ratshit to match up his memories of a quick-talking human whippet who liked rumpling his kid's hair and bringing him surprise gifts from commission checks he otherwise withheld as long as humanly possible from his needy wife, with the bony old half-dead bastard in the Caddy backseat—it had seemed natural to accept a telephone, lower his still-changing voice to sound older, and become a salesman like his footloose pop.

Mom, of course, had hated what young Wes chose to do. Most phone rooms in those days paid straight commish peeled off a wad of bills that might really have been used to choke a horse, and if teenage Wes Teagle struck out and sold zilch on a given day, zilch was exactly what he brought home.

But something cut and dried about that risk appealed to him, and Wes had begun getting the hang of it after ten days or so of timidly and precisely uttering the typed pitch they'd handed him into the telephone. Then he'd figured out that confidence—even when you no longer have an iota—nimble thinking, half-truths that weren't *ever* written down *for* the customer, *and* adaptability might be combined to create a sure-fire income-maker. Adaptability, he learned, meant transforming his manner and his message into whatever the individual at the other end of the brief connection wanted to hear. And saying what was expected, too, just short of the point at which the joker couldn't be made to pay up, regardless of how many goons the phone room operator sent over to collect the tab. All that took attentive listening, sounding upbeat with every prospect you dialed, the intuition of a stage mind-reader, and mercurially forming hunches. Also balls.

The payoffs for such effort, such performances, had seemed generous to the younger Wes. An established phone man wore what he pleased to the room, because ninety percent of the time he either sold the product or ad space or "brand-new sterling chance-of-a-lifetime with forty percent off" over the telephone or set up appointments for door-knockers like Purvis Richwine, Doc Jarvis or that sexy twist working Indy now, Lucia Mahorn. The good phone man developed a rep in his region, could feel free to tell some bad-ass like Levi Maxcraft to stuff it and get aligned with another operator inside twenty-four. He or she—Wes had known some beautiful broads in the business, beautiful in the sense of being aces at their job; and the basketball-playing Cheryl Conrad in the backseat who had given fresh meaning to the word *hooker* was a caller, a pro—played a dozen different roles a day, then had to invent another two dozen when the time came to move along and peddle something different.

And that *is one of the two fascinations about the phone room you cannot procure nowhere else,* Wes reminisced, grunting acknowledgment when Kenny nudged him in the ribs to indicate a sign at the edge of the road calling for a slower speed. Which meant they were beginning to tool straight into Stillwind Valley. *It's the* creativity *this profession demands,* he thought, accelerating just a bit. Sure: some people stayed in the racket because they were basically lazy and, once the basic skills were in place, you could always just scrape out a rudimentary living—and stay ready to kick your ass into a faster gear whenever more bucks were due.

And some men and women made it a career because it gave them a sense of honest-to-God power, it filled them to bursting with the knowledge that regardless of how often the sucker on the phone said no, or got rude as shit, it remained a possibility to make the SOB bend, break and blubber! An enriching feeling of genuine head-to-head conflict—warfare, even!—triumphantly won rose naturally from transactions of that sort. Jesus, there was so damned much practical psy*cholo*gy in calling total strangers on the phone at all hours! Wes still remembered a late afternoon when Doc Jarvis, before the wimp bastard went out into the field full-time to please one of his wives, got fed-up with some jackass who complained about being bothered 'cause supper was ready, and Jarvis hit him with an all-time Southport, Indiana, record . . . but not before Doc intentionally kept him on the line and made the discourteous turkey beg for the product! *Plead* with Doc to *let* him buy it at twice as much dough as the original price! But that marvelous bastard Jarvis kept him on the phone until supper was cold and the fucker's wife damned near *left* him!

That hadn't been the way for young Wes Teagle, however, nor the Wes who was verging upon middle age and making himself take one shot at *real* authority and independence, while there was still time. No, the rush he'd always got from phone work was knowing how infinitely creative he was and what a brilliant actor. Maybe the greatest creative talent and dramatic star in the whole world. He and Kenny Higgins had become close pals partly because Ken used his array of dialects and accents for much the same reason: to respond to a challenge cleverly, innovatively; in his own way.

—Is that tied to the second, the other *reason, I don't wanta fail in this burg or ever leave this racket?* Wes wondered, belatedly decelerating. The highway had become the main street of the unfamiliar town. Cheryl and Angelane Dubois O'Brien were pressing against the seat from behind him, staring out the Caddy's cracked and bug-encorpsed windows; in the rearview mirror he made out Ocie, his dad, leaning back with fragile arms folded like a goddam poison label as if to say he'd seen Agoura, California, Kansas City, Rochester, Tupelo, Mississippi, and Paris, France. *Because I got t'do everything my own way—like Kenny?*

"We're here, mite," the communist said needlessly, more for moral support than anything else, and emulated old Ocie without even realizing it. However—Wes observed—the bill of Kenny's soiled Baltimore Colts cap, which he wore to irk people in Indianapolis, was tilted back on his lineless forehead so he could see better. Wes turned right.

They were rolling creakily into range of a town square, postage stamp in the middle with rundown one-story shops appearing quaint as grandmothers' quilts on all four sides, nobody at all in sight and mid-afternoon silence folding in the aged Cadillac as if someone was making a bed. Sheesh, Wes mused, *this* is where the

Wesken Company must succeed or fucking perish?

But it was. It truly was. And he reminded himself that Stillwind Valley wasn't occupied by nothing but doddering oldsters protected from purchases by the boundaries of their limiting social security checks. That he and the others, and the rest of the phone room personnel yet to arrive—including the field salespersons they'd called in from Indy for direct approach—were not going anywhere they hadn't been *asked.* Uh-uh. Through a series of calls, Kenny and he had agreed to provide their services on behalf of the renovation of this very town square and all the stores encompassing it. Because Stillwind Valley wasn't, apart from its name, a new burg but a recently reopened one with an infusion of fresh blood—new, younger folks. Because widely established Kiper Research had chosen the town for expansion, and the citizens dwelling here today would not be the residents of the past, by and large. They'd be hip, contemporary people—maybe even eggheads; Wes Teagle loved matching wits with those who, in his phrase, were "super educated and super susceptible"—with fat, spendable, contemporary incomes. And probably nowhere much in town to spend them on!

"Hit the brakes!" Kenny shouted, bolting upright in his seat and dislodging his cap. "Stop the damn car!"

Noise—the close to deafening uproar of countless stereos or radios playing uncountable rock 'n' roll records at the loudest possible level—drowned out the familiar rattles of the Caddy. Drowned out, drenched, and totally defeated the company vehicle as Wes stopped it shudderingly against the nearest curb.

Ocie, his shout timorous: "What in Christname's that?" He leaned forward now.

"Hundreds of records and radios," Cheryl Conrad shouted back. On Ocie's other side Angelane muttered *"Sacre bleu,"* as if honoring her ancestors.

Kenny, shaking his head, retrieved his cap and looked apologetically at his partner. "Sorry, mate," he said, also yelling to be heard. "I thought we was goneta run over a bloody parade!"

"Maybe so." Wes, trembling slightly, was gaping at something through the window on the driver's side that the rest of them couldn't immediately see. "Maybe it is a parade."

Staring, the others finally saw what Wes had referred to.

A man, clearly young, athletically trim, clad only in a sweatshirt, dark-green shorts with matching socks and Reebok shoes, was jogging toward them on a line that would take him directly to the panting Cadillac. With the unidentifiable music blaring—there were too many songs for any one to break through—the jogger seemed to move soundlessly. Knees rising in apparent effortlessness, arms pumping economically, he might have been floating toward them in the shallows of still water.

It was only at the last second that he veered from a collision with the Caddy, circling round the front of it with just a minimal break of stride. He did not look at any of them, or the car.

Then he was gone.

2

Even before they had driven out of the town square and gone in search of the new apartment building to which they had been assigned for the duration of their complex sales campaign, the music—the ungodly racket—had stopped. Obviously, Cheryl Conrad mused, glancing with some concern at the recently startled, still ashen Ocie Teagle, *a lot of people who work in the square like rock music.*

Yet they had not seen a soul except for the silent jogger, and it was peculiar for merchants to play even bland Musak so loudly. The ex-basketball player—sometimes Cheryl wondered when a hobby that had ended a decade ago would stop being her number-one personal trademark or, considering her height, if it ever would—frowned but said nothing. The others were discussing something else; but it seemed improbable to her that many customers wouldn't mind being flooded with noise the instant they entered a store. Not every shopper grew up with rock music, after all. Yet it still might be that the store owners had turned their radios or record players up to welcome the newcomers—

Or alert everybody else in Stillwind Valley that they'd arrived?

That was silly. And there was another possibility, Cheryl reflected, watching through her window as a succession of small shops became an ill-maintained, almost decrepit residential area. *It was as if they were asserting their right—to do* whatever *they wanted. Establishing the fact that this is* their *town, not ours.*

Why was it that she didn't see anyone around now? Not that it was warm enough yet for people to be working in their yards or—a common enough sight almost anywhere in the state—shooting around at outdoor basketball goals. But where in the dickens were the people?

It took fewer than five minutes to locate the new Blackwood Apartments. During that time the old Caddy had meandered through a high percentage of the town and was on "the far northside," as Wes and Kenny had been told, virtually back on the highway again. But it was a short walk to the downtown area, assuming any of them ever wished to go there.

Angelane, Cheryl saw, was also appraising the exterior of the building, and the neighborhood. The two-story with a brick facade, isolated in the center of a long block without adjoining structures, was also as advertised—at least Cheryl decided, from the outside. While it was devoid of any intriguing architectural flourishes and its site in relation to the rest of the town gave it, for Cheryl, a remoteness that verged on enmity; it looked large enough to house those employees of the firm who planned to live in Stillwind Valley until the campaign ended—those in the Caddy, plus Clemon Sparrow and Darrel Brickowski, when they put in their appearance tomorrow. She supposed the recreation room was already temporarily outfitted with phones.

But the lot around the building was barren of trees and blotches of the last snowfall of dying winter looked like fading patches on the discolored shirt of a sick person who'd lost weight too fast. She half expected to hear an ambulance wail in the distance, or a rumble of freight cars—the kind she'd seemed to hear in the darkness of her bedroom every night of her puberty while her pale, betraying legs grew out before her like wild flowers with bone.

Abruptly, just as Wes threw his door open and Kenny Higgins moved to open his, Cheryl Conrad wanted several things enormously: a steaming hot bath; to get the first day of work and all those unfamiliar details that disturbed newcomers behind her; Wes Teagle, and, if he went on pretending not to see how fond she'd come to be of the four-eyed little conman, a joint; or three. He began crossing the bare thawing earth, gesticulating to his partner, and Cheryl's warm gaze was on his hipless backside. But then Ocie rose before her to climb down and the twisted S of the father's back, and his faltering descent, reminded her with real pain of how near she was to the close of her child-bearing years.

She realized she'd have to use her own game plan. Use this odd town Wes had never seen either to make him feel lonely and restless, or anomalous and horny. That would have to be her strategy while they were all in Stillwind Valley. And while Wes would be staying in one flat with his dad, aging Ocie'd have to sleep sometime!

Just a few minutes later Cheryl stood in the open doorway of the tiny and sparcely decorated apartment she'd be occupying, alone, annoyed again by the customary impression that the pate of her blond head almost brushed the top of the doorframe. Higgins, that lean Chicago charmer, paused only to peck the woman he swore he adored on the cheek before loping like a cowboy after his shorter, quick-witted partner. And Wes was already stomping off, adventure glinting in his gray, evasive eyes as if high on heroin, questing for the rec room headquarters and frantic to begin, now that they had "toured" the town, modifying their sales pitches. Well, damn him, then! Damn him, and Kenny, and—and communism!

Wondering if he'd ever even looked directly at her, already groping in her purse for the marijuana carefully stored in a Baggie, she thought as she had before that there were two problems when a woman fell in love with an SOB like Wes Teagle: He was simultaneously a hardworking, absolutely devoted phone man, and an unfeeling, overgrown brat!

Or was that, Cheryl asked herself, shutting and leaning against the door, saying exactly the same thing?

"Don't you 'buse that girl, Wilford. You hear?"

"I won't; I didn't lay a hand to her." His eyes flashed with despair, not anger. A sigh. "Don't you know I'm tryin' not to, woman?"

"Come right over here to Mama, baby. Mama knows it isn't your fault."

It took courage merely to move. To stand, and, when nothing further occurred that second, to cross the room on wobbly legs to her mother. That deed required sidestepping at least half of their few valuable or valued possessions, which littered the floor like the broken bodies of familial memory. "It's *not,* Mama," Thalia gasped, near tears again. She vanished partly into the woman's great, maternal bosom. The heavy wool tickled her nose but the sweater's scent and that of her mother kept her from smelling either the spilled liquids or the sweaty frustration of her father. "You know I wouldn't trash our things."

"And that's Jesus's truth, Wilford." Mama straightened to her full height of sixty inches. "This . . . is a good child." It was as if she were presenting daughter to unfamiliar father, or recommending her to some hazardous but obligatory employment. "Wilford, you stood right on *that spot* when it happened again, and my baby sat right in *that chair.*" The pointing black finger was unsteady but imperious; incontrovertible. It indicted him.

He responded by pounding, once, on the closest wall. "Look here! I didn't mean she made it happen on purpose. I've read about such things, Mary! I know they happen!" But then the middle-aged man wilted from the defiant gaze and sank into the chair his daughter had occupied throughout the latest bizarre visitation. He peered miserably over at the unhappy and bewildered girl. "Your daddy wouldn't hurt you, Thalia." Tears hazed his eyes, but he included Mary in what he blurted out next. "It's a fact of science that strange things like this happen only when there's a child present. One who's becoming a man . . . or a woman! They say it begins, somehow, in the child's mind, her private thoughts, and—"

"It can also happen," Mary interrupted him, her ominous and full-bodied vibrato reminding father and daughter of happier moments when Mary had witnessed during church services, "when there's *evil* in the house."

Faith confronted science and he had no idea what to say. "Nothing been right since we came to Stillwind Valley. Shit, I don't even know why they even hired me!" Wilford Boggs's tears rolled on his cheeks freely, yet he remained firm. "Either we got to send this child away 'til it all blows over or I got to give up the best job I ever had. We can't *afford* to do nothin' while everything we've worked to get, everything we've cared for, is plain *destroyed* before our eyes!"

Mary Boggs, who'd paid her husband's way through school by day labor, started to speak. She closed her mouth to think. Thalia, peering forlornly across the alienating room at Wilford, shook her head but spoke only to herself: *It's not me,* she insisted. She did her utmost to choke back the rising sobs. *It's not. Not me* or *my mind, causing it.*

"We stay put," Mary proclaimed at last. "This is all our home."

A framed black-and-white nine-by-twelve photograph of Wilford's long-deceased mother, one that had hung on the wall just inside the front door of every home the Boggs family'd had, clearly twitched and *squeaked*. It rose slightly, then, to disengage; it drifted off and away from the wall as if carried by unseen fingers. Then it hung—it was poised—just out of Wilford's reach.

Each of the features he had cherished and would give nearly anything on earth to see again in life seemed to etch themselves even deeper into his memory. He realized he owned no other copy of picture or negative. Lunging, his arms were outthrust, his hands groped for the photo suspended above him.

The wise, smiling, beneficent eyes melted and ran like mocking tears. The frame cracked asunder, as if someone plucked the wooden strips apart.

The old photograph burst into flames.

And the dark image of a much older, living person—a man—flared like a flash bulb before young Thalia's frightened vision. A smirk of a grin her father once might have described as "shit-eating" insulted all her family, and Thalia, held dear.

"I don't see why we have to revise the pitches," Kenny said when they'd shoved a couple of desks end-for-end to create their own managerial area. It was in the deepest corner of the recreation room, where they could keep an eye on the rest. Still wearing his Baltimore Colts cap, shoved back on his head so the wave in front showed, he'd propped one foot on his desk while the other was perched on the teetering rim of a wastebasket. Both sizable feet wore boots that Kenny said were made of Australian leather. Clemon Sparrow, who'd arrive tomorrow, swore he'd get them off Higgins someday, get them analyzed if he had to. "I wrote me bleedin' heart out, creating them masterpieces."

"They lack the real master's touch," Wes replied. He hadn't taken his seat yet. He was still trying to assign the desks properly, to keep the phone people who were particularly inclined to stop dialing and start conversing separated from each other. To achieve that without the independent crew complaining too vociferously, he had a surprise for them all: nameplates. A push-button telephone with a shoulder rest had already been installed at each desk. Wes shook his head then, retrieved a sign reading CLIFFORD MACY, and put it on a desk farthest from the managerial area. Cliff mightn't show up because he'd slipped off the wagon, but if he was there, he'd be hard at work. However ineffectually.

"You're fast becoming a Jee-kyl and Hyde, old dear. A fucking perfectionist."

Wes paused, glanced across at his friend and smiled. Amelioratingly. "Thing is, Kenny, your little pitches'd be fine and dandy in Illinois"—Wes pronounced "Illa-*noise*"—"but this here is Indiana!"

"Oy, he's *shtuping* around with his precious Hoosier *shtetls* again!" Kenny slapped his forehead dramatically. This was his "Jewish talk" and, while he was still in Chicago, it frequently had made the difference in good weeks or bad. There'd been less call for it in the hamlets, the *shtetls,* of Indiana, but Kenny was afraid he'd begin to lose both the dialect and the language. "Was it too much to ask I should become a *mensch* before I die?"

"Don't talk foreign, Kenny," Wes complained, lowering himself into the chair at the desk facing his partner's. "You know I don't know no real foreign."

"How should I talk?" His tan brows were lifted in innocence. "How?" The brows lowered in mock accusation. "Is this where I discover your true colors, Weston? Your secret *parvenu* antipathies?"

Wes folded his arms behind his neck and settled back, ignoring the way his eyeglasses had slipped to the tip of his nose. "I don't know nothin' about anti-pithies or anti-chovies, but there was never no bigotry back where I grew up. Not toward black folks or foreigners or persons of the Hee-brew persuasion." He blinked. "Well, truth was, we didn't have any colored people; or we didn't know about 'em, if we did."

Kenny sighed. "Here we go."

"Closest we came to one was my Uncle Falen. First man in our town who ever went to Florida."

"His *tan*—?"

"A few of the boys up from Kentucky got liquored up and there was some talk of lynchin' Uncle Falen, but nothin' came of it."

"Oh, stop," Kenny grunted, trying not to smile.

"They did go out onto my uncle's big yard in fronta the farmhouse with a good-sized cross. But nobody could recall what they was supposed t'do with it, and then the pastor over to the church, he found his cross was missing. Come after it."

"I'm relieved," Kenny sighed.

"Afore anyone knew what was going on, Uncle Falen and Aunt Noreen Eddie joined them out on the grass, and Reverend Nickpond was holding Satidday evenin' services, impromptu-like."

Kenny shoved the sales pitches he'd written across both desks until they rested under Wes Teagle's slightly pointed nose. "I surrender. Change the mothers!"

"Tell the truth, Kenny, Kentuckians was our foreigners back home." Wes leaned forward, adjusted his glasses, made a show of reading the crudely typed notes judicially. "For the most part, though, we just let 'em alone." He looked up at Kenny myopically. "Wasn't much else t'be done with 'em, fact is."

"What's your big Hoosier pitch?" asked the aspiring communist. He faked an irascible glance at his Sharp wristwatch. "Angelane might like to have something to eat before you or Ocie begin your next trip down memory lane."

"Well, the way I see it, our main task here in Stillwind Valley is to sell ad space for a keepsake program to announce the unveiling of some exotic statue a Dr. Dominique is donatin' to the town."

"Seems logical," Kenny said drily, "since that's what the man from Kiper Research contracted us to do. With all the proceeds going to renovate the town square and those crappy-looking old stores we saw on the way in." He smiled. "Not quite all proceeds, of course."

"Not quite," Wes agreed. He produced a shiny Cross pen from a pocket of his flannel shirt, bent forward, and drew a line through the table of advertising rates Kenny had proposed. "These are maybe ten percent too low—or lower'n the freight'll allow, considerin' the egghead burgers make good money over to the lab." He printed in higher rates with both precision and a flourish. "Acourse, they's no sense discussin' this with Professor Kiper or that Dr. A. Dominique. What they want is an amount of money they already fixed as our goal, and we'll by God *get* it for 'em!"

And the Wesken Company will just double its percentage, Kenny thought, marveling. "I'm not quite sure I see how that move is particularly a Hoosier touch."

"I ever tell you how Hoosier folks love their basketball?" Wes asked abruptly, glancing up.

Kenny waggled his palm and pursed his lips. "Get on with it. I'm listening."

"Then hear this," Wes began anew, resting his pen on the remains of the initial sales pitch and contriving to look excited. "The townsfolk here are miles 'n miles from any sorta professional entertainment, 'cept maybe movies. Must be starved for it. And on the way here, I saw a new building called the Stillwind Valley Auditorium. You notice it, Kenny?"

"Go on." Despite the noncommital answer, Kenny found his heartbeat beginning to pick up.

"What if we was able to sell tickets for a really big show over to the Auditorium but didn't bother tellin' Kiper and Dominque about it? What if they was tickets for a truly famous name?"

Kenny looked suspicious. "Like who?"

Wes looked in several directions, conspiratorially, before replying in a loud whisper, "Somebody who's funnier than Aunt Noreen Eddie or Uncle Felan but gettin' on in years. Someone who's known everywhere in this world. A really great comedian—first name of . . . George."

"George *Burns*?" Kenny rose halfway from his desk chair, gasping.

Wes said softly, "The one and only."

"But you don't know George Burns." Kenny began to redden. He dropped both big feet to the floor. "*We* don't know George Burns. Or anyone famous. Or have a prayer of getting him."

"Uh-huh."

"Man, we don't even know where he is or how to contact him!"

"I do," Wes murmured. "He's in Indi'nap'lis this minute. And he's been my friend for a 'coon's age." Wes hesitated, thoughtfully, modestly shrugged. "Well, he's not my best friend; you are, I reckon. But the thing is—I can get him for us."

Kenny Higgins' hazel eyes were huge. "And the plan'd be to arrange his appearance on the sly, sell tickets without informing Professor Kiper or Dr. Dominique"—he noticed Wes was nodding agreement, beatifically; reassuringly—"while the Wesken Company keeps everything over and above Mr. Burns's fee! Right?"

Wes scribbled energetically on a pad of paper for several seconds, then tossed it over the two desks to his partner. "I got it all figgered out and it's sweet as sugar lumps." He beamed almost paternally while Kenny eagerly began to read the information. "Folks can buy a block of four tickets for a dirt-cheap twenty-five bucks. We tell 'em that whether they attend the performance or not, half their money will be given to a nursing home. To build a home for the elderly in reopened and renamed Stillwind Valley." He frowned. "I haven't figured out yet if we really got to donate half the proceeds or not; but my ole buddy will be—"

"Hold on, mate!" Kenny cried. He was staring at the scrawled note in a mixture of incredulity and embryonic horror. *"Wait* a minute! This name you wrote here—"

The other cocked a brow. "What's wrong?"

"Wes, you wrote George *Byrnes."* Kenny gaped at his bespectacled partner, increasingly aghast. "It says right here: B-Y-R-N-E-S. Wes, partner, that isn't how George spells it."

"Sure it is," Wes disagreed. He stretched, made a long arm and gathered in his notepad. "Acourse, back when he appeared ever' night at the Fox Burlesque Theatre in Indi'nap'lis, he went by the name V.D. Byrnes." The smaller man's gaze swept Kenny's astonished features with the pure and sunny innocence of a newborn crocodile. "I give you my word, partner, his real name is George Byrnes."

Kenny exploded in Hebrew. "We can't make that work, you *cockamamie schnorer!* Not—not *shmontses* like that!"

"Do you mean the good hamburgers of this fine little town are gonna ask back the money they'd donated for the noble purpose of erectin' a shelter for the old and *in*firm?"

"They might. They bloody might!"

Wes spread his hands. "Then, the funniest top

banana since Scurvy will put on one hell of a show!"

"Wes . . . mate . . . old love—they will fucking string us up!"

With saintlike patience, with enormous slowness, Wes turned his head from right to left, to right again. "Uh-huh. No way, Kenny." A smile. " 'Cause we'll schedule ole George's appearance for approximately one year from now! Thirteen months sounds about right, don't it?"

"I see." It was a whisper. "And we will have taken the Wesken Company to some *other* town by then." Kenny's mouth remained open when he'd finished the remark of realization. Almost as deliberately as Wes had resolved his head, Kenny got to his feet and extended a long arm across the desktops to shake his partner's hand. "For a capitalist, my man, you are all right." His eyes widened with admiration. "Y'know, this'll really put it to all the bourgeois piggies in this burg!"

Wes Teagle, with appropriate decorum, cleared his throat shyly and picked up the Cross pen.

"Got another homespun Hoosier notion or two t'mention, partner. Coupon books. Home security systems." An irrepressible grin took twenty years off Wes's impending collection of forty. "What Doc and Purvis can do in Stillwind Valley oughta be magic t'behold. May even dream up an idea so's we can use that real looker from Speedway; the Mahorn girl. Remember the redhead?"

"Lucia Mahorn? Nope; I have no idea who you're thinking of, mate. My prurient interests are centered wholly upon Angelane O'Brien." It wasn't one-hundred percent falsehood. He added, as idly as possible, "A man is lucky if one woman during his lifetime looks at him the way

Angelane looks at me—or Cheryl Conrad regards *you.*"

"Shut up."

"I beg pardon?"

Wes was out of his chair, sneaking across the new phone room to a trio of windows draped with venetian blinds that looked out upon the street. Believing for a moment he'd been rudely told to shut up, Kenny watched Wes, saw him make a shushing sound and part two slats in order to peer outside. No light showed through; clearly darkness had come and Wes had imagined he heard a prowler. Kenny froze.

"It was just the guy," Wes said momentarily, releasing the blinds and turning back. But he looked puzzled. Fretful.

"What guy?" asked Kenny.

"The jogger." Wes shrugged, peeked out again before finally dropping the subject. "That . . . quiet guy. One we saw in the town square."

"All this time later?" Kenny asked, surprised. "Out here?"

"Yeah." Wes went slowly back to his desk, stroked his nameplate abstractedly before sitting. His gaze met Kenny's. "Close to the windows, you can hear it." He kept his expression blank but fumbled in his shirt pocket for a cigarette. "They're playin the music loud again down at the town square."

3

Never before in his *en*-tire life had he been a man who went where he wasn't wanted, and he'd always before sworn that he never by God would!

But Ocie Teagle had never before been seventy-three going-on-eternity, either. By God or by the faded fine print on one old reprobate's birth certificate—and by some gee-dee stroke of perverse Hoosier fortune that had stubbornly kept him alive and kicking customer ass through cities, decades, and experiences enough for a baker's dozen door-to-door salesmen and six whole gee-dee phone rooms.

And hated almost every minute of it.

Ocie paced the place he'd be sharing now with a son who was turning forty this year—how could Weston become middle-aged when it was only a few seasons ago when he'd turned the corner himself?—and found himself in the bathroom, staring at a rheumy-eyed old man in the mirror over the medicine cabinet. How? It was the same combination of screwed-up luck and back-asswards commonsense that had told him to clear out of Flanagan, Indiana, before his wife Ethel and his boy Weston began appearing to be good enough reasons for settling down. The same combination that had seen fit to pull him through a gee-dee heart attack powerful enough to turn up Bronko Nagurski's toes, and plunk him back down in Indiana t'die. Don't tell *him* luck wasn't no woman! Don't tell—

Told stories over and over about all the women he'd had from coast to by God coast, and he had poked his share. Women who'd make that young pinko's little French piece look like boys! But he'd always kept mum about bein' so tired after sellin' diddly squat for four days running that he'd just craved a comfortable bed to sleep in . . . some friendly, familiar place with his own things in it . . . somebody who gave a damn—somebody to do it all for.

Not that he was under any sort of death sentence, not anything like that, quite. Ocie splashed cold water on his face, shaking his head; he brushed back his sparse white hair with four folds of damp toilet paper and turned from the mirror, tried to leave the old man imprisoned inside the medicine cabinet. But the Rollo Cosmetic boys had carried him to a sawbones just outside Bethlehem, Pennsylvania, when he'd collapsed, and the wimp of a medic said flat out that Ocie would perish unless he called it a career and found some cozy place to rest his ticker. Which'd meant he had no choice left to him 'cept bein' back home again in Indiana where he could see the gee-dee candlelight gleam and smell the newmown hay till he puked! 'Cause Ocie Teagle'd made a small fortune in his time but spent it all, livin' the good life and—

And never made a true-blue pal or had a real girl after leaving home. Never owned anything he couldn't put on his back, stuff into a bag or cram into a display case . . . 'cept a junker or two. Tin cans his salesman 'buddies' had told him had lotsa miles on 'em when they'd turned back the gee-dee odometers! Never even found nowhere he liked better'n Flanagan, Indiana. And never got over learnin' that Ethel'd died, and never had the guts to attend the funeral—or to pick up a phone—a telephone, *for God's sake!—and wish little Weston Floyd Teagle a merry Christmas or a happy birthday!*

He had remained in this latest unfamiliar apartment their first evening in one more strange town and let Weston and his pinko buddy hightail it to their new phone room partly because he was purely bushed, partly because he was under no real obligation and didn't *have* t'go along, partly because all those young people with their crazy ideas was gettin' him down, and mainly because he knew damned well none of 'em wanted his company. Or he thought so, believed that, with nothin' said to the contrary by any of them. He didn't exactly blame Weston for not em-bracin' him or nothing since he hadn't hugged anyone himself or said anything nicer to 'em then "Which size do you want, ma'am?" in more years than he cared to count. He couldn't blame Wes-turning-by-God-*forty* for not having married, either, since the boy had evidentally tried to follow in his own wandering shoes and—

But why did it have to wind up this way; how did it happen that he'd never really earned anything like a small fortune, or saved a red cent of it? He'd learned the sales business from A to Izzard, truly worked his ass off in half a dozen states—even if all forty-eight was an allowable exaggeration—so why wasn't he People with a capital P the way he'd intended? Fact was, Ocie Teagle had never meant to stay on the road until it was time to pack up for the last time, nor meant to leave Ethel or Weston forever. He'd planned to drive back home to Indiana like People—in style—with beaucoup bucks in his pockets, presents for everyone from everywhere in the trunk of a new Caddy. And a genuine Cadillac straight from the showroom that he drove all the way home from some exotic capital, long and shiny and oozing success! What had gone wrong with the dream? What had he done wrong, or what hadn't he done?

With tears in his green eyes, Ocie caught a glimpse of a skinny little Stillwind Valley phone book lying next to one of those sporty new telephones, and his jaw set with renewed determination and spirit. He couldn't do much about the past or his bum ticker or the overall lousy fate he'd had dumped in his lap. He sort of wanted to make things up to Weston and didn't even know where to start.

But he could fend for himself awhile longer and not depend upon the boy to take him for grub and a drink—to entertain him, like he was stuck in some gee-dee home for old geezers. Eagerly, he dropped into a chair next to the phone and skimmed through the directory. He even got a bit flushed, the way he used to get when he was footloose and fancy free in some new town. He'd been a Mason, a Moose, an Elk and every other artisan or animal available since he was twenty-one, just like his daddy before him; any salesman who knew his asshole from a hole in the ground joined whatever he could, t' have a readymade base of operations wherever he happened to be.

Fewer than one hundred seconds later, Ocie

glanced up from the phone book, blinking his surprise. Across the small dining room of his and Weston's apartment, night shimmered like a dark curtain through a window with open draperies. There were no lodges, no clubs of any sort in Stillwind Valley; or if there were, Ocie couldn't find them listed.

He bobbed his head, once. A bar, then; or were they listin' them under *taverns* now? He leafed through the directory with a small, forced smile.

And drew a blank.

There was no ad or listing of a bar, a tavern, a night club. Nor, because Ocie remembered to check that, too, for a liquor store. The two drugstores in town were closed for the evening, according to the advertisements. There were a few restaurants shown, of course; people had to eat. But Ocie had wanted both companionship and a few cocktails. Beers, at least, if Stillwind Valley didn't have the right kind of license.

The drapes across the new, unfamiliar room shifted. From where he sat by the phone, the old man thought the windows were closed, but he'd had sworn the draperies moved. The building was new; recent, anyway. What kind of spooks haunted *new* places?

Okay, dammit, Ocie decided, abruptly very anxious to get out of the apartment and meet folks, mingle, exercise the unfailing persuasive charms that had never—almost never—failed to make friendships of a kind anywhere in the United States. Okay, dammit, he'd go to church.

He turned to the yellow pages slowly and with a rising, intuitive surge of apprehension, to C. He had belonged to Christ alone knew how many different denominations in his time. Because that was one more place to locate and secure a customer base, especially if a man wanted t'sell something like life insurance, or—

Ocie drew another blank.

He kept his gaze aimed downward for another count of two, unwilling to raise his head. To admit the impossible obvious.

There were no churches in Stillwind Valley, Indiana. Or none listed in the town telephone directory. And why in hell wouldn't they, routinely, be listed? What kind of gee-dee place was this? In all his travels, in all his seventy-plus years, he'd never once been in a town that didn't have so much as *one* bar or *one* Christian church.

Churches and bars were the first places decent people erected in a town, new or reopened.

He stared back at the blackness beyond the windows within three or four faltering paces across the new tufted bright orange carpeting and the notion occurred to him that what was going to come through the old Hoosier sycamores for him might well be the grim reaper.

She looked nothing so much to him, when he stopped in the shadows to peer down at where she lay on the bed they'd never slept in, as an improbable child. He thought privately that her frizzy dark hair was like Little Orphan Annie's except that the lobes of her ears always made him want to nibble on them. Her knees were tucked up to her chest, concealing her bosom, and the way she had carelessly pulled a blanket over the lower portion of her body suggested that Angelane had not meant to fall asleep.

Which was, Kenny mused, just like her. Since she would not want to offer the sacrament of her first night's sleep in a new place without Kenny Higgins sprawled out beside her.

It was like that ever since they'd met, or within forty-eight hours of it. From Kenny's standpoint, they'd fallen in love at first sight; it had never entered his head to question the fact. Some things—precious damned few—were givens, whether by the God he adamantly refused to believe in, largely because he had never believed much in Kenny Higgins, or because even phone men enjoyed a streak of good luck now and then. And this was the way it was: Whatever he and Angelane Debois O'Brien did when he was away from work, or his political activity, they planned to do it together. In lieu of marriage, that was their sacred vow.

Both Angelane and Kenny had been married before; once each. And each of them knew for a fact that their marriages would have worked out okay if they'd believed in that.

Kenny and Wes had tried to reach someone at Kiper Research, the professor who'd contacted the Wesken Company, or anybody, to get a tip about eating places in Stillwind Valley. Not surprisingly, at that hour of the evening, there had been no answer. Which was all right since Kenny had known by some long-dormant instinct Angelane had helped him discover that she wouldn't want to go out, that first night in town. But then he and Wes had phoned around and found no restaurants open at all.

Now he hovered in an awkward half stoop above his sleeping young woman, his hands and arms perilously clutching what remained of the snacks the crew had brought up from Indy; nacho chips, Planter's corn curls, a couple of off-brand candy bars and three golden Twinkies that were rather the worse for wear. Indecisively, Kenny tried to decide whether to awaken Angelane or not and at last turned away from the bed.

"Not," he murmured.

"Your Twinkies or your life," the sleepy voice declared.

"My Twinkie is my life." Kenny smiled. He dumped the small, gaily wrapped packages on the bed next to Angelane because she was raising her arms to him.

"What a foolish little thing to build a whole life around," she whispered, dispatching the blanket that had covered her legs. She proved to be naked from the waist down.

Kenny put out a long arm when his shirt had been removed, retrieved and slipped a popular goodie from its half-opened yellow wrapper. "Look," he observed brightly. "This poor thing has gotten all stiff, and crusty. Gummy, too."

"Cela va sans dire," Angelane said rather smugly. Most of the sleepiness had seeped from her unlikely blue eyes, but they somehow succeeded in seeming both drowsy and sensual. "I'm half-starved anyway."

"The problem with America," Kenny managed, "is that it's become a nation of junkfood junkies. Careful; don't kneel on the nacho chips!"

And later, pleasantly supine in all ways, Kenny peered with deep affection at Angelane's bare and curving back. She was avidly devouring a candy bar and had not uttered a single complaint about his failure to bring back a sack full of sandwiches. He counted down and tapped her fourth vertebra. "What about the corn curls?" he asked innocently.

He had not "spoken in Aussie," as Kenny liked to call it, since returning to their new apartment. Australian, Hebrew, Irish, Swedish, even Gallic, were Kenny's "sales aids." Around Angelane, he had confided in Wes Teagle once, he spoke only love.

But he'd never uttered a word to her relating to

marriage.

He did not for a minute believe Angelane's parents in Ohio would be overwhelmed with pleasure about the prospect of their already divorced and Catholic daughter tying the knot again. Certainly, not to a man who, according to phone colleague Clemon Sparrow—who exaggerated—"practically prays to Karl Marx."

But Kenny hoped Angelane knew that his primary prayer to any deity was that he would never be separated from her.

Most of the residents of town eventually went to sleep that inclement and late wintery night. Wes, grumbling about the possibility of his starving to death during the night, and uncharacteristically looking forward to breakfast, and Ocie Teagle, who'd kept the surprising secrets of the Stillwind Valley phone directory to himself, drifted off at midnight more or less. In Ocie's case, it was more.

Cheryl Conrad got to her hot bath, but it didn't help much; she remained lonely, even after she had smoked two joints. Her sleep was erratic and marginally erotic as well.

Young Thalia Boggs and her father, Wilford, slept eventually, but not until after two a.m. Mary, Thalia's mother, took longer because she was preoccupied with wondering when the next manifestations of evil were scheduled to begin, and destroy the rest of her family's lives.

The chief of police, a man named Magenheimer up from Indy, slept like a baby. So did the woman who usually shared his bed with him.

Unburdened by hard labors and bored because of too much time on his hands, the town undertaker and coroner spent a fitful night early on;

later, he began dreaming of busier and more fulfilling times, just ahead.

The jogger jogged . . . .

The Jagannath did not sleep, either, because it did not contain more than the thinnest thread of actual life. So far.

Albert Kiper, who'd been notified about the arrival of the Wesken Company within seconds following that event—who had been in the midst of seven utterly obedient people who might, judging by their spotless white lab jackets and their earnest youthful faces, have been college biology students—who'd listened with the other research teammates to enough rock 'n' roll music the past ten hours to satisfy his once insatiable passion—decided there was a remote chance for shuteye shortly before four a.m.

First, however, he had to telephone somebody whom he depended upon as if it were a case of life or death.

"They're here; the first of them. The rest will arrive tomorrow." And after he said that Kiper nodded and hung up, strode wearily back to the sofa in his private office in the Kiper Research building, slipped on his headphones and smiled with a mixture of satisfaction and anticipation.

He did not feel tense or anything about the fact that it *was* a case of life and death to pass the information along because the person he had called owed the same obligation to Professor Albert Kiper.

4

One blissful cheek cozily nestled against the soft hollow of Angelane's bare tummy, Kenny Higgins came to consciousness abruptly the following morning. It was, he realized instantly, blinking, an understandable reaction to some idiot hammering enthusiastically on the front door of their temporary quarters.

Kenny's drowsy gaze slowly met that of Ms. O'Brien, who'd cranked her neck from the pillow and was frowning. "Wes," they said in concert, knowing their man. Kenny added thoughtfully, "The *schmo*—the *khazer!*"

But he dressed quickly—beginning with his old Colts cap and working downward—and joined his partner in the nicely carpeted hallway with a piercing glare of unmistakable resentment. A lesser man might have fled.

Wes, not appearing to notice, trotted wordlessly toward and down the steps with Kenny traipsing in his wake. The bespectacled and shorter partner continued his alacritous pace until both chief executives had reached the

Wesken Company car in the parking lot. Kenny seized the opportunity to peer at his watch, and blanched. It was barely six a.m. "Git in," Wes commanded peremptorily, and took his customary station behind the steering wheel.

A peevish pause and Kenny did as he was bidden. But he slammed the door after him. There was almost no snow left on the Blackwood Apartments lot and the pre-spring sun was struggling to rise, but Kenny was freezing. "Why'd you knock us up, hoss?" he inquired querulously. The Caddy motor turned over as if it shared his feelings and those of the sun, and might change its mind. "Dear Jesus, Weston, if you'd remember the merits of the opposite sex—Cheryl, for example—you might permit other bloody people to complete their night's sleep!"

"I'm dyin', partner," Wes said startlingly. It got Kenny's attention. "Starvin' to death for sure. But I got to buy some food for my pore ole daddy, your woman and the Hooker, and I mightn't have the strength t'bring it back to them."

"Gonif!" Kenny exclaimed. Shivering, he leaned forward to turn on the car heater.

"But I didn't knock anybody up, Ken," Wes declared. Uncertain of his whereabouts when they'd reached an intersection, he turned left and began searching for a restaurant with carry-out food.

"That's just an expression for awakening decent people."

"Hoosiers take sex seriously, Kenny," Wes murmured. "Especially body parts." He waited until Kenny's brows rose questioningly. "Not *those* parts. We Hoosiers notice parts of the body nobody else cares a tinker's dam about."

"For example," Kenny said, sighing.

"For example, my Aunt Noreen Eddie had the

highest arch you ever saw. It was so far off the ground that when my aunt got on in years and took to sitting around, a family of field mice built thier home in the open space under Aunt Noreen Eddie's feet."

"I am a little hungry now that I think of it. Have—?"

"Since it rains a lot in Indiana, word got passed around the field mouse community. And whenever there was a big storm, *en*-tire generations of those little fellas held family reunions in the arches under Noreen Eddie's feet. When she died—"

"Y'know, I think I see a restaurant sign," Kenny said, "dead ahead." He pointed as dramatically and distractingly as possible.

"And when Aunt Noreen Eddie died and fell backwards, her pore ole legs shot straight up into the air and all the field mice in Oolitic County was homeless like that!" He hit the brakes, did it again. Once never cut it. "The governor back then had to declare the town of Flanagan an official disaster area!"

Kenny beat Wes into the restaurant by two full lengths.

But when they were both inside, the aging sign that had advertised Mother Quick's Home Cooking seemed to have been hung above the wrong door.

Wes's first clue was the pleasant, tart smell of fresh fruit instead of the hot and steamy fragrance of bacon and eggs frying. Wes loathed fruit, fresh or otherwise.

A number of tables with nobody sitting at them were covered with bright red-and-white checked tablecloths, but one glance by Wes at a menu he seized informed him he and Kenny were even worse off than a mere fruit stand.

"Granola cereals," he muttered, holding the menu at arm's length. "Herbal tea. *Honey* on all their crap!" He made a face and glared irritably at his partner. "This yore notion of a restaurant?"

"Some people might think so," Kenny replied equably. Then he curled his own lip. "But I'm not one of 'em. This is a *health food* restaurant, Weston—in case y'haven't deduced that yet."

"And here we are, alone again," Wes said softly. Kenny's faded brown eyes lifted in shared surprise. "Hullo?" Wes turned slowly, inquiringly. "Anybody here?"

An amazingly round face popped into view from the kitchen. It wasn't fleshy with fat nor was it old—Wes pegged the man's age at thirty, tops—but nature appeared to have begun the creation of his face with a juvenile perfect circle and progressed from there. One became aware of the enormous eyes, then how small the fellow was, only later, and in sequence.

His expression of startlement was the last thing Wes noticed. "Didn't hear you come in," the fellow said in a voice like a stage whisper. "Just opening up for the day."

"Don't reckon you're Mother Quick," Wes allowed, adding hopefully, "or that you have any real food on the menu?"

"Real food?" the small man repeated. He looked surprised again, but not angry. With a chuckle like a snort, he scooted nimbly to a radio perched on a ledge near his cash register and turned it on. Loudly. "Sorry I didn't have any music playing. As I said, we're just opening for the day. But my name *is* Quick; Roger Quick."

"Look, Mr. Quick," Kenny tried, "we haven't had a bite of food since late yesterday afternoon so we're in a bit of a mood for a regular breakfast. We need to take out—"

"*I* see!" the little man exclaimed. "I heard there were new people coming to Stillwind Valley." The round head bobbed. "Welcome!" He flashed a beaming smile but it soon dwindled. "I fear you won't find any of what you call 'regular food' in this town." While apologetic, he permitted a note of pride to enter his remark.

Wes had to yell to be heard over the radio. "Why not?"

"This town isn't your usual kind of place," Quick explained. "It's a scientific community and we're all health conscious here. Quite concerned with living in tune with nature."

But where does the constant rock music fit in? Wes wondered. "We won't find no restaurant here that serves food? No *McDonald's* even?" Two shakes of the cartoon-circle head left him incredulous. "What about a grocery store?"

"Around the corner," Quick said. "But it's more an old-fashioned general store—and they sell only natural foods."

No meat, Wes thought miserably. No sweets, Kenny moaned, and clarified it: "You mean we can't even buy any snacks in Stillwind Valley?"

"Not one cavity-causing chunk of candy, not a sack or sample of junk food," the little fellow answered promptly. "I could sell you some fruit to take out if you wish."

Both Kenny and Wes swallowed hard. "A big bag of apples and oranges then, mate," the former decided. He ignored Wes's glare of outrage. "And we'll want coffee, too—lots of coffee!"

"No coffee for sale in Stillwind Valley," said Quick, heading toward the rear of the restaurant. "However, I have numerous varieties of healthful herbal teas."

"Gosh!" Wes said mockingly, listening to his belly rumble.

Outside Mother Quick's moments later, Wes unlocked the trunk of the Caddy to reach inside. "I always keep a two-gallon can of gas back here for an emergency, y'know. And this is it."

"I don't get it," Kenny commented, watching.

"I'm gonna pour it over my head," Wes explained, glancing up at his partner, "and light one of my last Camels!"

And seconds after Kenny'd talked him out of it, they were heading back to their temporary quarters, the tall Chicagoan starting to devour his second apple. He caught a glimpse of a familiar sight, and pointed. "Look," he told Wes.

Wes followed the pointing finger in time to see the omnipresent jogger in green before he was hidden by the Stillwind Valley Auditorium. He was trying to decide what to say about the tireless athlete when his stomach groaned loudly and he reached into the backseat for an apple.

Because Angelane O'Brien did not man a phone she was elected by Kenny's and Wes's unanimous vote to drive to the closest town and stock up on "grub" —enough for days. The Blackwood Apartments were fully equipped, thankfully, with kitchen ranges and refrigerators, so the boys were in microscopically improved spirits by the time they entered their rec room base of operations.

Wes's pop, Ocie, already sat at the desk Wes had chosen for him—close to the managerial area, in deference to Ocie's age and experience —and Cheryl Conrad was already up. But the presence of the other three people, not only on time but early, was a surprise.

Cliff Macy, who was weakest in the telephonic

skills but most dependable in terms of hanging in there, doggedly working—assuming the humorless and stocky Macy wasn't at home nursing a hangover—glanced up and waved at Wes and Kenny without expression. Short, darkly saturnine except for the magenta tip of his nose, Cliff had singlehandedly begun his own lost generation. In his middle to late thirties, he was stranded somewhere between almost equal adoration of alcohol and the Almighty. He fought the former with fundamentalist salvation, along with inconsistent attendance at Alcoholics Anonymous soirees. At times when he felt privately that the Almighty asked more than he could deliver, Cliff studied what he called "the terrible Black Arts" and tried to conceal his fascination for the occult behind an unconvincing veneer of proximate biblical citation.

Lanky, pretty Cheryl folded into herself to pinch out the morning's second joint, then pretended to be lighting an ordinary cigarette.

More commanding than manning his desk and telephone, midway between the door to the makeshift phone room and the regal region Wes and Kenny had earmarked as their own, Clemon Sparrow sat like a massive black cloud. When he was "on his game," when the sales or appointments came almost faster than he could scribble orders down, Clemon made Kenny think of a black wave ready to crash with abandon upon some midnight shore in Africa. Except that Clemon Sparrow never crashed; everybody knew that. He was a survivor, a man who, at a mostly still-muscular forty-three, prided himself on the fact that nobody whom he called on any phone knew he was black unless he wanted them to know it. It was his one-man rebuttal to those who believed people of his race not only looked but sounded alike

But that was merely part of it. While Kenny had developed his reputation by adapting his accent speedily to match that of the party he was addressing, Sparrow was as selective—and practiced every ounce as hard—as an NBA player remembering to take the shots he really had in his own arsenal. The famous people Clemen "did" were dead, without exception; from the past, long enough in their graves to have left only their vocal inflections or levels seared in memory. And they possessed one further quality, Clemon's grand impersonations: The people whose voices he so flawlessly echoed had all been authority figures of one kind or another.

Using the adjective loosely, his favorite was Rod Serling. Whenever Kenny or Wes heard the black man singing "Doo-doo, doodoo; doo-doo, doodoo"—the *Twilight Zone* theme—they understood that a respectable sale had just been chalked up by Clemon (Don't Call Me Clem) Sparrow.

Darrell Brickowski, as the Wesken Company's namesakes entered the room, was already on the verge of reading a newspaper instead of going to work. "Brick," which he preferred to be called, was what Kenny termed a *kalyike.* That was Hebrew for Crippled. Yet the versatile word could also be used to mean somebody inept, or unskilled; and the way Brick fucked off, *kalyike* fitted him like a fine suit of clothes. Which none of the freshly-arriving phone men were ever disposed to wear.

Brick always wore jeans ready to rip asunder and a tanktop, regardless of weather. Pushing fifty but boyish of manner, motion and constant mood—cursed with both a wad of touched-up black hair that tended to fall over his street-smart eyes and a withered hand—Darrell Brickowski had the ability and know-how to have been the best man in any phone room. But a combination of his passion for incessantly keeping up on the news, as well as reading newspapers aloud and declaiming his views, and a tough-guy shoulder-chip approach that was meant to compensate for his crippled hand, had so far kept Brick from ever making much real money.

Each of the threesome coming to Stillwind Valley today—self-demonized but stubborn Cliff, muscular and ever-clever Clemon, gifted goof-off Brick Brickowski—had been married before. At least once each.

No one of them was presently married, or hoped to be.

Wes, who regarded Cliff Macy as something of a project and was unspokenly determined to keep the fleshy, born-again Christian on the path of sobriety, had paused to welcome Macy.

Kenny, grandly dispensing gifts of fruit and sealed paper containers, his long arm describing humanitarian flourishes, passed among them with a series of many "G'dy, mites!" Clemon took a negligent sip and almost spat the liquid back out. "That's no damn coffee," he said accusingly. "Never said it was, luv," Kenny retorted. He clapped the big fellow's broad shoulder, cheerfully. "Drink up anyway, then; it's said to be good for what ails you." He scored two points by shooting his apple core into a wastebasket next to Brickowski's desk, hoping Hoosier Wes would chance to notice the deft jumper.

But Wes, seeing that Brick had removed granny glasses after discreetly pushing his newspaper aside, was aiming a fake punch at his employee. "You wouldn't," Brick asked, pretending to cringe, "hit a cripple just for reading the goddam paper, wouldya?"

"He won't," Kenny called in reply, locating the sales pitch he and Wes had revised, slipping it under Cheryl Conrad's nose. "No way, Bricker. But we'll sic Clemon on you if you don't pull your bloody weight this time out."

"All I have to give is blood, sweat and tears," Clemon put in, from his desk. His Churchill impression was perfection.

"Do pass out the new pitch when y've typed 'er up, darling," Kenny told Cheryl, stooping to kiss her wide forehead.

"I wish you'd both get it through your heads that I am not your secretary," the blonde complained. But she lifted the portable typewriter she'd brought with her to the top of her desk and went to work with a frown.

"Elbows were big when I was a boy," Wes let Kenny know when they were both seated and facing one another. "My daddy Ocie's brother, my Uncle Irlin, he had such terrible calcium deposits on his elbow that a great knob grew out and kept gettin' bigger. One Friday night after Uncle Irlin had it operated on, the Flanagan High School team had its basketball stolen. They put brown paint on my Uncle Irlin's elbow knob, and used it for the center jump!"

Frowning, Kenny turned his head to see if the old man had been listening. "Is that true, Ocie?" he asked.

A pause. A nod. "Teagles lie only under combat. As I recall, Coach Clappers drove all the way t'Mount Maroney to git a real ball."

"By the time Coach got back, though," Wes picked up the tale, "the score was purty low but the Blue Dawgs was ahead. And sittin' right on the bench, there was Uncle Irlin—rootin' like hell for the kids and his elbow knob."

"Years after that," said Ocie drily, "every time a storm come up, my big brother Irlin made me drive over t'Mount Maroney t'rent the basketball. Just so he'd have something to press against his elbow." He met his son's gaze and nobody could possibly have sworn to the wink. "I'm willin' to bet that knob is still lyin' around thet ole house somewheres."

There was little for any of them to do until Cheryl typed carbons of the pitch. All three heard the newspaper rustle even before Brick began to read and discuss it aloud. Quietly, leaving Ocie, Wes and Kenny vacated the room and the building. Time had passed and Angelane O'Brien might have returned with real food.

"This is one goddamn crazy-ass newspaper they print here," Brick's voice lofted to the rest. "Front page has nothin' but town crap." *Rustle, rustle.* "Stupid movie page doesn't advertise anything but flicks you never heard of, with a bunch of kid actors."

"There've been more talented new actors come along recently than in years," Cheryl said by way of comment. She laughed. "Seems like every other one of them is named Tom." The typing began afresh.

Rustle, rustle. "Damn near every page refers to some doctor named A. Dominique, like he's the Big Man in town."

"Wes 'n Kenny said he and Kiper Research are the one's we're doing the job for," explained Clemon Sparrow. Cliff Macy's muted voice droned in the background; he was already lining up contacts.

"Here's a screwball goddam item." *Rustle, fold.* Brick spoke distinctly as he scanned the

newspaper. "There's an ad for some bird named Holroyd, who, apparently, is the only undertaker in town—and the town coroner!"

Cheryl's typewriter rattled. "It's a small town," Clemon answered Brick, muffling a yawn. "Oranges aren't too bad."

"Hey, but that's not the screwball part!" Brick's voice continued. *Rustle, rustle, rustle.* "I just checked again. There's no obit page!"

The typing stopped. "No obituary page?" Cheryl asked with surprise.

"Right," Brick confirmed. "Which must mean that no one's fucking *died* recently." *Slap,* the newspaper struck his desk. "So what do they need an undertaker, a mortuary, or a coroner for if nobody's dying?"

"Come get your sales pitches, gents," Cheryl called before answering Brick. "Maybe the mortician is just a—a born optimist!" A nervous laugh. "Maybe he knows something the people at the newspaper don't know."

"It says here in the pitch," Cliff Macy's voice intoned, "that we're going to use the same press the newspaper's printed on. The *Stillwind Valley Daily Sycophant.* You know; to print the program we're selling ads for."

"If we're stuck with really printing one at all," rumbled Clemon.

Brickowski was checking the newspaper's name for the first time. He hooted his hilarity. "*Daily Sycophant,* hey? The suckers around town probably call this rag 'the Daily Syco'! Get it? Psycho?"

Ocie'd been listening without watching; now, he turned his head in time to see Cheryl rise and move away from her desk to distribute the revised pitch to her more-ungallant colleagues.

She stared through the window and her voice was lower when she spoke; tense. "There he is again . . . ."

"Who, babe?" Brick inquired from his chair.

"The jogger," she replied. She sounded abstracted, one hundred untracable miles distant. "That strange, damned perpetual jogger . . ."

It all had to be achieved in logical steps, by minute increments, by pre-planned stages. He had explained that to the scientist—who should assuredly have understood it, but did not—and there was *no way* it could be rushed. He would not permit it. And he'd use the killing bird to halt the suicidal disposition to rush if he needed to.

The lab research had been essential, and remained so. Undeniably. The marriage between science and the ancient arts had always been possible, in theory; the efficacy of what was produced from the union was also predictable. He had never been one to scoff at advancement as a consequence of conventional means. That was what the *others* did.

But just like it was with most young people today, they who invoked such words as "modern" and "contemporary" as if they were magical terms—as if any of them had recently produced anything but destruction, death, and imagined conveniences—the scientist and his adherents were impatient. Rash. Fundamentally unreliable, even inherently uncontrollable.

Or so they could have become if the chief scientist himself had not so much to lose, and so very much to gain.

The doctor, who knew little sheer science, had utilized exactly the dispassionate reasoning of researchers far more successful than Albert

Kiper. Repeatedly, he had reminded Albert that the hazards and risks to which their associates were exposed were quite, quite within tolerable ranges. If what had been initially conceived as temporary proved to be just that, and some of them changed, or died—or worse—such dangers had been worked into the equation before the bonding of science and metaphysics brought them to Stillwind Valley. And all those hazards that were not, in fact, a risk—because they were both intentional and necessary—had likewise been factored in; Kiper had agreed to them from the outset. Sacrifices, each man knew full well, were as much an integral element of human progress as test tubes.

And just as much an element of the ancient arts to which the doctor and generations of his own family had religiously committed themselves.

Perhaps, he reflected, smiling with satisfaction at what he had just achieved, perhaps the scientist would once more be reassured that the major experiment was quite likely to be triumphantly, transcendently, successful—when he saw . . . *her.*

The doctor, curtailing his every hasty movement, using infinite caution, coaxed the night bird he had made from nothing—or from those elements of next-to-nothing on which alchemy and its sister, science itself, had been based—to the sturdy reinforced perch he had built for her. Ah. The *bruxsa* was truly beautiful, precisely as he'd anticipated. Beautiful in the way that the confidently, ruthlessly powerful, the magnificently murderous, was forever beautiful. The disconcerting glitter in eyes that had not existed in the world until this hour was a light of unearthly avarice and a naked hunger so consuming that he wished then nothing so much as to stare back at the eyes. Or, for the sake of retaining his own total liberty as an individual human being, never to peer into their defiling, disturbing depths again.

Each of those choices contained its own attraction and sensual appeal for the doctor. Because even should he surrender his body, intellect, and soul to the great and ravenous bird, he knew his reward would be an enduring sexual climax of similarly unearthly proportions.

He smiled, realized he'd have to create—or find—a meal for her. The thing was, man had relinquished the components of his individuality as well as his immortality for abundantly less impressive repayment.

However, but one of those human attributes would have to be surrendered by either the scientists or him. That which lingered should be quite, quite as fulfilling when humankind experienced it as its—

The remarkable white wings fanned out in reflex or some long-remembered craving to break its fetters and take to the air—he could not know its intimate desires, because it was female—and they brushed the wooden statue that was in many ways its own test tube and its own crucible. The singular focal point of all he and the scientist planned to achieve.

Smiling darkly, the doctor yanked cruelly on the chain that restrained the bruxsa, giving pain to it. He stepped back a single, respectful pace. She could not know she existed exclusively as experiment and demonstration, nor for one additional purpose.

While intelligent in her terrible alien way, and although she definitely would feed when he allowed it, she was as nothing beside the omniscient power of the *Jagannath.* Nothing whatever.

5

The temperature had warmed up by the next day and whether spring had actually arrived to stay or not, half the phone crew had a touch of spring fever and showed a tendency toward goofing off. Part of it was the home-cooked meal they'd devoured the night before, thanks to Kenny's lady, Angelane. Since she wasn't a working part of the crew, Angelane had not only brought the "real" food back but cooked it. Then they had topped it off with a company grand-opening beer party. It was no wonder they all liked Angelane.

Still, all had gone well that morning until about eleven o'clock when Kenny exercised his right as a full partner to order the crew not to pitch tickets for the so-called "George Burns concert" with all the proceeds hypothetically going toward a home for the golden-age folks, until that afternoon. Almost everyone in the room had laughed with delight about Wes's inventiveness, and they were eager to try the pitch. Kenny, however, wanted them to get their feet wet with what they had the legal *right* to sell. "Communists may be revolutionary," he explained to Wes, "but we're not necessarily dishonest." He also preferred that only one member of the crew experiment with the "concert" that day.

Wes went along agreeably enough with the handsome Chicagoan's outburst of scruples and himself selected the stocky Cliff Macy to test the outrageous ploy. Macy sounded like anybody, he reasoned; he could lie indefinitely without admitting the truth; that was one of his more effective abilities. But the main reason Wes chose him was that Cliff had been left out of last night's festivities, beer-wise.

By the time that determined little Macy was on the phone, radiating pride over his hand-picked "assignment," there were two other developments in the phone room. First, Wes had reached the dizzying plateau of absolutely believing that Burns himself *was* coming from Hollywood to entertain in Stillwind Valley; he thereby succumbed to the phone room operator's primary occupational hazard of self-delusion.

And Darrell Brickowski, having swiftly sold space for three ads in the program book—making the unveiling of the unknown Dr. Dominique's donated statuary sound like the Venus de Milo's second coming—was chattering away, aloud, about the contents of that morning's "Daily Syco."

"Here's a sports story the rag coulda put on the front page instead of more crap about the latest promotions of Kiper Research janitors or the 'famous' Dr. Dominique's latest goddamn bowel movement!" Brick used his good hand to bat back the wave of dyed black hair falling on his forehead and waited until Clemon, at least, was paying attention. "But instead, they stuck it on their shitty little sports page. Looks like the burg has a hero, wouldcha b'lieve that?"

"Tell us what, sir," Clemon said in a Murrow-esque *Person to Person* imitation, "is 'shitty'—as you've termed it—about the sports page?"

"They don't carry any goddam major league scores, that's what!" Brick scowled, shrugged. "But it looks like every third citizen made the page doin' *something* athaletic." *Rustle, rustle.* "The kid who oughta be in the front page headlines attends some consolidated high school nine miles off, but he lives here—his name is Jay-Jay Tedrick—and be damn if he didn't make the Indiana High School All-Star Team!"

Sparrow nodded his comprehension. No state had greater attendance at high school basketball games, regularly, than the state of Indiana; being chosen as a member of the team that annually played two games with a similar Kentucky all-star squad was arguably the highest honor available to a Hoosier student. "That is . . . impressive," Clemon said in his Ed Murrow voice, " . . . for a hamlet of . . . this size."

"Wait—wait!" Brick exclaimed, wriggling in his chair with excitement. "That's not the real grabber, man! You ready for this?" Suspenseful hesitation. "Clemon, this Tedrick kid? He's refused to report for practice or even play in either game!"

"Son of a bitch," drawled Clemon astounded. Although he wasn't a native Hoosier, he had lettered in three sports during his high school days and would have given almost anything to win such an honor. "There's got to be more to it than that."

"Maybe." Brick grinned as modestly as possible under the circumstances and rested boots-clad heels on his desk. He had succeeded in startling someone with an item from the newspaper; maybe he should have gone on to broadcasting the way his mom insisted. Brick hazarded a glance toward the rear of the phone room to see if Wes or Kenny chanced to be noticing his goof-off hour and tapping the glass on his watch, a trick Wes had picked up somewhere and frequently irritated Brick with. Then he noticed both Wes and Kenny were listening to Cliff Macy's pitch and abruptly remembered something else he had read in the "Syco." *Thump,* went feet to the floor; *rustle, rustle* went the Syco. "Here's something else that may interest you, Clemon. And it shoulda been on the front page, too, rather'n more bull-hockey about their fair-haired boy, Dominique."

"And back to you, Darrell," Clemon responded in the late Chet Huntley's intonations.

"Well, seems some little teenage broad named Thalia Boggs and her family has got themselves haunted by . . . whatchacallits?—poltergeists. Y'know; like the movie?"

"I can see why they'd put it in the papers."

"Yeah; right." Brickowski's brow raised. "But, on the goddamn *last page*?" A frown. "I mean, buddy, that's got to be a weirdo, big-deal news story in a burg like this one. So why's it on the back page?" *Rustle, rustle, rustle.* "Yo! Here's one for the fucking book, baby. You remember my telling Cheryl I saw an ad for a funeral parlor and for a town coroner named Holroyd—but no obituary page?" Brick hesitated for dramatic impact. Clemon then nodded.

But by the instant Brick actually expressed the idea to Sparrow, he was truly spooked. "Today, there's another ad—right here—for a *cemetery!* It even mentions somebody named Slaid who takes care of it. Tell me, Clemon: How can this town support a mortuary, coroner, and a graveyard geezer . . . when nobody has died?"

Neatly arrayed on stainless steel shelves immediately above the electric aspirator, exactly labeled, the creams and sprays, paints and waxes, powders and pastes awaited his deft use.

The embalming machine stood beside the aspirator, fairly humming its dignified readiness.

A glimmering cabinet lined with a complicated system of individually divided drawer space—almost as if he might at some point be asked to react speedily; salvationally—was within arm's reach of young, mustachiod Stancel F. Holroyd. Quickness or haste, though, were the very last requirements for any member of Holroyd's profession.

Encased in those immaculate drawers, nearly new, lay the meticulous and merciless implements of his trade, from scalpels to clamps, from pumps and basins and cleverly rounded bowls to injection needles with the awesome dimensions needed to give any average person a seizure born of sheer terror.

But apart from Stancel, no man or woman alive had been inside his tidy tile room. Fey of disposition, he remembered a sunny time when, attending embalming school, he'd caught a fellow student affixing a sign to the door of the dissecting surgery: NO ADMITTANCE UNLESS YOU'RE DEAD.

Giggling fondly, the undertaker recalled thinking that the sign would have been better with the word UNTIL substituted for UNLESS.

Suddenly playful in his idleness, the youthful Holroyd picked up and gently prodded a pair of plastic cusps between his eyelids. Bearing no kinship to the astrological borderline between zodiacal signs, such cusps were miniature picks used by morticians to prevent the deceased's eyelids from snapping open. James Moriarty, his favorite instructor for many reasons, had noted wryly that such little accidents inadvertently created new business. Now Holroyd opened his own deepset eyes and let the cusps drop into his waiting palm like plummeting little stars. "Peekaboo!" he said in a high, tenor voice, and giggled again.

When the phone rang, he almost did not hear it; the din from the rock songs playing on his stereo did not improve his hearing. Nudging the volumn control deftly as he passed, to turn the noise down only minimally, Stancel snatched up the receiver and chirped his name.

"They won't leave, regrettably," the caller announced. "That much is perfectly obvious."

The expansive whites of Holroyd's eyes turned the pupils into merrily anticipatory polkadots. "Does that mean what *we* think it does?"

"It means more than 'we' think it does." The dry voice paused, then added in a whisper of informative awe: "He did it. The bird lives."

Stancel F. Holroyd put his lips together and blew. "That man!" he said admiringly after the unsuccessful whistle. "I do believe you two genuises are succeeding in making it permanent!"

"I didn't call you to tell you that, Holroyd. I called to tell you this." He lowered his voice once more. "The bird . . . flies."

* * *

"To demonstrate our thanks for the support you've displayed by advertising in the official program," Cliff Macy read, his gaze rarely wandering from the pitch sheet, "I'm authorized to offer you and your family a chance to attend the concert!" Red-nosed as Santa's well-known reindeer, Cliff paused where it said PAUSE on the Cheryl Conrad-typed page.

On the other end of the connection, the customer was supposed to ask either, "What concert?" or "Who's coming?" And the man at the Trim Tim Health Spa opted for the former.

Little Cliff ran his pudgy index finger across the sheet to the appropriate follow-up comment: "The one at which one of our all-time *funniest* comedians will appear . . . on behalf of beginning to build a permanent home for our beloved senior citizens."

The devout alcoholic then waited where the typed word clearly commanded WAIT and found himself listening, in order, to a clicking sound and then a dial tone.

"He hung up," Cliff said simply to the nearby and listening Wes and Kenny. Looking aggrieved, almost as an afterthought, he replaced the phone in its cradle and folded his arms.

"Well, mate, the thing is," Kenny said in a not unkind fashion, "you followed the speech too closely."

"Uh-uh," Wes grunted, surprising his partner. He looked from Ken to Macy and back to Kenny, his expression wholly solemn, even grim. This was the sixth time Cliff Macy had peddled ad space for the unveiling of the statue, and then been disconnected. The tag-on pitch clearly wasn't working; or Cliff wasn't making it work.

Cheryl, from her desk, had watched the entire

proceedings and was concerned. She knew that just then in Wes's life, nothing was as important as comprehending the nature of the problem. Even if it meant his idea for the appearance of V.D. Byrnes was a bad one.

"I meant 'uh-*huh*,' he does follow the speech too close—but I don't think that's what is screwin' things up." Standing, Wes patted the alcoholic's arm to remove the sting from what he was about to say. "Ole Cliff always just plain reads the pitch out loud. But he's also been sellin' the ads! So it's somethin' else."

"Y'want t'know why it ain't clicking?" Ocie had maneuvered a path to the busy desk site. His eyes were agleam with their old emerald fire. "Or am I buttin' in where I ain't wanted?"

"Au contraire," Kenny replied before Wes, turning with a dazzling smile. "We're in this boat together. No one has more experience in these matters than you."

"I been listenin'. And everything is fine and dandy when Macy mentions the concert. Same thing even when he gits t'the cost of the tickets. After that . . . well, boys, I ob-served something very peculiar."

"Go ahead, Ocie." Wes had decided within five minutes of his roaming father's return home that he'd never call the old drifter "Dad."

"Well, sir," Ocie allowed, irritatingly clearing his throat, "if Macy gets t'the point of saying the proceeds go to build an old folks home, they hang up." He straightened, hitching gnarled thumbs under the front of the belt to heighten the drama. "And if Macy mentions 'George Burns,' well . . . they *also* hang up!"

Wes and Kenny swapped blank looks. "I don't get it," Kenny admitted.

"That's exactly right," Ocie said shortly, turning away from the younger man and walking slowly toward the rec room door. "You don't get the sale, *either* way." Back turned, his hand shot up. "It's upta you big cheeses t'figger out the end of the mystery." A curt wave without a glance toward them. He did incline his head in Darrell Brickowski's direction. "Gonna rest my aged bones awhile if nobody ob-jects; then Brick's havin' me over for supper at his apartment. We'll prob'ly watch cable news 'til I know everything that's happened in the world."

Brick laughed as the old man departed. Kenny smiled but told the others, "He's right. It doesn't make any bloody sense, Wes, but your father is right."

"Maybe," Wes said carefully. He lowered one ruminative buttock to the edge of Cliff's desk. His gaze met Cheryl's while his finely honed sales mind shifted gears. "But that would hafta mean one of two things: either folks in Stillwind Valley don't like George Burns and laughin'—or they just don't give one hoot in hell about their old people."

Early evening shadows crept across the phone room floor and a thoughtful silence fell. "The times," Cheryl said softly with a glance that included Kenny Higgins, "they are a-changing."

"Not that fast, luv," Kenny said. "Maybe that *way*—but I hope not."

"Here's what we're gonna do," Wes said, jumping up. He pointed a finger at Clemon Sparrow. "Clemon, start settin' up some appointments for the door-to-door people. Get out in the field yourself, if you want, just t'generate some revenue around here."

"Does that mean just Purvis Richwine and Doc

Jarvis?" Brick interpolated, leering, "or Lucia Mahorn too?"

"We'll accept any live bodies who can make a decent close," Kenny replied. "Right?"

Wes nodded. "Cheryl, you'n Brick can start tryin' the pitch for the concert tomorrow." He started for the door but paused, brows lowering above his glasses. "And *listen* to what folks say."

"Where are you off to?" Kenny called.

"To see what the night life is like in this here metropolis," Wes said. He winked at Cheryl Conrad and added, before bobbing out of sight, "I may check out the local talent, too!"

I'll even eat wheat germ or fucking grass at one of the make-believe restaurants, Wes thought with determination when he'd left the building and begun walking rapidly toward the town square, *if it takes that t'learn what's goin' on. What's wrong with the people in this town, and how t'sell em!*

Spring wasn't holding for the evenings in Stillwind Valley yet, however, and by the time Wes had reached the heart of town, he wished he had driven the company car or worn a coat. Yet out of the corner of one eye he caught a glimpse of first one, then several joggers drifting effortlessly up a rise of land. Even at a considerable distance he heard the sounds of rock songs conflicting as if in combat with each other and imagined, momentarily, he had seen the familiar, haunting jogger in green. An instant later, he realized that these were other people—

And began to encounter a startling number of both jogging and biking paths with mileage markers. Paths that led seemingly in every direction and, Wes thought with an involuntary shudder, nowhere.

Grabbing a deep breath and sucking on his teeth, all at once aware of how out of shape he was, Wes recognized the rundown neighborhood through which he was passing and knew the town square was only a few blocks off. Hell's bells, it occurred to him; *maybe this burg will be good for me . . . make us all healthier.* He hadn't really walked very far, yet he was huffing and puffing as if he were his father. A guy who was going to become forty years of age probably should take better care of himself—and, crapola, if it was gonna be constantly inconvenient to eat a decent meal while they were there, or buy a pack of Camels, he might—

Wes stopped walking; the town square was in view. For the first time he had a clear look at a sizeable number of Stillwind Valley residents. It was no mob scene but, at nearly six-thirty in the evening, the total number of men and women milling around in the square seemed fairly surprising to Wes.

And almost as many people were loafing in a small park at the center of the square. *Pee-culiar,* Wes decided, traversing an old, badly-cracked sidewalk and drawing nearer. At the curb he looked more closely at the townfolk gathered in the miniature park and perceived at their nucleus a freshly built limestone platform. Wes nodded; that Dr. A. Dominique was donating a statue and the platform was doubtlessly the foundation for it. The sales pitch Wes had written finally had some relation to reality for him, and that meant he'd need to firm up arrangements with the man at the *Daily Sycophant* who'd be printing the program with all the ads—assuming neither Wes nor Kenny discovered a way to side-step the cost at the last minute.

Wes turned from the park and the idling people with a disturbing impression that what he was seeing might somehow prove to be more fanciful than his own romantic approach to running a phone room. Why would folks flock to a platform where the statue was *going* to be erected? It wasn't there yet!

He continued to stroll, to mingle, wanting to work up an appetite that might let him dine at Mother Quick's or some other health food restaurant. Window shopping with animation, smiling affably, he tried to catch the eyes of other passersby and exchange a neighborly word. It was always harder to say no to a man you knew than to a complete stranger.

But almost at once Wes encountered two things wrong with the plan: First, the products and services suggested by signs on the shops in the square involved matters Wes knew little about, and it was hard to approach a stranger when you had nothing in common with him. It seemed that the town's merchants were single-mindedly devoted to maintaining good health, and Wes supposed he had lived most of his life as if he'd set out to ruin his. He shivered, feeling cold in various ways, and resisted the urge to cram his fists into his pants pockets as he walked. He saw health spas, suppliers of swimming pools and equipment for them, natural food outlets, pharmacies that seemed to sell nothing but medicine, home exercise establishments, athletic and sports wear stores; an occasional VCR rental outlet. Movies to watch alone at home were apparently the only means to what Wes Teagle considered recreation. He saw no bars, liquor stores, bookstores, ice cream or candy shops of any kind.

But it was the other people who concerned him —*unless,* Wes pondered the problem, *I'm plain imagining it.* Because persons to whom he gave his most charming smile—the three or four men to whom he spoke on one pretext or another and the merchants he saw whenever he stepped with amiable curiosity into a store—instantly glanced away. Ignored him; looked somewhere else, as if he didn't even exist.

And they shied away from him, unless he was flat-out going nuts, all but . . . fearfully.

Why?

He'd been trudging slowly forward, trying to sort it out, but he stopped then to regard his own reflection in a store window. The lighting was bad, however—evening was fast becoming night —and his features were indistinct, unclear. When a man inside the shop moved and chanced to glance toward him before looking away, Wes's own face shimmered and disappeared.

That moment, he felt more completely out of his own depths—cut-off, out of place, alone and unwanted—than he had ever felt before. He had to place one hand against the window, rest his weight momentarily against it, stare down at the feet of unknown and apparently unknowable strangers who passed without acknowledgment.

As a salesman, he had never understood the need other people seemed to have for their own kind. *He* was his own kind; he was *one* of a kind. He'd been an individualist on his own who survived by his own wits and by outsmarting others, for thirty-nine years; rarely had he even experienced the wish to love, or be loved. Young people of the past decade or more who explained their participation in crime, or drugs, on the basis of wanting to make or cement a friendship mystified Wes, and he'd scoffed at them, regarded them as spiritually and intellectually feeble, or feckless. On those very rare occasions when he'd allowed himself to review his own existence, his principles and needs, he had seen himself as not unlike an actor or writer, even the leader of outmanned but valiant military groups. The kind of man who did his own thing without the urge to talk about it or enlist a whole damned organization for moral support.

But I never turned forty before, he thought, slowly lifting his gaze. When his reflection didn't immediately show in the store window he moved his head, then his body, until he saw his dynamite smile beaming back at him. Feebly.

They *knew,* Wes decided, realizing how silly he'd looked, jiggling around to see his face; they *knew* he was leaving all his youth behind, forever.

But the realization came to Wes's mind then so shockingly—so overwhelmingly—that it brushed aside the surfacing self-pity and spun him around to stare at the features of the other people in the town square . . . to stare at and study them. And now he did not try to draw them out, to make acquaintances of them. Although they went on glancing warily at him, then averted their faces, Wes didn't want to rap now; he wanted only to appraise the residents of Stillwind Valley with all the experience and acumen at his command, and figure out the enigma that had just dawned on him:

He had seen, and was seeing now, *no* one—*nobody at all*—who looked *older than forty.*

Nor, now that he thought about it, had he seen a single person who seemed to be much past thirty. No old or elderly people. None at all.

Up the block, though—headed this time toward west of town and away from either the town square or the Blackwood Apartment building—Wes did see the indefatigable jogger in green. Not that far ahead of Wes, moving at a pace that looked somewhat slower than his customary gait, the man with the crewcut seemed nearly to lead Wes on, to beckon him away from the town square.

On impulse and wishing deeply now that he had driven the Caddy, Wes decided to do it—to jog after the athlete, see where he was going.

Then the younger man turned his head as if to be sure Wes was following. Their eyes met, and held. And the expression on the jogger's face would have been blank except, Wes thought, it contained defiance and mockery.

He was hustling after the man in green and stumbling breathlessly along a jogging path when it occurred to Wes that he had not only seen no one who looked as old as forty.

He also could not recall having seen so much as one small child.

6

Neither Kenny nor Cliff, whose idea going to the Boggs's house it was, had expected to go inside. If the place was actually under attack from poltergeists, the people who lived there would not exactly be in the most receptive mood for entertaining two salesmen. And if they were running some kind of hoax, for whatever reason, the family was unlikely to want to put on a special show for the men who were neither ghost-busters—the term leapt to Kenny's lips enroute to the house and instantly earned Cliff Macy's sternest frown—nor newspaper reporters.

But Cliff, who vacillated not only from sobriety to drunkenness but from quiet, Christian belief to a badly disguised absorption in the super-natural, had said he wanted "to get a feel for what Stillwind Valley folks are like in person." He felt badly stung by his inability to sell "concert" tickets while his two bosses had watched. And Kenny Higgins had always been a man who was game for almost anything. As a communist, of course, he was already convinced that the

Boggs's were pranksters "tryin' t'make a fast buck." If he didn't believe in God or the soul, he wasn't about to start believing in the devil or in ghosts.

The pretext for their night call was an attempt to sell tickets to see George Byrnes in person. Whether they sold any or not—*not* seemed probable to them, considering their reports of what Cliff Macy called "infestation"—they'd acquire information from Clemon Sparrow to pass along to the three direct salespeople coming in from Indy.

"I can't visit hell long, mate," Kenny said softly when Cliff had stopped his creaking old Chevy before one of the oldest houses in town. "My personal angel is waiting for me." And, when they were strolling with practiced nonchalance up a neatly kept lawn, he whispered a sudden hunch to Cliff: "Wouldn't be surprised if ol' Wilford and his folks were original residents, back when this town had another name."

"Wouldn't be nobody but self-employed farmers or coloreds who'd stay in a town with no one else around," Cliff replied softly.

Kenny glanced down at the red-nosed man and shoved his Colts cap back on his head. He wondered, as they reached the front door, if uneducated little Macy would be surprised to know that the word "colored" had different connotations in other parts of the world, and if he'd be able to understand what that said about the illogic of bigotry. Probably not, Kenny decided.

The door was not only ajar, but wide open. It was night, now, yet there was scanty illumination from inside the house. Removing his cap, Kenny put his head inside and called, "Hullo?" Gently.

Finding the gloomily lit front room reminding him of pictures he had seen of bombed-out London houses from World War II was a greater surprise to Kenny than the door being open.

Cliff followed the much taller man until they'd stopped not quite at the center of the room, turning slowly to look at such wreckage that it was nearly impossible to tell where a smashed chair ended and a coffee table with broken legs began. Liquid stuffs from the kitchen and, Kenny thought, from the bathroom had been liberally poured, willynilly, over the whole ruined mess, which stank.

They'd gone that far into the old house with a growing, dark feeling that they'd somehow been saddled by fate with the responsibility of discovering a horrid family of motionless corpses and of notifying the authorities.

And they found the bodies in what remained of the dining room. But they were still alive, functionally. An overweight woman; a man who had a table leg wrapped between large hands as if he intended or even hoped to strike someone; a girl in her teens. Exhausted, terrified, black of skin, sitting or leaning against an overturned dining table. Appearing both relieved and then disinterested when they'd looked up at Cliff and Kenny, and glanced away. The woman, Kenny thought, looked vaguely embarrassed, too; but she hugged the girl to her and managed to become the first to speak.

"What you want?" she asked.

"Missus Boggs," Cliff said, grinning, "we represent the Wesken Company, and we—"

"I don't think that this is the time for that, Clifford," said Kenny. While he had not raised his voice, there was a broken-bottle edge to what he'd said, and Cliff lapsed into silence. Kenny moved closer to the people, twisting his cap in his hands. "How can we help?"

"Shit," Wilford Boggs said. His smile was humorless. "Who are you? Kiper Research send you?"

Cliff's expression clearly registered his awareness of an opportunity to make his pitch, but Kenny's glance was daggerish. "We've just come to Stillwind Valley," the Chicagoan explained carefully without the trace of any accent, "but we read about you in the paper and thought you might need a hand."

Boggs shoved himself up from the smashed dining table, shook his head. He put out his hand, tentatively. "Need the sanitation department," he said sadly, "t'come haul our things away." He gestured. The gesture might have meant his entire house or the whole world. "It got everything."

"It?" Cliff inquired.

"Don't talk about it!" Mary Boggs said, still clutching her quiet daughter. The remark was a command. "Don't *name* it, Wilford!"

Boggs ran a big hand over the stubble of his chin, looking thoughtful. "I don't think it can do much more to us, Mary." His stricken gaze met Kenny's eyes with a hint of the courage, the character, the man must have had to have kept them all there even when there was no employment in a town with no name—and now, through a visitation from hell. Even Cliff nodded, understanding;. this was Wilford Boggs's *home.* "They call the damned thing a poltergeist," Boggs said clearly. "Usually, that means there's a child becomin' a man or a woman, and her unconscious mind—"

Crackling sounds—and an immediate scorching smell—interrupted Wilford Boggs. He, Kenny and Cliff and the woman turned their heads, searched for the source, felt sudden, smothering heat. Thalia Boggs broke away from her mother's grasp and, making a noise Kenny hoped he would never have to hear again, ran from the room.

Then he and the others saw the brown spots, no larger than a dime, materializing high up on the walls of the dining room. Before any of them had a chance to realize what they were or to do anything about them, they grew, fanned out.

"Fire," Cliff Macy whispered. He was momentarily frozen in place, short arms lifted from his rather pudgy body as if he planned to fly away. "*Hell fire.*"

"Hot . . ." Kenny gasped, backing away from the smudges even as they began to turn a deep, arterial red. "So hot . . ."

"Sweet Jesus," Mary Boggs prayed. But she was rising, trying to rush across the room in pursuit of Thalia, her daughter—not running from the fire.

"C'mon!" Kenny snatched both Cliff and Wilford Boggs by an arm each, still gaping at the reddening stains.

Cliff broke his trance-like state and followed the woman toward the front of the wrecked house, eyes huge and a handkerchief pressed over his nose and mouth.

Wilford Boggs, however, tore his arm free and drew himself wearily to his full height. "I'm not leavin'. Won't be driven out of my own house!"

"Man, this place is gonna *go*!" Kenny exclaimed. Tongues of flame stretched serpent-like from the brown and red splotches, and more brown stains were forming, gradually making a circuit of the room. The heat was becoming intolerable. "Boggs, you can't save it!"

Boggs had gone as far from Kenny as possible, stood beside the kitchen door, large eyes tearing. "The thing knows what it's doin'," he said, beginning to cough. There wasn't much smoke yet, but it was getting worse by the second. "Wants us out—but it doesn't want t'burn the house down."

"How can you know that?" Kenny demanded. Indecisive, he was half-turned to run but magnetized by this stranger's guts—and the odd premise he had just enunciated. "Let's get out of here!"

"Go on," Boggs barked, shoving the kitchen door open. Kenny saw no evidence of fire there. He saw only the pieces of dishes and glasses, silverware strewn on the floor and bent as if a mad psychic had been at work. "Go! I'm *ordering* you out of my house!"

Kenny paused. Then, "You've got it," and he was back into the front room and jogging toward the door. Perhaps Boggs was correct, after all; and if it got too hot for him in the kitchen, there was probably a back door to the house.

Cliff was leaning against his Chevy, trembling. Loping toward him, looking for Mary or Thalia Boggs and seeing neither of them in either direction he looked, Kenny thought how small Macy appeared, how fundamentally little and fragile all people were . . . if you went only by what was on the outside, in plain view.

"You've seen your spook at work," Kenny said, pausing to peer back at the house and realizing with surprise that it seemed unharmed from there. Passersby, had there been any, would never have known a hundred miniature fires were burning inside the building.

"I didn't see no poltergeist," Cliff murmured. He nodded when Kenny showed surprise. "That's right, you heard me." He bobbed his head determinedly. "Maybe the work of Satan. Might even be the Almighty tryin' to get those coloreds to leave."

"I don't follow you," Kenny snapped. "I don't get it."

"I studied the occult, Ken. Wanted t'know my enemy, and the Lord's." His close-set eyes gleamed in the darkness. "Whatever evil spirit is at work, unless it's a real demon—a creature born in hell itself—it only does certain things. Because if it ain't a demon, Kenny, that means it's an exhuman being, and it's also ruled by the number of man—a six."

"Dammit, Macy, make sense!" Kenny exclaimed. He was still trying to figure out where Thalia Boggs and her mother had gone; possibly a neighbor took them in. "You saying people are all born under a six? What the hell does that mean?"

"It means," Cliff said, nodding, "we're bound by routine and so are those spirits who were people once. We, and they, can only do certain things that are a part of us."

"Make your point," Kenny prompted him, opening the door of the dilapidated Chevy and staring to get inside.

"Poltergeists tear down things, throw 'em around," said Cliff. He got into his car, too, and fired up a grudging engine. "They can talk through people sometimes, and they often curse like the devil himself—say awful, vile things." He looked a last time at the seemingly-ordinary Boggs home, edged the Chevy away from the curb. "But they're *not* firestarters. That's something else entirely."

Kenny's light brown brows raised in further startlement. "Are you telling me, you *plosher,* that what we just saw was a hoax? That it was all faked for our benefit?"

"No. Dear Jesus, no." Cliff steered their way back to the Blackwood Apartments, smelling of perspiration from a day's work and the terrible heat they had both experienced. "It wasn't faked. But Kenny"—he turned his egg-yolk eyes toward his colleague and boss, and they were filled with concern and superstitious awe—"I don't know what was happenin' to them poor people."

It did not make sense that Kiper Research hired no one as old as forty, or that people in their twenties and thirties had no small children—

Or that Wes Teagle was chasing after a total stranger at the end of his first full day in Stillwind Valley, and doing it while the night got darker and darker.

But that was just the start of it, Wes thought, really gasping for air now. It made no sense that other strangers gaped at him in the town square as if they were snooty white folks in the pre-integration south and he'd turned black overnight. He had also heard what Brick reported from the newspaper—that the town had a mortuary, undertaker, coroner, and a cemetery with nobody in it—and *that* didn't add up.

And it sure as shit stinks didn't make a lick of sense the way the silent, snotty young guy in the green jogging outfit practically came to a damn *halt* whenever Wes looked as if he couldn't run another step.

Panicky thought: He had no clear idea where in hell he was, either. That wasn't a big problem because he had spotted a couple of phone booths enroute to their destination—whatever that proved to be—and he could always call Kenny, ask his partner to come pick him up. The farther the jogger led him, loping forward as effortlessly as ever, the more Wes knew he would be phoning Kenny.

But what might very well be a big problem occurred to the Hoosier then.

The half-naked kid ahead of him, knowing Wes was a stranger in town, might have concluded he had money and could have lured him into the countryside to roll him. And the skinny bastard might know karate or another of those flashy martial arts they were undoubtedly teaching somewhere in Stillwind Valley!

With the full formulation of the scary thought, Wes intentionally slowed down, pretended to be more tired than he was—which took one hell of a lot of acting ability. This time the jogger didn't glance back, and kept going. A three-quarter moon shed its light on him and Wes saw the youth's nearly skeletally thin form through globules of cold sweat, those white knees rising and falling like pistons in a machine; and Wes wondered about cutting across a weed-strewn field to his right while he had the opportunity.

But that'd be like denying his own manhood, his own credo! Wes squinted at the jogger, his heart racing, suddenly aware of sprawling shadows everywhere. Dammit! White men in their thirties who kept their weight down and their hair on weren't *used* to getting apprehensive, anxious about being attacked by just one other bird; it wasn't *manly!* Yet for the first time since Ocie had vamoosed when Wes was only a tad, Wes was experiencing fear, learning how people of the opposite sex and others were obliged to exist in modern cities, and detesting it. But he was out in the *country,* dammit—how could he regard it as "opportunity" to make a mad-ass dash to nowhere across a frigging vacant field . . .

"Golden opportunity," he recalled the term; he and Kenny Higgins's word to describe this town. Before they'd been there. Deep inside, he had also imagined how he'd teach the yokels or eggheads—whatever they were—a thing or two. Instead, they were already teaching him, and the only question that remained was—*what?*

Or putting it differently, unless the athletic pile of bones that appeared to float up a hill without even breathing hard really did intend to beat the crap out of him, *why* had he led Wes out into the middle of Nowhereville at night when they'd never even spoken to each other?

Wes's toe caught on something; he stumbled, cried out in alarm. Flailing his arms and recovering his balance, he looked up fast, certain he had not let the jogger out of his sight for a second.

Before now.

The rise in the road was a splash of vivid moonlight, and deserted. A part of Wes's mind that always coped well registered the fact that it hadn't been an utterly soundless parade, after all. Because a rhythmic, metronomic *pat-pat-pat* of jogger's shoes on the lonely road had disappeared with the jogger.

Still lurching up the hill, legs aching, lungs increasingly protesting the unaccustomed exertion, Wes cast searching looks of bafflement and beginning fright to the left, to the right—

Saw, at the summit of the incline, the start of an eerie wrought-iron gate. The long arc of ensuing fence dwindled into the distance as if concealing from night-sight a concentration camp. Or heaven; or hell.

He had ascended to the highway's highest point, and tufty clouds like bruised fists were poised for attack across the face of the moon. Wes was an exposed target, felt nude. He was also unable to read the ornate sign that he had just noticed at eye level on the fancy gate; then the lunar nightlight went out behind cloud cover.

Shaky, listening for any traffic that might climb the incline, he fished his Djeep lighter from his flannel shirt pocket and stepped closer. Unsteadily, he flicked the lighter, saw the obedient flame surge up to illuminate the legend on the sign before him: STILLWIND VALLEY CEMETERY.

Once, the fire winked, coyly; then it went out. Wes's grip on the Djeep had slipped. Now, though, he did not wish to relight it. Instead—without fully realizing he was doing it—Wes tiptoed several hesitant steps down the other side of the hill, unwilling to raise his gaze from the noiseless graveyard, keeping contact by running his cold fingers along vertical bars of fencing that felt like bone.

The cloud cover abruptly dispersed. Moonlight like milk spilling washed over the sight Wes saw, and he spasmed and dropped his lighter in a fringe of grass on the berm of the road.

He'd never seen a new cemetery before.

He thought the unbroken ground was strange, horribly unnatural. Gaping, he trudged another few paces forward. It was as if the winter that had just passed had perfectly filled in those pits man excavated, tidied up enviously, expunged the evidence of human passing. Worse, he decided imaginatively, fingers still grazing the vertical rods of the cemetery fencing—*Who or what did they keep in, or out?*—it was like the place was pre-haunted . . . as if the expiring souls of those persons yet to depart had silently lifted from their sleeping forms in intuitive knowing and come to inspect the forlorn earth in which they'd reside. But they *had* left their traces; Wes sensed it in his fingertips, his toes, the reflexive jumpy part of his lower spine. And—

"Omigod!" he said aloud, staring through the bars into the dark place, trying to absorb what he'd seen then. Darrell Brickowski had said nobody died; the *Syco* didn't even have an obituary page.

But it carried advertisements for the cemetery and Wes had just perceived, in a sweeping glance of fresh alarm, the caretaker's traditional *who-in-hell'd-stay-here* small house and, to the rear of the structure, something else . . .

A freshly opened grave.

Who's it for? Wes wondered, and *Where'd the damn jogger GO?* The fence seemed to jolt his shivering fingers like electricity, and he was whirling to run back up the hill and keep going down the other side.

And it was when he had begun wondering frantically how far he'd need to go to locate once more the telephone booth from which he could call Kenny that the noise of mammoth wings flapping tore Wes's gaze up, to scan the bleak skies.

Framed fleetingly by pale light from the moon, soaring from blackness into blackness, was something of truly unreasonable bulk and muscle. It looked full as a sated tick, or a glutted buzzard.

Yet it was like no bird Wes had ever heard of, sleek but corded with power, vulturish in ambience yet bigger. He thought he was able to detect talons that opened and closed, rendingly, and a wide but pointed beak capable of consuming a man.

He was not absolutely sure of anything except the enormous, graceful, beautiful wings. Wings that looked soft, warm and suffocating. White as snow . . . as crisp, clean bond paper . . .

As a person dead for days.

When Wes finally reached the phone booth and stumbled inside, holding the sliding door to and watching the sky in case the bird returned, he learned that the phone was disconnected. By someone having cut the cablelike wire, just below the aperture wherein change was returned.

He had not remained at Brick's apartment longer than it took to eat the supper Angelane brought over—part of a casserole—and regain some of the cockiness provided men like him by masculine companionship. He and Brick had swapped partly true anecdotes about the life of a salesman; then Ocie had begun to yawn, and finally announced that he needed some shuteye.

What the old man really wanted was renewed courage to get out into the town awhile that night, on his own the way it'd always been, in the hope of locating a carton of smokable cigarettes. Even filters would do, if that was all they'd hidden somewhere behind the counter, tucked away with the men's magazines. He had not doubted that the town fathers put some kind of ignorant gee-dee ban on smokes in Stillwind Valley, but he doubted a lot that there was no mechant in town willing to cater to his customers' demands. Every town, anywhere, had its addicts to nicotine; and they also had smart merchants who provided what folks wanted. Ocie was sure of it.

So he hiked the meaningless blocks downtown, glad to use his legs once more, not minding the wintry chill lingering on the evening air at all.

Ocie checked out several shops within the town square, stubbornness growing. Once, he wondered if he had actually seen his son Wes across the way, trotting up a path as if he was following someone. He'd speedily concluded he was wrong; his son had never been one to expend physical energy needlessly, even when he was a little kid. Just a trick of lighting from the old buildings, and maybe two eyes that were in their seventies now and had already seen too many strange sights.

The young birds he asked about covert caches of cigarettes were nearly rude in their denials. They gave him funny looks, blinked and retreated to their cash registers, or rearranged their displays. But that was okay, because *how* each of them said no merely lent Ocie confidence that they were lying in their teeth. All he required was one practical storekeeper who had use of an extra sawbuck.

Returning to Indiana at his age, Ocie saw, pushing open the door to the Coomer Pharmacy, had permitted him clearer insight into his own motives. Also fine; because he'd spent seven decades learning what other folks were all about. And he knew, as he ignored the counters crammed with vitamins, diet food and health aids, that he was as much in need of having his own way as he was of smokes. Bad enough the way busybodies passed laws opposing cigarettes without such fancy scientist-type fucking *ordaining*—Ocie was sure Kiper Research was behind the outrage—that merchants couldn't even sell 'em! He'd tried to be an honest man according to his own lights; he had seen more changes in what they called society than any man should—

Behind him—out on the street or maybe issuing from the shop he'd visited last—rock music blared as if the lunatics of an asylum had captured a gee-dee Dixie band. Ocie paused, glared back the way he had come. What he realized sent chills trickling a path through his aging body: Every time he'd left a store and walked on to another one, the noise—the rock—had started up again . . . .

"Do we have a prescription ready for you?"

NOXIE COOMER read the name tag on the yellow pharmacist's jacket. "Don't b'lieve so, Mr. Coomer, but—"

"Then we have nothing in this store for you. Nothing."

Ocie frowned. The average-size kid pharmacist before him had spoken in an unmistakeably rude fashion and wore an unmistakeably rude expression. Coomer held his ground, folded his arms, glared at Ocie. "Reckon you have a coupla cartons of—"

"You will not find cigarettes anywhere in Stillwind Valley," Noxie Coomer stated. "I must ask you to leave."

Ocie had the words "Now hold on" forming on his lips when he grew aware of the other customers converging from various aisles until all five—no, six; all men but one—had hemmed him in. Ocie stared at them in real amazement. The men were pretending to poke around in the vitamin displays, but the single woman, taller than Ocie was at seventy-three, with biceps implausibly muscled and tanned for the season, was within arm's reach. Staring him down, fists doubled.

"Nothing," Coomer repeated. He pointed to his door. *"Now."*

"You infectious, diseased old bastard." The source of the epithet was evident to Ocie without the need for him to look her way. "You foul relic. You despoiler."

"You musclebound butch cunt," Ocie said distinctly, at last.

But by the time he said it, he was hurrying through the door of Coomer's pharmacy, the amazon was nowhere in sight, and Noxie Coomer was hurrying after him, a sign in his hands.

CLOSED, it read. And a window shade was drawn on the other side of it, blocking out the old man's view of the store completely.

He began the long walk back to the Blackwood Apartments, dimly aware of motorcycles in the distance rumbling like warning thunder, completely aware of the embarrassing tears in his emerald-colored eyes.

Part Two

The Condition of Youth

"We will not bury you; we will just outlive you."
—Tom Hayden

"Magic is the art of causing changes in consciousness at will."

—Dion Fortune

"All people must be helped to regain the condition of youth."

—Charles Reich

7

By Friday night Wes and Kenny had swapped horror stories, bringing each other up to date on their harrowing adventures. They'd played down what had happened for the benefit of the other phone people, knowing they were tense enough about the trouble all of them were having selling anything but space in the program.

When Wes finished relating his story about the jogger, the cemetery, and the great bird with white wings, however, he had promptly received one of Kenny Higgins's periodic prolonged stares; the kind Wes usually got when his partner was waiting for the punchline to one of his Hoosier stories.

But the only punchline Wes had to offer involved his long, weary, scary walk back to the apartment building—when two additional phone booths he'd located also housed phones with the wires cut.

"It could've been vandals, luv," Kenny proposed. He gave a not quite surreptitious wink to

Angelane, who brought them each another beer and kept a straight face. "Punkers, out for a bleedin' spin, y'know."

"I recall a monster beaver," Wes began dreamily, acidly, "over t'Oolitic County, in my boyhood. Had the reputation for bein' able to fell a tree in less time than it took our local champeen, name of Elroy Ostermeyer." He gazed languidly over the beer can at his friends. "I reckon, however, it wasn't likely the beaver who got those phone wires. Might have been Elroy, 'cept he's maybe seventy-nine or eighty now."

"That largish bird you saw," Kenny retrieved the thread. He sipped his Bud slowly, knowing it was the last of what Angelane had bought in nearby Walterville. He planned for her and him to drive back the next day for more, and also to stock up the swiftly emptying food supply. "Sure it wasn't blue?"

"The bluebird of happiness dumping on ole Wes?"

"Why not?" Kenny gestured broadly, crossing long jeans-clad legs. Even at home in his own apartment, he still wore the faded Colts cap. "I mean, there are normal people—probably—who've seen the Abominable Snowman—"

"Snowpersons," Angelane put in, the way her friend Cheryl might have.

Kenny snickered. "—Who believe in the Abominable Snowperson, and the Loch Ness monster. What's wrong with a Stillwind Valley Bluebird of Happiness?"

"Nothin'," Wes growled. "But what's wrong with a town without folks even as old as you or me? People without little tads?" Still clutching his empty Bud can, Wes freed an index and pointed with it. "That one girl, Thalia—the one you met—she's disappeared, right?"

"You think there's a connection?" Kenny inquired.

"Hell, no," Wes said sarcastically. "I'm just a dumb Hoosier hick. I'm just willin' and eager t'believe the crap we've discovered here in a coupla days is normal as blueberry pie!"

"Bluebird-berry pie," Kenny amended, straightfaced.

"Kenny and I are old enough to have had children," Angelane murmured. Perched on the arm of her lover's easy chair, she brushed with fingertips at the wave of hair protruding from beneath his cap. "Young children. But we don't."

"You aren't married," Wes explained quickly, and instantly regretted it. Kenny's wide mouth had become a line. "Yeah, I know. If you don't believe in God, and you don't cotton much t'most laws, what's the point t'gettin' hitched?"

"There's a bit more to it than that, Weston."

"I'm sure there is." Before his best friend could launch his whole sociopolitical argument, Wes sighed and got slowly to his feet. "I'm still tuckered out from all that walkin'. And you two have some flicks t'see."

Kenny, he knew, had joined a VCR club just off the town square that afternoon, renting both the player and a few movies. Wes had caught a glimpse of them on a table by the door when he'd entered the apartment.

"No reason you can't watch 'em too, mate," Kenny said hospitably, jumping up. Angelane followed suit, smoothing her dress. "You're more'n welcome."

"No reason?" Wes grinned. He hugged Angelane, shook Kenny's hand. "One of 'em is X-rated." A sigh. "Single men don't watch them things if they enjoy their shuteye—or I *should* say, 'unattached,' men." Awkwardly, he pulled open the door to the hallway, then paused, smiling. "I sure as shootin' don't care t'see no damn dirty movies while my ole partner's lady is present!"

Both Kenny and Angelane laughed, saw him out, and the petite brunette carried the empty beer cans out to the small apartment kitchen while Kenny turned on the television and VCR and slipped the movie Wes had noticed into the latter. He'd felt both romantic and horny all day and, while he knew Angelane basically objected to everything about the idea of sexually explicit movies, he also had known times when they'd both enjoyed their own physiological reactions to them.

"Do you want some popcorn?" she called brightly.

Kenny grinned, raised his eyes to the ceiling. "Not until the second film. All right?" *Gawd,* but he loved her! He supposed a part of the great attraction Angelane had for him, and always had, was linked to her proper Catholic upbringing. She still swore inexpertly despite every effort of the phone crew—some effort, Kenny'd have sworn, intentional—and while he made the second man with whom she'd known a sexual relationship, he was ready to bet a bundle that there'd never been a third or fourth.

"Was it a good VCR shop?" She was back with coffee for both of them and, he noticed, an old shirt of his. Which meant she was going to sew on a button or something and pretend not to see what was happening on the TV screen. "Lots of good movies?"

"Not really," Kenny said. He shrugged, went back to his chair. The rented film's blank lead-in was blinking its way through. "Almost everything they had starred these young kids who've come along lately; didn't see a single old classic. Did have an amazing collection of instructional tapes—aerobics and other exercise stuff."

"Why did you join then?" she asked. Already she'd threaded a needle and was setting to work.

He looked at her blank expression, amused. *Because I wanted to get hot watching other people make it,* he thought. *As you darned bloody well know!*

"It's called Arnt's Video," he said. The title of the film had sped by while they were talking and he'd forgotten what he'd read on the box, but that didn't matter. Neither did the names of the "actors," which Kenny scarcely knew. "Owner is Pritchard Arnt, and he seemed like a nice bloke. Friendliest I've met so far in Stillwind Valley." Pointedly, Kenny nodded toward the screen. "He even recommended this flick." He chuckled. "Arnt claims he has a knack for knowing what kind of erotica his customers will really like."

"What a peculiar talent," Angelane said softly. Very fleetingly, her bemused but reproving gaze met his.

When he looked back, the motion picture camera was traveling—hand held—down the corridor of an apartment building. No people were shown. Probably either a chippy's pad, Kenny ruminated, or a place with a make-believe virgin and Daddy out of town. Then there was a dissolve and, when the images on the screen were restored, viewers were not only inside the apartment but inside a bedroom. And, from the doorway, focused on a bed where two people were already naked.

Blunt and no-nonsense, thought Kenny, shifting in the easy chair. *And no buildup; no introduction to this twosome. Who says I like that?*

A tight close-up of two beautiful bare breasts inclined him, then, to change his mind slightly. They were hanging forward, dangling, and it was instantly clear to Kenny that the breasts *were* the kind he preferred, and what their owner was doing.

"Want some more coffee?" asked Angelane.

"What?" He blinked over at her, focused on her familiar, beloved face, the cute frizzy dark hair, the way Angelane was keeping that sweet face polite and composed. All business. "No, I'm fine," he said. "Thanks."

The movie girl's buttocks were raised into the air, photographed with what passed for loving precision from behind and somewhat below them. Between her legs the camera showed the base of a man's penis, the rest of it concealed by buttocks and the girl's mouth. It was, Kenny decided, an altogether adorable ass. For the first time he began to respond, physically, even though he liked to know what the players in such flicks looked like; facially. Rather preferred to know their names, too; something about them beyond their anatomical details. The prone man, he saw when the camera swung round to a different angle, wasn't as well endowed as these chaps generally were—is it really true they're all gay, or bisexual?—and that was a plus. He'd seen girls in these things with practically no titties at all, but a guy who merely looked like a guy was rare. Oh, Christ, look at what she's doing with her tongue, I love that!

"Isn't it," Angelane said clearly in her everyday tone, "rather grainy?"

"Grainy. *Is* it rather grainy?" He repeated the query as if doing his utmost to give the solemn, distracting question his earnest attention. Clearing his throat and trying to keep her from seeing him do it, he shifted once more in his chair and groped, rearranged himself. "I suppose it is, really. Definitely grainy."

"You sure you wouldn't like more coffee?" she asked innocently. *Silly, silly man. Why do you men put yourselves through that, when we'll do practically anything you ask of us?* From an end table, she'd raised a silver coffeepot her mother in Ohio had given her for Angelane's only marriage; it had indicated she was ready to rise and to refill Kenny's cup.

"The coffee," he said. Tearing his gaze away was all but painful. Light from the radiating television screen glinted in the silver finish, cloned and exaggerated the sex partners.

Coherent thought escaping him, perspiration dripping from under the bill of his Colts cap, Kenny had to look back to the picture on the screen; and when he did he gasped. The "actress" had mounted the prone "actor" and the sniggering camera eye was trailing up her body from where they were joined. Little on earth thrilled Kenny more than that sexual position, yet part of him remained miserably, distantly aware that he had not answered Angelane politely, or lucidly; and that the deep-set navel in the soft stomach flesh, the rising breasts with the extetnded nipples, the dark, damp, rather bushy hair of the young woman in the film more than made up for the grainy quality of the picture . . . even the ridiculous way the director was apparently waiting until the last second to frame the actor's faces. As if their *facial features* were what those who rented the cheap flick yearned to see, might even remember!

And then the world changed forever.

Angelane emitted something quite like a powerful electrical current that he felt, which shocked and made Kenny turn instantly, staring at her. A sound she made, too, reminded him remotely of one other terrible feminine sound he'd heard only recently. For a wonderful moment of relief, of release from his immediate concern, he believed her to be laughing. Because Angelaine had sunk deep into the cushions on the couch and both small hands were raised to her mouth as though suppressing inexplicable hilarity; but her lips were twisted into a terrifying grimace he could not remember seeing before on anyone's face. The vibrations Angelane gave off, he saw then, accepting it as fact, were all too obviously related in no way to amusement.

His presence of mind was barely intact enough for Kenny to peer back in reluctant inquisitiveness at the TV, and to stop gaping at the naked woman's sweating, working, beautiful and familiar body long enough to discern her features.

"Oh, no," he gasped. "God—no!"

Then the moviemaker showed Kenny and Angelane the man's face.

Only white kids could consider giving up the chance to play on the Indiana High School All-Star Team, Clemon Sparrow had decided before going to Jay—Jay Tedrick's home. Usually it meant a full scholarship and a diploma, and Clemon had been resentful when he arrived at the teenager's address. He'd gone up the drive and crossed a short stretch of walkway to the front door with his jaw and meaty shoulders set, aching to tell the brat off.

He'd had the opportunity. Now, departing, he heard Jay-Jay's young voice from within the house saying a single word that put it all in a different perspective . . . and mystified Clemon Sparrow.

What Clemon himself had chosen to do that evening was not, he believed, exactly stealing a lead from Doc Jarvis, Purvis Richwine or that blond Lucia Mahorn, whom the other dudes drooled over. Wes had told him to set up appointments for the direct salespeople from Indy, and Clemon had.

But the big bro of the hotshot hoop star had asked for someone to come over before next week, and no salesman passed on a chance like that. Especially when the carrot Clemon had dangled in front of the sucker's nose was expensive gym equipment with a discount. Not that the discount would be discussed, of course.

When he had gotten inside the house and started his pitch, rusty after merely manning the phone the past six or eight months, Clemon found out why Grady Tedrick was eager to buy muscle-building stuff for his little brother: Jay-Jay, a predictably blond, crewcut guard with a jumper that reminded folks of Rick Mount during his Lebanon High days, wasn't entirely convinced he should thumb his nose at the All-Star Team. Or college, either. He hadn't said so with words, but Clemon, a great professional listener, was ready to bet money on it. Within minutes he was certain Jay-Jay Tedrick was eating his heart out over what his big bro wanted instead.

Obviously, twenty-seven or twenty-eight-year-old Grady Tedrick, roughly a decade older than the kid, was trying to bribe his blood. Buy him off with a set of muscle-building shit ol' Charles Atlas might've used to kick a whole *beach* into a bully's face. Why, Clemon had asked himself, nodding, trying to stay out of it, *does big bro care so much that Jay-Jay hang in Stillwind Valley?*

He found out. For the elder Tedrick, the world began and ended at the town limits. Grady hadn't even wanted the boy to attend the incorporated school in Walterville, but the law'd demanded it. "He doesn't need college because I can get him on at Kiper," big brother had rumbled, talking more to Jay-Jay than to Clemon. "Our educational program will prepare him fully for the kind of career his intelligence is geared for."

I can't keep out of this, Clemon had thought. Jay-Jay was like some tiny tot perched on a chair, skinny knees up over his face like bars. "He's almost old enough to vote," Clemon remarked softly, aware that he was slipping into the voice of Martin Luther King. "In an emergency, they could draft him. Shouldn't Jay-Jay decide, Mr. Tedrick?"

The shit hit the fan then. "There are outlets in Stillwind Valley for almost anything we'll ever need," Grady'd said, fists doubling. He stood, feet spread, braced. The bastard wasn't nearly as tall as his little brother, but he made two of Jay-Jay horizontally. "Do you want me to buy this exercise equipment or not?"

Clemons had stood, too, learned that he was somewhere between brothers in height but probably didn't weigh as much as Grady Tedrick. He sure as shit wasn't in that kind of condition. Ordinarily, he'd have tried to mollify the man, remember what he was there for. Clemon had made big sales to honkies who'd called him that word, and adored it.

But he wouldn't have adored compromising with Grady Tedrick. "I don't think so," he'd said. And, keeping his gaze on big bro, added to the teenager: "Go for it, Jay-Jay. If you don't, man, you'll kick your own ass off and on forever—the way this man's whipping it now."

And he'd gotten through the front door without having to fight his way out only because the basketball player'd squeezed between Clemon and the wide-shouldered motherfucker.

And trembled on the drive leading back to his own Cutlass Sierra—not because he'd been scared but because he'd had enough sense not to want, *ever,* to fight a white man on his own property.

Which was when he overheard young Jay-Jay uttering the word that mystified him. He didn't so much shout it as *weep* it out, wail it at the butt-end of other words Clemon didn't quite get. Perhaps there was sarcasm to it; he'd admit that. But he had a terrific ear for the inflections of a human voice and didn't think so.

And by the time he'd slammed the Sierra door behind him and glanced back through the thickening shadows at the frame one-story, he was pretty damned sure Jay-Jay Tedrick had called his big brother "*Faaaaaather.*"

Before he could peel bewilderedly away from the curb, Clemon, the old house, and the night itself were jarred by a blast of too many pop songs to count. From where the Tedricks lived, and houses for blocks around.

And between two homes he passed, Clemon made out a familiar figure, jogging inaudibly, climbing a hill as if he were a wafted autumn leaf.

Wes saw few of his cronies on Sunday. Since Cliff and Brick had preferred to maintain their homes in Indy, their lack of contact didn't surprise him.

But the one time he'd buzzed Kenny, wanting

to work out a four-handed pinochle game involving Angelane O'Brien and, for want of a shorter woman, Cheryl Conrad, the phone had rung and rung with no one picking it up.

He hadn't walked over to their apartment because it dawned on Wes that they'd probably taken the company car over to Walterville for supplies. Real food; more beer. But Kenny generally asked if Wes had plans for the Caddy and, when Wes went out to buy a Sunday paper, he'd been able to drive into town to get it. A glance at the mileage indicator let him know Kenny hadn't touched the Caddy.

So he'd been stuck playing a card game called Skipbo with Cheryl, since Ocie'd hardly put his ole geezer face out of his bedroom and seemed to feel under the weather. Wes was dimly aware that Cheryl, wearing red shorts that made her legs look like two three-pointers, was asking if he felt lonely and volunteering to plug up the gap in his life. He was also aware that, eventually, she wanted him to leave her alone so she could puff on her weed without a lecture from Wes. He had seen two buddies—damn good phone men—flush themselves down the toilet after graduating from pot to coke, and had turned into a moralist where drugs were concerned.

But by eleven-thirty Monday morning, with no word from Kenny, he'd turned into a worried friend. So he phoned the Chicagoan from the rec room, conscious that Ken and Angelane might've gotten into it; then he waited for about four days to hear Kenny mumble, " 'Lo." And when Wes asked him amiably where he'd been keepin' himself, Kenny explained that he'd been trying to tie up a carnival pitch for the company.

The tone in the voice Wes knew best on the

planet Earth immediately told him Kenny was lying. "Bullshit," he said clearly after a minute or two of rambling oral fiction. "You got problems, Kenny. And I thought that meant *we* got problems."

A beat. "Not this time."

"Then you must've finally did it."

"Did what?"

"Assassinated the president; overthrowed the gover'ment." He inhaled. "Anything else, 'cept blowin' up a church or two, means I got the same problems you got." Wes drummed his short fingers on his desk blotter; he was huddled into the phone, to prevent the rest of the crew from overhearing the discussion between two partners. Friends. "Tell me."

"I can't, hoss." Kenny'd never been so emotional before. "It's too personal."

"I'm a person."

"You're a phone man," Kenny replied. Forced a laugh.

"And that makes me the only kind you can talk to. 'Cause, we don't got nobody else, Ken." But Wes startled himself with the remark; a tingling chill nipped the nape of his neck. He knew, the fast way he knew when a sale was made, he'd discovered the key. "Where is Angelane?" he asked. "Let me talk to her."

"No." The single word seemed to balloon, begin to seep Kenny Higgins's life breath. He whispered. "I can't, mate." Silence for a long count Wes knew better than to interrupt. "She went back to Indianapolis. She's *gone,* Weston."

Wes could not have been more astonished if his partner'd told him he had shot the president. "She left you? Angelane?"

The implied shrug was a phony. "Works out

that way." Kenny dropped the pitch of his voice. "I think they've driven her off." He didn't clarify the meaning of the remark. "I think they're trying to drive us all away."

"Aw, Kenny." Wes didn't know what to say. "Tell me what happened."

He sighed, a sound beyond exhaustion. "Remember the flicks I rented? The ones we were gonna watch?" That was how Kenny began his recitation of umblemished truth; haltingly, almost but not quite disbelievingly, he continued almost without pause till he was at the very last of it.

"The man and woman . . . having . . . sex," he whispered; "the two in the—X-rated film . . ." Ken stopped, nearly too humiliated to finish. Wes thought for a second he'd hung up. "Weston," he said finally, blurting it out with abject repugnance, "they were Angelane, and me."

Wes closed his eyes. He'd had the impression his partner might say something like that. And it made Wes Teagle's heart ache.

Where Angelane Dubois O'Brien was, Kenny Higgins could not be far away.

8

Nobody called a town meeting. Apparently, they simply found themselves getting together at Coomer's Pharmacy that Monday night, the way they had ever since Albert Kiper opened the lab in Stillwind Valley. The way that revolutionaries, anarchists, terrorists, people of certain political or theological or scientific obsessiveness had always known when to gather.

Or perhaps it was merely that one or two of the dedicated employees of Kiper Research—or the others who had received certain pledges and assurances—had noticed the expression on the unpretty face of Police Chief Hemmer M. Magenheimer earlier that day. Certainly word had been passed, by covert whisper or nudge, and all of them wanted to know what the local law had on his mind.

In his days of youth and yore, the chief had been Sgt. Magenheimer in Indianapolis; he had possessed a solid reputation. Not entirely impeccable and not for solving crimes, but for stubbornly doing what his superiors told him he should do; for public relations activity, such as unctuously addressing schoolchildren; and for effectively flexing his muscles to threaten gypsies, vagrants, and returning drunks. The sarge had known just how far it was wise to go in the matter of presenting ladies of the night with a choice between him, for half an hour or so, or a week in the slammer. He'd had even more skills with which he was less likely to regale his grade-school audiences.

No one in Coomer's Pharmacy Monday evening knew how much time had passed since Hemmer Magenheimer's halcyon days on the big city force and none of them wished to ask. It was enough, with his craggy features, croaking voice, boldface brows and freshly restored, feathery dark hair that he was, without question, one of them.

"The small one with the specs came by this afternoon," the chief began. Ostensibly, he was confiding in Noxie Coomer, he who operated the pharmacy. But he would have to have been blind, or dumber than he usually acted, not to be aware of the townfolk massing to hang on his monosyllabic grunts. "One who sounds the way Willie Nelson looks, that one."

Coomer, who didn't look thirty but had improved his reputation when it got around that he was the first to throw the old man out of his store, made a show of busily filling a prescription. He didn't have new black sideburns like the chief, but his tan seemed more advanced, improbably, than it was a week ago. "That old bastard's son?" he clarified. "I tossed the old one out." Noxie made a face. "Tried to buy *cigarettes* from me!"

Moon-faced Roger Quick, who ran Mother's restaurant, leaned nearer to the policeman. "He and his commie friend think they outsmarted us by going over to Walterville to buy their food. Not a one of them is a vegetarian."

"They bought beer, too," Mary Barbara Bomwell improved the details of the vile picture. Buxom as well as brilliant but something of a professional virgin where men were concerned, she had also bettered her reputation in Stillwind Valley by swearing at seventy-two-year-old Ocie Teagle.

"Came t'see me about that partner of his," the chief said tersely. He lifted the cover of his notebook, glanced down at a note he'd made. "Higgins, Kenneth. Ran a tracer on him in Marion County, but he's just a crackpot. B'longs t'some fringe fronts, is all." He snapped the notebook shut and included all those who had spoken in his visual survey. His gaze came to rest on Pritchard Arnt. "That dodge with the dirty movie was ill advised, Pritch. Put 'em on their guard."

"It got rid of the woman," Arnt argued, as emphatically as he dared. Smily, surfacely amiable, the man who ran the video-tape store might have been in his middle twenties. He used too much Pierre Cardin aftershave in hopes the legend was true and people usually edged away from him sooner or later. "Chief, she's already taken the bus back to Indianapolis."

"For a smart guy who has as much to lose as any of us," Magenheimer said, "it was a dumb goddamned move."

"Don't pin all the blame on me," Arnt said hastily. "I could never work out the trick with the camera!" He pointed, affability gone from his face, leaving it sallow and frightened. "Grady Tedrick learned how to do it when the doctor was showing off, one night. Filming Higgins and that whore of his was *his* idea."

Grady, gripping the paper sack containing the Vitamin Cs he'd bought from Noxie Coomer, glowered but said nothing. He was present without his younger brother.

Magenheimer straightened. He was too blocklike or evenly proportioned for that to make him appear taller, but his blue uniform tightened ominously at the neck. "The doctor," he said, almost loudly, "does not show off." He pivoted quite slowly on the ball of one foot and included everybody in the drugstore in gaze and comment. "You've all taken it on yourselves to chase them away? Is that correct?"

Roger Quick bobbed his blob of a head. Stancel Holroyd, the undertaker and coroner, did not. Neither did the caretaker, Vernon Slaid. The others detected the trap and did nothing with their heads, apart from watching the chief silently, closely.

The latter slipped his notepad into a blue pocket and sighed hugely. "Has it occurred to you people that *they* might not approve?"

Pritch Arnt whitened. Mother Quick nearly spoke but thought better of it. Noxie Coomer became busy as the devil with his few prescription orders, while the amazon, Mary Barbara Bomwell, edged away from both odiferous Arnt and the adamant apprehensiveness stamped into the chief's fleshy face. Grady Tedrick, looking pale, mouthed the words *I'm sorry*.

"We've all been cautioned about taking action on our own, people," Magenheimer said softly. His eye caught a glimpse of a handsome Vitamin E display and he removed one bottle and slipped it thoughtfully into his blue blouse pocket without glancing at Coomer. "I think you're confusing these sales types with the Boggs family—the old residents, et cetera." One black brow lifted with significance. "Not that I'm saying the doctor or Professor Kiper have chosen to confide in me personally; but from experience, people, my bet is that there'll be some . . . *uses* . . . for the Wesken Company." He rebuttoned the blouse pocket, slapping it for emphasis.

"That makes sense," Coomer confessed. "Those itinerant hillbillies *were* asked here." He nodded ruminiatively, then turned up the blaring rock 'n roll on his store radio.

"But I have no intention of supporting that concert!" exclaimed Mary Barbara Bomwell. "Considering our sacrifices and everything we've striven to accomplish, the idea of practically *importing* old people is repellent!"

"Perhaps it would help if you perceived the humor in the situation, Mrs. Bomwell."

The speaker was Dean K. Stamper, her Kiper Research superior, a biochemist from the east who had quietly advanced the world's knowledge of the *dura mater* or collagen sac that separates the skull from the brain. Rail-thin yet giving the impression of someone who'd lost weight so fast his facial flesh hung in folds, Stamper had recently begun to explore ways of identifying aging cells, and replacing them without destroying vital proteins. He succeeded in projecting an image of gravity without looking older than his mid-thirties. Mary Barbara, and the others, knew that Professor Kiper depended not only on the team and on the doctor but on Dean Stamper; even Chief Magenheimer peered at him with respect.

"I mean, my dear," Stamper continued, clearly amused by the way his entrance had silenced them, "that the proceeds from their projected concert are reportedly to be used to construct a home for the aged and infirm." His marble-hard brown eyes, which seemed to adhere to his face after his weight loss, instead of peering from sockets, shone with his own version of amusement. "Should our efforts prove not to be long lasting, despite the good doctor's essential donation, mightn't some of us be glad we cooperated with the Wesken Company?"

Chief Magenheimer took two steps back from Stamper, much the way amazonian Bomwell was disposed to avoid Pritchard Arnt's proximity. These scientists; he might owe them his ongoing existence, but it was downright scary how they dared to speak the unthinkable! Finding himself near the front door of the pharmacy, he started to push his way into the square. Night air snapped at him, made him shiver and hesitate.

"That girl. Thalia Boggs." He glanced back at Stancel Holroyd, avoiding Dean Stamper's strange eyes. "She get there in one piece?"

"Relatively speaking," Holroyd answered him archly. "She's on hold until I get the word."

Nodding, the chief turned to depart. At the same moment a bone-thin youth in green jogging costume bobbed past the door. His motion was wraithlike. That close to the policeman, it was evident that his skin glistened peculiarly, his crewcut hair was actually mosslike, and he gave off a sickeningly sweet smell.

"Poor son of a bitch," the chief said, shuddering. *I guess they had to begin somewhere,* he thought, and left.

"I did search the place, mate," Kenny insisted. "Went over it with a fine-tooth comb, as they say. No trace of any photographic equipment. By the way"—he shoved his Colts cap to the back of his head, grinning fondly at Wes—"I do believe you saw the bird."

"Ain't that somethin'?" Wes said with a laugh. "I've just about made up my mind I imagined it all. Except the jogger, and the cemetery." He shook his head wryly, not without an element of sadness. "You sure you won't change your mind about leavin'?"

"No way, Weston. Two good things have happened to me in my life, and the prettier of the two is in Indianapolis, alone. But you're a big boy. Besides, somebody has to keep the 'ken' part of 'Wesken' alive and kicking till things work out." He jabbed an index finger pointedly, eyebrows cocked. "Are you certain you won't change *your* mind about leaving? This is a rather strange place and the concert is going nowhere. We can break the contract one way or the other."

The partners stood awkwardly at lonely midnight on a cheerless road heading south, the only spot from which Kenny could catch a bus to Indianapolis. Despite every effort on Wes's part, Ken had insisted that their "company car" stay in Stillwind Valley. It was all part of the perfectly mandatory, mutual pretense that Angelane might somehow recover from her embarrassment, that she and Kenny might soon rejoin the rest of the phone room people as if nothing had happened.

Both men knew, however, that there were humiliations a woman could surmount and others no one had a right to ask her to overcome. And a real friend of Kenny Higgins's would not ask him, ever, to remain separated from Angelane for anything as transitory and ultimately meaningless as business or money.

"Since you placed that printing order for the unveiling program with Harlan Rowe, at the

Sycophant," said Wes, keeping it light, "me 'n Ocie don't have no choice but finishin' the job here. Thank God we got another coupla weeks left on the sales campaign."

"Someone had to keep your Hoosier ass out of the hoosegow," Kenny remarked. He jostled his single suitcase and stared off into the distance. Wes had not asked why he hadn't taken the movie back to Arnt's Video and raised hell, punched the man's lights out unless he told Kenny the truth; he'd settled for Wes asking the police chief to investigate, and, from what Wes'd said, Chief Magenheimer was obviously part of it —whatever *it* was. Maybe Wes knew about what had happened in Nam, and afterward, even though he'd never told either Angelane or Wes.

"This ole road out here," Wes began, igniting one of his last three Camels—he'd had five but given one to his father when he'd been caught lighting the fourth—"reminds me of when I was beginning to date back in my teens."

"I'm surprised you weren't ten at the time," Kenny said, grinning. "Or nine. Why does the road remind you of that?"

"Goin' on hayrides," Wes replied succinctly. "All the fellas liked gittin' a gorgeous Hoosier girl snuggled into the hay and messin' around." He threw up his index finger, cautioning Kenny. "Don't get me wrong; we wasn't doin' anything with what they call the private parts of those girls. Us boys on hayrides, we wanted t'feel up the girls' earlobes. Or toes, if we felt bold as brass."

"Foot fetishes began among Hoosiers, then?" Kenny prompted him.

Wes surprised him by nodding. "It wasn't 'cause we thought toes were sexy but because they was the only portion of a woman's *an*atomy we got t'see naked till at least three years of marriage."

"Go on." Kenny saw the headlights of a bus in the distance, matching dumb eyes gleaming in the head of some huge beast. *What am I leaving Weston to contend with?* The bespectacled little guy was only phone-room smart; he was so naive about the essential self-serving apathy, sociopathic greed and buck-passing, the inability to take entirely independent action on the part of other people, he might well prove to be more vulnerable than Angelane. The working world wherein he and Kenny hid out seemed intrusive because it was exactly what it seemed to be—because they were rarely dependent upon the decisions of superiors who pretended to be on the same corporate team and didn't validate their deeds or their beliefs by seeing if other people agreed. Phone work was brash and direct during a period of cool hypocrisy so titanic most people didn't even understand their own actions and never owned up to their own real motives. Most salespeople lived their working lives with a complete realization that little was permanent any more except those deals that were signed, sealed and delivered that week, even that day. They knew the world was in flux, refused to pretend anything to the contrary even when they yearned to prefer the old ways—but they insisted upon getting a piece of the action this time. Money was no longer the measuring stick grasped by people with power; the knack for influencing other persons, bending them to your will, was.

Yet the only thing Kenny had ever liked about it—aside from Wes and a few other chums—was that he got to spend each day in fantasyland making a few things real by virtue of contacting folks who imagined they preferred reality and couldn't remember what it looked like unless they paid for it! It kept the sleek public sharks at bay awhile longer and provided a clearer lesson in the truth of life for their customers than anything else that happened to them. What was occurring here, in Stillwind Valley, would probably have appeared to be fantasy to outsiders; Kenny was fearful it might prove to be more real than Wes was ready to cope with. It had all the lying signs of modern actuality.

"One more Hoosier story," he requested, watching the next beast that would devour him draw closer. But it was all right. You might lose your life in a town like Stillwind Valley; you stood a chance of losing everything in the big city, where everyone pretended to know what was going on. But love awaited him there. "One more and I'm history."

"Knew a wild boy," Wes obliged, "name of Sissel Brinkerhoff." Lazily, he picked up his friend's suitcase before his friend could, wished t'God Kenny'd taken the company car that awaited him at the side of the road. "Ole Sissel mooned Flanagan, Indiana. By unsnappin' the top of his overalls and showin' his chest."

"Surely," Kenny cooperated, "they arrested the *meshugener*."

"Had t'have a big-timey attorney come in from New Albany just t'git Sissel a fair trial." Wes nodded. "The lawyer proved temporary ignorance—"

"Temporary *ignorance*?"

"And his grandpa was got out of the retired Masonic home just to explain the facts o' life to

Sissel. Grandpa Brickerhoff, though, had plumb forgot. So, next thing y'know both Sissel and his aged granddaddy were dropping the tops of their overalls all over Oolitic County and laughing like fools!"

Ken was stepping into the bus by the time Wes finished and handed up his single suitcase. "*Mazel tov,*" Kenny said softly. His hand shot out.

"God bless you, Kenny," Wes said, grasping the hand with his own. "See ya when they're breakin' ground for the ole folks home!"

God again, Kenny thought while the Greyhound lumbered back onto the road south and he watched his oldest friend dwindle into the distance. *Why should I believe in Him when nobody else does, but Wes Teagle?*

9

When he returned safely to his apartment after seeing Kenny off, relieved he had encountered no great, white-winged birds by sky or grave-quiet joggers by road, Wes was surprised to find Ocie still up.

For one moment—until he noticed how the old man glanced away, as if avoiding conversation—Wes almost imagined his father had been worried during his absence and was glad to have him back.

Ocie had donned the most flamboyant pajamas Wes ever saw. He was sitting in the easy chair he'd earmarked as his own, hours after arriving in Stillwind Valley, and was watching an old movie on Channel 59. That channel was Wes's favorite, too, because they made an effort to locate horror films that were either classics or not part of the usual packages other stations tended to get. This movie was *The Intruders,* not occult but one featuring two masters of horror; William F. Nolan and the late Charles Beaumont. Wes thought he'd see part of it over and took his own chair on the far side of the TV.

"Where'd you get them pjs?" he inquired, willing to chat. It had been hard, lately, getting two words out of Ocie.

"Cain't help it they don't fit right no more." He crossed, uncrossed, recrossed his legs, and Wes saw for the first time the distinct fragility of his father's limbs. Ocie had not eaten much of what Angelane cooked; with her gone, would he simply starve himself to death? And why? "Man loses weight when he gets older 'n his apptite ain't what it was."

Wes started to speak, closed his mouth. He wanted to explain that he'd meant the garish colors, the wild pattern of the night garments; but it made him feel like a wild-eyed, apologetic little kid to consider explaining. He attempted a different tack. "Saw Kenny off. He's gone, now."

Ocie's eyelids fluttered. Without that, he'd have seemed not to have heard what Wes said. But he sighed, at length, cleared his throat the way he did. "Just as well," he intoned.

White-hot fury surged like bitter bile. "What was that?" Sitting ramrod straight, Wes struggled to beat back the outrage. "Ocie, dammit, I know you don't cotton t' Kenny's politics. Neither do I. But he's my buddy and this company needs his—"

"Just as well"—the green eyes flashed—"for his sake. If he is your buddy, Weston, be glad he's gone. Maybe the guy's a hell of a lot smarter 'n you are. Or me."

Wes stared at his father, trying to analyze and understand the rather cryptic observation. Despite its measure of amelioration, there was a kind of tension to the old fellow these days. But it clearly requested that Wes not push, not force issues.

Now Ocie, silent, appeared to be fighting for the right words. "Your pal Higgins. He's all right." He shrugged his spiny shoulders and his pajamas moved in a tidal wave of color. "Not a bad sort, I s'pose—compared t'folks in these parts."

Which was the closest Ocie Teagle had come to mentioning anything nice about anybody in Wes Teagle's presence, and Wes bobbed his head in agreement, working at perceiving what the hell was going on in the old man's mind. Just for a second, when he studied the sharp-nosed profile, sensed the bull-like stubbornness that was startling in such a small and fragile person, he believed his father had aged greatly these last few days. But it wasn't that; not really, not if you appraised him the way a sales-minded man did it.

It was as if some inexpressible emotion, something darkly personal, was haunting him and he wished to confide it but couldn't. "You aren't," Wes began again, carefully, "spendin' as much time in the ole phone room as I'd thought you would."

"Don't sweat it. We all make mistakes."

The comment—it was a joke, wasn't it?—made Wes chuckle uncertainly.

"Y'don't figger on screwin' up when you're starting out," Ocie continued, still tiptoeing through his vocabulary as if one slip would cast him to the sharks. "But you do. Afore long, you're *pointin'* to 'em, saying, 'There's one. There's another one! Hogshit, Ocie, another . . . another!' And then you stop countin' birthdays, you count up the mistakes instead." Ocie shrugged, still staring at the TV screen and William Shatner doing his level best to play a bigot. "One night, y've got enough mistakes to count yourself old."

The younger man's smile was more uncertain than his laugh had been. "I reckoned a fella does what he figgers he should, in his seventies. Maybe does what he wants."

"You figgered that, did you?"

Wes's fingertips crept toward his shirt pocket, the last of his Camels; but he knew Ocie would want one. When he needed a smoke Ocie wasn't too proud to speak up. What the hell kinda priorities was that for a man? "Look. With Kenny gone, we could really use some help tomorrow."

Silence fell between them again. It was difficult to tell, with the television set providing the only light, if the space was filled with all those days when they'd had no contact with one another or with whatever had happened to the old man since they arrived in this pee-culiar town. Ocie cleared his throat. "You serious?"

"Sure," Wes retorted, frowning, "I'm serious. Any fool can see we're minus one now. Short-handed." He spoke as earnestly to his father as he was able. "I'm askin' you to pitch in." A grin. "Just that, Ocie; to *pitch* in!"

One final pause. "If I'm really wanted," he answered, turning his head, looking somehow fresher, more in control. "I'll give 'er a try. But I want t'be honest with you, Weston." He stood, steadily if not quickly, switched off the TV. "I'm not sure it'd do any good in *this* gee-dee burg if y'hired the best gee-dee salesman in the whole country."

"Well, we'll find out," Wes said, jumping up and clapping Ocie's shoulders. Ocie'd already begun trudging toward his bedroom. " 'Cause I jest talked him into givin' it a try!"

No response. The bedroom door closed in Wes's face and the old man hadn't turned back.

Ocie certainly seemed correct in his prophecy. With Kenny Higgins away, the space sales of the Weston Company promptly plummeted while the impossibility of selling tickets to the V.D. Byrnes concert began to appear completely unsolvable. Even with Wes and his father pulling out all the stops and staying on the phone for hours, everything the Wesken Company tried to peddle—honestly or not so honestly—was met with apathy or hostility, and rejection.

By late that week, spring seemed to have come to Stillwind Valley to stay awhile, but the phone room was frozen in the throes of terminal winter. Part of what got Wes down was the lack of even a phone call from Kenny or Angelane to lift his spirits.

But he'd never been the kind to surrender to the inevitable, since that meant going belly up to reality, and there was a prodigal father just a few feet away, fully capable of saying "I told you so" and looking like nothing on earth could please him more. So Wes requested Cheryl Conrad to telephone Dr. A. Dominique, suddenly determined to learn exactly what had gone awry and why the townsfolk treated them as if their initials were "VD." And while he was at it, Wes thought he'd try to solve some of the other mysteries that were starting to make Cliff Macy long for a bottle and Darrell Brickowsky spend half his time reading the *Syco*.

Blond Cheryl was back at Wes's desk inside of a minute, taller than ever with Wes seated behind it. "Considering how many times we see his name in print, you won't believe this. But Dr. Dominique has an *unlisted* number! He isn't even in the yellow pages." Her eyes opened wider. "So far as I can find out, Wes, nobody even seems to know where his office is located—where he practices!"

Wes sighed. He muttered something Cheryl believed was cursing; then he said it more distinctly: "*Kiper.* Set up an appointment for me with the scientist who runs that big ole laboratory, Albert Kiper." He let his feet drop from the desk to the floor; to Cheryl, his expression at that instant was a lot like his father's. "Cheryl, honey, somethin' downright weird is goin' down around here—and we ain't goin' down with it until I find out what's happenin'!"

She left but again returned swiftly. Wes glanced up at her expectantly.

"You have a personal appointment with Professor Kiper," she reported, looking flushed with excitement. "In his private office right after the lunch hour on Monday."

"Please overlook my apparent bad manners," Kiper murmured. He'd shaken hands warmly with Wes; then, sitting, he'd seemed almost to vanish behind his massive desk. "It's so hard to decide where hospitality ends and interference begins. I trust your accommodations at the Blackwood Apartments are satisfactory?"

"They're fine, Professor." They were, actually, and the realization rather surprised Wes, defused his drive toward getting to the truth. He hadn't reflected about it, but everything Albert Kiper'd promised on the phone was precisely as advertised. Wes could also appreciate the fact, now that it was drawn to his attention, that neither the scientist nor the hard-to-get Dr. Dominique had interfered in any way with their phone operation.

"I've heard," Kiper said, chuckling with silent apology, "that you've driven over to Walterville for meat. Afraid the vegetarian emphasis in Stillwind Valley is mine. And the doctor's, of course."

"Seems a mite odd that a whole town—"

"You're right, of course, you're right!" Kiper smiled as if Wes had aced a gracious tennis opponent. "My fault for not warning you, about the food as well as the absence of cigarettes and alcohol." He appeared to pull himself up straighter in his chair, but it didn't make the small man seem taller. "Let me see if I can explain my own oddball psychology: It seems unthinkable to you that another man would not prefer a juicy two-inch Porterhouse for dinner to some concoction that resembles a bowl of inedible grass. Right so far?"

Wes allowed as how it was.

"It's the reverse of that for us!" Kiper exclaimed. "Never occurred to Dr. Dominique or me to warn you." He leaned forward minimally, small fingers on the edge of his wide desk. "Of course, you won't find many modern scientists who *encourage* smoking."

"What I don't get about all that," Wes said impulsively, shifting in his chair and glancing idly through glass-partitioned walls at young men and women in white lab coats, clearly hard at work, "is how y'make the whole town go along with it."

"I see, *I* see!" Kiper smiled. It was the reaction of one tennis player to a passing shot he could manage to return. "It's just that Stillwind Valley is the modern equivalent of an old-fashioned factory town!" He looked questioningly at Wes, decided he hadn't yet made his point. "In the old days, the ruthless men who operated factories pretty much got by with running their towns the way they wished—because their towns would close down if the factory moved away. D'you see?" He welcomed Wes's quiet nod. "Well, I don't hold the mortgages of the people who work here or behave like Simon Legree; I pay top wages to a lot of gifted fellow scientists of many disciplines and they, I'm happy to say, agree with my various personal policies."

The implication—if it wasn't Wes's inference—that the employees had *better* agree with the boss's policies didn't escape Wes. But that wasn't exceptional; he'd done business with modern companies himself at which employees were expected to work out and lose weight, tolerate unreasonable dress codes, date the "right" people and vote the "right" way . . . or seek other employment. It was the American way, Wes thought wryly, had been for a couple of decades.

His gaze wandered, met through the glass partition that of a big and buxom woman who walked immediately to a cadaverous-looking youth with eyes that looked stuck on. He seemed to make a point of not staring in Wes's direction; but Wes had seen unreasoning detestation in the female eyes before she turned away. The two of them against the backdrop of test tubes, beakers, and gleaming machinery made Wes remember the jogger. But he couldn't imagine a logical way of mentioning him, the freshly opened grave in the cemetery, or even what had happened to Angelane and Kenny to Albert Kiper. The man who hired virtually everyone in town might govern numerous aspects of their existence, but he couldn't be expected to know what was going on at a graveyard or a VCR store—or why some skeletal nutcase spent most of his damn life jogging all over town!

And Wes wouldn't have mentioned his solitary

glimpse of an immense bird with snow-white wings to the poised, well-educated gentleman across the desk from him had Albert Kiper personally elected to buy all the ad space in his program.

"Well, here's the thing, Professor," he began.

"Dr. Kiper is fine." The small scientist, recrossing his legs, alternated them. He was one of those men who probably never sat with his top leg sprawling, knee parallel to the floor, Wes decided. He was the sort who kept the top leg compressed against the lower as if he were either trying to rub something up, or contain one that was already on its way. "Better yet, make it . . . Al." He beamed. It was as if he had never before considered having his first name shortened to that and he adored the brevity, the simplicity, of the notion.

"Albert," Wes said emphathetically with a nod. "I can go that far." He caught his breath. "Albert, I got some of the best damn phone personnel in the Midwest. Experienced folks. Folks with a track record nearly as fine as mine. But you see—"

"Sales are *bad*?"

Wes blinked at the younger man, startled by an expression of real caring. Albert Kiper had kept him on his toes ever since Wes had arrived at the big new brick building and had been promptly and politely shown to Kiper's office. For one thing, the scientist couldn't have been over five feet in height or thirty years of age. Most of what height there was began at the waist level and went up; the legs looked dwarflike but probably weren't. Most of what age Albert Kiper had, for a man with his power in Stillwind Valley, resided in his nearly colorless eyes and an expression in them that seemed to alternate between businesslike shrewdness and a dreamily romantic light that was, for Wes, like staring into the mirror. His hair, while it didn't need trimming, was arranged in a glossy pompadour heaped upon his head as if Kiper was trying to appear older or signaling some surprising sexual preference. Had Wes tried to guess at the latter, he'd have said bisexuality. Or was that just because "Albert" was so small and weighed so little that his movements were effortless, like those of the unknown jogger?

"Sales will be much better now," he said grimly, confidently. Kiper stood. The motion did rather little to improve his size, but other-directed anger—or outrage—hardened the rather soft features. Startlingly, he whipped out of his suitcoat as if he wanted to strike someone, and the glimpse Wes had of the small man's biceps and pectorals, pressing against his immaculate shirt, left him with very few firm conclusions about Kiper. "You should have come to me sooner, Mr. Teagle. We want the goodwill and cooperation of this town's citizens and the proceeds from the program. We expect the people to appreciate the generosity of Dr. Dominique."

I wondered who you meant by "we," Wes reflected.

Kiper's next comment surprised Wes as much as its predecessors. "We do think it best, Mr. Teagle, for you to desist in attempting to bring a concert to town." It was devoid of threat, the comment; but it was exceedingly firm, and Wes wondered who'd told Kiper about ole V.D. Byrnes. Or maybe the question was, who *hadn't* told him? "I did compare Stillwind Valley to an old-style factory town, but there are some marked differences." Kiper went from behind the desk and led Wes easily toward the office door. "This is a youth-oriented town. Old persons, alas, are a reminder of those things that each of us would avoid. As you may have seen for yourself, there are no elderly—as residents." While Wes wasn't tall, he made two of the scientist where they stood at the door. "No time to go into details, but Stillwind Valley is, in numerous ways, a town of the future."

"How's that?"

"Only a couple of decades ago, experts were predicting a society of specialists. They were right, but not precise enough." Kiper pushed the door open, allowed Wes to precede him. "Now, well, it's safe to say the future will be run by those who are considered either scientists—or nonscientists."

"In'tresting," Wes said, passing over the same richly carpeted corridor through which he'd entered. It enabled Albert Kiper to exit or enter without going through the laboratory. The rug, Wes noticed, was the same color red as that in the Blackwood Apartments.

"Of course, you doubt me," Kiper continued softly. "That's because my colleagues in the nuclear community have had such an abominable press that the average man thinks he loathes science." His nod directed Wes past a number of doors that were unmarked, closed, probably soundproofed. "In reality, people worship science. You depend upon it more than . . . anything else."

I do? Wes wondered doubtfully.

"Granted, it can be a love/hate relationship—the kind people once experienced with God. Which is why religious belief plays a vital role in the future of Kiper Research itself, why we've worked hand in hand with Dr.

Dominique, whose donation has unusual but unarguable religious connotations. But more and more people are part of the vast, nuclear family. As well, you lose sight of the constantly growing importance we all place on computer science."

We do? wondered Wes.

"Modern science without the convenience and marvelous speed of computers would be unthinkable." Kiper sighed. "There'll always be those, of course, who follow in Father's footsteps. But 'Father' will be unemployed before long unless his menial labors place him among the service industries. Sure, there'll be the uneducable, the lazy; some with skills in areas apart from science."

He'd been padding so steadily behind Wes he had virtually shepherded him toward the door. "I thought communications was the big thing. And I wonder where phone rooms fit in?"

Kiper stopped. "Communications is part of the big picture. Directly or indirectly, smart, successful people will soon be earning their livelihood from the world of science." He patted Wes's arm, urged him forward. "You're a survivor. It's those 'fathers' I mentioned who concern all future-oriented scientists."

Like Ocie? Wes mused. Was it possible that Kiper could explain what had upset the old boy? "Why *is* that, Albert, exactly?"

"They're living longer and longer, according to all indications." The small man sounded put upon, irked by what he'd had to admit. "With less and less to do—because they have less and less ability or strength to use on behalf of the emerging society."

"Emerging society" had a familiar ring to it. "I know a lot of smart old birds, Professor," he said mildly.

"They never remain that way, face it," Kiper snapped. "Each of them inevitably must possess less endurance, less strength. Diminished mental faculties."

"Sure," Wes murmured. "But ain't that the way it's always been, and the way it'll always be?"

"Absolutely *not!*" Kiper exploded. "*No!*" He expostulated the words, startling Wes Teagle. They'd drawn within a few yards of the outer door. "It must not be the same in the immediate future, Mr. Teagle"—Kiper was calmer now, more controlled—"because there are too many of us now without enough for people to do or enough room for them to live." He started to reach around Wes to open the door and his breath was candy-sweet on Wes's cheek. "If society is to continue sustaining the aged at all, they must be made brighter, physically sturdier, intellectually reliable. They must be able to contribute."

Another door swung wide, back up the corridor. The dignified man who'd spoken with the amazon type—very thin, with the flesh of his jowls and cheeks sagging—peered expectantly at Kiper. Before the door slid shut behind him, he had been followed by a burst of screeching rock music that sounded piped in, to Wes; like Musak.

"Albert, how in the world can you folks work in that racket?" Wes asked.

"What racket?" Smoothing back his high pompadour, Kiper appeared not to know what Wes meant. At last he laughed, amiably. "Every age has its distinctive sound, my friend—music that chacterizes or symbolizes its mood of aspiration and dread, magic and militancy." Heartily, he shook Wes's hand and looked him straight in the eye. "Your business will pick up at once. You have my word on it."

He shut the door and Wes, on the other side, looked at it without moving for a moment, uremic spring sunlight trickling along his spine. The names of the musical groups he'd heard with some regularity since coming to Stillwind Valley came finally to mind. Megadeth. Iron Maiden. Groups that were part of what rock fans called Heavy Metal, a music of hostility and group rebellion. *Metalmania*, some called it.

The musicians on the recording that was playing for the dubious benefit of all the Kiper Research workers, Wes realized, were called the Stormtroopers of Death.

The door opened and both young and beaming scientists stood in the doorway with an afterthought. "Sell those ads as quickly as you can, Mr. Teagle," Kiper encouraged him, glancing at Dean Stamper, who nodded. "We just got word from Dr. Dominique." He caught his breath and the smile widened. "The *Jagannath* will be ready for its unveiling in the town square next Friday evening!"

10

It took until the next day, Tuesday, for Albert Kiper's word to prove good. Which was how it had to be, since his news about an unveiling of the statue at the end of this week left the sales crew with very little time for making money.

But with sunlight flooding the phone room, around 9:45 A.M., Cliff Macy began to click—selling two quarter-page advertisements and one three-quarter, the largest ad he'd ever sold for Wes or any other phone room operator! Even Darrell Brickowsky saw a chance, then, to make some money, so he put down that morning's edition of the *Syco*, and did.

And Ocie, who knew how to abbreviate a pitch and what to emphasize—who had a knack for adapting to the moods and mannerisms of the people he talked with, without resorting either to dialects or impersonations—could scarcely write his orders up fast enough. Wes, seeing his happy, flushed face, winked at Cheryl Conrad, who positively glowed with delight for Wes's father.

Cheryl and Clemon Sparrow, under the prompting of Wes Teagle, concentrated upon making direct appointments for the salespeople coming in from Indy that afternoon. Both the ex-basketball player and the conscientious black phone man had been told to "go with the flow," to sell space primarily but to stick with the products that seemed to be selling best for them.

Albert said we had t'knock off sellin' the concert, Wes had ruminated—but Kiper hadn't said a thing about the *other* goodies Wesken had going for them. And their success or failure would dictate whether they remained in town awhile or had to rent space in Indianapolis.

By the time two of the three Indy people roared into Stillwind Valley, everyone on the phone crew—not just Clemon and Cheryl—boasted a stack of sales call slips. The townsfolk had gone on a buying spree! And some of the appointments lined up for the direct salespeople, Brick bragged, always delighted to spread good news, amounted to no more than driving over to the business—or the house—introducing themselves and writing up the sale!

"Doc" Jarvis glanced dubiously at Brick as he thumbed through the blue sheets handed to him. "Wouldn't kid a kidder, wouldya, buddy?" he inquired. "At least twelve times phone men have told me shit like that. I wound up having the dozen worst days of my life."

Brick waggled his functioning hand, raised a brow. Doc was both the oldest and the most experienced of the pros Kenny and Wes had lined up at the time they were breathing life into their dream. There was no point in trying to convince Jarvis, because, unlike those salespeople who worked with such a head of enthusiastic steam that it slopped over into their own lives, Doc was absolutely sales-proof. An adamant, completely goal-centered guy in his late forties who'd seen it all and found most of it bullcrap. Like Ocie, he'd been outside so much his skin was leathery, like that of certain baseball managers. But Doc was also a master of economic motion, the kind of direct salesperson who has his body halfway through the door one second and was off down the street rapping on another door seconds later. His method was playing the percentages; Jarvis totally believed in the premise that if you knocked at enough doors and talked to enough people, you made a living automatically.

Which was why he scarcely spoke to Wes, who disliked and immensely respected him, or shook hands with Ocie, who instinctively liked and felt challenged by Jarvis, before he was back on the streets of Stillwind Valley in his late-model Toyota—

Certain he had found himself in a town that was no better, no worse, and in no important way different than any other.

Purvis Richwine, in his own rundown '79 Trans Am, had followed the older Doc up from Indy. Chubby, with a receding hairline, pink-cheeked as a babe in arms, the twenty-seven-year-old Richwine was a sociable man who prided himself on his flexibility. "Whatever," succeeded by a shrug, was his personal catch-phrase. Convinced he had a "calling" that he hadn't yet discovered and inclined to believe he'd find out what it was by rapping with as many different people as possible, Purvis wasn't even sure he'd remain in sales. He knew how big-hearted he appeared—anyone who met him, however casually, might expect a sunny call or drop-in visit—and how harmless he seemed to women. All his options were open, particularly where the opposite sex was concerned, and his cleverly opportunistic, even courageous soul was neatly concealed by both appearance and cheerful personality.

Wes knew about Purvis's surprising skills and was happy to see the kid, while Ocie instinctively disliked him and privately wondered why his son or the pinko had hired him.

"Where's Lucia?" Purvis asked. He wore spectacles that made him look owlish and craned his plump neck in the hope of finding Lucia Mahorn lurking in a corner somewhere. Wes was the only other person in the room who knew Richwine's spectacles were made of clear glass. They exaggerated his innocent demeanor. "Gosh, I was hoping to see her. At least."

Cheryl glanced disapprovingly at both Purvis Richwine and her employer.

Then she saw the vision entering the phone room and studied their faces with amusement.

Some women, Cheryl knew, dressed down to boost the merit of their professional claims as individuals capable of succeeding in the so-called man's world. Not Lucia Mahorn. Once, the redhead had told Cheryl confidentially that she'd decided after her first marriage failed to take what the Almighty'd given her the most of and "show a little appreciation along with a little skin."

The vision swinging its way between the desks in the phone room remained true to her word. Brick's elbow jerked and spun the *Daily Syco* into the wastebasket as his gaze settled on two gorgeous legs exposed as thoroughly as Lucia's double split skirt could allow. Ocie's expression did not alter but he was clearly absorbing the entire, ambient wonder of the vision. Purvis Richwine, standing, contrived to step to Lucia's side in a movement that was deferential, and one that facilitated the best possible glimpse at her spectacular frontage. The cleavage of Lucia's blouse, Cheryl decided with a mixture of envy, annoyance, and amusement, provided a living endorsement both for the generosity of the Creator and the ingenuity of her brassiere-maker. Poor Clemon, Cheryl observed, did *his* best to nod and appear casual when Lucia swayed past his desk while Wes, who'd said he once dated the vision, was clearly an unabashed admirer of Lucia's remarkable red hair. Whether it came from a bottle or a beauty parlor or not, blond Cheryl didn't know. That it topped off the vision of sensual beauty and made late-movie or middle-aged men think of Rita Hayworth and Susan Hayward, Cheryl was sure.

What Lucia and her hair made other men think about—particularly those she encountered during her sales calls—was much more obvious. Nobody, cetainly not Wes Teagle, would ever suggest that the vision toil in the confines of a phone room.

She went directly to Wes's desk after touching Cheryl's hand and offering a smile that was altogether different from those she had just bestowed, and asked—in a breathy voice that nevertheless carried—"Well, Weston, what do you *have* for me?"

For the next ten minutes—until Lucia had taken her sales slips and departed—nothing about the phone room was the same, and nothing whatever was accomplished.

After Lucia was gone in a swirl of long hair and perfect, pivoting hips, Clemon summed it up for everyone in the voice of the late newsman-adventurer Lowell Thomas: "On the rolling desert sands with El Lucia, it was hot, ladies and gentlemen . . . very, very *hot.*"

Around four o'clock Wes punched the buttons that should have connected him with either Kenny or Angelane in Indianapolis. He let the phone ring and ring, drumming his fingertips on his desk blotter while he waited. His partner's desk loomed nearby, untouched, unoccupied and unused. No one answered.

He found Cheryl studying him sympathetically, affectionately. "I don't like this," he told her.

And when she attempted to cheer him up by carrying him a tottering stack of complete order sheets for ads in the program he repeated the sentiment for his father, who was grinning like he'd discovered a goldmine. "I don't like this, either," Wes complained.

Ocie, eyes dancing, got up from his desk springily and perched on his son's. Clearly he was overjoyed to be back in harness with a successful sales day. "Why in the worl' is that?"

"Somehow Albert Kiper told 'em t'buy like crazy, and that's what folks are doin'. Like we raised our hands like good little boys 'n girls and said 'May we?' and teacher gave his permission. It's like—"

"It's like the Wesken Company might make it, after all," Ocie said with rare, unevasive pointedness. Whatever had perturbed him appeared to be in the past. He winked boldly at Cheryl. "I ain't much for giving advice, Weston, but this here's been a hard marketplace. So when ya run into pushovers, son—push 'em over!"

"You're right, you're right," Wes sighed, staring at the telephone on his desk. He wanted badly to talk with Kenny, or Angelane; why didn't they answer?

Abruptly, he found himself wondering what the unveiling of the statue would be like—and Dr. A. Dominique, whom they'd finally get to see.

And also wondered what in the hell a Jagannath was!

11

Nobody had ever known that the fabled "Doc" Jarvis, widely respected by his peers throughout several counties surrounding Indianapolis, said "*Hut*-two-three-four, *hut*-two-three-four" as he walked from house to house.

Or that he sometimes pretended to himself that he was either a drill sergeant about to lead a crack squad of fighting Marines into battle, or, times when sales were brisk and Doc felt good, General Douglas MacArthur. Either way, his intentions were pure, noble, and American, patriotic to the teeth—

Because he hadn't followed in the footsteps of his father, a career G.I., and he'd always feel guilty about it. So Doc had set out over twenty years ago to make himself believe that the way he made his living was similar to a soldier's life, and that if he *had* done what Dad wanted him to do, the sky would've been the limit, he might well have *become* another MacArthur, or Eisenhower.

Or a topkick, at least. Tough as nails, resourceful, the kind of hardbitten old son of a bitch who never asked his men to do anything he wouldn't do himself because he'd do *anything* to make them fit and ready, or to lead them safely into ferocious combat. Sure; sure, there'd be losses, a head-count. But they'd be acceptable, because the dogfaces he lost had sacrificed themselves for a purpose, and they'd been ready enough—trained so gawdamn well by M/Sgt "Doc" Jarvis that they gave a helluva lot worse than they got, and took ten of the enemy for every one they lost! And they'd be grateful to Doc for giving them a purpose, making them men—

And when the last thing they whispered was his name, it would be with reverence. Not the emotion that had suffused the real Doc Jarvis when his own Dad died after getting the shit beat out of him in a drunken bar-room brawl.

"*Hut!*-two-three-four," and Doc trekked doggedly up and over another lawn in this newest enemy town he had to take—what the fuck was it called? Stillwind Valley?—while he strove like hell to ignore both the arthritic pain in his legs and the small of his back and the growing-like-a-weed realization that he could not conceivably remain in direct sales past this coming fall.

Not if he ever wanted to see fifty years of age. Not even if he hadn't quite put in his thirty years of combat against the dregs of humanity that hid out behind the facades of Everyman's homes and businesses—alternate perspective: the pathetic citizens huddling in the homes of their occupied towns and cities, waiting to be liberated by M/Sgt "Doc" Jarvis.

Because a sumbitch who had a right to be called "Doc" had said he had a bum ticker.

Then I'm going out with a blaze of glory, reflected the direct sales champ of at least a county or two that sometimes included Indianapolis. Or had, twelve-thirteen years ago when he'd still been married to Josephine and his third wife had provided him with a shot of adrenalin, of motivation to show Jo she hadn't screwed up the way her Ma said. That salesmen *could* make good husbands, be steady providers, come home regular at night and be true, despite the perfectly accurate bullshit Doc's first two wives had spread around about him. That he *could* be a good father to Jo's two kids, even if he hadn't the foggiest gawdamn idea what had happened recently to the two brats he'd fathered. *Men, now, Jesus,* he thought, *one in his late* twenties *for God's sake!*

. . . Why didn't this sucker come to the door?

Doc shifted his sales kit to his left hand, bit his lip to help ignore the way his legs were trying to lock—and to halt a twinge of pain in the vicinity of his heart that was doubtlessly indigestion—and glared at the slip of paper in his right hand. It matched the address on the well-maintained, enormous house, and Doc jabbed his middle finger into the buzzer up to the second knuckle practically, listened to the gawdamn chimes ringing inside the place like it was a fucking church or something. Where the hell *was* the bastard? He tried to read the name, but Cliff Macy's handwriting had grown worse with every year of periodic drunkenness he'd lived and the damned scrawl was unreadable.

Unthinkable: that he'd been given a really bad lead, or that Cliff, whose initials were on the paper, had made the appointment up. The former, once admitted, meant Doc'd wasted some of the precious time and energy he had left, and some of this day's daylight. Once, the time of day or evening hadn't meant diddly to Doc;

but now he was middleaged and got to looking dirty and tired, and even the Man of the House who came to the door after dark usually squinted at him like he was a gawdamn perv or something. The latter possibility—that Macy'd invented an appointment out of whole cloth, presumbly to reach some dollar total for the day Cliff had set himself as a goal—was a matter of breaking a cardinal rule. The Eleventh Commandment. And direct sales types genuinely believed it ought to be a case of justificable homicide if they grabbed the—

"Home security system," Doc read aloud, softly, making out a part of Cliff's hand-writing. Sumbitch. The rich bastard who lived in what was unquestionably the best-looking house Doc had seen in Stillwind Valley had showed an interest in the most expensive sales package either Doc Jarvis or the Wesken Company fucking offered! The commission on an HSS for *this* mansion . . .

The door was unlocked when, trembling with his own daring, Doc tried it. It swung back with just a teeny squeal, lights out as far as Doc could see, and no one in sight. As if nature, maybe God himself, had created the opportunity. Assuming Doc could find as much nerve as he had possessed the last time, maybe seven years ago.

The nerve to enter the house, stalk in, throw open a windor or two, pull the cellar door and the back door ajar—and *wait*, cocky as crap, for the owner to show his face. Then say, arms folded and looking as much like Karl Malden as humanly possible, "Do you *realize* what could have happened here this afternoon?" And point out that nothing was missing, but *everything* could've been taken—the whole gawdamn house cleaned out—because the owner of the place had not protected himself, his loved ones, or his priceless possessions with the proper kind of home security system!

All it took was nerve. Balls. And it couldn't miss. It meant a commission any sumbitch in direct sales would talk about for the next year . . . good booze, steaks . . . car repairs—maybe even a trip back to see Jo and the kids for a weekend. Maybe—

Hut-two-three-four, Doc pumped himself up, stepping into the house; *hut-two-three-four!*

The interior of the old mansion didn't seem to hold any surprises and was, Doc decided, bum ticker doing excitable things he couldn't curtail right then, just about what he'd expected. Except for the question of where the Man of the House was, considering Cliff Macy had set this up, and why he'd said to come over unless he was really interested. Not that it was impossible for the sucker to be a joker, a clown of some sort; Doc had met plenty of them over the long years, SOBs who thought the way another guy made his living was funny, something to fuck around with. *Through the enemy lines now, men, follow me! Bayonets ready!*

A distinct, very brief *rolling* noise. From deep in the house. And Doc froze, display case raised as if it were a weapon, all his senses on full alert. The sound had happened just once; it went *BBrrrt,* like that. A rolling noise.

Or could it have been a *very big, well-trained attack* dog?

"Uh-uh," Doc whispered to himself, starting forward again, heading—he hoped—toward the cellar. To his left, he saw drapes, went to them through pools of darkness that made him feel as if he was wading, felt around behind them and encountered the lock on a massive window. Doc unlocked it, ignoring his heartbeat, paused to tug on the window and raise it, two inches, three.

BBBbbrrt.

Spinning, trembling, Doc sought the source of the sound.

But it wasn't repeated. All he knew for sure was, it wasn't an animal of any kind, he'd have staked his life on that. *We stake our lives on two things, men, our training and the element of surprise.* Doc passed through huge rooms filled with things he couldn't quite make out in the shadows to the rear of the house, and discovered . . .

A door. To, he found when he'd opened it, the cellar. And he descended the steps, carefully, display case covering his wildly beating heart, free hand groping for and clutching the railing. He took four steps down before he realized he should maybe have switched on the lights. *But darkness is an ally, never fear, boys, because it covers a multitude of sins—and your asses!*

Half stumbling, cursing aloud automatically in surprise, dropping the sample case—and aware at the outreaches of his senses that it'd snapped open and thrown everything-but-the-kitchen-sink display items halfway across the fucking floor, Doc reached the cellar—

Then saw something *massive* crammed into the shadows at the far side of the cellar that apparently stretched the whole depth and width of the house. Massive, and unidentifiable at that range and in that odd darkness. Unidentifiable but *very* big—too big to be a person yet shaped, roughly, like a human being.

Shaped roughly like a human being and going *BBBbbbrrrrtttt*—

Because it was rolling toward Doc somehow. The sumbitch had something like tires or wheels, and it was moving fast, amazingly fast, coming out of the shadows into the faint illumination provided from the first floor of the mansion, *rollllllling* toward Doc as he glanced down at the handful of artifacts of his life on earth, strewn on a dark cellar floor—

Be a man, willya, f'chrissakes, boy—Dad, dying—and, *I'm going out with a blaze of glory*—M/Sgt. Jarvis; and Doc was moving with his military briskness of yore, scrabbling around grabbing things up off the floor and cramming them into his case willynilly, simultaneously scooting discreetly away from the foot of the cellar steps to try to retrieve *all* his precious sales tools, his heart thudding like pounding pistons, casting terrified glances back up at the immense what-in-the-hell-*IS*-THAT that was *rollllllling* toward his heels *BBBBBBBbbbbrrrrrttt* and seeing a fucking face, starting to shriek like a goddamn madman—

Then glimpsing, at the top of the steps across from the What's-that—framed in the murkiness gathered inside the cellar door like glommed-up molasses at the bottom of a bottle—a guy in his underwear . . . or a uniform of some kind . . . a skinny, unspeaking young guy who was jogging in place.

Doc looked back, saw *it* loom above him like a moving mountain, made out the awful features that were carved into it but that seemed at the salesman's last instant of life to twist into a smile flashing ivory teeth like elephant tusks—BBBBBBBBBBBBBBBBBBBBbbbbbbbbbbbbbbbb-rrrrrr*ttttttttttT! Screech*. Stop; silence.

Pad, pad, pad, pad down the cellar steps; scoop! *Pad, pad, pad, pad* up the stairs, *pad, pad, pad, pad, pad* through the house, *pad, pad, pad, pad* down the front lane to the sidewalk white with sunlight. *Eyes*, watching from behind neighbor curtains.

Dump. Down beside the trash cans, partly in the street. Motionless.

Pad, pad, pad, pad, back up the lane to the front door; *"Hut-two-three-four,"* the jogger counted off, scarcely breathing, nearly inaudible, but distantly liking the cadence. *"Hut-two-three-four!"* Front door closed, him on the outside, cutting now across the front lawn, almost drifting, almost floating, utterly effortless. Going for some exercise.

Neighbors' doors, opening. Neighbors, stepping out to See. Staring.

Seeing the body sprawled mostly on the sidewalk as if knocked there by some reckless driver who drove on. Knocked there after a car had *rollled* over him.

Doors closing, neighbors on the insides. Going about their business. Going about their exercises, their part of the experimentation. Going about their listening to the sounds of violent protest, rebellion; of youth recovered.

12

The guttering that edged the whole perimeter of the embalming table was on a slight slant—at the head of the table, or body—both to contain the draining fluids as tidily as possible and to empty them, unobtrusively, into a wide-mouthed container conveniently placed on the floor.

Any skilled embalmer, particularly when he was the mortician and the town coroner as well, prided himself on curtailing the chance splash, on not getting any on himself or even on the immaculate offwhite tile.

But at that happy moment, late on Tuesday afternoon, Stancel Holroyd was so relieved and glad to get back to work that it wouldn't have bothered him a whit if the electric aspirator had gone completely out of control and splattered yecchhy body wastes all over his nice whites.

Except, of course, that someone else was with them in the room—with Stancel and the white male corpse. Someone alive. And even though that person's presence customarily made

Holroyd ill at ease, disposed to chirp nonsensical comments in his high-pitched squeak of a voice, it remained a matter of pride to prepare *this* pale, naked body as capably as possible.

The initial step, of course, was a massage. Of the dead man. No self-respecting embalmer left a subject he'd worked on with one knee bent, as if it had attempted to flee; the limbs had to be coaxed into an appearance of suppleness. Although this aspect of his work always gave Stancel a certain uncommunicable, quiet pleasure, he was aware of the necessity to move on to the arms. Vernon Slaid at the cemetery would require a casket four feet deep with the arms the way they were: thrust out from the body, frozen by rigor mortis with one hand fisted and the other clawed, as if the man had tried to fend something off. They had to be manipulated, too.

By the time he'd tugged the lids over the eyes and affixed them with the small picks called cusps, the undertaker was sanguine of mood, content in his work, and busy injecting wires into the corpse's jaws, twisting them in preparation for sealing the mouth shut. As usual, there was difficulty in making the closed eyes and lips match so the face didn't look bewildered, or quizzical, then another problem with the excess wire. Stancel Holroyd solved both problems by poking the surplus wire out of sight entirely in the mouth and artistically molding it until a half smile materialized.

Now, he realized with sunny professional anticipation, rubbing his palms together, for the actual embalming! It was a matter of a fleeting moment to opt for the femoral artery and the vein adjacent to the groin in preference either to the jugular and carotid or the auxillary artery and subclavian vein near the armpit. *Zip!* went the excision, *poof!* went the artery and vein as Holroyd lifted them out. "I'm in the mood for love," Stancel hummed and the strings were tied, the needle poised above the artery. With the drainage forceps plunged into the vein of choice, *zap!* went the injection . . . and *chuggg* went the embalming machine as it coughed to life and began to pump its more-or-less sustaining fluids into the formerly living man.

"Three batches are necessary for the job," Holroyd said aloud, chattily. His slender fingers gently, lovingly worked with the limbs as well as the ears, sidestepping the disgusting possibility of purpling. "Formaldehyde and alcohol aren't the only ingredients of the fluid, you know. It also contains emulsifiers." He glanced affably towards the corner, smiled. "Exactly the kind contained in ice cream! Of course, sir, this is only the arterial embalming procedure. Still have the bodily cavities to go."

The first batch entering, gurgling audibly, succeeded in a general cleaning-out process, while the second and third—assuming the embalmer was on his game—produced a bright coloration that suggested a lifelike, healthy rosiness.

"There!" Holroyd patted one cheek, then the other, beaming on the corpse. "Now isn't that ever so much better?"

Nobody replied.

Hours passed. Employing a shining instrument called a trocar, which he attached to the embloating aspirator, Stancel switched melodies—to "Love for Sale"—and excavated both bloody residue and wastes, then refilled the cavity close to the navel—where he had begun that procedure—with a concentrate powerful enough to kill any nasty little lingering microorganisms.

"Doctor?" he said questioningly, looking very pleased with himself.

"Interesting. A shame it will be necessary to . . . ah . . . alter the facial expression." The second living person in the room pointed. "The other," he began. "Is that Thalia Boggs?"

"Oh, yes," Holroyd murmured. His glance was accompanied by a distasteful twitch of his mustache. The *bruxsa* had left him with a very trying task. And it was a shame her parents hadn't had the sense to leave town. Stancel wasn't much for the female gender, but Thalia Boggs, unlike the other person, who must've been pushing forty, was young.

"I was given to understand she was black."

"But she *is,* good doctor." Holroyd stepped toward the youthful corpse, spreading his arms in a gesture of explanation. "That occurs, sometimes, usually after a black person has been exhumed." He followed the still-pointing, demanding index finger. "It's mold that . . . well, leaches pigmentation from the skin."

"I wondered," the other man rumbled. "The child looks—almost pink."

"I'm less certain about the soapy texture and why that's occurred," Stancel remarked judicially. He rubbed a thumb against the dead shoulder, ruminating. "I wouldn't concern myself with it, sir. No one will be seeing her, isn't that right? No viewing in her case?"

But the doctor did not appear to have listened to Holroyd's gratuitous comments. He was striding toward the white male corpse with the artificially rosy cheeks and the faint, unnatural smile.

"Watch," he whispered.

* * *

Jay-Jay Tedrick spent as much of the first warm days of spring as possible shooting baskets at a goal and backboard in his backyard. Grady Tedrick was pretty sure the high-school All-American had that nonsense about playing in the two Indiana-Kentucky games out of his system; not forgotten, of course, but abandoned. And they would be "helping" him forget, equally of course.

He watched as Jay-Jay took every kind of shot known to basketball, hitting most of them, and Grady didn't feel remotely remorseful. The boy would benefit just as splendidly from what was being achieved at Kiper Research—and because of the astonishing things Dr. Dominique was reportedly accomplishing, in partnership with Kiper—as he would himself. And when Jay-Jay ultimately forgot how to pass, rebound, fake and shoot, he'd be content with the long, contributory life planned for him here.

Grady wrinkled his nose. Undeniably, Kiper knew what he was doing and actually needed what he called the "complementary cooperation" of bizarre abilities borrowed from every nook and cranny of the world. But it wasn't what a man like Grady—a research biologist with nearly twenty-five full years of experience—thought of as a marriage made in heaven. Or under ideal laboratory conditions, which amounted, for Tedrick, to the same thing. Unquestionably, the doctor was brilliant.

But it was painfully difficult to think of the man and his work as theologically based, the way Kiper insisted it was. Hell's bells, nobody else in science considered voodoo religious and *vodun*, it's correct name, was only *one* tiny element of Dominique's bag of tricks—or expertise.

Swish, and a fall-away jumper dropped through. Dribble, head fake, reverse dunk, *swish!* "Combined the best features of Oscar's floor generalship, Keller's zest, Mount's outside shot, and Alford's cool under pressure," they'd said about Jay-Jay.

"Who cares?" Grady asked the spring sky. A robin that had been perched on a telephone wire raised into the air as if it'd discovered urgent business elsewhere. He wouldn't allow that boy to waste his life on something as transitory, risky or pointless as athletics. The conditioning of sports was fine; there was purpose to that. *He'll follow in my footsteps whether he wants to or not,* swore the youthful, square-shouldered man at the window, but then he banished the wording of his pledge as outmoded and old-fashioned.

Yet it was true that Jay-Jay's alternative, at this instant in the regenerated history of small Stillwind Valley, was a far shorter life than even the countless, ordinary people elsewhere had been stuck with and always would be.

Damned near as short, Grady reflected, as the lives of those illiterate middle-aged phone people!

The living guest at the embalming, a powerful icon, hesitated for a moment over the bare male corpse on the undertaker's table. He was, so to speak, praying. Considerable time had passed since last practicing Oriental rites, he was not Oriental, and he had never been so much a devout believer as a highly advanced professional student . . . with a knack for adapting the practicable theories, tested knowledge, and seminal faith of various time-rooted religions to his overall goals. Just as his fathers and grandfathers had "borrowed" from elsewhere in the world—in an open-minded, truly scientific fashion—whatever ancient magick worked harmoniously in concert with the *Jagannath*.

Because it was the latter that steadfastly served as the matrix for all the apparent miracles brought off by the family Dominique, and the Jagannath that had received all their potent, germinating prayers since they'd stolen it.

Whenever it came to a question of personal belief, Dr. A. Dominique had always been able to believe whatever served his purposes for the period it took to achieve them—passionately; singlemindedly.

So those miracles he had wrought before coming to the world's center of influence and accessible power were the products of a combination of wide-ranging, multi-source facts; suspension of his own credulity; temporary but absolutely impassioned faith . . . and the Hindu statue of antiquity, the great wooden artifact of quite a different culture to which the doctor's family had become illegal heirs, centuries ago. What was extraordinary about him, personally, was basically twofold, apart from his remarkable appearance: A. Dominique had not been satisfied with the boundaries of his power, with geographical or cultural limitations. And he had understood and accepted the fact that fulfilling his ambitions in the United States of America meant that he would have to become the first of his people to cooperate with contemporary science.

The numerous degrees he had earned, including that which entitled him to refer to himself as a medical doctor, amply testified to his intellectual flexibility. The fact that it might also be seen as evidence of the man's moral bankruptcy had meant nothing whatever to

Albert Kiper when A. Dominique showed that he could deliver.

Now he curved his large body like a question mark above that dead man, prayers said and magickal selections long since made. This important demonstration depended upon the adroit combination of rituals from two nations, China and Tibet. He elected to bypass evocation of the *ch'lang shih*, the Chinese vampire, in preference for the secondary, undersoul of that demon called *p'o*. It was delicate to evade the intermediary *hun*—the oversoul—but necessary because the latter kept the demon in balance, and it was not some neglected devil-thing of the past that would be in charge of *this* experson-ation!

The doctor nodded, and Stancel Holroyd turned on his tape player, exactly where Dominique wanted it.

Tibetan faith replaced Chinese at the point where *overshadowing* began; the process of summoning the *kuei*, or evil spirit within this prettified white corpse, so that it would animate the body yet leave its direction in Dr. Dominique's hands. The product of the complex rites—a *rolang*, or dancer—would no longer decay, no one would be able to detect that life had fled its fully governable limbs, and the rolang, totally indebted to the doctor, must then do what was asked of it. It would continue its mockery of the living so long as it remained up-right—

And danced.

Holroyd caught the next signal, turned up the volume. This recording was an album of singularly angry, rebellious, harshly taunting sounds that even the mortician found vaguely frightening, offputting. But he watched Dominique carefully, forewarned that the body should be revivified just as a specific band of the album began to play.

Inhaling, the doctor rested one knee on the table beside the dead man, prepared to straddle it. But the man had not been young; he'd have infinitely preferred the female, Thalia Boggs, not because of gender, race or other such factors but because what remained of her flesh appealed to him. All those older than thirty-five years of age, Dr. Dominique found repulsive.

No other would, however, do for the present purposes. Holding his breath, the *shaman* clambered up on the table and reclined in a full-length embrace with the deceased. Upon the deceased. A stranger passing by and glancing in might have liked to believe that the doctor was merely administering a particularly intimate variety of mouth-to-mouth resuscitation. Indeed, he was breathing into the mouth and the nostrils beneath him in steady, husbanded spurts. When nothing happened initially, he inhaled and this time prolonged the unnatural procedure, forcing each gasp between the wired lips and the nose to last as long as possible.

This time, when he'd expended his own human supply of oxygen, Dominique distinctly felt the cold form spasm . . . *shiver* . . . and he pressed his blunt but deft fingertips to the nose to give the dead man the full benefit of air from his own nostrils. He virtually spat a series of short, stacatto breaths into the crack between the lifeless lips, as well—

With the result that the corpse definitely and undeniably shuddered, the length of its body. It gasped, was suspended momentarily between

Stillwind Valley and eternity; then it inhaled. Dominique thrilled to what he had accomplished, stared down into the garishly made-up features. Painfully, laboriously, it *breathed.*

The doctor was off man and table instantly, emotionally drained yet freshly excited, invigorated. At his post, Stancel Holroyd took his cue, threw up the volume of cacophony all the way—

And it sat up. It struggled, like a newborn child, to open its eyes. Muscles everywhere in the cold anatomy twitched, as if from ague. When it succeeded in parting its eyelids, the cusps Holroyd had affixed snapped across the room like discharged bullets. It snorted, *Mmmmff, mmfff,* as if to clear its head, and twisted its neck; whether it strove to identify the pain of its death or marveled that it had no feeling, was not evident. Ooze dribbled from the recently-closed cavity near the navel, ran freely. Yet except for the eyes being open now, its amused expression —Holroyd's gift—had not changed. Neither doctor nor undertaker, despite a long vocational kinship, could move.

The cadaver, however, could. And did. Standing unaided, wobbling in place, it gaped blindly for another moment before seeming to recognize its benefactor by means of bizarre instinct and tentatively, awkwardly, pawing out with one white foot.

"Dance," Dominique demanded.

A blank stare. Then, clumsily, shamblingly, the *rolang* minced a hideous, rhythmic path toward the doctor, moving in perfect time with the deafening metalmaniacal music bursting off the insulated white walls. And with each pounding beat, every unnimble step, the being choked healing air into its straining lungs, attempted to improve its minimal mimicry of the living.

Enroute, however—feet from Dr. Dominique—it paused; stopped.

The rolang had found on the floor a hat it had owned prior to being murdered, and it wanted to wear it. With a lopsided new smile that produced a clanging, tinny sound from its torn lips, the regenerated man clapped the hat foolishly, almost endearingly, upon its head.

"It can't speak, can it?" Stancel Holroyd whispered.

"It can," the good doctor said softly, putting out his arms. "When I wish it."

13

Ever since the moment she had known for a fact that her marriage was down the tubes and she'd have to fend for herself, Lucia Mahorn had considered herself a realist, and it had paid off in big bucks. Not *really* big bucks, perhaps, not the ones that seemed almost overweight to the touch; but bigger ones than she'd seen for herself, *earned* for herself, during the part of her life when she'd tried to be a genuine person instead of a clever body. Which was all of her life until just before the divorce.

Sometimes, privately, she regretted having decided to flirt her way to economic security—"flirt" was a euphemism Lucia insisted upon, because it covered a multitude of sins—and really wished it had been possible to make a decent living decently. Many of those nights she spent by herself, however rare they were by any kind of honest comparison, seemed not so much lonely times as opportunities to rest and—nobody knew this but Lucia—to feel guilty. Guilty because she was earning more money than the women she used to know; guilty because she'd chosen to channel an excellent intellect into vocational activity founded mostly upon cunning and hypocrisy; guilty because she frequently enjoyed the company of those male customers who'd only buy her wares by sampling her more personal wares—and guilty because half the time she didn't feel guilty at all and thought she should.

But there was also a generous amount of time like this Wednesday morning in a challenging little town filled with men who probably never saw anybody remotely like Lucia Mahorn, drenched with sunlight and wearing no more than Lucia's law allowed, when the fact of the matter was that she *liked* feeling desirable, *liked* feeling beautiful, and knew that most of the men she'd met would *like* feeling beautiful, desirable Lucia Mahorn.

And if she felt like it, it wasn't even impossible that she'd meet a sexy hunk at Tim's Gym—her sales destination—and let him. Everything was feelings, when you got down to it—Lucia giggled; "when you got down to it"—just like the old song had it. Just the way she hadn't felt like stopping by Wesken today and rapping with either Wes or Cheryl, and therefore knew nothing about the fate of her fellow direct salesperson from Indianapolis, Doc Jarvis.

Just like she didn't have the slightest inkling that within minutes she wouldn't feel anything but dead.

She certainly didn't feel suicidal.

Her first clue, which she ignored, was the sensation of being stared at, of eyes positively *fixed* on her. She'd stopped the gorgeous rebuilt Jaguar XKE in front of the store, two blocks from the town square, taken out a brush and begun to fluff up her beautiful red hair. With the top down, she'd fully intended for people to notice her, but the feelings she had seemed different from that—worse even than the sort of stares perverty types gave her. It was the kind she had dreamed about a few times, as if hundreds or maybe thousands of men were looking at her. Except it was more like only two or three perverts, actually; or one with the kind of intensity that had always made that dream turn into a nightmare and eventually awaken her, leave her feeling soiled.

It wasn't a stare that shared, definitely not in fun.

It was the kind for a perverty guy all by himself, and it wouldn't be "fun" even for him.

He'd given up the straight caretaker job in Indy for the same reasons other folks in Stillwind Valley had come there, but the secret reason Vernon Slaid had was that he missed digging graves.

He hadn't told anyone that because it wasn't the sort of thing other people—except grave-diggers, and the one he'd met was pretty strange—understood. And just as that sissy Stancel Holroyd was obliged to be lonely because he was a mortician and coroner, Vernon also didn't get to meet a lot of other folks. Fact was, it had been a smidge easier t'be sociable when he'd lived in the city and admitted to being just a caretaker. Folks could imagine him mowing and trimming grass, maybe, putting flowers on the stones and then spraying water around. Socially acceptable crapola like that.

But no one Vernon Slaid had ever met could smile honestly or nod his understanding if Vernon so much as hinted at how much he enjoyed (1) digging a hole in Mother Earth with the realization firmly and pleasurably in mind that he would very shortly be (2) lowering a human being into the ground where it'd rot, and sooner or later get et by those ugly little pale things he'd got to see once at an exhumation, and then (3) know the human being was turning into the only clean thing Vernon had ever seen: a skeleton. Which was the most satisfying thing on or in the earth, in Vernon's estimation. People the way you could tolerate 'em, people arrived at the destination Nature planned for them all along, once the nonsense of what went before was done and forgotten. Skeletons didn't talk back, or criticize, couldn't give you jaundiced looks 'cause they had no eyes, wouldn't give you no unwelcome out-of-the-blue bastard brats or filthy damned diseases, and they displayed the sheer, perfect *order* of Nature. They had the same number of bones, from skeleton to skeleton, lest a fool physician had got to 'em first; mostly, they even looked the same. That was Nature's organization, symmetry, and it was the natural look everyone deep-down sought from their killer diets.

He couldn't even figure out why he'd ever given up digging graves all those years ago, for a few extra bucks! Especially now, when he was excavating not just a single grave for one body-to-become-a-skeleton but two—with an assignment for a third tomorrow! Why them bigshots didn't want four, or more—since it was pure fact they had bumped off more sales folks than that, and the black girl was a part of his current order —Vernon couldn't figure, either. It wasn't efficient, like the time Mother Earth had proved to him, personally, how right he was to believe in her order and symmetry. That was the night he'd got up the nerve to dig up an old black corpse and find out for sure that the skeleton was just as white from skull to bony toe as Mother Earth seemed to have promised him.

Vernon Slaid still marveled at that and also wondered why the hell he'd come out to this re-opened town that reminded him right off of a re-opened grave. Just like the rest of 'em, he'd chosen to live; maybe for a real, long while, dammit. Incredibly, he'd turned down the chance that had escaped him all his life to become a white, pure, symmetrical skeleton himself, clean and forever grinning.

I flat chickened out, he admitted to himself, staying honorable but sighing again. He jabbed his spade into a pile of dirt he'd drawn from the womb of the big Mother, thankful Kiper and Dr. Dominique had not positively insisted on his using mechanical assistance. He paused, not because he was tired, but to make the virtually erotic satisfaction of this moment last as long as possible. The sunshine felt exhilarating on his trim, bare chest and muscled back, his sturdy young arms. Vernon pulled the waistband of his smelly work pants away from his freshly flat belly and peeked inside.

Then, wondering as he had a hundred times why that didn't have a nice, white bone inside it, too, it occurred to Vernon Slaid to get rid of his bushy, bristling, chest-length beard.

Now that it was coal black again and his blue eyes wouldn't even squint menacingly, they didn't scare nobody no more.

Where Lucia Mahorn had parked—out in front of Tim's Gym—there was an incline. There was meant to be. When the feeling of eyes with immense intensity focused on her was overpowering enough, Lucia was obliged to open the door of the gorgeous rebuilt XKE with the sloping fenders, and get out, leaving her sample case on the other bucket seat.

Only for an instant did she have the opportunity to wonder if this, or something like this, was what had happened to Angelane O'Brien. She'd gone to her and Kenny's place in Indianapolis before driving up to Stillwind Valley and it had been boarded over. But thoughts about others, and thoughts for herself, were promptly banished.

Up the street, before she turned toward the front of the Jaguar, Lucia noticed—quite distantly—a skinny, odd young man in a green jogging costume coming down the hill like something blowing in her direction. She paid no lasting attention despite the way the jogger definitely included her in his grim, unfeeling, automatic sort of gaze. As she hurried to the front of her car to determine how far ahead of it she'd need to run, and how fast—as well as to position her head and neck just-so on the pavement—Lucia became aware, vaguely, of the all-but-inaudible whisper of the youth's shallow breathing, and she sensed his steadily pumping pace in vibrations from the pavement.

Several customers of Tim's Gym gathered before the store to look at her. *That should do it,* she thought, feeling businesslike and probably less self-consciously desirable than she had since her ex-husband had betrayed her with her own best friend. There was a feeling of planning to what she was doing, of intellectually calculating the solution to a problem. Dusting her palms, smiling to herself, Lucia bent into the XKE and, catching her breath, released the emergency brake.

Then—because the slightest pause would ruin the plan—Lucia spun around and raced down the hill with her beautiful red hair flying behind her like a banner, and with the carefree, athletic zest of a young girl. *I can make it in time,* she thought, *I can* do *it!*

She was lying in the street at precisely the right angle, in front of her runaway car, with a second to spare!

And when the jogger in green drew abreast of the newly dead woman crumpled on the pavement, his gaze flicked from it to the rebuilt Jag just at the moment it careened with a resounding crash into the brick two-story building that housed the *Daily Sycophant.* When he jogged on, effortlessly, radios in the hands of onlookers went on or were turned up.

Then nobody was around to report the "accident," and it was silent except for the distant twang of electric guitars.

14

Despite the way he'd enjoyed a wonderfully rejuvenated couple of sales days on Monday and Tuesday, Ocie Teagle was already decked out in his screaming-hot pajamas when Wes got home Wednesday evening. The old man had left the phone room early without saying anything to anybody, and still had never explained why he had moods when he seemed hurt, or a thousand miles away.

Now, seated perfectly erect in his chair across from the TV, Ocie didn't exactly appear sick or even exhausted from his adventures on the telephone. Just . . . troubled again, Wes thought. Distant. Probably the news about Doc Jarvis dropping dead of a stroke, Wes decided, nodding at Ocie and ambling out to the kitchen for a beer. *Must've been a bad reminder of how old he's getting hisself.*

Craggy-faced Chief Magenheimer'd come to the phone room to tell them personally, which had reminded Wes that Doc left no survivors—at least, nobody who presumably gave a damn.

Then the coroner named Stancel Holroyd had phoned, saying that a hit-and-run driver evidently rolled over the body but stressing that the stroke had killed Jarvis. Impetuously, Wes had agreed to let Holroyd's mortuary handle things right there in town. While the chief asserted that his department would look for the bastard who left Doc in the gutter like a dead cat, he also admitted there were no clues. Not even paint from the vehicle that'd struck the salesman.

Until the second Wes discovered there was just one other Bud left in the apartment refrigerator —and precious little food—he'd suffered no powerful emotions linked to his colleague's sudden death. They'd been professional buddies at best. Respected one another's abilities, but never friends the way me and Kenny was. At that point Wes eased the refrigerator door to and sobbed. Abruptly, an upwelling of tears made him blink, lashes spotting the lenses of his glasses; and for the first time Wes seriously wondered if it was time to get the Wesken Company out of Stillwind Valley. If it was remotely possible to go on pretendin' for another hour that livin' there wasn't very likely injurious to all their health.

He leaned his short, angular, turning-forty-soon body against the humming coolness of the fridge and shook his head in worry. Maybe he was just missing Kenny and Angelane. He sure missed Angelane's cooking, that was certain! Neither he nor Ocie was eating properly. And worse, that day during the lunch hour they'd gone over to Mother Quick's in the company car, too busy with their work to bother making sandwiches or soup in somebody's apartment.

Horseshit, he'd even halfway *liked* the damn vegetable crap that Roger Quick cooked!

Or was it, he pondered, and popped the tab on their penultimate can of beer, more than that? Was something else happening that he couldn't recognize? Wes took a long pull, got half mad, half scared. Could it be that Ocie and he were starting to adjust—to become absorbed by the town . . . were actually beginning to follow the course of least resistance, and just fit in the best they could?

Cheryl had actually dated some joker from Kiper Research last night, to Wes's total astonishment. He might have even suffered another emotion or two, when he found out. And Clem Sparrow, just as amazingly, had gone gee-dee *jogging* after work yesterday, Tuesday. Finding that one out had made Wes feel strangely let down. Betrayed.

What kind of fool place was it that made an outta-shape, in-your-face, independent bird like Clemon Sparrow try to get some exercise or made an athlete like tall ole Cheryl Conrad go out with somebody else, instead of waitin' awhile longer for him?

And what kind is it that runs down strangers like 'possums?

Wes had meant to ask Lucia Mahorn to hang around that night, go out with him on what woulda been their second date. First time, despite what Wes adroitly advertised around Wesken headquarters, nothin' much had happened at all. But she hadn't stopped by the phone room that morning, a surprising break in Lucia's routine. He assumed she was already headed back, this evening, to Indi'nap'lis.

I gotta call Kenny tomorrow, tell him what's

happened to Doc, he thought, uncomfortably lonely that moment, strangely grateful his father was present. He snatched up a quarterful sack of out-of-town barbeque chips and took them and his Bud back out to the front room, wishing for the first time since he was a kid that he could say just what he wished to Ocie. Experience whatever it was some sons appeared to get from their fathers.

"How many times was Jarvis hitched?"

Ocie had spoken without turning his head, which remained aimed toward the television set. Apparently his hearing was still good, Wes thought, shrugging and dropping into his own chair.

"I dunno." Wes held up the sack of snackfood. "Two, three times."

"Figgers." The age-spotted hand waggled, declining the barbeque chips. "No one stays married forever to any kind of salesman. Mebbe you're smart."

"How do you figger?"

The elderly shoulders moved in a shrug beneath the loud pjs. "Not gittin' married. Goin' it alone."

Wes didn't break his staring gaze at Ocie's non-committal profile. "Dunno," he said for the second time. "Gits lonesome sometimes." He hesitated, experimented with a joke. "Bein' married must be better'n spending ever night with an ole geezer like you."

Ocie answered as if he hadn't heard his son. "Prob'ly nobudy'd have you, anyway." He cleared his throat noisily. " 'Cept mebbe that baseball player."

"Cheryl?" Wes pretended surprise. "It was basketball she played."

"Whatever." Another colorful shrug. "S'funny."

"What is?"

"They gonna bury Jarvis in a town he never saw 'til t'other day; it'll be over in minutes, with nobody t'mourn but us."

"Yessir, Ocie," Wes replied sardonically, faking a chuckle. "That sure is a riot."

Ocie ignored him. "I'm sittin' here getting older by the minute, stuck with spendin' ever night with a forty-year-old bachelor who can't get it up anymore, and—"

"I won't be forty 'til—"

"When I kick the bucket, and then you," the old man interrupted, staring across the front room at the TV, "and there prob'ly won't be more'n twenty year difference in time, they'll bury us the same way they do Doc." He shook his head slowly, very slowly. "It'll be over in minutes."

Wes opened his mouth to reply, found himself unable to judge the extent of the old man's seriousness. *I just don't know him well enough.* Then he observed the note upraised in Ocie's hand, fluttering between the spare fingers.

Without speaking, he went and fetched it. He read the words of the message with the combined assistance of illumination from the flickering television set and evening sunlight coloring the closest apartment window: "Come over for a decent meal, if you want," it read. Although the note wasn't signed, the writing was Cheryl Conrad's. Another, additional sentence was underlined: "And maybe for snacks."

"I already et," Ocie said when Wes revolved his head to peer inquiringly down at him. "Get your butt over there; don't keep the lady waitin' forever." He swiveled his own head to stare up at his son; not the faintest evidence of kidding in his wrinkled face. "I must've taught you *something* about manners. Afore I left your mom'n you."

Wes started to squeeze the bony shoulders affectionately, thought better of that. He went to clean up, changed shirts, was dimly conscious of a certain tentative excitement—a pleasing anticipation—that he couldn't remember experiencing for years.

He was headed for the door leading to the hallway when Ocie's dry rasp of throat clearing halted him with an arm raised.

"Your mother. She was a good woman, Weston."

He almost turned back. But chose not to. "That's a fact," Wes agreed.

Ocie did not reply to that and Wes, his lashes suddenly moist, closed his hand on the doorknob and turned it.

"You was a good boy, son."

Again, Wes froze. *Son.* He caught his breath, began to turn toward the chair before the old TV; the word *dad* was on its way toward formulation with the tip of his tongue prodding the center of the roof of Wes's mouth. It was easier for a child to say "Mom" because you simply moved your lips, as if you meant to kiss somebody.

Ocie's usual chair was empty, and Wes heard the bathroom door closing, quietly.

He managed the same controlled, dignified effect with the front door.

She had been so adamant about appearing casual at dinner—if he showed up, at all—that Cheryl had neither fixed her hair nor cleaned up the apartment. What the hell; he'd seen her only an hour or so ago at work. Besides, they'd seen each other in good times and bad already, in the phone room, so there was no way she could fool Wes into thinking she looked different away from work.

But she had managed to smoke just one joint, since Wes hated drugs, and cooked a nice roast. It was the last of the meat Angelane bought in Walterville, and Cheryl knew she needed to take her best shot since she was a rotten cook. *All this,* she thought as she went to answer the doorbell, *and I can't cook or stay straight either.* Home ec had bored her crazy; Mother'd been too busy trying to find a sub for Cheryl's pop to pass along her own limited expertise in the kitchen; and Cheryl's devotion to refining her hook shot and learning how to hold on to a rebound had combined to make Cheryl—in her own never-expressed, private phrase—"the best catch this side of the Red Army woman's barracks!"

But at the last second, before opening the door, it occurred to her to kick off her shoes, thinking, *This way I'm only one and a half times taller than he is.*

Then Wes said immediately blessedly, "I'm starved," gave her the goofy grin she knew he usually saved for his best customers and real girls like Lucia Mahorn, and she was pretty sure her strategy was working this time—the game plan she'd selected when they arrived in town—*it seems like months*—with Wes finding himself in unfamiliar territory, too, and getting lonely enough to want to spend some time alone with her.

Lordy, Cheryl thought, smiling him through the door and ultimately into a chair in the dining room, *it's wonderful being irresistible.*

Throughout the longest dinner in history—*thank you that the roast isn't too tough, Jesus, but why didn't you remind me to find out if he likes it rare too?*—Wes kept up a steady barrage of patter and his corny Hoosier jokes. She remembered every time to agree with or laugh at what he said, as the occasionally mystifying topic of the instant seemed to demand—

But her feeling of appreciation that Wes's gab was preventing any deadly silences was supplanted, first, by her realization that he was almost as ill at ease as she was, and second by becoming aware that if she didn't do or say *something* that registered on the little guy—made him recognize her as an individual, maybe even an enjoyable female human being who could conceivably be more than an ex-basketball player or a damn laughing machine if the moon was just right—she'd have gained nothing at all from this perfectly ghastly event. It would wind up being a tie game, and there might not even be an overtime.

But there were only two things to do when the clock was running out in regulation.

Play hard-nosed defense—which depended upon who had possession of the ball—or go for the score.

And the trouble with this particular matchup was that Cheryl didn't have the foggiest notion whether she or Wes had the ball, or worse, whether or not he was even on the goddamn floor!

. . . Cheryl realized abruptly that Wes was staring thoughtfully at her. And it occurred to her that she had no recollection of the expression he wore.

"That was delicious," he said. He gripped the cloth napkin she had put on his plate before the meal above the rim of his plate; then, almost as if he were reaching one of the most difficult decisions of his life, he let go of it with one hand and reached out to touch her. "Thank you."

"Why, I'm glad you enjoyed it, Wes." Another difference about his manner came to mind and she put out a hand to touch him. "You said that without your Hoosier accent!"

He grinned, shrugged. "Sometimes I can't remember exactly the way it goes." Sighing, Wes leaned back, simultaneously contented and looking as if he were revealing a secret sought by several international spy rings. "Kenny likes it. He and Clemon think they're the only phone guys who do things with style to help their sales pitches."

"You've been talking that way as a *sales aid*?" Cheryl demanded, incredulous.

"Hell, it was real enough mosta my life," Wes declared. "I haven't been back home for almost as long as Ocie's been away. But folks who hear me 'that way' don't take me as a phony, or as pretentious. When I'm as smart as they are, it's a pleasant surprise—not a turn-offy kind of shock!" He chuckled gently at Cheryl's expression of astonishment. His brows dipped behind his glasses; he might have been seeing her as she was for the first time. "You got purty hair."

Cheryl flushed, automatically touched the blond nape of her neck. " 'Purty,' " she repeated, and shared his laugh of amusement.

"Why don't you look tall," he began, "when you're sitting at the dining-room table?"

"I have no idea," she murmured, and glanced away. For a prolonged moment, she considered the need to take the last shot of this game and wondered if she dared to go for a three-pointer. Arguably, there were better ways to win than what coaches called sacrificing yourself. On the other hand, you didn't get to the tourney every year. Not in your thirties.

Barefooted, she stood and walked deliberately around the table to where Wes sat, a questioning expression taking form on his boyish face. She knew how tall she seemed towering above him with her hands on his shoulders, but it was clear to her then that he might never put the ball into play. "Y'know, I just realized that there's something you've never found out about tall women, Wes."

Hesitantly, he raised his arms, encircled her waist. Squinting up at her through the thick lenses of his glasses, he looked ridiculously young to Cheryl. He wasn't however. "What don't I know?" he asked her.

"That we're no taller than anyone else," Cheryl replied softly, "when we're lying down."

The cost of the effort Ocie had put into trying to replace Kenny Higgins that week was high, and dear, but he'd kept it to himself the way he had most things throughout his seventy-three years, good or bad. A man alone in the world became selfish in a fashion other men rarely became, unless they wound up aged widowers. At least, he had the pride of holding on just as privately and as tightly to the crap nobody'd want him to share.

Not that he could, anyway. Nothing Ocie had was infectious or contagious, unless it was how youngsters were exposed to old folks and sooner or later got it through their heads that they had the obligation to get old and die, eventually, too.

Ocie had filled the bathtub and soaked in hot water for nearly an hour after Wes went over to Cheryl Conrad's, trying to pretend it was

Lourdes. Showers were for young bucks in a rush, baths were for the old who knew they didn't have to, and a time came when hot water—inwardly or outwardly—was the only cure left to believe in. Medical doctors seemed like miracle workers and they were, maybe, for quite awhile. You got older, worn-out and frazzled, they prescribed a pill or liquid shit in a bottle or poked your skinny arm with a hypodermic, and there was another chunk of time added on. So you kept goin' back, gettin' more pills or liquid or shots, till the moment came when you noticed—halfway from here to there; midway through a sales pitch—that the chunks were getting smaller. Shorter. So you went back to the doc one more time the way you always had, explained the new—or the somewhat different, or maybe realized there wasn't no way to put in words how you felt—ailment, and he came up with a different medicine or another shot—

'Cept he took a lot longer afore he came up with it. As if he had this top-secret checklist and he'd been markin' off what he'd already used, and he knew there wasn't much crap left to try before he had t'go over to the next column—

Which was where all those gee-dee things that'd plagued you over the years had been put back on, somehow. Bigger'n they was thirty, ten, five years ago, angry as hell 'cause they'd been delayed in gettin' at you, never truly stopped for good at all. The stiffness in the joints, which had come one joint at a time, came running at your whole gee-dee body all at once, like a gang of barkin' dogs outside a new customer's house. Lungs that'd been reported by the medico as "a bit cloudy" turned into threatening thunderclouds that defied the penicillin and the occasional cutback on smokin' and got black with fury like a tornado. And the heart that'd been "maybe a trifle irregular" had stored up all the disappointment, stress, loneliness and unshared excitement until the neat healed-over cracks from where it had broken a dozen or more times was ready t'just bust open.

So you took longer hot baths like the water was some sorta amniotic fluid in reverse, went to bed earlier and earlier, and told yourself . . . now . . . that you weren't really seein' things, when they slipped into the bedroom to get you, you was just misinterpretin' ordinary things 'cause of the darkness—

And what you had t'do when you not only believed you saw somethin' that definitely did not belong in your bedroom but you almost heard and smelled and felt it in both your bones and your sneaky gee-dee heart, was to turn on the lights. *Can't. Want Mama, where's Mama.* Put out your trembling arm just the way you did when you were a small boy who'd been punished for somethin' he hadn't done, and left alone in the house. Fumble for the switch on the closest lamp, bring a little light to the subject, and made the "somethin' " disappear.

'Cept it was no easier than it had been six, seven decades ago. The darkness was not mother's remembered gentle sustaining lulling fluids but the inside of the borne-down coffin that'd been made now and, somewhere, waited for your occupancy. And when you sensed that something drawing nearer, when you heard rustling noises, inhaled odors akin to smells from the interior of a giant, suspended cage, and its leaden heaviness made the whole room seem to go askew and leave deep shadows within shadows inches from the bed, it required even more guts than it took for a kid to. . . .

Reach out . . .

Grope for the switch on the bedlamp . . .

Catch your breath . . .

And hurtle light with all its undeniable clarity into every corner of the bedroom so that you could see, looming above the bed and you—

???*What*???

Great meaty bulk. Power in a shroud of *feathers:* penetrating feminine eyes of innate knowing . . . but of knowledge conveyable only by means of hideous, instant *DEATH.*

. .. Deeply plunging, surfacing soft *breast,* heaving, *surging,* concealing lustful, avid, panting *HUNGER.* An enormous *beak* with gee-dee *lips* outlining it, compressed in a kind of inexpressible *leer.*

> . . . sweeping out from a muscled torso and sinewy body, rising like things with erectile tissue, *wings* of purest virginal *white*—white like snowy clouds, like enveloping impossible *arms* that spanned the bed . . . the *room . . . the world—wings* of unfathomable and intricate layered *beauty,* rising, twitching wings that stretched *wide,* then began to *CLOSE*—

Six-inch gashes appeared in the bedsheet at Ocie's sides, the cloth ripped by his own nails. Pressed back into the pillow, leathery aged features contorted in a grimace that only at the last moment began to choose stark terror as its primary motivation, the old man felt already half devoured by a traitorous heart that became a kettle drum, an out-of-control jungle rhythm that spread the way the *bruxsa's wings* were reaching, swooping down to enfold him. In its intelligent, summoned, knowing eyes Ocie Teagle saw mirrored—twice—the face of the one woman he had loved, the first of those he'd left behind.

In her two faces he saw resolute gladness, and joy.

In the consuming beak that parted, then, separating the smirking lips, Ocie saw deep inside the image of a man who was even larger than the night-bird, taller, more powerful than any human being he had ever seen. Yet, around the image within the slavering maw, Ocie also caught a glimpse of an ambience of age . . . especially depicted to him, maybe, created in an outline of sizzling crimson flame. *Come,* the human giant intoned from the belly of the *bruxsa,* and crooked his gnarled figer. *Come to death. Come to eternity.*

The lovely white wings flapped once, brought his pain-wracked body almost tenderly against its soft and yielding bosom; and the rending bill of the great beak closed.

For a moment Wes didn't know where he was exactly and was frightened. Not because it was a particularly different place, but because it was so much like his and Ocie's apartment, but feminine. Frilly, despite a glittering trophy near the window.

Jerking once in sleep-fogged fear because somebody was in bed with him, Wes awakened fully, smiled, and patted Cheryl's pale, partly clad rump with a feeling of foolishness.

But what woke him up?

For another instant he thought the noises he heard were in the building and swung his legs over the edge of the bed; stood. Then he knew the sounds that had brought him to consciousness were outside the Blackwood Apartments, and wondered why he felt apprehensive—as if terrible things were going on and he should *do* something.

So he stayed erect and padded barefoot across Cheryl's bedroom floor to a place beside the shining trophy, pushed away the blinds as quietly as he could, and looked out at the night world of Stillwind Valley.

Three people—a quick glimpse of his Sharp watch told him it was almost four A.M.—were jogging. The trio had just passed the building, evidently, and they were trotting up a hill without a sound—except for rock music wailing with numbing energy from a source Wes could not identify. The omnipresent, skinny youth in green was one of the trio; Wes felt certain of that.

But for the most fleeting of moments, he'd have sworn that one of the other joggers was Doc Jarvis.

Wes grabbed the windowsill with his hands, braced himself.

The third member of the trio, right before all three of them were hidden by the rise of the street, wore a cap that looked a lot like Kenny's.

They were headed more or less in the direction of the town square.

15

After he learned why he had felt so apprehensive in the middle of the night, discovered his dead father and then attempted to do all those ghastly things human beings are obliged to try to do when they're least equipped to do anything at all, Wes took the ancient pattern of misery another, characteristic step forward.

He blamed himself for what had happened.

Or if not specifically that, he told Cheryl while Ocie's body was being removed from the apartment building, and Cheryl was doing her best to comfort him, he felt "awful damn bad" that he had not "been there" when his father needed him. Forgotten entirely for the time being were the decades during which Ocie Teagle had never been present for Wes.

"Right, sure; absolutely." Cheryl nodded with sweet sarcasm. "You're an acknowledged authority on how to save sick old fellas who are having heart attacks."

"We don't know for sure that's what it was,"

Wes argued.

"All right, it was probably a lot of things. Which makes my point even more valid, hon."

Wes peered up at her from where he perched on a hassock in her apartment, arms dangling to the floor in melting despair, face a mask of anguish. "Well, shit, if I'd stayed home last night Ocie wouldn't have had to die *alone.*" Until then, he had retained a measure of self-control. Now his voice broke and he had to fight to utter the rest of it distinctly. "It's awful t'die by yourself."

From the chair next to the hassock, Cheryl put out her long arms to hug his face between her wrists and forearms. "Listen to me, Weston. If you're scheduled to die at Market Square Arena in Indianapolis with a Pan American basketball championship being played, and seventeen thousand people crammed into the place . . . you *still die alone.*" She squeezed his face affectionately. "That's how it goes. We're born by ourselves, 'cept for Mom, and—"

"Did you see *his face*?" Wes whispered. At that instant men from the coroner's department passed their open door, the man who'd given Wes life carried between them on a stretcher. The face was concealed by a sheet. *We're no taller than anyone else when we're lying down.* Wes pulled Cheryl's left hand from his cheek, squeezed back hard. "Cheryl, he was flat-out terrified—he looked like he'd been *scared* to death!"

She leaned forward, kissed his temple. "Maybe he knew. Maybe he just looked like that, and it was pain."

"D'you think it was fast?" Wes asked.

"I think so." Cheryl nodded. It was a lie, partly; she had no idea. And she was dealing with her own sense of guilt. If she hadn't written the note to Wes, asked old Ocie to give it to him and taken Wes away . . . Tears rushed into her eyes. "I hope so, honey." She stood, tugged at his hand. "You can call the coroner—his name's Holroyd, I think—from the phone room after while."

Wes yanked his hand free. "Can't work today." He shook his head. "No way."

"Yes, you can," Cheryl said stubbornly. She seemed seven feet tall, standing above him then—and different, today. Changed. It got through to Wes Teagle then that he might have done more than share lovemaking with the tall blond woman Wednesday night. He might have formed a relationship. "Because you have to check out the programs today."

"My God," Wes replied, blinking his surprise. "I'd forgotten all about it." He got to his feet, feeling wobbly, feeling as if everything in the world of Weston Floyd Teagle had changed forever in a period of time that amounted to days, and felt like months. "The unveiling and dedication of Dr. Dominique's statue is tomorrow!"

"We can't be positive without an autopsy, but yes, I'm fairly sure it was a heart attack." A pause. "There may well have been other . . . complications."

"An autopsy?" Wes lowered the receiver from his ear, making a face. Cheryl, listening, gave him an expression of what-next? For a count of two, maybe three seconds, Wes tried to think as clearly and as much on behalf of another human being as he ever had. Finally, he sighed, glanced down at the mouthpiece of the telephone as if it were something disgusting he had to take. "Let's skip the autopsy, Mr. Holroyd. Ocie wouldn't've cottoned to that one bit."

"As you wish, sir." The precise, affected voice was preoccupied, possibly disappointed. Almost rude. "I reported it to Chief Magenheimer, of course, and considering the age of the deceased and his history of recent illness, there's no official obligation. But—"

"I'd like the funeral t'be as soon as you can make it," Wes interjected. He had noticed Harlan Rowe, the newspaperman who both edited and published the *Daily Sycophant*, wandering into the phone room and peering around questioningly. "There's nobody to notify, just the way it was with Mr. Jarvis; so you—"

"I'll do the best I *can*, Mr. Teagle." Stancel Holroyd was clearly piqued. "I'm quite busy these days, you know, and the aged require rather . . . special . . . attention."

"Yeah, I noticed you were gettin' busy," Wes murmured, raising his eyes, looking soberly, somberly, into Cheryl's. The remembered image of a new grave when no one had yet died formed in Wes's mind and he knew with a cold, sick feeling at the pit of his stomach that he'd noticed other things, as well. Things that didn't add up.

But one of them—how the town coroner and mortician knew Ocie Teagle had a recent history of illness when he hadn't even conducted an autopsy—did not occur to him until the connection was broken.

Odd, the way people died, sometimes in numbers—sometimes with things that connected them in one way or another, like the old saw about movie stars dying in threes—and other folks just took the word of total strangers for what had happened. Like they'd never read or seen a murder mystery, hadn't heard about husbands and wives killing each other for their lovers, never gave a second thought to reports of "accidents," or what doctors said, or the cops, or coroners.

Odd, the way that Holroyd had spoken to him on the telephone. As if old Ocie's sudden death didn't amount to a row of beans, or was expected. As if there was no need whatsoever t'show Ocie's only son the sort of artificial but polite sympathy mortuary fellas generally did.

Odder, the way that Holroyd had spoken to Wes—

The way, Wes realized uncomfortably, he and most younger men had sometimes treated Ocie, and all older men . . .

Wes felt eyes on him. Harlan Rowe had given Brick a copy of that Thursday's *Daily Sycophant* as if he'd known how Darrell loved to read newspapers and was wending his way toward Wes. Then, however, he dropped the *Syco* on Cliff Macy's desk and when Cheryl smiled inquiringly at the middle-sized man, he handed a copy to her.

Rowe had the page proofs for the program on which they'd all worked so hard, but he paused before putting them in Wes's hands and looked expectant. *Oh, horseshit,* Wes thought as he realized the reason for the newspaperman's hesitation. *He wants t'be paid.*

"Ain't this a shame?" Wes asked, moaning the question and moving his head from side to side with sad embarrassment. "I'll just bet you'd like t'be paid for the printin', Harlan."

"I'll just bet you're right, Mr. Teagle," Rowe replied evenly. He held on to the proofs. A man of indeterminate age but one of the older-appearing persons Wes had seen in Stillwind Valley—Harlan could have been slightly beyond his middle thirties, a round-shouldered man with a beard flecked with silver, which came to a point

—the newspaperman seemed adamant. Not menacing, by any means; adamant. "That's customarily how I have done business, here, in Kokomo, Thessaly, Carmel, one or two other Indiana towns: payment on delivery. I'm as Hoosier as you are, Mr. Teagle."

Shit, though, thought Wes, *the proofs aren't the actual programs;* but he decided to save that alibi till he really needed one. "Well, Harlan, that's how the Wesken Company does business too!" Grinningly, Wes pulled open his desk drawer as if looking for something. He managed a disappointed sigh. "Trouble is, my partner and my father made the arrangements with you—not me. I'd hoped to find our copy of the order, but it don't seem t'be here."

"Can you ask Mr. Higgins or Mr. Teagle?" suggested the bearded man.

Gotcha, Wes thought automatically. But he remained somber. "Kenny's over in Indi-nap'lis on business for a week," he explained. "And I thought you might have already heard the bad news from the coroner's office." Wes's lips quivered. "My daddy passed away suddenly, just last night."

Harlan Rowe's head and pointed beard shot up; his rather colorless lips parted in amazement. There might even have been other emotions suggested by his expression. "I hadn't heard, no," he said softly. To Wes's surprise, the newsman had gone white as snow. "I'm distressed to hear that. I liked your father, Mr. Teagle."

"Everybody did." Wes's brain raced, tried to sort things out. He had the impression that Rowe was telling the truth. That he might not be part of whatever was going on. "Folks said, 'Ocie may never pass over 'cause the Almighty isn't that cruel to his flock, and the ole devil would be afeared Ocie might change his place forever.' That's what they said."

"I thought he was a lovable old grouch," Harlan Rowe said in reply, setting his mouth in a pale line. "Here." He rested the proofs under Wes's nose and immediately turned to leave.

Startled, Wes called after him, "What about your bill?"

Rowe called something in reply but Wes, irked because he'd made a completely Unteaglelike blunder, couldn't be certain he'd understood properly.

It'd seemed that Harlan Rowe's parting comment was, "That's the least of our worries—mine or yours!" Whose side was he on?

Dammit, he had to call Kenny, notify him about Ocie! Wes gave the proofs to Cheryl, asked her to have Brick, Cliff Macy, and Clemon Sparrow read them, too, to be sure the spelling was correct in the ads they'd sold. Proofreading—reading generally, in fact—had never been one of Wes's long suits.

Punching out his partner's number, Wes waited, watching Cheryl's long, slender, fair-skinned form move quietly from desk to desk. A relationship? With a tall woman? He shook his head, couldn't dislodge the memory of them together in her apartment, how exciting, how fulfilling she'd been. Harder yet to dislodge the recollection of Cheryl that morning, keeping him from abject loneliness, from taking all the responsibility for his dad on his own shoulders. *Nobody t'mourn but us.* Moistness on the inside of his glasses again. *Your mother was a good woman.* Ah—a clicking sound! Wes leaned forward with anticipation, near joy, yearning to hear Kenny's accents.

But it was the unfamiliar, uninterested voice of

a woman. A telephone operator, reporting the almost impossible.

She stated clearly the fact that Kenny's phone had been disconnected.

White sound, drained and empty as an ocean devoid of life, roared in Wes's left ear. Disconnected? A *phone* man without a *telephone?*

Black face, anything but empty; intelligent, thoughtful. Sympathetic. "That guy Holroyd called," Clemon Sparrow informed him. "Ocie will be . . . well, ready . . . Sunday evening. Funeral's Monday."

"Thanks, buddy," Wes grunted, half smiling.

"Anything I can do?" There wasn't a trace of an impersonation, of a famous voice, in Clem's melodic inflections. Taking the big dark hand that went out to him in camaraderie, Wes faintly shook his head. What really got to him about the behavior of everyone in the phone room that day was how they hadn't pressed in the slightest for news about the future of the Wesken Company—which was theirs, too, for now. Nobody'd been phony, like they'd known Ocie twenty-five years and found him adorable, or come up to make matters worse by mumbling crap that couldn't help. These were genuine people, and he just wished Ocie was there to appreciate it. And Kenny and Angelane O'Brien.

Where had they gone to?—Because it seemed pretty obvious, now, that Kenny and Angelane hadn't gone back to Indy. Angelane, in theory, might have been so upset about the movie that she actually left Kenny, but Wes doubted that, didn't believe it for a second. The two had never been lovers, they'd been *lovers!* Could Stillwind Valley have—

Reddish face, spooked, scared; Cliff Macy's. Plump hands clutching the proofs of the program, eyes big as saucers. Plump hands, trembling. "Nobody told me what kind of statue that doctor is donating," he hissed. Which was how Wes characterized the way the little ex-alcoholic, occult-loving born-again Christian had spoken. Because he didn't recall having heard a real man *hiss* a message at him before. Not like something sinister, or evil—but as if he had things to say about matters that were.

"Phone people don't really *read* the publications they sell ads for, Cliff," Wes began gently, spoofing his friend. "Come t'think of it, pal, I don't believe *anybody* reads them things!"

The moon-shaped face jerked. No, it said clearly, don't *joke* about this. Obviously, Cliff was fighting for control, and losing it to his convoluted belief system. "I can't remember for sure whether I heard about it or not, Wes, and mebbe I wasn't listenin'. I don't see *how* this could be the—the real thing." His voice was rising and others in the room glanced over, concerned. Brick unconsciously massaged his bad hand and recalled when an outburst of Macy's emotions had led to a two-week toot. "Lordy, it *can't* be, Wes—but evil things have been happenin' here and this town is so . . . so *wrong,* it's like it's Godforsaken, or—" Cliff swallowed, seemed on the verge of hyperventilating. Nibbling his lower lip, he inhaled, said, "I ain't proud of it but I've studied it, Wes. I *know* the adversary."

"The who?"

"The adversary! The opposition to the Lord!" Sweat poured off the alcoholic's crimsoning features. "Haven't you ever in your life heard about . . . about *it?*"

Wes glanced at Cheryl, made a glass-raising motion; she nodded, went to get water for Cliff.

Wes's gaze fell to the *Syco's* front page where it lay on Cheryl's desk. "Not sure I follow you, Clifford," Wes said gently, quietingly. "Heard about what?"

The small man was getting redder of face, and Clemon was rising, heading back to help calm him. "You don't know a thing about the *Jagannath*?"

But Wes scarcely heard the question.

He'd become aware of something familiar about the photo on the front page of the newspaper; he was recognizing the sensual features of Lucia Mahorn, and he was realizing what the headline said. Turning pale.

"Thousands upon thousands of people died under its wheels!" Cliff Macy explained, struggling to get his employer's attention. "Wes . . . I think it's here. In this town!"

16

"I should appreciate a straight, definitive reply." He held his neck and head erect in hopes that his folds of loose skin wouldn't sag so much and mar the dignity of his approach. The bright brown eyes appeared to roll, searchingly, at the outer limits of the protruding lids. "*Do* you feel he's getting out of our control? Or if you don't care for that question, are you concerned in the slightest that he is starting to require more . . . sacrifices . . . than we were told about at the beginning?"

"Please, Dean, refrain from the tendency to recast either of us as a crazed scientist from some television late show. Or, for that matter, as humanitarians. We're research scientists, and we have a job to do." Querulous, he passed a hand over his massive, glossy pompadour. "You knew what the score was before you came down from the east, and you agreed that extraordinary science demands extraordinary methods. Particularly when we are involved with a man like Akeem."

Dean K. Stamper sipped the vitamin cocktail he was sharing with his dwarflike colleague, smiled. "That's not precisely an evasive answer, I'll grant you. But I doubt it would fetch you much of a test grade." He raised his palm. "I've just been working with some elementary arithmetic, and our associate's column of figures is thriving. For example, it appears, on the surface, that there wasn't much to gain from scaring that old man to death. His energy level was already exhausted."

"He loathes the elderly. Need I remind you, D.K., that it's an emotion shared by everyone in the community?"

"You needn't. But it's primarily a view we are *obliged* to hold, if our experiment is to succeed—not a feeling all of us automatically or innately possess."

"We should. Each and every one of us." Kiper frowned. "Possibly I *should* remind you that my initial theory involved the way that all people, upon meeting a stranger, first categorize him in regard to his age. Other valuations, such as skin color, similarity of geographical or educational backgrounds, are secondary. Young people sometimes are deficit of ambition because they measure their accomplishments by their individual age. In contemporary 'cave dwelling' apartment living, condominiums, et cetera—entire communities are formed according to age." A slight, smug smile played on Kiper's mouth. "The realization of that fact led to my decision to relocate Kiper Research in a reopened town; in Stillwind Valley."

"I know all that," Stamper said. "However—"

"Please; allow me to proceed." Kiper looked as tall in his chair at the gleaming desk as he could. "It occurred to me that each of us cooperates with such categorization, even seizes it gleefully. Think of the teenagers; think of how each of us looked forward to becoming legally a man. Despite advancement in our own fields of interest, and despite an increase of *decades* in life expectancy since the turn of the century, people cooperate with social expectations instead of reason, logic; we dread turning thirty, declare ourselves middle-aged at forty, old at sixty-five." Albert Kiper allowed his dreamy mood to be reflected from his drab, colorless eyes. "It was I, not Dominique, not you, who was able to envision a society in which intelligent, modern people would spurn such pointless classifications and aspire to the longevity promised by our bodies themselves—and do so with the complementary methodology of science and collective will on the one hand, continually reinforced, magical belief on the other!"

"I don't mean to appear ungrateful," Stamper said. "In all probability, I would be senile now—or dead—if you hadn't contacted me." He shrugged. "That's true, of course, of nearly everyone in Stillwind Valley. Yet the age reversal we've achieved may or may not be permanent. And while the Doctor's feathered creation was his proof that he can hold up his end of the bargain, the damned thing is getting out of hand!" He shifted in his chair uneasily. "I have no quarrel at all with the sales persons, Higgins, Jarvis, or Mahorn. Clearly, the regeneration technique—"

"It's combined Oriental magick," Kiper put in tiredly, yawning. "It's called a rolang."

"Actually, I don't want to *learn* the fellow's pseudoscience," Stamper commented with a delicate shudder. "I'll grant you he's come a long way since he came up with that—that bizarre, perpetual motion machine running around the streets. But the Boggs family has not been driven out despite what the bruxsa did to the daughter—"

"They're completely under control so long as they believe the girl might be alive. The Tedrick boy is also being controlled." The tiny man pointed across the desk. "I don't intend to let you forget, Stamper, that it's the energy produced by Higgins and the others that *sustains* the regression for you and me—for all of us!"

Dean Stamper's restless marble eyes settled, focussed on his colleague's colorless orbs. "That damned statue of his had better prove as effective as his bird and his zombies," he said softly. There was no threat because that would amount to absolute self-incrimination. But there was regret, and the beginning of an urgency bordering upon desperation. "In accord with what we're doing here at the lab. I didn't intend to regain my youth and sustain it indefinitely at a nonstop cost of life." Stamper looked away, the odd, brown eyes once more roaming. "I'll never approve of the independent steps taken by that monster Holroyd against Higgins's woman."

"If that's it . . . ?" Albert Kiper shuffled papers on his desk.

"Not quite." Stamper rose but kept his feet where they were. He leaned forward microscopically. "The questions I put to you at the start of this conversation were based upon my impression that Holroyd is not the only one behaving erratically; idiosyncratically. We're aware of what our esteemed colleague can do with mind control, with hallucination."

"Get to the point, Dean, please," Kiper moaned. He glanced pointedly at his Omega wristwatch.

"I shall." Stamper caught his breath. "Do you think Akeem is getting out of hand?"

"No." Kiper shook his head, firmly. "I do not." He saw the other scientist pause, then nod and turn away. "But if he is," Kiper continued, freezing Stamper in place, "would you mind telling me what in the name of all that's holy we can do about it?"

"Jagannath means," Cliff told Wes, oblivious to the other phone people drawing near, "lord of the world."

Cheryl saw Wes's shocked expression and put the glass of water on the desk beside Cliff, went to Wes consolingly.

"Imagine how evil that idea is, Lord of the whole *world,*" Cliff said to Clem, catching his arm and peering wide-eyed at him. "See, it was a thing almost fifty feet in height, a Hindu statue—them heathens believed in it—and they pulled it through the streets on an enormous wagon . . ."

"Lucia," Clem said, staring where Wes and Cheryl were looking; "aw, damn." They hadn't picked up the newspaper; it was as if doing so fully acknowledged her reported suicide.

Brick was there, too, and looked solemnly at the others after glancing down at the *Syco* front page. "First Doc. Then Ocie. Now Lucia." He scowled bitterly, angrily. "We're fucking targets!"

"You better hear me," Cliff told them. Farthest away, he had not seen Lucia Mahorn's picture nor comprehended what they were saying. "If this town worships that statue, it's idol worship, people."

"Come here, Cliff." Wes, quietly, tightly.

"Believers were called pilgrims, and they hurled

themselves right under the wheels of that Jagannath—they was *crushed* to death." He started around the desk, politely curious but still wrapped up in his own discovery. "Folks in our part of the world heard about it when the statue disappeared but called it a *juggernaut*—somethin' that smooshes whatever's in front of it." At Cheryl's desk, Cliff followed the sadly pointing fingers of his colleagues.

And sank heavily into the chair that had been Kenny's. "She shouldn't've done that to herself," he sobbed. His round eyes filled with honest tears. "That pore girl."

The alcoholic's genuine affection galvanized Brick, who glared at the others as if defying them to disagree with what he had to say: "I don't understand why but this damn town is out to kill our asses!"

No one disagreed; all of them began to think about leaving at once. Wes, however, surprised the others by reaching out to take Cheryl Conrad's chilling hand. "They're buryin' Doc today and Ocie's funeral is Monday. I got to stay around." He peered toward the phone room windows, dimly recognizing what a beautiful spring day it was in picturesque and deadly Stillwind Valley. "I don't know why all this is happening either but I'm going to go to the unveiling of that—that Jagannath tomorrow and try to have a chat with the police chief, Kiper, and Dr. Dominique, too." Although myopic, Wes's eyes blazed through the thick lenses. He hugged Cheryl. "You and everybody else best get out of here tonight; after dark. But since I hafta stay for Ocie anyway, well . . . there's a lot to be set straight. Including what's happened to Kenny and Angelane. I'll have your checks in the mail by Tuesday evening."

Cheryl pulled her hand away from his. "Angelane was my friend." She succeeded in manufacturing a thin smile. "And I may have been the only other woman who ever liked Lucia Mahorn." She looked into Wes's eyes, steadily. "I'll be here, too."

He opened his mouth to argue but saw that glint in the athlete's eyes and knew she had other reasons for remaining there. That he was unquestionably the primary one.

"I gotta see that son of a bitch, Dominique," Clem said flatly, "in person."

"I've heard that shit about 'the check's in the mail' too many times to be fooled," Brick growled. He dumped that day's *Syco* in the closest wastebasket. Wes clapped his arm in appreciation.

"Well, me too," Cliff put in. He was a trifle shaky when he arose, but the color in his face had been replaced by conviction, and steel. "Besides, I hafta go on a sales call—right now!" He headed toward the phone room door. "Mebbe I can get a line on what's happenin' while I'm at it."

"Hold on—the program's already printed!" Startled, Wes noticed Macy had a sample case under one arm and appeared about as much in need of help as a sailor on the carrier *Forrestal*. "You're not gonna try to sell tickets to the George Byrnes concert, so what *are* you pitching?"

"Well, a man called here yesterday and wanted somebody t'come see him."

"It's a miracle," Clem said, glancing at the ceiling in mock awe.

"Said he was the man Doc was s'posed to see before Doc got run over." Cliff flushed. "That gives me the chance t'sell a home security system and make some real money!"

Then he was out of there and Brick, grinning, was tipping two fingers at the temple to Wes. "I never understood before why you and Kenny tolerated that sanctimonious character. Y'know, maybe he really is a salesman!"

Cheryl glowered at Brick. "Salesperson," she corrected him icily.

The remnant laughed.

Except Wes, to whom they turned curiously. "I don't like little Cliff goin' out in this neighborhood with everything happening the way it is. And there's something else I don't like."

Cheryl mouthed the word What? silently.

"Maybe he just didn't drive up from Indy today and I hope 'n pray that's all there is to it." Wes sighed, looked at each of the others in turn. "But none of us have even seen Purvis Richwine since he went out on his sales calls on Tuesday."

The address in trusting Cliff Macy's note wasn't the same one Doc Jarvis visited. His caller had simply said it was, to be sure someone came.

This large building was next door, almost as well-maintained and as imposing as that of Dr. A. Dominique's home—in whose basement Jarvis had been killed—but it wasn't a private residence.

Yet one living man dwelled there. The two-story was a combination coroner's office and funeral home.

The resident embalmer had felt rather "funny" recently, lightheaded and irascible. Given to fantasies. Although he'd been badly overworked of late, he was a glutton for punishment, for steady production, and yesterday he'd found himself phoning the Wesken Company both out of impulse and eerie curiosity to see which one of the phone personnel would respond. It did not matter to him especially, however.

But the arrival of eager, earnest Cliff Macy made Stancel Holroyd lose his bet with himself and that provided him with the needed impetus and pique—

With which to waylay and overpower Cliff without a struggle.

Up-close and personal experience in swiftly locating susceptible areas of the human anatomy with dexterous fingers clutching an ether-drenched cloth made it impossible for Macy even to know what or who attacked him. The fact of Cliff's own emerging courage and surprising new willingness to help others meant nothing to a man whose incipient insanity was being released through a complex variety of chemical reactions and eruptions.

Nature presents the raw materials and aptitudes; it doesn't play favorites.

Piling the chubby body on a spotless table was the matter of a moment for someone with Holroyd's present turn of mind. For a workaholic, he had been idle far too long; the greedy, almost middle-aged man who had come at his bidding served a multitude of salubrious purposes, among them a scarcely realized inclination to work himself to death.

Yet his rotund little victim was not dead at the time he was placed, unconscious, on Stancel Holroyd's immaculate table.

But Holroyd embalmed him anyway, and then he was.

Humming a merry tune from the late forties that might have earned him a sharp reprimand from Albert Kiper or Dr. Dominique, Stancel diligently shaved the face of his new corpse, applied makeup with a hand that tremored more on occasion only, then deposited the somewhat garish results in an open, wooden coffin he had set up across from many similar white tables. Upon one of the latter lay a motionless young woman whose sweet blue eyes were forever closed; a person of charmingly mixed ancestry whose previously frizzy hair had been thoughtfully restyled by Holroyd himself.

Perspiring freely, the single, living man in the big two-story building depressed his cadaver's nearest shoulder until the body was turned just so; efficient morticians did not allow the loved one to appear altogether flat; lifelessly prone. He capped off his considerable labors by resting a half circle of rubber contrived for such ultimate occasions upon the round belly of the late Cliff Macy, and cupping the pudgy hands around it.

As natural as life itself, the happy undertaker complimented himself.

That Thursday evening, Purvis Richwine showed up—wreathed in smiles and buoyant with good health.

He'd earned a small fortune in the field, and he became pathetically dejected when Wes was obliged to spoil his week of sales triumphs with news of the deaths. Just then, Wes hadn't thought it necessary to express a newly evolved opinion as to why Purvis hadn't been assaulted or worse. But it was obvious when you thought about it.

Purvis Richwine was nowhere near thirty. There'd been a chance he might fit in with the youth-seeking residents of Stillwind Valley.

Minus Purvus, the Wesken Company had gone en masse to Doc Jarvis's burial—the simplest of affairs, since it largely consisted of the caretaker lowering Doc's remains into an open grave. Wes had nudged Cheryl, indicated with a glance the others present.

But they'd been allowed to depart the cemetery without incident and had joined forces in Wes's apartment—believing in safety in numbers—and eventually told the rest of the story, and their dark suspicions, to young Purvis.

It was hard for him to understand why, in some ways, they all seemed to look forward to the unveiling of the statue on Friday.

Especially after they gave up on Cliff Macy returning, an hour past midnight, when Cheryl led them in a prayer that was not offered for Cliff alone.

17

Any crowd of three or more people carries with it the tension of anticipation. It expects things, and desires them, and it only differs as to the degree of its intensity and the extent of its outer control.

This one didn't seem likely to have a lot of the latter. They had ruled out seeing Chief Magenheimer last night on the basis of Wes Teagle's observation that doing so could only let the townsfolk know that the phone crew was on to them, and not quite as stupid as they'd apparently believed.

The next to worst thing about a crowd—and it is at this point it can, in theory, become a mob—is that those persons who share the expectations, the common desires, forget very quickly that they are part of a crowd.

The worst things about it are when such people remember it and recognize their power, come mercurially to cherish it—

And when part of the crowd is not, really, a part of it.

Wes, Cheryl, Clem, Brick and Purvis used their experience-taught dramatic ability to pretend, at five that Friday evening, to belong, to blend in with the other citizens. They had never striven harder to do anything—Clemon was reflecting upon the virtues of invisibility—but their success was a mixed bag. A few people pretended just as enthusiastically not to notice their presence, to treat them just as frostily as they were able—

But the overwhelming majority of people gathered in the town square was all too clearly aware of their presence at once. They stared at the Wesken Company in discomfiting silence, and the emotions in their faces ranged roughly from repugnance and instinctive dislike to hostility and malevolence.

"I feel like Jim and Tammy Bakker at Jerry Falwell's birthday party," Purvis admitted, standing as close to the others as possible without becoming intimate.

"I feel like Eddie Murphy attending a cross-burning," Clemon grunted, dark eyes sweeping the crowd.

Neither man had felt constrained to whisper but had spoken in his normal tone of voice. Loudspeakers ringed the Square, and militant heavy metal clamored away as if a team of strong men was whaling at suits of armor with mallets from an old Korda movie.

Wes, wondering when the last time was he had seen Clem Sparrow go two or three days without an impersonation of anyone, nudged Cheryl and attempted to catch the other's eyes. "That's Albert Kiper."

As subtly as they were able—but the overall effect was that of a small group of tennis fans apprehensively watching their hero's return of service—the phone people turned their heads in the indicated direction.

The founder of Kiper Research, as well as Stillwind Valley, was seated on a folding chair with a handful of other local dignitaries on a small platform raised at the heart of the town square. With his miniature legs crossed, observed in contrast with the size of other, ostensibly normal persons, Kiper looked queerly doll-like. They'd posted themselves on the outer fringes of the gabbling assemblage, ready for flight. At that distance, it seemed to Wes that Albert did not literally seem young, *per se*. The notion bothered him for a moment until he was able, to his own satisfaction, to describe the man: Kiper appeared *without* age, that instant; the way a human-shaped form of porcelain can convey a caricature of life with none of the realistic "character" of frown- or laugh-lines and wrinkles.

Day was dying steadily in the west, humidity had adhered their clothing to their skins, and the small scientist reminded Wes in that dwinding wave of illumination of the way some photocopies looked when shrunk. The details remained, but they were somehow too fine, altogether too obviously no longer in accord with the plan of their makers—or the original copy.

"*That's* Kiper?" Cheryl asked incredulously. This time, being a polite woman, she'd whispered. It was as if she had learned the director of the CIA was also the bearded lady in a circus.

Wes, his eyes gleaming with brave humor, nodded. "Ain't he somethin'?"

Cheryl slouched beside him, getting smaller. She made a face. "Something else," she said.

Each of them continued to contrive to seem disinterested in that which truly, deeply magnetized their attentions. But unfailingly, despite small talk, despite even the peevish or disgusted and loathing expressions on the boyish and girlish faces bobbing around them, each employee of the Wesken Company turned back to it.

That for which they had arduously and cleverly sold advertisements in the programs that now littered the grass in the town square, discarded as if disease-bearing, poked its head against the lowering sky. The statue, erected upon its long-waiting foundation and guarded by one of Chief Magenheimer's limited force, stood near the town daddies, fully concealed beneath a large, canvas cloth. No feature of it, save its bulk, was visible. Several ropes dangled from it in readiness for the magical instant when the Jagannath would be exposed to the public for the first time in hundreds of years.

"I don't think it's all that big," Brick said, trying to estimate the monument's size from where they waited with the rest of the crowd.

"S'big enough," Clem Sparrow growled.

On the other side of the draped statue, Wes noticed, seated entirely apart from the dignitaries on the platform, was a man whose feet and lower legs could be detected from time to time. Nobody present glanced his way; no one went within yards of him, although there was a walkway beside him and several stores that might usually, Wes thought, be popular with these townsfolk. Except that each store appeared locked up, deserted; even a restaurant that Wes had previously noticed, and Coomer's Pharmacy, were closed for the event.

"Looks like every man, woman, and thing in town is here," he remarked to Purvis Richwine. But since he knew Cheryl could hear him, he didn't add what passed through his thoughts: *I've never heard of a whole town being shut down and everybody present and accounted for. Except for a highschool basketball championship, maybe—or in newsreels of the German people gettin' together to hear ole Adolf speak.*

And they hadn't always come out—necessarily—on a strictly voluntary basis.

Sensing another presence, maybe a different one, Wes looked around, then up. He was filled with terror although he couldn't instantly locate the watcher, the one with eyes burning into him. At first he saw nothing he hadn't already seen. Run-down old business buildings that the proceeds from Wesken's initial sales campaign were intended partly to restore. Slightly familiar young faces including those of Pritchard Arnt, who'd rented Kenny and Angelane the shocking videotape; the vegetarian restauranteur, Roger Quick; distinguished biochemist Dean Stamper, whom Wes met at the exit from Kiper Research, now seated next to Kiper on the platform. A black couple with faces that quested, questioned desperately. And there were those glimpsed during Wes's brief passage through Stillwind Valley as a person may perceive the faces in nightmares through shimmering veils of imagination, half truth and deceit.

Then upon the roof of a dilapidated building to the west he saw perched on the very edge, staring soundlessly down into the town square and directly at Wes, a figure in green, pale and thin, jogging in place. A quality about him Wes could not identify—perhaps it was the fact that he'd never before seen the jogger stay in one place, possibly it was now he'd chosen Wes from everyone else present as the object of his blankly threatening gaze—made Wes shiver with fear.

And when the residents of Stillwind Valley broke into spontaneous applause, turning their heads with a rising shout that momentarily overcame the din of rock noise blaring from the speakers high on the deserted buildings, Wes imagined for an instant that they were cheering for the jogger . . . rooting for him to vault from the roof onto Wes, and madly pound him into the earth.

Instead, it was just that Kiper had stood and marched to the microphone that awaited the evening's speakers and was tapping on the face of the mike the way any innocuous amateur speaker tended to do. For a moment Wes laughed inwardly at himself, at what appeared to have been an instant of cowardice. It got worse, looking at Albert. Why would anybody be afraid of a fella that small?

"Napoleon was virtually that tiny," Cheryl said as if reading his mind. Actually, she had her own fleeting doubts and was reassuring herself that the nightmare was valid. "Even Hitler wasn't a lot taller than that."

The heavy metal shriek became muted. Not turned off, but down.

"Welcome. Welcome, one and all," Kiper said, looking once at Wes and Cheryl, smiling. The microphone yowled and Albert frowned, disconcerted; he stopped speaking into it from half an inch away. To young Purvis Richwine, then, the danger was over, ended. Had probably never existed. With his diminutive stature and ridiculous mass of wavy hair piled atop his head, Kiper made Purvis think of instructors, ordinary teachers he'd had a mere few years ago. "This is a momentous occasion for each of us, and a penultimate point in the progress of your company . . . and your beloved new town."

Clemon's liquid eyes sought his employer's. Black brows raised in silent question. Wes, shrugging, found his own terror of the scientist, the town's people, their much guessed-at covert purposes and unspoken plans, starting to slip away, dissolve. What could be more American, more apple-pie normal, than the residents of a town with little to do gathering in the town square on an early spring evening to watch the dedication of a statue?

But he realized then that he had not seen, in person, such utterly rapt attention given to a human being before this crowd and Albert Kiper. It could've been simple to believe that they weren't all that attentive with the pulsating pseudo-music still audible as a backdrop, but they were. They listened to the little man with a fascination that was abnormal or, in any case, beyond Wes Teagle's experience.

And despite the fact that Wes scanned the crowd again in a revived hope of learning his conjectures were false, even paranoid, there was not so much as one child present, not one woman or man dwelling in the so-called golden years of human life.

And with the exception of Chief Hemmer Magenheimer, Professor Stamper with his drooping, weight-loss flesh, Harlan Rowe of the *Daily Sycophant* and the no-age-at-all little male doll at the mike, the citizens of Stillwind Valley might've been born in the same damned year.

What was even worse, Wes finally perceived—wondering at how easily he and his friends were lulled into a willing sense of false security—was how fast they could forget Kenny, Angelane, Doc Jarvis, Lucia Mahorn, the disappearing Cliff Macy, and Wes's own father, Ocie. Not one of them was enjoying this "momentous occasion"; none would ever enjoy even those occasions that lacked moment.

Wes glanced at the rooftop; the jogger was gone.

Kiper kept his speech of introduction short. Wes looked back at the scientist, realized he was winding it up, saw the rest of the man behind the draped statue whose legs and feet they had observed earlier as he unfolded himself to approach the lectern. Approached it in approximately two strides, while the music from the speakers was cut off abruptly—entirely—and the silence in the Stillwind Valley town square became a quietus of awe, of totality and wonder and latent terror.

"My God," Cheryl whispered from Wes's side.

" . . . This great man who is generously donating a statue that had been part of his family for decades," Albert Kiper was saying, looking up . . . *up* . . . *UP* at the enormous colleague joining him at the mike, dwarfing him to an insignificance that amounted, almost, to nonexistence. "—Our glorious physician, our benefactor, our dear friend from Nigeria . . . *Dr. Akeem Dominique."*

The dark, umbrageous good doctor seemed to be almost eight feet tall, and he was indisputably black—the largest and blackest man any of the members of the Wesken Company had ever seen.

"Sweet Jesus!" Clem Sparrow said softly and wondered, with Cheryl Conrad, if the powerful, beaming figure peering down at them possessed a hookshot.

Part Three

Try to Be Alive

"It is easier to develop unusual powers than to control them."

—Colin Wilson, *Mysteries*

"Absorption into the masses is comfortable for us. . . . It frees us from the terrors of the extreme isolation of being an individual alone . . ."

—Katherine Ramsland, Ph.D.
The Psychology of Horror and Fantasy

"Try to be alive. You will be dead soon enough."

—William Saroyan

18

It was, Wes reflected while he gaped up at the immense man on the platform, a funny thing about age. Although his attention was absolutely riveted to the doctor and he was more afraid than he had been, he still found himself marveling at the varying effects of the aging process as well as about the individual, distinctive ways that each of us speaks.

". . . doubtless could seem secretive to the outer world, if people from elsewhere happened to drop by Stillwind Valley and inquired about our activities, our plans."

Wes stared. Where Kiper appeared to be no particular age, apart from having grown up, Akeem Dominique also gave no obvious clues to his years of life upon the planet but was certainly not as young as the other residents of Stillwind Valley. How and why that could be, considering that Dominique and Kiper were definitely the "town daddies," Wes could not understand. As to the dark titan's speech patterns, he had presumably traveled so extensively and lived in so many places that, in the very fact that the ubiquitous doctor seemed accentless, Wes was aware of a certain rootlessness.

". . . because we have our existence at a time in history when any man or woman who dares to aspire to the fulfillment of his or her dream and achieves a position of prominence is expected to rush to the media, or subject himself, or herself, to it for the closest conceivable scrutiny." *Chuckles from the crowd.* "And it is also because all of us are perpetually seeking answers to the increasingly complex, universal questions; and because each of us has been repeatedly deceived —dare I say cheated? —that we find ourselves devoid of the faith, or trust, which is required in order to fulfill even the smallest dream."

There was another reason, Wes worked it out, that the big fella semed to possess an accent when he actually had none. TV newscasters often sounded accent-free and their roots, too, were concealed; but they emphasized certain syllables, stressed—at some unconscious level—favorite words, letters, terms. And Dominique, while he didn't exactly address the crowd in a flat monotone, projected the clear impression that he needed not to convince another, living soul of what he was saying . . . nor to woo his audience into liking him. How he differed from the scientist Kiper, age-wise, was linked to the giant's dignity or gravity of manner. There was a starkly committed, undeviating earnestness that invested him, for Wes, with the sort of character tiny Albert Kiper altogether lacked.

". . . we aren't secretive, apart from the understandable fact that no research laboratory is precisely eager to report its findings in advance of the evidence—prematurely—and not restricted or exclusionistic beyond this point:

The gift that Albert, his employees, the "civilian" supporters of Stillwind Valley—*'crowd chuckles'*—and I plan to bestow upon humankind *begins* here—and will be given, first, to each and every one of you."

The Wesken people glanced at one another, not without hope. In fact, Wes realized, Dominique hadn't hesitated to look down from where he towered above the lectern and microphone—virtually eschewing the latter with his sonorous rumble of a bass voice—as if being certain to include each phone person in what he was so carefully saying.

"I'd like to remind each person in the crowd gathered here, this evening, for the unveiling of the ancient statue I'm donating to our community, of those salient reasons why Professor Kiper wished to reopen the town and bring so many of you here—and both how, and why, he enlisted my support." Dominique, it occurred to Wes, addressed crowds in a fashion that was somewhat paternalistic but not truly condescending; not authoritarian, or devoid of humor. While his mellow, resonant voice was neither very warm nor sentimental, it contained an apparently sincere quality that fully matched the regular, refined ebony features. Because only a bigot wouldn't have considered the titan handsome—and it further occurred to Wes that the doctor probably did not have a drop of Caucasian blood. None of that seemed anomalous to Wes, as a Hoosier; the Ku Klux Klan had virtually succeeded in moving in to Indiana four decades ago, but the man who'd led them, in going to jail had inadvertently managed to cleanse countless Hoosier hearts of the taint of bigotry.

If he's a liar, Wes concluded, squeezing Cheryl's hand and knowing she, too, had begun to relax slightly, *he's the best I've ever seen. And a gee-dee wonderful salesman, t'boot!*

"Selflessness had virtually nothing to do with it," Dominique rumbled, pausing, "but so did . . . selfishness."

Brick was clearly captivated by the gigantic physician's remarks. It reminded Wes of how most of his own customers had always badly wanted to buy what he was trying to sell. He'd taught Cliff Macy that customer resistiveness merely *seemed* to the customers the easiest possible reaction to a sales pitch—and that removing their anxiety at the same time you indicated how they'd benefit by nodding their heads yes made everybody relieved, and happy; particularly the salesman or -woman.

Then he noticed that Clem-the-unconnable and oft-burned-by-life Cheryl were now on the verge of saying yes to Dominique, and he made himself wonder if big ole Akeem was offering such a terrific product that it could override the lives of half a dozen of their friends.

"In the year nineteen-twenty, were you a Caucasian male," the doctor intoned, "your life expectancy at birth was fifty-four point four years. Two decades later, the figure stood at sixty-two point one years; and when you became twenty, the life expectancy was seventy point three years." Dominique dropped his voice, but it had the effect of making his listeners still more acutely attentive. "A white male born in nineteen-sixty had the right to expect to attain the age of sixty-seven point four, and in nineteen-eighty-two, a year after his twenty-first birthday . . . he could look foward to reaching the age of seventy-three point two." He whispered, "A white female born in sixty, when she achieved the tender age of twenty-two, theoretically could relax in the comforting knowledge that she would live precisely *eighty* years."

Dominique paused, drew himself erect. The man's height, Cheryl perceived, however anyone might like to think first of his handsome face or voice—his accomplishments and his remarkable speech—periodically intruded, made it impossible to consider any other factor. The doctor was almost a foot taller than Wilt Chamberlain, nine or ten inches taller than Kareem Abdul-Jabbar or Ralph Sampson. What he weighed, Cheryl could not even guess to herself, but Dominique appeared well-proportioned; power and good health—vitality; virility—exuded from him. And like Larry Bird and Isiah Thomas, he didn't even seem to sweat!

"Some years back, concerned citizens expressed their apprehension concerning the matter of overpopulation. Despite a slacking-off of the birthrate, that concern remains with us—but it is not as dominant a problem as one other." Dominique braced mammoth hands on the lectern supporting his microphone, raised fine brows. "You know I refer to the basic question of what we're to do with the old and infirm. Consider. More females under fifteen and *over* thirty-five are delivering their first child than ever before. Thus, each stride taken by Professor Kiper's colleagues causes the average age of earth's population to ascend; to an outsider, it could appear that our own activities contradict human need." He let those remarks sink in before proceeding. "Not quite two hundred years ago, half of all persons were under sixteen years of age. By two-thousand thirty, a fifth of us—by the most conservative estimate—will be sixty-five or older. Are we, once more, behaving irresponsibily as scientists and supporters of the scientific community?"

Sounds that way, young Purvis Richwine reflected privately.

"The aging process eventually disables and ends life; the best the sturdiest, of us," Dominique declaimed. "While it's true that three of every four men are still employed between the ages of fifty-five and sixty-four, the fourth is not. Ultimately, he becomes a burden. Twenty-eight percent of the elderly annually earn less than the federal poverty line, five thousand, one-hundred dollars. The same percent of those under age thirty take care of their older relatives—one way or the other."

Cheryl whispered hotly to Wes, "Then seventy-two percent *don't!*"

"Those helpers, mostly women," said the doctor, "average sixteen hours a week providing such care."

"I wonder how many hours a week their moms spent taking care of them when they were young!" Cheryl said somewhat more loudly. Wes nudged her when angry stares turned her way.

Intense, immense, Dominique bent his neck to peer at them, then at the other phone people. "We have found a solution for these problems," he said slowly, clearly. The brilliant black eyes were smouldering fires. "An answer we can all . . . live with."

Brick glanced fearfully at the covered statue, half expecting it to throw off its cloth and come alive.

But Dr. Dominique simply raised his hands, spread them. "It is *not* immortality—because those who quested for it failed." The huge hands spread wider. "Nor is it an answer that directly improves the well being of the already aged . . . for that, too, is a demonstrated failure.

Eventually, you see, they perish." His eyes opened wide as did his arms, the palms turned up in a gesture of generosity. "The solution we provide has never been attempted by the merging of new and old, science-fact and magic-faith." He straightened and, though his mouth was well above the microphone, his majestic voice carried. "Instead of trying to live forever . . . we will simply *remain young.*"

The silence that ensued was total. Wes, who'd believed he was prepared for anything, jumped and felt his mouth drop open.

"We have taken around us, therefore, the appurtenances of youth," the giant explained. "Music, running; exercise. It is why we shall not consume any food that is not entirely healthful."

Why, he's talking to us, Cheryl thought, shocked by the realization. *The others know why they came here—so this speech is meant just for us. Why?*

"By remaining young we shall not become hindrances to others, or to ourselves. Instead, we will remain productive. Useful." Akeem Dominique smiled blissfully. "Today, there are seventy-five-year-old men in nursing homes, and on golf greens. Only a quarter of those exceeding eighty-five spent even a single night in hospital during a year of study conducted by Longino, the gerontologist; yet the typical oldster from that group didn't complete a year of high school. 'In studying this group,' Longino stressed, 'we have to be aware of youth-creep.' And so the chance to achieve the fundamental desire of our time falls to us in Stillwind Valley. The mindset of people today is eager to cooperate with evolving nature. That is obvious since the symbols of what we do now were the millions of ordinary persons who began to diet, and exercise, during the 1970s."

"I haven't tried to lose a pound since high school," Clem muttered, tucking in his belly.

"We noticed," Brick said acidly.

"So the climate is ideal," declared the doctor, "for reaching our objective: sustained youth. We will become the people who utilize their faculties fully for the first time; we shall continue to enhance our skills and our knowledge—on behalf of the unborn." Gradually, the physician's handsome features had taken on the dreamy cast Wes observed earlier on Albert Kiper's face. "We shall learn to understand youth, what it means, truly, to be young . . . by experiencing youth *longer* than anyone has before. And doing so, we shall push back the boundaries of progress—and life itself!"

An unprovoked burst of applause made Dominique dab at his moist eyes. "Evolution itself focused its primary creativity on our development. Primarily, however, our physiological development." He stared briefly toward Kiper and others with him on the platform; they shocked Wes by nodding, glancing away. "Most men strove to cooperate with natural evolution through discovery and research—but others centered their energies upon the *mind,* the *soul.* They were the clergy and metaphysicians, the magicians and occultists." His unflinching gaze rolled over the faces in the hushed audience. "The occult is that which is hidden, and Albert Kiper concurred with me that it was time for the occult to come out of the closet . . . because as biologist Lyall Watson wrote, 'we are now beginning to rediscover more of our extraordinary gifts.' "

Then he moved closer to the draped statue, and Brick made the sign of the cross, mentally. "Alchemy was in vogue until Boyle's *Sceptical*

Chymist in 1661. When Black proved the concept of quantitative chemistry and Priestly came upon oxygen, it seemed quite, quite dead." Akeem Dominique seized the longest of the ropes dangling from the statue between his two, powerful hands. "Yet early this century, Rutherford revived alchemical claims by turning nitrogen into oxygen. The key to alchemy is changing one thing into another. Much was lost, my friends." He shook his head ruefully; then his expression lightened. "But is isn't too late. Consider the development of silicon, for example."

"This is gonna be the sexy part," Wes told Cheryl, grinning.

But Dominique abruptly changed the subject and brought him a sense of guilt followed quickly by fresh alarm. "Mr. Wes Teagle and his associates," the doctor said directly, looking at Wes, "nobly aided us to generate income with which to restore this square." He let his arms droop, crossed one over the other, beaming. "Without their efforts, performed in the face of their own tragic misfortunes, the run-down structures you see around us would stand as poor monuments to the deeds we're striving to accomplish. You merchants have a right to occupy buildings commensurate with the necessities of life that you provide us, and the Wesken Company has made that possible." He threw out one arm, beckoning. "Come, Mr. Teagle! *Join* us here, where you belong . . . *please!*"

Wes was stunned; astounded. Reluctant and lingeringly apprehensive at first, he was spurred forward by good-humored shoves from Brick and Purvis Richwine. He raised a hand to balance himself for the leap to the platform, then glanced inquiringly back to Cheryl Conrad—

And found himself feeling as if he were flying.

Akeem Dominique had hauled Wes to his side as easily as if he were an infant. Then his hand was being swallowed up by the doctor's in a gentle, congratulatory shake.

Clemon and Cheryl tittered. It was, Wes knew, the contrast between the black man's size and his own. He was fully unprepared for the way Dominique looked, up close; as a boy, he'd had the opportunity to meet the first great scorer in NBA history—George Mikan, who stood roughly six-ten. But *this* giant was at least a foot taller than George.

He was even less prepared for the instant when Dr. Dominique started to clap his massive hands; steadily, rhythmically, insistently—

And the way the people of Stillwind Valley, Indiana, one by one, followed suit. Gaping out at them through the layer of night shadows coming on as the minutes passed, Wes realized the applause was spreading, made out smiles of long-belated welcome and apparent friendship on the faces of pharmacist Noxie Coomer, "Mother" Quick, Chief Magenheimer; Arnt, Tedrick, even the other men and women with him on the platform.

It was, he perceived, the mortician who was first to reach down and retrieve one of the official but idly discarded programs into which the whole Wesken Company had put so much work. And when others in the crowd saw what Stancel Holroyd was doing, flashes of white paper fluttered to chest and waist level, matching the gleam of grinning, healthy teeth revealed in hundreds of heretofore antagonistic faces.

Young Purvis, who privately believed his fellow salespeople had simply struck out and gone home, realized immediately what the acceptance of the townsfolk meant to his commission-making potential. Impulsively, he raised his right hand, tried to exchange high fives with Clemon Sparrow.

"Uh-uh," Clem growled. "We still haven't seen the statue."

"I'm told," Dr. Dominique's bass tones rumbled into the microphone, his black eyes twinkling, "that the Wesken Company has *many* products to sell—and that they even have the ear of a famous comedian who might be persuaded to entertain us in our auditorium." He motioned to Albert Kiper with a long arm. "Let us not be somber, Professor, while yet we have our youth! Since that will be a very long period of time, indeed"—he clapped Wes on the shoulder, numbingly—"let us toil industriously together but also *enjoy* life!"

With an uncertain, crooked grin, Wes watched Kiper stare blankly at the abruptly playful giant, shrug, and actually attempt his own lopsided smile.

"Time," said Dr. Dominique, turning back to the people ringing the platform, "for the unveiling." Instantly, everyone subsided into silence. "For the information of those who are not part of Professor Kiper's scientific team, the statue you're about to see—which I am about to donate—was stolen from India and used as a tool of political leverage between nations for more than a hundred years. Then, however, my family saved, housed, preserved and protected it . . . for centuries."

Most of those present turned their attention toward the draped object. From where Wes stood now, next to the doctor, it reminded him of pictures he'd seen of dead persons encased in body bags—except it was upright.

"My father's father's father cherished and venerated the priceless object that becomes your own this evening." Tears showed in the giant's eyes and his lower lip trembled, Wes saw. "Whether it possesses magical properties or not, as tradition asserts, isn't for me to say. But in the way it has not changed, appreciably, for centuries, it seems to me a worthwhile symbol of our own important quest. It sustained my fathers in their youth, as it did me." Dominique's fingers tightened on the rope. "My friends, my colleagues . . . my new and permanent family . . . I give you—the *Jagannath!*"

Folds of canvas slipped and slithered from head and shoulders as if the icon of antiquity were divesting itself of clothing. People gasped; breaths were inhaled, sustained. By prearrangement, a spotlight sought to halo and expose it with clarity, but the lighting man wasn't professionally skilled and a globule of pale illumination darted here and there like an unidentified flying object whose pilot was bewildered by his audience.

Then it found the wooden head of the statue and settled.

What the Wesken Company as well as the residents of Stillwind Valley saw was an undeniably aged, rather clumsily carved creation mounted on wheels that appeared fixed; permanently immobilized. The features of the thing were at once foreign and improbable. There were a large nose, large ears, a crude gash suggestive of lips, or a mouth . . . and dull, utterly unconvincing wooden eyes that stared without animation at nothing in particular—seeing nothing. Dead; never living.

Cheryl felt as if she was losing both weight and height in the flood of relief that ran through her body. "It's just about as scary as—as the Soldiers and Sailors Monument, on the Circle in Indianapolis!" she said to the trio of men sharing her view of the unremarkable icon.

"Almost, maybe," Brick said with a slow grin.

From where Wes stood, making himself touch the *Jagannath* and getting no sensation of viability, no shock of current, he saw Clem Sparrow turn smilingly toward young Purvis and slap his upraised palm with an attitude of indescribable relief.

19

The next day, a Saturday, Cheryl drove with Wes in the company car to Speedway, Indiana, where Lucia Mahorn was to be buried. On the way there, unlike the trip back to Stillwind Valley, neither of them had much to say. Or, more precisely, neither Wes nor Cheryl had formulated their views about the unveiling ceremony to discuss it objectively.

There was rather little about the town located due west of Indianapolis to indicate, at times of the year other than April and May, that an internationally televised race was annually run off at an outdoor track bearing its name. Speedway looked, ten months out of twelve, not unlike Stillwind Valley would have appeared from a helicopter whose pilot was not particularly observant. Probably the primary difference between Speedway and other Hoosier towns of the same general size and age was how its citizens were inclined, by and large, to like the 500-Mile Race considerably less.

When Cheryl and Wes made their way to the

tiny Protestant church at which services for their friend were being conducted, they acquired an immediate inkling of why Speedway's good people were lacking in enthusiasm for the great money-making event. Already this year, ardent 500-Mile fans and other persons with a lot of time on their hands and money to burn were beginning to arrive; traffic seemed heavy for such a small town, but that was only the start of it. Visitors' inclinations were to view Speedway as an extension of the racing facility itself and to consider the people who lived there year-round mere adjuncts to their own fun. While plenty of residents turned a tidy dollar each year by selling lemonade or offering their driveways and back-yards for parking, more of them lived ordinary existences and did not. The absence of a sign plugging something for sale often seemed an invitation to a certain type of 500 fan. By mid-May, Wes knew from having been there a few times before, the normally tidy streets would be strewn with beer cans and littered with food wrappers, discarded souvenirs and more disgusting things—enough crap, as he told Cheryl, to make a movie director think of inventing a monster made up of discarded junk and burned-out automotive parts.

Nothing about the race was on the minds of Lucia Mahorn's parents, however. To positively no surprise on Cheryl Conrad's part, they bore little or no resemblance to the dead woman. Sadder, she thought, photographs of Lucia from high school—the parents passed them around during a hideous half hour afterward, at their house—were almost as difficult to match with the flamboyant salesperson they had known.

Her real hair color turned out to be an unexciting forgettable brown.

Returning to Stillwind Valley, much of the bouyant mood Wes, especially, had displayed after his warm reception by Dr. Dominique was dissipated and both he and Cheryl sensed the need to talk. Deep inside, the tall blonde had never believed Lucia committed suicide, and seeing the many subtle, terrible ways her parents had sought to argue against it without actually saying so had convinced her. As a consequence, the idea of purposely driving back to the town—she hadn't even been certain they'd be permitted to leave for Lucia's funeral—seemed foolish to her. No, idiotic—except that she knew it was a waste of breath to try to talk Wes out of being there on Monday, for Ocie. And wherever Wes was now, Cheryl had decided without having the foggiest notion when she'd become adamant on the point, she intended fully to be.

So they spoke about it because they had to, but haltingly, circuitously, each aware of some level of the other's feelings and careful to avoid an expensive quarrel. When Wes unreeled an array of hypothetical explanations for the sudden deaths in their circle of associates, Cheryl considered it remarkably imaginative and mentally gave him credit for that. She'd always been the sort of person who had enough detachment to locate insight, principle or humor in an opinion that was otherwise ridiculous to her, and each of his theories stood up well enough by itself, as far as they went: Lucia had lived a post-divorce life that was "unnatural" to her, she knew it was hard on her Mom and Dad, and she was guilty enough to virtually behead herself. Ocie and Doc Jarvis had been ill; either man would still be alive if he'd taken better care of himself. The black girl, Thalia, had just run away and was probably perfectly healthy somewhere, except maybe she was pregnant and hadn't known how to tell her folks.

It was when they were added together along with the pecularities of Stillwind Valley itself and one was asked to accept so damned *much* in such a brief period of time that Wes's obvious desire to believe they were safe—and that the Wesken Company was entering upon a period of tremendous success—was untenable. Cheryl was reminded of the dozens of demises following on the heels of John F. Kennedy's assassination; to her, the best argument for a conspiracy theory had nothing to do with guns and bullets; it was the death of so many men and women in the span of a year or two and relatively few of them anywhere near Ocie Teagle's age.

There was also the fact that Wes was oddly able to gloss over that the whereabouts of Kenny Higgins, Angelane O'Brien, and Cliff Macy remained unknown.

Lacking candor, the chat inevitably disintegrated well before they approached the town limits. It seemed to Cheryl that it broke down because there was not yet bond enough between them for her to risk being honest and imperiling a relationship for which she still had high hopes. And he didn't want to risk giving up his rutting rights. He was like an ambitious boy who'd rediscovered an old talent.

The last time they'd entered Stillwind Valley together, Cheryl thought, with all the others, Wes had considered her too tall to be a desirable screwing partner. Or maybe he had actually shifted all his sexual drives to sales, or running a company; it was difficult to be certain. Now, though, they had slept together. In the way of what they called modern times—which often made Cheryl feel deprived of the rights earlier women had taken for granted and made her see herself as stripped of the right to exercise her own, keen will because it jeopardized what other females wanted or expected from her—they were friends now. Sometimes lovers; they could even be mated in the fashion that still mattered most to Cheryl, if you possessed Dr. Dominique's kind of belief. God knew she'd tried for it not to matter so much; but as an individual person, she'd never quite got past the conviction that an unmarried male lover constantly kept in mind his right to—

"Want me to hop over to Walterville, buy some good grub?"

Cheryl stared straight out the windshield. She told herself she was being unreasonable, but knew that was her cue to say yes, the way he wanted. To signal and 'fess up to her essential fragility as a human being, that which the doctor and Albert Kiper so palpably preyed upon: Admit she was reluctant to return to Stillwind Valley without at least being armored with normal *food*! So *he* could stock up on the customary "grub" he wanted even more than she did, and smile his smug awareness of her self-confessed unwillingness to *die* before her time—while he reveled in her dragged-out "weakness" and it refilled his tank of stupid male courage!

A tiny shriek she could throttle, mash down, without sacrificing anything she hadn't already relinquished and half-smothered a thousand times, screamed tinnily in her guts. At that point she wondered if she or her mother or her *great*-grandmother had ever for one instant had the unthreatened liberty to say just what she knew to be true without also knowing what the consequences were—without having to have thrown in her face the single scrap of information about her sex that every heterosexual man in the world was born understanding: that she could not tolerate being considered less than worthy due to her femaleness, and subsequently becoming no longer worth tolerating, humoring, teasing, or arguing with at all. . . .

Cheryl peeked at the man at the steering wheel, saw how apparently calm he was, how goddamned perpetually confident or cocksure—and what was the derivation of *that* word? She pushed back the most forbidden thought of her gender, the temptation to wonder or even to determine why she cared about *him* at all. But maybe Wes possessed enough real belief in those individual rights he loved rapping about to relocate his sense of humor in a timely manner and be honest enough to go to Walterville despite what she was going to say. *God knows,* Cheryl mused, *I don't* want *to eat any more of that crap that passes for food in Stillwind Valley.*

"I don't care," she said aloud, lying.

"Okay," he replied promptly, expressionlessly, without an iota of reflection, without the slightest sign that she had surprised him or that he knew he'd be eating food he loathed this week. Instead of thinking about their danger, she was wondering, when they reentered Stillwind Valley, which one of them was the bigger fool. And why it was apparently so easy for men to hate and fly into rages when all she was ever able to mount was either resentment or cocksure men.

"You beautiful ole car," Wes said lovingly, kissing his fingertips, tenderly pressing them to the dashboard. The Caddy had made it again. He promptly opened the door without asking Cheryl when she wanted to be with him. Above the Wes-blessed finger kiss, a checkered flag he'd bought in Speedway and mounted under the Caddy's wide rearview mirror ceased fluttering even before he was through the door and striding unhesitantly toward the apartment building.

The next day, a Sunday, Wes played cards in the phone room with Clem and Brick—who showed up with a sack of Arby roast beef sandwiches from Walterville. Cheryl washed and set her hair, bathed and smoked grass, alone; and the parents of Thalia Boggs attended services at a small Baptist church in the neighboring town. They prayed they would eventually find their missing daughter and pretended, with the practice stemming from years of experience, that the whites attending services weren't staring.

It hadn't for so much as a moment occurred to Wilford Boggs that the Man—whether Kiper, Dominique or someone else entirely—wasn't trying to get him and his family to give up and leave town, nor for a second that his daughter, Thalia, wasn't alive. All people have a range of forbidden topics, some of which, as individuals, they are good at avoiding. It also had not occurred to Boggs that Thalia might be pregnant, because he was a father who'd made it a point to know his daughter well. His major regret in that area was that Thalia found it very difficult to return the favor.

It hadn't for an instant occurred to Mary Boggs that anybody wanted them to leave, except perhaps the evil spirits in their house, nor that her daughter Thalia was still alive. Because respectively she knew for a fact that they were good folks, decent and God-fearing folks, and Thalia'd known exactly what her mama expected of her and had always done it. Unquestioningly.

She also knew that her husband, Wilford, was chockful of forbidden subjects and her major worry wasn't that he might have to give up his fine job, but speak of all that he had wisely refrained from mentioning.

Police Chief Hemmer Magenheimer was waiting in his official car when they got back to town, flagging them down, and it didn't take more than a moment for both Mary and Wilford Boggs to perceive that almost everything they had believed was either wrong or warped out of shape for good, and that the only thing forbidden to them now was happiness.

They followed him docilely to headquarters, stared at his white, mountainous profile with shaggy brows that belonged on the face of an Old Testament prophet, looked down at the tattered remnant of a girl's dress that he drew from an incongruous manila envelope. Wilford couldn't have described a single article of clothing belonging either to his wife or daughter but recognized it as Thalia's at once. Mary Boggs covered her husband's board-stiff, out-thrust arm with one hand and the enormous bloodstain on the torn frock with her other hand. Boggs didn't even quite touch it and didn't put his arm down, either, for quite awhile, but he got around to nodding, and making noises in his throat that sounded more like strangling than acknowledgment.

"When she run off," Magenheimer said carefully, ungrammatically, yet sounding as if he were reading from a script, "she crossed old Milford Bridge east of town. Bottom fell out—not where cars cross so's we'd notice it; along the edge." His gaze stayed on the manila envelope in his hands but his brows frowned. "This here's a big piece of the dress that caught afore your girl fell into the crick."

He offered more data but no clear expressions of grief.

That Sunday evening, then, most of the possessions they had left after the poltergeist infestation were crammed into the trunk of their car and Wilford and Mary Boggs were ready to leave. She'd called Kiper Research, unasked, thinking it was the thing to do; he'd assured her two more times that the body he'd seen at the Holroyd Mortuary was probably Thalia's. He didn't quite understand why Mary hadn't insisted upon helping identify their girl, but that was a small, a very small, relief. "Drowning . . . being in the water a long while . . . sometimes does that," Mr. Holroyd had told him. The man hadn't looked startled or offended when Wilford asked that Thalia be sent to a funeral home in Walterville.

They stopped on the bridge over Milford Creek while Mary got out to find the hole, and did. There were even bloodstains, she assured him when she climbed back into the car. When he scarcely nodded and didn't drive on, off the bridge and toward whatever life awaited them in Walterville, she stared through the windshield without asking him why and simply waited for him to explain; if he wanted to.

At length, however, without speaking immediately, Wilford sighed heavily and crossed the rest of the bridge. Then he shared her silence, her thoughtless rumination, for several moments.

"Those phone people," he said at last. "I was thinking about going over to the Blackwood Apartments."

"All right," Mary said softly. Then she turned her head. "Why?"

"I was thinking about warning them," Boggs replied.

She nodded. "Well, that might be the thing to do."

"Yes, it might," he said.

"The Christian thing to do," Mary added.

Wilford nodded. It was dark now, the road to Walterville was unlit, and the sky seemed to begin an arm's length from the roof of the car. If you looked at it just so, in the rearview mirror, you could almost imagine that a portion of the sky was thicker, darker, occupied. By something large that drifted along in the wake of their car with silent sentience, and a care taken to be sure they kept going.

"I loved her so, Mary," Wilford said. *But she's gone,* he thought.

"I know," Mary said. Her sigh was a shudder. "She knew you did, Wilford. Thalia knew that."

He blinked back tears, reached up to adjust the rearview mirror, realized quite dimly that his heart was beating erratically. "Maybe I'll call them after we get settled in," he said.

The skies behind them were clearing now. Mary patted his arm, glanced out her window at a handful of lights sprinkled like shining sand. The place where they'd be starting over, alone. "You do that, honey," she told him, wishing he'd shut up so she could begin to pray. "You do that."

20

"Dearly beloved, we are gathered here," Vernon Slaid mumbled, squinting now and then at some notes he had jotted down for the occasion, "at the site of the Stillwind Valley Cemetery."

On the lip of the fresh grave he'd dug Sunday afternoon, Vernon seemed self-conscious in the role of clergyman and in the presence of the deceased's loved ones. He'd shaved off his nearly coal black beard, even bathed, but the dead old fart's offspring kept eye-balling him 'stead of cryin' his heart out like he was supposed to. It wasn't his fault it was rainin' cats and dogs, or the wind was howling 'n kickin' up dust around the bottom of the coffin. Wasn't even his fault the old booger was dead, even if it did seem like a right smart idea.

"If anyone can show just cause why this man, Ocie Teagle, should not be dumped in the earth and joined in Paradise," the caretaker rasped, "let him step forward now or forever hold his peace." He glanced up sharply, shrewd-eyed, ready to pronounce Ocie headed for heaven—

And the four-eyed little SOB who was the old fart's son stepped forth, obviously pissed as hell.

"That's my *father*, you idiot!" Wes told him. Some tall, skinny blonde was tryin' to hold him back.

"Well, why don't ya go with him, then?" the caretaker snapped back, and grabbed his spade. His blue eyes blazed as he whipped it behind one brawny shoulder and stood that way, poised for a moment. "Allus did like the i-dee of two skeletons for the price of one!"

The spade whistled in an arc toward the base of Wes Teagle's skull—

"Are you all right?"

Wes blinked, slopped some of the Southern Comfort in his glass. Clem had bought it in Walterville early that morning, before Ocie's interment, and this was meant to be a wake of some kind. Except it wasn't much fun so far—maybe you had to be Catholic, Irish at least—and Wes suspected he was getting a bit high. "I'm fine." He stood, stretched, wobbled, sipped. It hadn't been awful at the cemetery today except for random clamors of rock music clanging dutifully from Slaid's queer little building. "Guess I was day-dreaming about how it *could* have gone."

"That caretaker!" Cheryl agreed, shuddering. "What a horror!" Slouching to seem shorter, she touched Wes's wrist. He had been distant ever since they got back to town, and she couldn't quite judge how much of his withdrawn mood was due to his father's burial. "I think you made the right decision about our silent prayer for Ocie. That Slaid character would've made an awful mess of it."

Wes glanced around the phone room without

seeing it, or anybody. For one night it was a rec room again. And it had neither rained nor been windy today; incongruously, the sun had shone as if they'd gone to see tennis at the Sports Center in Indy. "I just wish . . ." He allowed the rest of it to fade. Sighing, Wes looked back at Cheryl, his face purposely blank. "I just wish I'd been able t'say something . . . decent."

Without speaking, she considered his expression until her woman's eyes detected the tears lurking like shamed things in his. "You just did," she said, brightly, and smiled.

He looked startled. Then he thought about it. "Thanks," he offered simply, hugging her.

Then, however, his surviving trio of male sales friends were at him again, prodding him with their persistent unconscious reminders of his gender—*The one that gets killed most in wars, because they never start them, they always think they finish them,* Cheryl mused. Helpless, she watched them utilize their seemingly unvanquishable masculine slaps and spirits, quips and coarse affection, their collective eagerness to get him drunk enough to dry up his unshed tears. He was hurt, showing blood, and they were relentless. It was like watching a man floating precariously on the surface of a sea of semen and trying not to drown, a mating dance of smaller mammals with no intercourse and no clear objective apart from the avoidance of actuality.

Before Wes was borne off by them to the bar where pretzels that seemed shaped roughly like DNA were pressed upon him, and each of the others managed a single terse, tough-minded grunt of awkward praise for "the sweet old bastard" who'd by-God fathered Wes, Cheryl was fairly sure he recalled again the expression of stark terror on Ocie's motionless features, and that Wes's resolve to remain in Stillwind Valley had weakened. If not that, yet, she reasoned, peeking into her commodious purse for reassurance that she had brought her pot—contemporary women didn't need pans too—Cheryl felt pretty certain he was no longer positive of their safety.

But now Clem, Brick and Purvis—meaning well, of course; they always did—had taken their macho turn, laughed danger in the eye, and if she never learned anything else about the gender since Date One at almost age thirteen, she knew one unarguable fact: Whether the salmon went out to spawn or just show off, whenever they did it in unison not even depth charges, or Akeem Dominique, could make them back off. Jostling, joking, and rubbing their crotches when they thought nobody was looking, they had just turned it all into a fart-blowing, finger-flipping friend-to-the-end time—and if Cheryl Conrad herself stuck around until the end came along, she was going to be blown out of the water along with cute little D'Artagnan and his Three Mouseketeers.

Right before she tucked her pot-containing purse under her arm and exited the rec room, Cheryl was filled with a fresh hunch, one that took shape—for the first time—as inescapable conviction: That Dr. A. Dominique and Albert Kiper had really wanted them to stay—and to stay docile—but just for a brief, alloted amount of time.

And that had to mean, logically enough, that she, Wes and the rest of them had been cleverly trapped in a covert, quiet web that had to stick together only until something perfectly terrible occurred. . . .

* * *

Before the *Syco*'s Harlan Rowe showed up and his piqued revelation sent the small universe of Stillwind Valley spinning, Kiper and Dean K. Stamper—who seemed to be Albert's friend—attended the wake in Ocie's honor. That brought the civic duty scenario full circle since Dominique had furnished enough floral arrangements at the cemetery that morning for a sinecure of suddenly dead, retired salesmen. They didn't stay long; Darrell Brickowski got simultaneously drunk and indiscriminately abusive, and the scientists took their obviously reproachful leave during the period that Wes and Clemon Sparrow wrestled Brick into Kenny's old apartment. But they stayed long enough, with Cheryl, that she was obliged to chat with them and to gauge their genuine, individual menace with the foggy yet relaxed outlook of someone who had already smoked grass that evening and privately planned to smoke more.

Immediately, both scientists seemed guarded and monosyllabic to Cheryl, and she was ready—in menace gauging—to award them high marks.

That was especially the case when she had fished a Lucky Strike from a sequined case in her purse and accidentally revealed her portable cache of pot. Dean Stamper's strangely popped-out eyes clouded over with discreet annoyance, and Cheryl knew he'd be sure to tell his friend Kiper what he saw. Maybe even the good doctor.

After the two scientists departed but before Rowe arrived to try to collect his printing bill for the program, Cheryl returned to the privacy a bathroom door provided and Wes began pontificating to Clem and Purvis Richwine. The latter, however, was fighting sleep, drifting off faster by the moment, which led to Wes's next philosophical notion.

"Y'know, fellas, not even those eggheads at Kiper Research know *why* people sleep. That's how smart they are—or aren't!"

Clem glanced at the drowsy young Richwine. "I used to think, Wes, it was because people got *sleepy.*" He raised a dark brow. "That's not a scientific enough reason?"

"Uh-uh, no way," Wes told him, waggling an upraised palm. He wasn't drunk yet, just buzzed. But he also knew that pretending to be smashed was the socially acceptable next step at such an occasion. "According to them egghead signacests"—that's how the word came out—"sleep don't serve any purpose; I read that somewhere. And I got t'thinkin': If they keep folks awake a long while, folks get real strange; they act weird, or nuts . . . know what I mean?"

Clem nodded. "Whatever," Purvis mumbled noncommitally, burrowing his prematurely balding head into the pillow on the sofa set against the rec room wall.

"So *I* figger," Wes continued doggedly, "this means that half of a guy's brain is sane—and the other half is crazy! And the way you keep the looney half in control is"—he hoisted his current drink, carelessly, and it drooled from its glass lips—"by just *sleepin'* through it! You see? We sleep because, whenever folks begin usin' the nutty part of their minds, they automatically drop off and don't hurt anybody. Like it!"

"Sorry I couldn't make it to the cemetery this morning," Harlan Rowe interrupted; "for your father." He had entered the room unnoticed and, with his silver-splashed pointed beard bristling, he looked aggressive. Determined to collect on the printing bill, if not truly malicious of intent.

"As I told you, I rather liked the kind of man he was. Direct. Uncompromising. Honest." The last word was clearly a hint at Wes for action.

"Well now, I got that piece of paper made out for you already!" Wes cried. He smiled like a man does who loves to give money away. Groping and clumsy, he reached into his hip pocket for his billfold, then dropped it to the floor. But finally he yanked it open, fumbled around in it and located the check. "Here you go, Harlan!" He handed it over with a flourish, as if bestowing a gift.

Clemon watched the proceedings with enjoyment; Purvis was already soundly asleep.

Rowe read the amount and turned incredulous. In a burst of quick thinking, Wes, an hour before the wake, had already made out the check. "This is for half of what your firm owes me, Mr. Teagle," Rowe observed. Slowly, his frown became a glare. "I suppose that neither surprises nor distresses you."

"Not really, Harlan," Wes said, standing. "To tell the truth." *Because I want to figure out whether you're fish or fowl,* he reflected, still mentally hazy but wanting information. *Just whose side* are *you on, anyway?* "Mosta the folks in town who bought ads for the program haven't paid us yet. I figger I'm being generous t'you. For all I know, Harl, some of them will never pay up." He smoothed his hands out as if he'd just dealt very forthrightly with a problem and everything was tied up in a nice package. "I wanted you and the *Syco* t'have half of what's owed you, right now!"

Purvis was continuing to doze, even occasionally to snore; but Clem, who couldn't remember the last time he'd passed out, was attentively following their printer's veering expressions.

For a moment, Rowe did not retort at all, except by folding the scrap of blue paper and sliping it inside his own billfold. "I think you're a scoundrel, Mr. Teagle," he murmured judiciously. "But I don't think you're as damned smart as you imagine."

Wes cocked a brow, affably listening "Y'have something specific in mind, Harlan?"

Rowe paused, either reining in his temper or trying to arrive an an important decision. Then he half turned as if ready to depart. "I think you should know they found your missing friend," he said softly. "They found Cliff Macy."

There'd been no public ladies' room in the building when Cheryl went in quest of one, earlier. Instead, then and now, privacy proved to be a question of going back to her own apartment bathroom.

But this time when she started down the hallway with her key already in her hand she sensed the presence of somebody else at the end of the corridor. There appeared to be nothing to see, but good basketball floor generals were attuned to the proximity of others, and Cheryl's ball-handling instincts insisted someone was there.

Her first impulse was to unlock the door as quickly as possible, and dart inside. But the idea of hurrying like that, admitting to the panicky feeling this town was generating in her, rubbed the athletic, independent spirit of Cheryl Conrad the wrong way. This was not Detroit, or Chicago; it wasn't even Indianapolis—and there was enough weird damned activity going on in Stillwind Valley without beginning to manufacture perverts, mentally, with which to scare herself!

So she merely paused outside her apartment, tapping the key ring restively against the heel of her outstretched hand, listening intently and also craning her neck to see who it was.

Who it was was shadows, nothing more—for another instant. A black mass—the evil ambiguity of that term disturbed her—the size of a man. Even men. Partly out of sight, round the bend at the end of the otherwise empty hallway . . .

Moving, Cheryl thought, into the faint illumination of the subdued ceiling fixtures—then *seeing* who it was, just at the second he headed toward her, *ran* toward her—

Rushed toward Cheryl, while she jabbed the key futilely at her front door lock; heard the pounding, masturbative pulse of rock music more with her half-stopped, tremblingly tensed body than with her sharp ears—

Realized then she had selected the *wrong* key, just as he came racing up behind her, deadpan and dead-looking—and threw out his arms, thin arms to grasp and embrace her . . .

"It'll be the lead story in the *Syco* tomorrow," Harlan Rowe explained. "I thought I should do that much." He looked back at the dismayed, shocked faces, white and black. "Apparently, your friend Macy . . . just . . . died. Like the others." He held Wes Teagle's fast-sobering gaze with his own eyes and quietly stroked his silvering beard. "From what I hear, he was a lush; so maybe that contributed—"

"He was a recovering alcoholic, you motherfucker," Clem Sparrow exclaimed. He was on his feet, knotting big hands into fists like dark tornados. Then the shock overcame the fury and he turned away, sadly. "He was *trying,* man. Jesus, he was *trying."*

"What'd they *do* with him?" Wes couldn't recall ever feeling more chilled with anguish, not even when the father he had scarcely known stared sightlessly at him from his lonely deathbed. He hadn't asked Ocie to come home; but he had felt responsible for Cliff Macy. This was *not* better than starting silly little skirmishes at a neighborhood bar. "Where is Cliff . . . now?"

"Well, you aren't going to like this." He put it together with exaggerated caution. "As I get it, while everybody else was at the unveiling Friday evening . . . well, some assistant or friend of the coroner embalmed him."

"Say *what?"* Clem shouted.

"It could have been Holroyd himself, of course, I saw Stancel in the town square later." He glanced around the room as if listeners might be concealed beneath the phone tables and desks shoved against the walls. "There was . . . something . . . that didn't sit right with me."

"What?" Wes demanded, incredulous that other things apparently had.

"They—well, they buried him. Saturday morning."

"Without any religious services? Without prayers?" Clem took a step toward the publisher. "You must be fucking kidding. Macy was *religious;* he'd have wanted a decent Christian burial more than anyone else in this town."

"Oh, he knows *that,"* Wes spat. He stepped between Clem and Rowe, snatched a handful of the latter's shirt and pulled Rowe closer. "Explain, dammit! Get the rest of it out—*now!"*

"Look, don't blame *me."* Hastily, Rowe raised his hands in a defensive posture, palms out. His face looked distinctly middle-aged when it was full of apprehension and mounting fear. "I'm the one who's breaking the story tomorrow."

"It's too damned late!" Wes snapped. And the full realization of how accurate his remark might be began to sink in. *Was* it too late for the rest of them . . . for everything? And how in hell had he just forgotten about Cliff, Angelane, Kenny? "Why didn't you do your job before now?"

"I've always done my job." Harlan Rowe lifted his head, attempted to muster a measure of pride. "The *Syco*'s been run the modern way, with interesting stories off the wire services, chatty columns, nothing very deep or done in analysis—but with every effort on my part to please the town fathers with what I printed and to satisfy the advertisers. I've never made waves before." Abruptly, he shook his head sadly, seemed tired. "Crusading? That's for younger men, fiery guys just starting out."

"You used t'be like that, Harlan," Wes said quietly. "Didn't you?"

Rowe smiled forlornly. "How d'you think I wound up in a burg like Stillwind Valley?" He straightened his shoulders, managed an expression meant for Wes and Clem that contained a remnant of arduously overcome prior defiance. "But this one, well, I don't like it any more than you do. I was really shocked about your dad, just as I told you. But I couldn't be sure his death was due to anything but old age or illness." Rowe made a face. "It looks to me as if your friend Cliff was the victim of somebody's chemical inbalance."

"You talked to Chief Magenheimer?" Clem demanded.

Rowe nodded. "Yep, I phoned the Maggot.

According to law, the coroner should have reported it to the police, but he didn't."

"What did the chief say?" Wes followed up.

"He confirmed what I've thought all along," Rowe answered with a sigh. "That he's quite a bit older than I am, and got the whole treatment; the entire ball of wax." He scowled. "All I got was a right to turn out the *Syco* and a little help in retarding the aging process—not that Magenheimer admitted any of it in so many words."

"What did he mean by the 'entire ball of wax'?" Wes asked.

"I've never gotten the details of the procedure, not even Kiper's or Dominique's different roles in this. But the Maggot told me to let sleeping dogs lie, then he just hung up."

"Well, he's not hanging up on us," Wes declared, gesturing to Clem, "because *we're* gonna be across the desk from him! You wanta come along?"

The newspaperman blinked, considered and sighed. He walked toward the rec room door, paused only briefly. "I said what I had to say in tomorrow's *Syco,*" he said shortly. "I wish you luck—but this may be the last decent night's sleep I get for a while. Take care."

While they talked about whether to awaken Purvis or not—and decided against it—Wes recalled his sleep theory and realized he was probably wrong. Because it seemed Harlan Rowe had been dozing a long while and maybe now, like the phone people, he was finally waking up.

But when Wes and Clem reached tiny police headquarters, just around the corner from the town square and up the street from Mother's, they were astonished to find it locked! As nearly as either man could judge, there was nobody inside the building at all.

"What'd he do with the guys in the cell or drunk tank?" Clem wondered. He struck the closest, barred window with a frustrated fist. "Whoever heard of a police station locked up at eleven o'clock at night?"

"It is int'restin'," Wes said mildly. Ruminating, he turned and peered into the gloom. It was humid again, the air was heavy; he was ready to believe they weren't the only people afoot in Stillwind Valley. "I recall readin' in the papers that there used t'be very little crime in Moscow; leastwise, near the Kremlin." He began moving toward the town square, aware that Clem would follow. "And I remember wantin' t'go to church after I busted up with a lady friend, several years back . . . 'cept it was ten o'clock at night and the church was closed."

"Vandals," Clem murmured.

"Vandals, second-storeymen, hitmen, terrorists—a church is where you go when you want t'do some heavy prayin'." Wes glanced back at his associate who was murky, indistinct, in the shadows cast by the run-down old buildings; structures from an earlier time, when ordinary people had worked in them. "So I drove around and around, figurin' any kinda church'd do, really. All of 'em claim they have the ear of the Almighty. Right?"

"They were shut, too?" Clem asked from behind his friend.

Wes's bespectacled head nodded. "Up until then, I'd never imagined God closed for the night." He paused and, when he continued, spoke more softly. "I was fairly sure grief didn't. And sin."

"You make me remember something else," Clem said. He did a hasty shuffle-and-skip to catch up and fall in stride. "Remember how surprised we were that there were no regular restaurants, not even a McDonald's, in this place? No bars? But Wes," he argued, his plain, decent features earnest and apprehensive as they drifted among the shadows, "who the hell ever heard of *any* American town . . . with *no church at all?*"

Wes caught Clemon's elbow, stopped them both short. He had heard what the other man said and was similarly startled by the facts. However, Wes had learned that morning that Stillwind Valley contained no churches or synagogues or temples—when he'd attempted to locate a minister to "say some words" for his father.

What shocked him now, and the reason he'd drawn them both to the edge of the town square area and halted, was because Wes's entire attention was gripped by the amazing amount of activity occurring in the miniature park at the heart of the square.

Where the large wooden Jagannath Akeem Dominique had donated rose like a phallic symbol of prehistory against the soft bosom of night, almost half the number of people who'd been present for the Friday evening unveiling were gathered round the ancient icon.

"Listen!" Wes said.

"I don't hear anything," Clem whispered in answer.

"Thet's because they're just standin' out there, looking at the dumb thing. Without movin'. Not making a sound."

You don't know a thing about the Jagannath? Cliff had asked him. *The adversary . . . the opposition to the Lord?* Wes's heartbeat accelerated. What was the rest Cliffy had said—and what, he wondered while he and his friend gaped in openmouthed mystification at the silent crowd, what was it Cliff Macy himself had not known about the statue—and the town?

"I'll bet that's where Chief Maggot is, right now," Clem said huskily. "Among those . . . those praying people."

"Kiper and Stamper probably went there, too, after they 'paid their respects,' " Wes whispered sardonically. Then he inclined his head and started back, with Clemon, toward the company car. "Thank God we didn't park any nearer than we did," he said when they were far enough from the square and the park. "Tomorrow, if you're game, we're goin' back to see Magenheimer—while it's broad daylight!"

"I'm game," Clem assured him, opening the passenger door of the old Caddy. "And after that, I think we'd better think about getting our butts out of this weirdo town."

Wes fired up the engine as quietly as possible, thought about the other man's suggestion, and—at length—nodded. After the things Harlan Rowe had told them, including the hints about the police chief's active participation in the town daddies' "sustained youth" program, he realized that no amount of money or acceptance was worth this jeopardy.

So both men slept uneasily that night, and Clem dreamed that the culmination of all that had happened was coming up on them like a hound dog chasing the escapee from a chain gang.

Fast. And deadly.

Willing to kill, if no one restrained it.

21

He woke up wearing his usual daytime costume of badly faded skin-tight jeans and an old tanktop—both of which he remembered wearing to the wake—but they smelled of booze he had spilled on himself, and alcoholic drool.

Pushing fifty, despite how young he usually appeared in the mornings, he didn't find the phenomenon entirely unfamiliar so he brushed his touched-up, lank dark hair out of his bleary eyes and tried to go back to sleep.

Being dirty, reeking, and still half intoxicated were no causes for concern for an unmarried man.

The first of the two things that prevented Brick from embracing Morpheus, or at least getting a decent grip on him, was a belated stirring of mild curiosity about his whereabouts.

Shoving himself halfheartedly upright in bed with his fully functioning hand, he tried to pierce the middle-of-the-night darkness of the unfamiliar room with his bloodshot eyes but failed. Finally he muttered "Fuck it" and dropped back on the mattress where the long-missing Kenny Higgins and sweet Angelane O'Brien had slept during their brief visitation to the peculiar hamlet.

Then the second thing brought Brick's eyelids popping open again, along with a knife-edge glimmer of daylight human awareness.

It was an irritating query posed unconsciously in his brain, involving *why* he had awakened. And it was promptly answered by another area of his mind, however improbably or unrealistically: "By the parade passing by."

—*What* parade? . . .

Struggling upright again, Darrell glanced toward the window across the alien room, at which juncture several other issues either occurred to him or took place in fact.

He heard the sounds of many walking or jogging human beings dwindlng in the distance—along with a heavy, oddly ominous rumbling noise—and thought, groggily but with some sleepy satisfaction, "Oh, *that* parade."

He didn't have the slightest clue how long they had lurked beneath the window or, more precisely, lurked at the foundation of the Blackwood Apartment building, trying to discover if he'd returned to Indianapolis as usual or if he had stayed overnight and, if the later was the case, *where* he was.

He realized that he was still in Stillwind Valley, had not departed the building, and assumed that some of the other fellas had brought him there when he almost certainly passed out.

He lay down and went back to sleep without giving a damn that the parade had once more passed him by, or understanding that his life itself had been spared by an inebriated state that the people participating in the parade would have considered sufficient reason, alone, for assassination.

And he awakened alive on Tuesday morning with no conscious memory of the little he had experienced, plus an excruciating hangover that he swore he would never forget.

Except that he would, in a way, since *this* was going to be the last day of his life. He didn't remember anything on Wednesday.

Other people woke up during the period of time between midnight and dawn, but they weren't allowed to go back to sleep.

Not in the dictionary interpretation of the word *sleep*.

Cheryl Conrad was not one of their number.

Scantly.

They'd gone to bed at the usual time for most of them; the hour varied from house to house, as it did with the majority of basically ordinary people in any town or city. And whether they went to sleep soon after their heads hit their pillows or not depended upon the usual things: whether they were well, or feeling poorly. Neither of the doctors—it's a fact—had to make a house call or make arrangements for anyone to be sent to a hospital in Indianapolis. Whether they had sex, or not; whether they read, or gabbed awhile. Whether they discovered they were hungry and went flopping around in their slippers in search of a midnight snack. Whether they were plagued by insomnia or guilt that night; or had a quarrel.

Two men beat their wives, one of them until she was unconscious, and the other one swore she was going to leave him. A third husband beat his eldest son because he'd had a piss-poor day; a fourth stared longingly in at his young, sleeping daughter but fought off the most forbidden impulse. Another man slept with his neighbor's wife and never got out of their bed again.

Only one woman personally initiated violence without provocation, but that was because she was drunk as a skunk. When she'd got all the bitterness and bile out of her system for the last time, and both her mother and her husband had taken her abuse equably enough, she wept copiously and said she was sorry. Mother and her husband said okay; neither believed her, but there'd been nothing exceptional in her behavior so all three of them had planned to go on living the same way they always had.

Only a handful of the people used any kind of drugs that night—except for Gladys Waldale, who took all her sleeping pills and was subsequently passed over until thoroughness led the visitors to slash her throat anyway—because it was a small town and the next day, Tuesday, was a work day. Several residents slept very well for a while because they had performed acts that might reasonably have been called saintly. One girl, age fourteen, became pregnant and would have suffered through a living nightmare if she hadn't been slaughtered. About the usual percentage of talented people, most of them young enough that they were still trying right up to the time they died, had written songs or stories or practiced pirouettes or piano lessons or sung melodies or strummed energetically on their guitars or painted pictures or enacted scenes or vocal impersonations before their mirrors and tape recorders. More young people than that had engaged, the afternoon or evening before, in practicing with a basketball; not as many had played catch, passed a football, run track, or done their chores without being reminded.

Six people—three males, three females—had become certain they were in love, Monday night; five of them were right. Crime involving human victims had not occurred before the visitors came to call, although a couple of teenage boys whose dates had said they wouldn't do it managed to set off the meek and unresponsive alarm at Pfaff's General Store, then ran like hell.

They could have gotten away with it, too, giggling like idiots, since high probability was the only thing anybody could have pinned on the boys. It's hard to say, since everyone knew what wild, likable young fools they were and it's conceivable the town might have ganged up on them to teach them a lesson. That's a moot point, anyway.

Because they didn't survive the Jagannath either.

It is also impossible to say who got it first or to offer a statistical evaluation setting forth the facts about how many people were stabbed or strangled, blown away with rifles and shotguns, or simply beaten to death by a rain of fists. The fists, apparently, of numerous assailants in most cases, since there wasn't much evidence of a struggle. The likelihood is that most of the people were stabbed—not always by knives; the silent killers were generous in their expenditure of imagination—or, if clubs of every kind may be tossed into the mix, beaten everywhere on their heads and bodies until there was no life left in them.

. . . Or crushed. Crushings—being mashed like a roach and ground into the earth or the floor until a lot of the corpses appeared more like silhouettes or shadows than former human beings—might well have topped the *modus operandi* list.

For example, Nellie Arnt, seventy-six, who had written a letter to her nephew, Pritchard, and left it where she'd remember to take it to the post office that was located at the rear of Pfaff's General Store, was not identified for several days.

A man named Oliver Quick, age eighty-one, awakened to the presence in his room some three hours before dawn of another man whom he loved. "What brings you here at this hour, Roger?" he asked. But when there was no audible reply and the interloper drew close to his bed, Mr. Quick experienced just under two seconds of doubt that the man who subsequently slit his throat and then leaped up and down on his body was actually his son.

Another moot point.

The overwhelming majority of men, women, and children who died in a period of time that was later placed, as a reasonable estimate, at fewer than fifteen minutes, bore no relationship to those who wantonly murdered them. Even those people who were kinsmen did not perish because there was anything personal about it.

The aged woman whose drunken daughter had slapped her around had never seen any of the grinning young people who killed her in an amazing and simultaneous array of ways; neither had her daughter. Her son-in-law, who got a very good look at all the strangers because he strove with all his might to defend both women, lived just long enough to wonder why they were doing it and to think how much they reminded him of the youthful couples who sang in the church choir with his wife and him. While it cannot be said that they resented his hitting back as long as he could, that group of assailants did nearly as much damage as the Jagannath did—

To the man and wife who came awake to a strange, frightening sound outside the house they'd just rented and occupied. *BBBrrrttttt!* it went; *BBBBrrrrrttttT!*

"Oh sweet Lord," the woman groaned, following her husband as he hurried down the unfamiliar steps and through the front door. "What now, what now?"

It rolled over her right after they were both outside.

Wilford didn't notice it, wasn't able to help, because he was swinging his arms and fists as freely as he might at the biggest bird he had ever seen, and becoming painfully aware that its long, white talons were deep in his right shoulder and the meaty part of his throat. Red streams were pouring down his pajamas as if a faucet had been turned on and the night-bird was forcing his face to turn into its bosom so the mammoth white wings could enfold him, smother him. It was too much, everything; he stopped flailing out with his arms, paused because of the pain and because he really longed to give up.

Which was when . . . *BBBBrrrrTTTTTTT!* . . . steamrolled him out of his earthly troubles.

Both husband and wife, who were not known well in the community because of their brief residency, were found undeniably, indescribably dead.

There were no unusual marks on his neck or shoulders, however.

Which was not the case with those who had been killed in their beds by less overtly supernatural means.

* * *

Purvis had always been an early riser, and possessed the kind of mental equipment that went off like a reliable GE alarm clock just before six A.M. So he was bounding enthusiastically off the sofa of the Wesken Company rec room base of operations at his self-appointed time, wondering only momentarily where he was and what had happened; then he was ravenous for breakfast.

Both his considerable appetite and his ability to rise early were based on desire, and a fondness for the simple things in life.

He also possessed the sort of system that always curtailed his liquor input by the most elementary of means: he tended to go to sleep before he'd had enough to get drunk.

Not in the least dismayed or concerned to find himself alone on another sunny spring day with at least five decades of ever-thriving achievements ahead of him, and the disciplined imagination of a five-hundred-dollar whore, Purvis drew the conclusion instantly that everybody else was in his or her apartment whether asleep or awake—"Whatever," he said cheerily after he'd taken a morning whiz—and besides, today was going to be a big day.

Most of them were.

"This is the first day of the rest of my liiiiiife!" he said aloud, trotting like a plump gelding into the parking lot of Blackwood Apartments and literally rubbing his fleshy hands together—"and all that very profitable crap!"

What was to worry? Even if there had been some oddball shit going down, Wes had mentioned that everyone would leave him alone since he was young the way they were. But today was the day after the night Kiper and Stamper had both showed up, and the biggest cheese of all, King Krafty Dominique himself, had sent half the flowers in the damn *county* to see ol' Ocie off! Talk about customer *acceptance;* talk about goin' out and taking *orders*—man, there'd be no selling to it, this was fucking duck-soup time!

"Duck-soup and ea-sy sales," Purvis carroled, firing up the motor of his '79 Trans Am. "Purvis Rich-wine nev-er faaails!" He headed the car in the direction of neighboring Walterville, where a hearty breakfast could be had by all—if they had his appetite. "Gonna make me some muhhh-uh-neeee!"

The old, rundown Trans Am purred its way round a bend in the road, cleared a bridge like an angel floating on a cloud—and Purvis himself was a cherub with a golden touch, a golden arm, a golden—

"Jesus H. Christ!" he cried, slamming his right foot on the brake so hard that the Trans Am hung a looie and damn near piled his ass into a ditch. Mouth open, gaping and disbelieving the evidence of his own sunny senses, Purvis automatically fumbled with his ignition key to restart the motor, which his shock had temporarily killed.

—*They haven't seen me yet, have they?* he asked God and presumably Jesus H., craning his neck out the window he'd instinctively rolled down to get a better, more comprehensible view.

To his right, fifty yards farther and over a slight rise, lay the Stillwind Valley Cemetery. He hadn't cared much for it, but he'd seen that before.

Beyond it, eerily sloping up another incline like the steedless knights in the old Monty Python movie—backlit by dawnlight and dripping with shadows, sunshine and gore—hundreds and hundreds of people were simply . . . walking. Not jogging, or running hard; not hurrying in any fashion, but walking—

Filled with a quietus akin to the new headstones in the graveyard ahead, stiff-legged as the zombie undead from the old Late Show.

And while Purvis was virtually frozen at the Trans Am's snazzy black steering wheel by disbelief and dismay, a part of those emotions generated by his growing realization that he had *met* some of those marching men and women, that he fucking *knew* some of them—

They just kept coming. Not at him, but appearing to float noiselessly above the rise. Floods of people, looking as if they had been dipped in or baptized by barrels of blood, looking either totally out of it or distantly, peculiarly puzzled . . . blank and as sallow-faced as corpses in ambulatory caskets.

"Why, it's almost the whole damn *town* of Stillwind Valley!" Purvis whispered, as if his own logical salesperson's intellect, when the problem was stated, could talk him out of an unreasonable idea.

The sole answer Purvis got was the rush and surge of his own motor when he'd slammed his foot down on the Trans Am's accelerator and striven harder than he'd ever tried before to do anything just to get the hell away from there.

What *followed* them rumbled over the incline just when Purvis found a dirt road and cut into it as if the lord of the world had been after him.

22

It was fewer than forty-five minutes later that a vastly experienced and usually dauntless newspaperman awakened from his sound sleep with axe-blade alertness, and stared at the ceiling above his head as if he saw terrible things oozing out of the cracks. He had been all over Nam, in Seoul and at the 32nd parallel, even islands in the South Pacific, yet nothing had inured him against such instants of panic and paralyzing fear as these.

Unlike many others who had been roused from sleep totally without warning that long night, Harlan Rowe did not sit bolt upright in his bed. His predecessors hadn't known what came to get them and were largely motivated by the unexpected; the unknown.

For a handful of seconds, Harlan Rowe had a sickeningly graphic and clear image of gory evil, and awful death.

That picture remained in his mind's eye for only another few moments, however, before that inner eye that everyone knows about and no one has ever truly seen cleared, as if bathed by psychic Visine. The conscious mind is intended to inform the unconscious mind, not the other way round, not directly; and the oft-maligned latter is customarily more subtle, assuredly more protective.

When the horror faded and was gone, Rowe felt abruptly ill, shaken. *A man my age oughtn't to have nightmares like that,* he reminded himself, sternly, before recalling that he wasn't, actually, a man of his age; it belonged to somebody else.

By the time he'd lowered his legs over the side of the bed and tried to trust his wobbly knees, almost every trace of dream memory Harlan had known upon awakening was gone.

So it was that he discovered he was "all bloody" with honest consternation, raising his seemingly rusted arms from his sides and gaping at them as if he had grown tentacles since Monday night. "What the devil?" he asked, aloud and not unreasonably, but was accorded no answer.

In the corner of his bachelor's bedroom, across a wooden chair, Rowe's clothes from the preceding day were untidily littered. He was a Virgoan; he always read astrology columns and knew himself to be a methodical, efficient person. But the mess he had made of his garb wasn't what disturbed the editor/publisher/printer.

What did was the trail of blood running between the clothes and the chair, on one hand, and his reddened bare feet, on the other.

That, and the fact that he was naked as a jaybird. Stark; literally bare-ass—and he always, *always* slept in his old-fashioned armless undershirt and even more old-fashioned BVDs. Even when, in a past he'd begun to think about regenerating, he'd persuaded a woman to spend the night. He didn't even possess a *memory* of the way the entirety of the female form felt against his masculine form; even in the revived, personal fantasies that he'd permitted himself of late, sensing a stirring which Harlan knew to be the palest echo of what Kiper, Stamper and the rest were enjoying first hand, he imagined his Manhood modestly poking through the light-blue fly in his old-style shorts and The Woman shyly, hesitantly, lowering her silk step-ins. If he'd had his own way about it and had been able to deduce a way to get decently clean, he'd have taken his *bath* with his underwear on! He didn't like being naked, didn't want—

. . . He perceived then, with some degree of certainty, that he'd climaxed recently. Sexually. Rowe closed his eyes, fleetingly. Then, gazing reluctantly down his somewhat scrawny white shape, gingerly touching it, he felt the faint mocking viability of tell-it-like-it-is sensual pique, and was absolutely positive he had.

Just as he was positive he had not . . . been . . . with a woman. Because that was the one thing Harlan couldn't conceivably have forgotten and he knew it, shaking his head and not even wanting to know what he'd really done. There were things a man could banish from his thoughts successfully, simply to go on staying alive in today's world. Others, well, nobody over sixty ever entirely forgot because sex had been special in the past, it had been hard to *get*, just as much so as it was when one became—

Consciously unsought, a flicker of the recent past played across the screen of his unconscious mind like one of those disgusting horror movies kids everywhere—or kids elsewhere; the normal and real kids—enjoyed.

And the ugliness of the images he'd seen, because of how real they'd been, had to mean two things: that the secret lusts he'd tried to keep more from himself, even, than anyone else, were unavoidable now. And that he had somehow engaged in hot-headed, misguided, perverted passion of the variety that did not have to involve intercourse itself, directly. The kind in which hard-up, utterly selfish men with private wells of hatred that had always tried to overflow found extremely . . . *different* . . . outlets. For those drives they had kept forbidden, even in fantasy, even from themselves.

When had he begun to hate, to crave the sort of violence he had seen anew in memory? Just *what* he'd done, personally, was unclear and certainly best forgotten—*That's right, forget it! Blank it out*—but it was something no decent man, no professional man, had the right to forget. Because, if his memories were real, it was news. Rowe's glance touched the still-wet, stained clothes on the chair and the trail a bitch in season might have left. *It was me, though. And I did something exciting, incitingly, disgustingly, arousingly dark . . . perverted . . . evil.* Which would have to be reported in the *Syco* just the way today's edition covered the unauthorized interment of Macy, the salesman. *Something . . . murderous?*

But . . . what? Harlan cursed the day he had agreed to come to this town and work for Kiper and that African Negro—*no,* black; *Negroes and niggers and coloreds went away even if my thoughts didn't.* What *had* he done, exactly? Guilt ate at Rowe, crunched his memories and drooled them out toward awareness. Yes, he'd have to cover it, print the truth . . .

But what *was* it?

* * *

Wes awoke later than usual and later than he'd meant to, ignored the headache that perversely reminded him he was Almost Forty Years of Age, and rushed to the phone room. It was already well past the lunch hour and he felt drugged.

He was so set on picking up Clem Sparrow and driving over to police headquarters to confront Chief Magenheimer that it didn't occur to him for another five minutes that only Clemon and Brick were there in addition to himself.

Cheryl—and Purvis Richwine—were not.

Incipient panic, throttled: *Well, they had other crap to do. Maybe they were hungover worse than I was, and maybe Purvis just went out in the field.* Worry; worry. Minutes later: *Shit, they simply aren't in yet; don't make it a big deal!* He saw Clemon Sparrow evading his gaze, knowing Wes was worried.—*So what if it's afternoon and she's never late?* Well, he couldn't go with Clem to see Chief Magenheimer until he was certain Cheryl was safe, and Purvis, and—

And Wes realized with a suddenness that stunned and all but devastated his living spirit how very bleak and deserted the Blackwood Apartments recreation room-*cum*-phone room looked today. No, not "looked." *Was;* it was a fact.

Wes had to sit down.

He remained at his desk while the minutes crawled by and his worry deepened, reached depths only those capable of love can ever know. He wondered with horror how many of them were gone now. He could count empty desks the way a teacher did at school, except the people wouldn't be back in their chairs tomorrow. And he didn't really want to add 'em up, reach a total, because—

With two more . . . out . . . this moment, God Almighty, did that mean what he was after was just a *subtotal*?

We're gonna need new people; replacements. He had to be businesslike. Practical. *For Cheryl; for Kenny?* He glanced at the door for the fiftieth time, wanting her or Purvis to enter each time Brick or Clem went silently to the john, or returned. *Or does it matter, is the company dead completely? I don't even know what those two are doing—unless they're waiting, too . . .*

He began upbraiding himself for having gotten tight last night and becoming so fascinated with what half the gee-dee town had been doing in the square that he had never *thought* of Cheryl, couldn't even remember the last time he'd even *seen* her at the wake—because he was busy bein' a buddy, a pal, one of the guys—*trying t'act like Ocie would, always guessing how he'd handle stuff and I figured he'd just get lit.*

Around three, Wes started struggling to achieve some sort of overview of their situation. It wasn't just essential to learn why Stancel Holroyd or some secret aide had killed Cliff and buried him, probably to conceal the fact; it was important to protest what had happened to *all* their missing, or dead. To insist . . . *but how d'you 'make whole,' that's that legal term, human lives gone forever? Who or what can replace the first woman I've cared about in years?* Okay, if the chief refused to help, they'd talk with Dominique! It was possible he was not involved in the same way Kiper and Stamper were; it could be that he was bein' used, so maybe he could be talked into pitching in, if they used the right words, then—

"Talked into," Wes muttered, burying his face with anguish in his palms. *Pitch in; right words!*

The solution to every problem in life for a Hoosier hick like Wes Teagle came down to convincing somebody, peddling something . . . if just a point of view! He'd considered himself a doer, a man of action, and simply *sat* there like a bump on a log until—

"You ready for that visit to the Maggot?"

Clem. Good, loyal Clem, gazing patiently at him; ready. Wes felt bleary-eyed but looked up with a feeling of deep gratitude. "I thought another twenty minutes." He shrugged. "T'see if she . . . they . . . checked in."

"When did you call her at her apartment last?" Clem was certain Wes had.

A shrug. "Four-five minutes back. But that doesn't mean—"

The phone beneath Wes's nose rang so abruptly, shrilly, it appeared to him that it also leaped an inch from his desk.

"I'll bet that's her now." Clem said it softly; prayerfully.

Wes couldn't remember feeling more relief. Grinning, phone at his ear, he began enunciating the company name . . .

"The town, the whole goddamn *town,* Wes!"

Purvis. Virtually hysterical.

"Walterville, I mean. Listen"—Purvis took what seemed to be a minute to inhale or find the control to say it—"Wes, they've *killed the whole town!"*

Gasping, Wes met Clemon eye to eye, held the phone out from his ear so that Clem might also hear it.

"Purvis, you slow down now, okay?" Wes tried to ignore his own frantic heartbeat. "Now: What does that mean?"

"Aw God, Wes, it means what I fucking *said!"* the voice from hell exclaimed. "Jesus, Wes, I came over here for *breakfast.*" Purvis sounded as if he were marveling at anything so absurd. "And . . . and they're dead, man, the people—everybody. Wes, the *entire town,* every man, woman, and child . . . little kids, just *smeared,* old folks—"

Wes rose slowly, steadily from his chair, blinking in Clem's direction. It was difficult to put credence to what the young Richwine was saying. Until he saw Clemon's solemn eyes fill with tears.

"They were all murdered in their sleep." This time he said it softly. Somehow it sounded worse. "They . . . they were strangled, and shot; they were—smooshed; flattened." Purvis swallowed and it conveyed the impression, over the phone wires, of his choking back both tears and vomit. "They had their throats cut; their faces were caved in, eyes cut right out . . . sweet Jesus, man, I saw one poor old fart with his head just hanging by a *thread . . .*"

So horrified he would have believed nothing whatever could distract his attention, Wes was looking past Clemon Sparrow when he realized—almost as if he were reading it in a letter, so quietly did she enter the room—that Cheryl Conrad had staggered through the doorway.

Staggered. Barely conscious. Hurt *Oh God they've HURT her!*

Wes dropped the telephone into its cradle.

" . . . Almost got my ass, too, baby," Purvis was going on, his blood churning through his veins as if it sought an escape route. He had a headache and it was almost blinding him but he wasn't aware of it. "But I circles around behind the mob, see, down this bitty side road? And . . ."

And I'm talking to a dead telephone, Purvis

thought, understanding the truth finally, nodding brightly. It was one more almost unbelievable piece of data weaving crazily through his insanely scattered and overloaded sensory system. "*Uh*-huh," he grunted. "I am telling this man who's my boss and my friend about a town that has been wiped out overnight, and of *course*, he hangs *UP* on me! Of course; naturally."

Putting on a ghastly, pale smile, Purvis nodded his acceptance of his maddening new lot in life and pushed the phone booth door back so the terrible rotting stench could get at him. "Got it, Wes," he muttered, stepping outside, "got it got it *got* it!"

So he played this game with himself for the next couple of seconds, pretending he wouldn't raise his head and look. He'd merely go back to his Trans Am, hum a little tune, start the motor, drive back out on the road—the road heading for any other place on the earth but Stillwind Valley—and hope to *God* the Trans Am didn't begin a fucking conversation; or sprout wings; or turn into a goddamn pumpkin!

And he actually had the door on the driver's side open, and one well-shod foot inside, before he lifted his head and his gaze as nonchalantly as he could—

To see devastation everywhere he looked. A harmless patch of dirt and grass with friendly looking houses on it, a handful of businesses, a church in the distance, Olivey's Bar & Grill down a side street *and bloodbodieslimbsstainsBlood; ex-humanity of all ages, yessir, the whole spectrum, a prone or chopped-up mangled motionless MUSEUM of the senselesslymind-lesslytheylookfuckingFUNNYthatway DEAD.*

"Awwww, God," young Purvis Richwine prayed,

and sank to the ground to lean against his open car door. "*Aw!*"

The shadow of something wide-winged and fluttering spread across part of a field, a couple locked in a lasting embrace, the front of the '79 Trans Am, and cherubic Purvis.

He didn't look up, however. It was too much. Whatever it was, it was too much. "Go away," he pleaded with it, chin on knuckles and elbows on knees. "Willya just get lost, please?"

It did. For good.

23

For interminable minutes after Wes, Clem and Brick had made her comfortable on the couch in the large room, Cheryl refused to tell them who had hurt her, referring to her assailants as "they" and "them"—or why.

Wes's first concern, of course, had been the extent of her injuries and her mental state as well. Akeem Dominique was the only physician they'd heard about in Stillwind Valley and they still had no idea where he practiced. In any case, Cheryl refused to permit any of them to call for a doctor, batting at Wes's fussing hands and generally waving all three men away—except when Clem brought her dampened paper toweling to hold against her scratches, along with a cup of cool water.

Basically, Wes decided, feeling less confident about his impulsive conclusions than usual, she didn't seem seriously hurt. But he had one lingering concern he finally had to put into words: "Did they . . . do anything sexually? Did they rape you?"

Cheryl, to the astonishment of the other phone people, leaned back against the couch and laughed. For one awful instant they were afraid she might lapse into hysterics.

Then they realized that her amusement, although wry and rueful, was genuine and, for all three men, the mystery deepened. What in the world was funny about the possibility that Cheryl had been violated?

"Y'wanta tell us what happened now?" Wes inquired, his emotions a complex tangle. He sought to keep the asperity from his voice, but he'd just hung up on a friend who claimed that an entire town had been annihilated and this woman for whom he had a high regard, and deep affection, thought the notion of her own rape was a laugh riot.

"You characters know I smoke a little grass sometimes," she began at last, sipping from the glass Clem had brought her. She averted her gaze from Wes's burning eyes. "Okay; a lot, dammit." Cheryl shrugged. "It's a rotten habit, okay, but I've never gotten into the heavy stuff like coke."

"You do know that's the next step for people, usually," Clem said gruffly, almost paternalistically, surprising her. It wasn't a question.

"Gaawwd, they're doing twenty-first-century science in this burg and I'm living in a nineteenth-century moral environment," Cheryl marveled. She shrugged again, embarrassed but happy her friends cared. "So after Kiper and Stamper left, I went back to the apartment for a joint, and there was a . . . man . . . in the shadows."

"Who?" Darrell Brickowski asked, leaning toward her. "Did you see his face?"

"Oh, yeah." Cheryl shuddered. "You remember that—that creepy jogger we've seen all over town? The skinny one who . . . never seems to make any noise when he jogs?" They nodded, exchanged apprehensive glances. "Well, he grabbed me before I could get inside the apartment. He looks even worse up close. When he opened his mouth—"

"Christ," Brick muttered, shivering, "these weirdos aren't a bunch of *vampires*, are they?"

"Let her tell the story, man," Clem growled.

"His tongue was almost black!" Cheryl said, her vivacious eyes opened wide in memory. "That startled me, caught me off guard. They all have terrible breath, did you notice? So next thing I knew, I was waking up in—"

"Waking up?" Wes, beside Cheryl on the couch, holding her hand—and all but mauling it—hung onto her every word. "Did he hit you or what?"

Cheryl shook her head vigorously. "He must have, since I had these marks when I woke up in that big house." She touched her forehead and cheek with her fingertips, then a knee-calf. She still wore a pretty party dress she had donned for Ocie's wake, but the skirt was ripped, and one sleeve, while some of her scratches looked to Wes as if they'd been made by human nails. "Apparently I did struggle, some; then I was just . . . out of it."

"Sure you hadn't already smoked pot?" Clem asked a bit contemptuously.

"I hadn't even gotten *in* to the apartment," Cheryl retorted, giving him a frown. Conveniently, she ignored the fact that she had been returning to her apartment a second time.

"Whose house was it?" Wes asked, squeezing her fingers.

"I never saw it before," she replied, wide-eyed. "But it was near Holroyd's mortuary." Suddenly the recollection of her ordeal was so vivid that she came perilously close to tears and finished her glass of water in a swallow, fighting for self-control. "There were more of them. A *lot* more of them . . ."

Wes was on his feet, fists doubled. His face was scarlet with fury. "Name 'em," he coaxed.

Cheryl stared up at him. Her lashes were wet; the pupils reflected her amazement, her terror. "I c-couldn't tell because they w-wore masks. Or more like *hoods*, actually; they went all the way over the head."

"How awful, baby," Clemon said tenderly. He stood beside Wes, a vein working in one dark temple.

"Cowards always wear masks," Wes muttered. "Bullies never say who they are."

"Were they just plain hoods?" Brick asked. "No details?"

Tears shone on Cheryl's cheeks. "No," she whispered; "they weren't ordinary." She fumbled for a cigarette from her purse, the strap of which was broken. Wes lit it for her. She looked up at him and the others. "They were . . . like the statue. Not exactly, but you could t-tell what they . . . represented." Anger colored the tear-dampened cheeks as she turned her head to look out the window across the phone room; it was getting hot, humid, and it was a day for other pursuits than this. For happier times. "The masks were all the same and it was as if they represented another side—another face—of the Jagannath." She shook her head again, unable to explain adequately. She added, inhaling, "An evil side."

For a moment no one spoke.

Then Wes, reaching down, cupped her soft jaw in one hand. "What did they say, honey. Did they tell you why they kidnapped you?"

She met his concerned gaze with unabashed tears. "They said they m-may still kill me . . . but they won't do it if . . . if I quit using drugs!" She sobbed. "That's just the way they put it, but I think it was a recording and the voice was muffled. 'We won't kill you if you agree to stop using illegal drugs.'"

"Sons of bitches!" Clem hissed.

Cheryl slumped against the end of the sofa, both angry and humiliated. "That's why I laughed when you asked if they'd raped me . . . because I was almost murdered by a b-bunch of hooded, moralistic damn do-gooders!"

"They will pay." Wes said it tightly, intensely. He leaned forward to kiss her, then glanced around at the others. "I'm gonna find out who that freak of a jogger is, and the rest of 'em, and what the hell is goin' on—and they're gonna *pay!*" He whirled toward the door.

"Hold it," Clemon barked, catching his arm and holding on. The grip hurt. He addressed Cheryl softly. "How did you get away?"

"I didn't actually 'get away' or 'escape,' " she answered haltingly. "The weird jogger was gone when I woke up in a sort of study in the old house. He came back and I saw him trying to speak, to say something to a short man in a hood. He could scarcely speak, I think."

I'll bet the short man was Kiper, Brick thought.

"Then most of them—one was definitely a woman—took off." Her expression held the terrifying events close, became one of bewilderment. "That's when they tied me up and b-blindfolded me—as if there was something they didn't want me to see. And then they just kept me there until today, this afternoon . . . when the jogger guided me outside with his clammy hand, removed the blindfold and—just closed the door. Locked it!"

"That shows what little regard they have for the law in this town," Clem said slowly, angrily. He turned to Wes. "Let's go give him something new to respect—what bastards like them *can* respect!"

"No," Wes replied, clutching Clemon by the arms and including Darrell Brickowski in his comments. "I won't be hurt while I'm actually inside police headquarters and I want both of you to stay here." He inclined his head toward Cheryl. "I'm gonna talk with Magenheimer, that's all. Do it nice and legal." His lips formed a grim, determined line. "If he won't do anything, I'll come back here for you guys and Cheryl, and we'll try t'get a little justice in Indy."

Both Clem and Brick began to protest, yearned to argue the point, to accompany him.

But both took another look at Cheryl and realized how vulnerable, how exhausted and hurt she was.

She doesn't even look tall now, Wes thought, kissing Cheryl's cheek.

Then he was through the phone room door and running down the corridor to the steps and the parking lot, before either Clem or Brick realized that what he'd said didn't quite add up. Because if all he intended to do was talk with the Maggot, there was no reason why all of them—including Cheryl—couldn't wait in the old Caddy and drive to Indianapolis from police headquarters.

He'd meant it with all his heart and soul when he had promised Cheryl that they were going to pay.

For bullying and frightening and hurting her, and for what had happened to all of Wes Teagle's suffering colleagues—his family, in a way—in Stillwind Valley.

Besides, he ruminated, spotting the small building he and Clem had found locked up just last night, and observing how relatively few denizens of the town were afoot in mid-afternoon, *she doesn't know yet about Walterville . . . and whatever happened there, and she shouldn't. Not now.* Because for all he or the rest of them knew, the chief was somehow a part of the horrors Purvis had described and there might well be greater hazards here—close to the town square, and to the ancient Dominique statue—than there were in the Blackwood Apartment building on the fringe of town.

Wes slammed on the brakes; they squealed, and he stopped right in front of police headquarters. No one around. He paused, then opened and reached into the glove compartment, drew something out. What defense he might have against armed and maybe crazy town daddies, Wes did not know, but he also didn't care . . . because he was on the offense now, not the defense. He was angrier, more fed up, more needing to strike back, than he had ever been before.

Yet there was, he saw, peering down the sidewalk and then hurrying toward the front door, another "besides." Wes even faltered momentarily.

He had suddenly realized why the bastards who had kidnapped Cheryl had eventually chosen to blindfold her . . . because *somebody else* had arrived in that unknown house, after the others.

And only one man, Wes thought, one hand raised to the chipped door of the police headquarters but feeling freshly vulnerable, *one man* in the *whole town* could be instantly identified by anybody, even if he wore a hood or mask on his head . . .

"Chief's busy," a uniformed cop grunted when Wes had virtually demanded to see Chief Magenheimer. Obviouslly he knew who Wes was, but there was no glitter of interest, or concern, in his eyes. "Got someone with him."

"That so?" Wes glanced toward the inner office, the door of which was ajar a foot or two. There was a glimpse of a man in street clothes restlessly pacing back and forth. "Well, I can't wait, officer. I need t'see him now.'"

"You can wait 'til hell freezes over!"

"Then I'm in the right place," Wes drawled. He leaned on one arm, held the other behind his back.

The smile curling the unwrinkled lips of the young face was as uncaring and cold as the lyrics of the tune blasting from a radio on his desk. "There's just one way you're gonna see the chief today," he said simply. He lifted a big ring of keys which, Wes presumed, fitted the few cells at the rear of the building. Then he jangled them, pointedly, the smile turning colder.

"You've got that right," Wes retorted—

And the battery-holding butt of the big Eveready flashlight Wes had pulled from his glove compartment swung in a deadly accurate half circle and caught the uniformed youth on the point of the chin.

Tumbling over his desk chair backwards, he wasn't even unconscious on the floor before Wes had sprinted toward the inner office, kicked the door wide open, and balanced the weighty flashlight between both hands, menacingly. His heart had never throbbed so loudly—

But he was about to discover that it could beat more noisily, more rapidly.

The long-legged man in street clothes who had been pacing in front of Chief Magenheimer's desk turned to face Wes, smiling without surprise but with considerable endearing charm.

"G'd'y, mate!" he piped in an utterly familiar and much-loved voice.

Part Four

The Forces That Threaten

"Normal longevity at the present level of human development may be scientifically determined as being one-hundred, twenty-five to one-hundred, fifty years."

—Alexander A Bogomletz, *The Prolongation of Life*

"We lived in a perceived world . . . of sequential cause and effect—a world in which space and time are limiting factors . . . What then if these basic laws . . . are threatened (and) we are faced with apparent evidence that they may be illusions . . . ?

—Lawrence LeShan,
The Medium, The Mystic, and The Psysicists

"If we fail to face who we truly are, and thus fail to develop ourselves as human beings, we leave ourselves defenseless to forces which threaten to annihilate our human integrity."

—Katherine Ramsland, Ph.D.,
—*The Psychology of Horror and Fantasy*

24

"Kenny, where in the heck've you *been?* I must have tried t'phone you in Indi'nap'-lis a hundred times and couldn't reach you." Wes soared with relief; he was overjoyed to see his pal —his partner—again and almost threw out his arms to hug him. Yet some vague and vagrant sense of the wary about Kenny, of distance or "wired" neutrality, kept Wes's arms merely raised for another instant. He squinted into Kenny's face. "You all right, ole buddy? Or you been sick? I've been worried about you."

"Sick?" The tall man repeated it, worried the word, even mauled it—not as if its meaning was foreign to him, but as if Wes's question might contain an insult or a challenge. The lips of the wide mouth turned up at the corners, stayed that way a moment longer than seemingly normal. "Do I *look* sick, old love?"

Then he shoved the faded and now filthy Colts cap back on his long head and the tannish, fluffy brows snapped into a quizzical formation that was boyish, endearingly familiar; for a moment.

Yet the expression appeared queerly practiced. More precisely, it was as if a small, unimportant button deeply recessed in Kenny's brain had been depressed, or a miniature switch thrown.

Yet he did appear well, Wes thought; filled with a restless vitality that was quick and darting; birdlike. Kenny hadn't stopped moving or sat down since Wes laid eyes on him. There was color in the cheeks, at the temples, even if it looked splotchy, and the mouth that smirked at Wes was rosy; carmine. Most of all, despite the routine, good-humored banter of their exchange, the lanky Chicagoan sounded as if he were speaking from the inside of a barrel; on a recording or perhaps from a TV hooked up to a VCR. Nonplussed and alerted to danger in a deep-down, intimate way he'd not experienced before, Wes began to wonder—with no enthusiasm and with a willingness to be proved wrong that was towering—if his dearest friend had somehow been . . . tampered with.

But there was much to clear up. "I asked where you've been," Wes said, not quite curt. He swiveled his head, looking for Chief Magenheimer, but his chair behind a sturdy, file-strewn desk was empty. "It's been tough titties lately, Ken. A lot's happened." He yearned to tell his partner about Ocie, and the others, but felt unwilling to test Kenny's reaction.

"TCB, Weston," the tall man said quickly, winking, his body bobbing restlessly. "*Big* B—for Business."

"That's good t'hear," Wes nodded, simultaneously aggrieved that he had been burdened with so much responsibility, so much loss, and willing to overlook almost anything now that Kenny was back. "I knew you never really wanted t'stay in the Midwest so I thought, maybe, you'd just boogied out of ole Hoosierland. You wanta explain why you didn't lay it out for me? We're partners, right?"

"The opportunity is right here in Indiana, hoss. Right here in Stillwind Valley, Weston." The light-colored brows arched down in a memory of his former, kidding confidentiality. The voice seemed almost to issue, by remote hook up, from another source entirely, and he kept moving closer to Wes. "But I couldn't tell even you."

"Ain't that somethin'?" Wes said, feeling distinctly uncomfortable and beginning to perspire. "Where the hell is Chief Magenheimer?"

Kenny's finger—it was incontrovertibly Kenny's finger but it felt hard, careless, stony—tapped hurtfully against the center of his chest. "Mate," Kenny's voice said, the word exactingly enunciated, "I got us a lead on maybe the biggest deal in the history of the Wesken Company!"

"Well, shit and Shinola, buddy, that won't take a whole lot," Wes replied. He made himself grin but knew it came out badly. For the life of him, he couldn't decide if he should be frightened. "Where's the chief?"

"And the real beauty part, hoss, Weston," the tall man went on relentlessly, "we won't even have to leave town to take full advantage of the deal!"

"Gosh!" Blinking, the smaller, bespectacled Wes edged back a cautious step, trying to gauge his risk, if any, trying just as hard to understand what had happened, what was so terribly wrong. So ghastly. "That's a God's blessing, ain't it?" he asked, letting just a bit of the sarcasm show. But Kenny, who'd worked so hard at atheism, didn't take the cue, didn't show a flicker of humor. And why did he *move* like that, all herky-jerky? Wes put his palms between his own chest and Kenny's prodding bullet of an index finger. And it occurred to him that it was as if Kenny were dancing, alone, drifting to and fro to the sounds of an awful music only he heard playing. "What're you doin' in the chief's office, Kenny? Where is he, anyhow? You know?"

Nearer to Wes, Kenny's breath was abominable. No well man had ever smelled that badly; it was the stench of sewers backed up, a smell from some deep part of the earth where seeping blood and rotting things went. But that didn't mean he was mentally unbalanced. "Dr. Dominique and Professor Kiper have given their endorsement, mate; Weston. Why, it'll be worth a fortune. Mate. It'll make us a lot of money, Weston. Hoss."

"Don't breathe in my ear, man, I won't follow you anyplace," Wes said; but the humor he'd intended slipped as if he had put his foot in something moist, and festering. Yet what he'd just said himself reminded Wes of how they had been, of the playful nature of their unlikely friendship. He saw a way to test the tall man and put on his solemn, storytelling face. "Earlobes is important to Hoosiers," he began, trying to face the other, " 'cause we got earlobes at least three, four inches long."

No expression. No answer. No "Oh, no!"

"Cousin Crayola Passwater was too dang poor t'buy new earrings so the night of the senior prom, in June, she rummaged around in a box with Christmas decorations 'til she found two big shiny ornaments the same color, and stuck them hooks right into her lobes." Trying to breathe shallowly, he faced the lanky figure hovering expressionlessly above him; grinned. "So my Great-Aunt Bonabelle said they looked fine but didn't quite cover up cousin Crayola's dangly lobes. So the two of 'em done strung tinsel right behind her earlobes . . . just let it fall right down around the Christmas bulbs. Natural-like. Y'know, Kenny, my cousin Crayola, she won a prize for the prettiest girl at the prom that June!"

Tiny muscles behind the splotchy cheeks tightened like rodents about to pop out of Kenny's mouth and, for the first time, Wes saw that his partner wore rouge, and lipstick.

"Then all the high-school kids turned out the lights," Wes finished, wanting to cry but ducking under a long arm and hurrying to the chief's desk where he hefted his weighted flashlight—"and that whole graduatin' class sang 'Oh, Holy Night' pretty as you please!"

The tall man's body turned spastically, almost in segments. The wide mouth created a tentative smile, again.

And laughter pealed from him, roared from him . . . jubilant hilarity geysered from a mouth that strained wide, almost cracking, and exhibited a tongue as black as the unbeating heart of the planet. And he went on chortling, cackling ridiculously, reinventing as best he could the quality of titanic laughter. His head was thrown back so far, the Colts cap fell off and dropped to the floor, unnoticed. For Wes, it was the saddest thing he'd ever had to see. The hair was matted, tangled; dirty. The legs kept jiggling, ceaselessly.

"Aw, old friend," Wes whispered, wanting to cry, "what did they do to you?"

At once the lips clapped shut, the puffy brows went up, half questioningly. It looked genuine. "Do?" Kenny's eyelids fluttered. "Who?" He stepped—danced—after Wes, paused. He shook his head and small, almost invisible things moved in the shadows of his hair. "They? Who, mate?" He pawed out toward Wes. "Who, Weston . . . hoss?"

"How do I know who?" Wes felt he might begin to weep. But he had to get out of there and backed round the edge of Magenheimer's desk toward the door.

He found the Chief behind it, crammed there, feet and legs partly protruding. There was one quick glimpse of hair like snow and an aged, very dead face. It stared at Kenny's boot.

"They want to meet you at the phone room, Weston," the voice said with exquisite care. "Soon. To discuss the deal." Smirk. "Old Hoss, old love." He stopped his advance, however, danced in place, swayed from side to side as if he held an invisible lover close. "The doctor and the professor." His body turned in a complete circle without missing a beat and his eyes were nearly dreamy—and Wes knew they weren't right, they weren't, in ways he couldn't figure out, his old friend's eyes. "We won't even have to leave town to take advantage of the deal."

"Kenny," Wes said, edging toward the office door, sick at heart and afraid he was going to be more conspicuously ill. "Where's Angelane?"

The tall, thin body missed a beat. Instantly the torso slumped, visibly, as if quiescence was dangerous to the health. "Angelane?"

"Your real, old love, Ken," Wes explained. The tears in his eyes were partly for her, and Cheryl, partly because he sensed that it was all right for the Kenny-thing to do to him what he'd apparently done to the Maggot but that data, or order, refused to compute in the altered brain. Still, he had to get out of there, now. Alive. "Aw, man, where's Angelane?"

Grotesquely, the long legs regained motion, dipped, swayed.

But the professionally made-up features showed a pain they might otherwise have never displayed again. Confusion registered. And a look of tragic, infinite, bewildering loss. "I don't know," Kenny said, almost like himself. Human grief flickered in his eyes. "I . . . forgot her."

Wes took a breath, stepped past the unconscious young cop in the outer office. It seemed safe to leave, then. "Try thinkin' for yourself, Kenny, and remembering. That's why we were put here."

Close to hyperventilating and to tears that would never stop, he was outside the building. It was almost dusk and there was no one on the street, there were no metallic shrieks of imitation music, and Wes's basic emotion then was relief to have escaped . . . something. He opened the car door but refused to look back to see if Kenny was following him, unwilling to abandon their friendship to so much suspicion. Dropping onto the driver's seat, under the steering wheel, he felt he'd put on a ton.

Immediately a comment of Akeem Dominique came pointedly to recollection: "The key to alchemy is changing one thing into another."

But in Kenny's case, to *what?*

With a shudder, and concern that the car engine might fail him, it also entered Wes's mind like something slithering into one ear that this—right *now*—was the time when he could run. When he had started the Caddy and driven a few blocks from the immediate location, he realized, finally, what had been meant by a "moment of truth."

If all he was was *exactly* the same man he'd

been when they had come to town, filled with dreams and high hopes, he could opt—right now, there was nothing to stop him, probably—to save his own ass, aim the jalopy south, and head for Indianapolis.

Escape. For life.

He had slowed the company car among the new shadows, now let it idle at the side of the road that led to the Blackwood Apartments. When he peered down at the dashboard he saw that the gas tank was half-filled. Which meant there was plenty to enable him to get to Indy, driving straight through.

Probably enough, too, to drive back to the apartment for . . .

Cheryl. Wes nodded to himself. For everybody, sure. But mainly to save Cheryl. Only problem with that was whether the old Caddy would keep running at all, or not; he'd known for weeks it didn't have much left.

Wes slipped down slightly in the seat, both to be more comfortable, and think, and to provide a smaller target. As a rule, he reflected, a man had a chance to weigh the question of love; to consider whether to propose marriage or, the less demanding way kids had been doin' it for a while, to propose livin' together. They'd begun the same way as modern young folks but that was about the end of that tune! 'Cause movin' in together was a big step, a really *serious* step for a dude Pushing Forty, one who had never been with a woman on a regular day-in, day-out sorta basis. Worse, for him and Cheryl, they knew each other even less than most of the youngsters today did . . . or so he imagined.

He lifted his head to glance out the rolled-down window to see if he'd picked up a tail, the way gangster flicks put it. The fact that he hadn't was cool; the ongoing absence of anybody on the streets or the road seemed offputting, inexplicable.

The thing was, no kind of fool went to save his girl and risk his life in the process unless he pretty damned sure knew his own feelings. Dominique was a gee-dee giant; Albert Kiper probably knew more ways t'kill someone with drugs, undetected, than anybody Wes's side of a crooked NFL trainer.

Hell's bells, he couldn't even be sure people had ever died for love, whatever anyone said. Folks said a lot of things; ask somebody who knew.

Wes sighed and longed for a smoke. *Shitfire,* he thought, *I couldn't even buy a cigarette in Walterville now, if Purvis got it right!*

No, people talked about sacrifices all the time, from today's war, sports—with athletes puttin' million-dollar-a-year legs on the line—to hero-types writers thought up for survivors of nuclear attack. According to what they wrote in papers, movies and novels, everyone was cut out from birth t'be a hero or a villain and wars were there t'find out which one you were. And there was no kinda person inbetween; there was nothin'. When the world got itself nuked there'd be these big, horny guys who could not only get it up yet despite deep-fried, radiated lungs, and right off they set out lookin' for girls to rape. They rode motorcycles, smilin' evilly, with sidecars for tamed girls, or their stash; or stripped-down chassis with engines just tuned up last week especially for the occasion.

Then there were those *other* guys who made it and who had been waitin' for Meaning all their lives, the chance to Sacrifice. They drove station wagons or pick-up trucks—and stopped at red-lights in nuked-out cities—wore glasses they never even *missed* when a big horny guy busted 'em, and they always had to get somewhere . . . they had Purpose—or understood it—for the first time in all their dumb existances. They'd defend a bunch of real puny folks inside some farmhouse or hospital, a church or a school, and teach a widowed mother's punk-mouth kid what Living was all about. By dyin'. Or, at least, Wes figured, gettin' everybody *else* killed—'cept for the widowed Mom and the smart-ass kid. Even if writers of stuff like that didn't haul in the horny guys on the hogs 'til the end of the story, the ex-wimp who lost his specs always managed—with the kid's assistance—to wipe out everyone who was left.

Folks, the way Wes Teagle looked at it then, weren't like that. Much, at least. He had never met anyone on a motorcycle who wasn't weird, one way or the other, anybody in a hot rod who wasn't your basic showoff or a cheapskate cuttin' monetary corners, anyone in a station wagon who didn't look down on those who weren't, or anybody in a pickup truck who didn't crave a station wagon, rod, or motorcycle far more than he did widowed Moms with smart-mouthed kids.

And mosta the folks he'd known who could barely wait to risk their lives for something didn't put much value on them to begin with!

A grin happened, spread. Then a soft, rather self-contented chuckle. Maybe it shouldn't have been there under the circumstances, but you could only hack so much horror in life and then you had to smile or give it up. He liked what he'd worked out about sacrifice and meaning so he was enabled to make himself a nice, clear mental picture of Cheryl, Ocie, Clem, Brick, Cliff,

Angelane, and Kenny, too, plus see his own grimy and bespectacled mug in the company car's rearview mirror. *Weak-eyed guys with dirty glasses have it all over others, Wes decided. When you wanted t'see things differently, all y'had to do was not clean'em.* You could even look inside.

It was getting darker so Wes sighed and raised his hand to shift gears. Sure, Cheryl was the best reason to go back to the Blackwood. And she'd already been hurt. But now he knew that if nobody was left of the Wesken Company but him, he probably wouldn't even show up in the mirror! He couldn't be sure yet what the town had done to Kenny, or even what Kenny was, but it seemed to Wes then that vampires were just ex-salespeople who'd needed to be reminded what it was t'be alone in the world.

With that attitude, Wes felt like a man in an expensive new station wagon right up until he'd parked at the curb, rushed up the lane to the door of the apartment building, and found Harlan Rowe tucked neatly into the entrance way.

All of the publisher's exposed flesh was crisscrossed with wounds like sloppy Christian tattoos and they were oozing like treacle. Most of the copious, ardent pumping had already taken place and it was obvious—once Wes, shakily, had made himself take an enormously reluctant, closer look—that the murderer had avoided the main arteries in preference for just hacking the newspaperman to death. *Good Christ,* Wes prayed, *if he'd had grease pencil and wanted to, the killer could have played tic-tac-toe!* And this was *recent,* Wes realized, freezing in his kneeling position; this *just happened.*

—He sensed even more than he heard the presence, sensed imminent, carved-up awful death even more strongly. Having stooped to peer at the man who'd wanted it all both ways, he had to straighten and spin more or less simultaneously, and expected a knife in the throat or the back every inch he moved.

Nobody was very near him. No one living. But while darkness' initial progress was more stealthy than sinister, Wes gazed out across the Blackwood lawn, up the sidewalk that rode an incline some distance before disappearing from sight, and was able to identify a peculiarly running man as the likely killer—by a piercing glint of light on his upraised scalpal.

Then he recognized the partly averted face of the murderer, too: Stancel Holroyd. The coroner who doubled as the mortician. Glancing back at Wes that instant just long enough to recognize *him*, too—

Then stop. Stop his inexpert, heels-to-the-side stride, halted in place with an abruptness that looked almost impossible to Wes. Unnatural.

And to stare at him with a recognition that reminded Wes of how a helpless experimental animal felt when he'd been carefully rested on a lab table, petted, and then gazed up at the disaffected, totally dispassionate person who was undeniably going to eviscerate—disembowel—him. All that and more—more that was unreadable, seemingly out of it, even insane—showed in Holroyd's intense gaze. He was different in some manner; perhaps chemically altered. Modified.

Holroyd turned. Raised the scalpel, still dripping slightly, over his head. Planted his feet as if readying himself to charge across the pavement and the Blackwood Apartments yard, directly at Wes. He yearned to; that was definitely there to be read in the effeminate features. And there was an elusive quality about the undertaker that indicated a bizarre youth that was rushing at him inside, in the reverse way that old age sometimes appeared to charge at the elderly. Motionless that instant, the youthful quality couldn't be understood. Wes just knew that Stancel Holroyd's principle expression in the embryonic shadows atop the slight rise irradiated both madness and the vapid, unreasoning, hate-filled stubbornness of a very naughty, neurotic child, over-sized and armed. Casting swift glances of fear from right to left, pissed at himself for leaving the heavy flashlight in the company car parked at the curb, Wes found nothing more useful for defense than a yellow sheet of typescript that had clearly fluttered away from Harlan Rowe's sprawling hand and arm.

And when he glanced back up, bracing himself inwardly for the undertaker's run and lunge, he wasn't sure at once that the twilight skies over the terrible town had not played tricks with his myopic vision.

Holroyd emitted a fiercely happy, high-pitched squeal, and plunged the scalpel into his own lower belly.

Aghast, Wes stared incredulously as Holroyd wrapped his long arms about himself in a shiver of involuntary agony or a hug of chemical ecstasy—it was impossible to know which it was, at that range—and then at how the scalpel seemed to extrude from below the navel, obscenely, refracting seeds of twilight like solder-hot sperm.

All but soundlessly yet with a jarring psychic impact, the body collided with the ground and only then did it begin to bleed. Silence ensued, but Wes had no chance to recover from the shock of either Holroyd or Rowe before he caught the faint yet unmistakeable noise of footsteps.

Hollow, somehow militant footsteps, well beyond the bleeding undertaker. Brisk; youthful; collective footsteps, almost organized. *In step.*

Not out for a jog, Wes understood. Because they were marching.

Although he listened inently, the thrum of his overworked heart prevented Wes from being sure that they were moving off, or coming closer. Trembling, he turned, bent to snatch up the yellow sheet of paper which it appeared that Rowe had wanted to bring him in the phone room. *Jagannath,* a glance informed him, was Sanskrit. It was hard to concentrate with the matching cadence in his ears, with the light uncertain, eerie.

Then he realized he had a news story in his shaky hand. For tomorrow's *Sycophant;* for an edition that would never see print. Harlan's own life substance, in spilling, had blotted out much of what he'd written. Wes, alerted, made out "first time in history one." Nettled, then, he looked up and around. He was so nervous by now his skin seemed ready to crawl off his wrists, forearms, and legs.

But this time it was just nerves; no marcher was in view. He thought, though, that he heard murmuring voices. Stancel Holroyd could have been an advance scout and *he'd* gone straight to the apartment building, seemingly mad. But what had happened? Was it what Kiper Research had made him take? Perspiring, Wes tried to hear what the residents were saying, the mob. But he could only be sure their number was growing . . . that they seemed to be picking up new people from the houses they passed. Eventually, he saw with a surge of fresh terror, it might be everybody who lived in Stillwind Valley. Everyone.

Staring back down at the bloodstained paper,

he finally read what Harlan Rowe had meant to communicate: "First time in history one town literally *killed* another town."

Wes's mouth opened. The concept frightened him badly. But while he was making himself absorb it, trying to consider its ramifications, he noticed one particular word Rowe had underscored four times, thrice in red pen: *juggernaut.* The fourth, also red, was in blood.

Somebody shouted and Wes jumped, quavering. They weren't pointing him out, however; not yet. They were calling unintelligibly to each other. What were they saying, trying to do? *What,* Wes wondered frantically, *do they want*?

He forced himself to climb over the body crammed into the entranceway. Sweating heavily, he shoved the door open, went inside. The mob was headed for Blackwood, that was clear. And they'd gone crazy, or crazier; they might go berserk—or had. With no time to waste, determined to collect Cheryl, Clem, and Brick, pile into the Caddy and drive like hell—like "the lord of the universe" was on their heels—he struggled up the apartment stairs, staggered down the hall, and pushed the door to the Wesken Company temporary phone room all the way *open . . .*

Without remembering that it was only closed at night until he'd seen Professor Albert Kiper and Dr. Akeem Dominique there, already, the latter grinning his sleek welcome. They'd been waiting for him.

25

He'd heard the expression "work yourself to death" all his relatively long life and hadn't really believed it was possible. Desirable, maybe; not the worst way to go, but probably not within the realm of possibility.

Then he'd gone with the others last night, and at just about the time he was caving in the head of some teenage boy without realizing he was having so much fun, it had occurred to Vernon Slaid simultaneously (1) what he was doing and (2) that working himself to the point of death might be conceivable after all.

The cemetery caretaker, cognizant at last of his murderous actions but enjoying them far more, had gone on killing strangers with the rest of his town's denizens, pretty damn sure he wasn't the only sumbitch who'd come to and proceeded with the annihilation as if he hadn't known. But he was no hypocrite, like mosta the high-toned scientist types, and he'd become increasingly preoccupied by the challenge he'd thought up for himself.

Without losing an iota of enthusiasm for the chore at hand, of course. Vernon had always possessed the knack for doin' more than one thing at a time, even if so-called experts did swear it was impossible for a sane man.

Then this evening, all bright-eyed and bushy-tailed, he'd begun to act on his impulse, to accept his own challenge, both because it was high time to seek the skeletal perfection that he knew dwelled within himself and for more pragmatic, less idealistic reasons: Slaid knew that the doctor and Kiper were gonna try to convince them hoky salesmen to cooperate, to go along for the ride—with long and healthy life as the bait, the carrot—and Vernon knew damn well assholes like Wes Teagle and the others wouldn't do that. Not because they was idealists, the way he was, hisself, or cause they understood the whole flow of life-into-death and found it good, as Vernon did; but 'cause they was too common. Too much like the ordinary, mine-run sorta men and women who always got tensed up if they knew that they was gettin' called on the shit that they claimed to've believed in all their lives. They lacked the vision, and they never understood any better'n anyone else did how purty death was—once it got rid of the skin, and the muscle, and worked itself down to the pure bony goodie part.

They thought folks had rights. But Vernon Slaid, a man of the earth, knew just how many rights anybody had.

So he took action to assert his, untouched by the virulent reaction that most of Stillwind Valley had finally had to what the professor and the doctor had cooked up, and, leavin' the damfool science types and the other idjits to this evening's parade, he'd started digging graves. As many as he could before he dropped dead.

All the sweet, soft, crumbly, worm-squirming graves Vernon had longed to dig all his life.

Miles of 'em, it seemed like, 'cause the cemetery might still be new but it was gettin' broke-in purty good, rows and rows and rows of yawning pits, empty still yet Welcome Wagon cavities in Good Mother Earth's brown belly . . . and he forced himself t'keep goin', not to stop, not to pause for a breath or take any kinda break but t'keep diggin'—each and every modern contrivance that would've speeded up the task eschewed, each and every smoothly functioning restored sinew or muscle in Vernon's body straining, aching, and protesting—demanding he quit—while Vernon just snickered and even laughed out loud at the exquisite and vibrantly throbbing warning signals going off from head to booted toe.

This was the right folks had; or folks such as Slaid. Men who had never bothered to make a buddy, or learn to love, even t'like anybody living including himself—and he was by-God asserting that right by accepting the challenge of working himself to death, with the kind of fucking-mad single-minded perserverance folks like Vernon Slaid always had left, at the end.

Dominique and Albert, they hadn't promised nobody immortality, he knew that; he'd got that vital point stuck in his lunatic's brain right from the get-go. They had talked about gettin' young again, about startin' over, livin' awhile longer and, most important of all to him, they had given him the chance to do what he preferred to do, *liked* to do—

Even down to meeting his own crazy challenge and winning.

The agony that couldn't be vanquished by blind, selfish, bullheaded determination began in the center of the chest and took off in every damn direction like a ravaging pack of wild dogs, going "yeahyeahyeah*yeah*." At the time, Vernon was proceeding nicely with another grave—a couple of the most recent ones, he'd observed in a vaguely comprehending fashion, had turned out sorta lopsided with weird angles and bottoms that wasn't perfectly flat—and he was perched on a hillock of dirt. He began lifting a shovel, and the mad dogs ate up his guts: *zap!*

For the only time since he had been a warped little sumbitch, a both unadorable and unadored child, Vernon almost believed in God at the instant he tumbled face forward into his shallow pit. Dislodged dirt dropped on his back feeling the way sunshine does to some men.

He discovered just enough willpower and life left to roll over on his back, and work the muscles of his face with the same kind of dumb, feverish self-command that had seen him that far.

He wanted to arrange his features just so, so his skull would have a really happy, purty smile when all the flesh had gone.

"I imagine you have a number of questions at this point," Dr. Dominique said in his deep, rumbling voice. "Professor Kiper and I are here to clear them up for you, Mr. Teagle."

Wes almost laughed in the giant's face. "I'm not even sure God Almighty could 'clear up' the questions I have," he said, and worked his way around the seated pair to a nearby desk. He sat on the edge, folding his arms, noticing that Dominique and Kiper at least had the commonsense not to want to shake hands.

"I'm not sure God Almighty would," Cheryl said softly from her own desk. She was sitting behind it, in her chair, looking physically improved, but clearly frightened. "He has nothing to do with this."

"I suggest you shouldn't be too sure of that, Ms. Conrad," the doctor said softly. "Allow me to apologize for the way you were mistreated last night. It was not my idea."

"You were *there*!" Cheryl exclaimed, crimsoning with ire. "No one else in town is your height." She shuddered. "If *anybody is* . . . anywhere."

Dominique's brows and manicured index finger lifted marginally, without menace. He and Kiper sat side by side on the couch, the former towering over the latter. After he'd spoken he paused to let his message sink in. "It was I who made them release you," he said. Smiled. "Things had begun getting a bit out of hand. And where I come from, madam, many males approach my height."

Amazing, thought Wes, realizing that these two —the doctor, at any rate—actually imagined they might explain it all away. He was far more appalled by a sudden acceptance deep within himself of the remote, real chance they had to pull it off.

"In a way, nobody is responsible for what happened to Ms. Conrad," Albert Kiper dared to say.

"I loathe it when I'm sitting right here," Cheryl said tensely, "and people talk through me as if I were invisible."

"Apologies." Kiper was apparently composed, despite the way some things seemed to be going wrong for them; the small man's colorless eyes darted constantly and his hopefully height-building pompadour looked rumpled. "The chemical aspects of our sustained youth program always contained elements of risk. Unpredictable factors, if members of the group failed to follow their prescribed regimens. By the way, you people were there when the Jagannath was unveiled, so you've already opted, tacitly, to be part of—"

"I never agreed to be part of what you pricks are doing!" Brick blustered. He and Clem Sparrow were at their own desks, but whether from choice or because they'd been directed there, Wes didn't know. Something about the way they all looked, however, sent his inventive imagination on a danger-fleeing tangent . . .

"Hold," Dominique said. Kiper had started to argue Brick's point, but the doctor, seemingly desiring to prevent an aggressive debate, had raised a wide palm. Presumably, Wes saw, he wanted to press on quietly—and in the direction he chose. "In the sense of gaining your full understanding and acceptance, Mr. Brickowski, that's quite true. And in fairness, how could we expect otherwise when we've yet to present a total explanation? That's why we're here this evening."

The way that the big man contentedly folded his arms furthered the tangential impression disturbing Wes, but he couldn't quite define the feeling. A surprise attack occurred to Wes. "Your stooge from the *Syco,* he's in the entranceway to this building," Wes announced. "Dead. You fellas arrange for that?"

Little Kiper's lips parted. He looked surprised. Displeased.

A light that was largely unreadable flickered in Dominique's dark eyes. He sighed. "That would probably be the handiwork of the coroner, Mr. Holroyd."

"Probably," Wes snapped. Dominique's candor and adaptability privately dazzled him. But he laced his fingers, leaned back from his seat on the desk and locked his hands over a knee. He didn't doubt for a moment that these two had ordered it. "But Holroyd's dead, too. Killed himself with his own scalpel."

Albert gasped audibly. He and the doctor both looked genuinely if mildly shocked; seeing their expressions gave Wes a moment's impression that he had the upper hand. Clem Sparrow, he noticed, unaccountably reticent, was watching the proceedings like an alert hawk. "Gents," Wes said helpfully, "if all that is some kinda chemical reaction, well, I'd hafta say it's back to the test tubes and the ol' drawing board!"

"What a charming and witty expression of concern," Dominique said. He permitted himself the luxury of a toothy smile. "My thanks"—he peered closely, curiously at Wes—"for being the bearer of macabre yet glad tidings!"

Wes stammered, "W-What's that?"

The black giant pursed his lips. "I am not a hypocrite, sir. And I am not saddened by Mr. Holroyd's loss." He exchanged a glance with Kiper, who frowned. "At no point, you see, was I asked to provide psychological evaluations of the research team or the town support team. And all along, I feared Holroyd was both unstable and, like Ms. Conrad, an unfortunate person who sometimes resorted to . . . unwise chemical aids." He turned to Cheryl, shrugged. "Consider the dreadful ramifications."

The buck passing, Wes realized, was brilliant—and bewildering! Dominique was disavowing responsibility for a man he hadn't chosen and, by defining the man as innately unstable, limiting Kiper's culpability to his hiring methods!

"He probably was a bit, well, out of balance," Albert said grudgingly, staring directly at the enormous man beside him on the couch. He nibbled on his lip, worried it. "Stancel Holroyd knew the risks, if he went off on his own. That they included the chance of tragic side effects."

"—Which all too obviously," Dominique said, seizing the opportunity, "extended to his attack upon your friend, Cliff Macy—and goodness knows how many others!"

Neat, Wes applauded, mentally. By the time they were through talking, every gee-dee thing that had happened would seem like it was either the mortician's work or an act of God!

"You knew there'd be side effects?" Cheryl asked, frowning.

Kiper nodded, then let his chin sink ruminatively to his narrow chest. "When you operate this kind of fairly large-scale experiment, and confidentiality is paramount to success, you can't make team choices based on really thorough investigation. Mistakes are inevitable." He peered up, abruptly, at each of them in the phone room and the passion of his convictions lit his colorless eyes with inner fire. "All of you think my rules that exclude certain foods and drugs were based on some Hitlerian urge to become a petty dictator." His small hands fisted and one shook, faintly. "But that's film horror. I'm real-life science."

Dominique cleared his voice delicately. "In fairness, some food or drink combined with the professor's vitamins and medicines could be expected to produce unpleasant side effects." He beamed on the much smaller man as if reinforcing his ongoing collaborative spirit.

. . . And Wes achieved his elusive, unconscious comparison: With each of the Wesken Company people seated at desks in growing shadow, Dominique and Albert Kiper addressing them from a different and facing location, it was as if they all found themselves in school again. Except that Kiper and the doctor weren't so much teaching a class as selling them a bill of goods . . . and monitoring the rest of their lives, however short a period that proved to be. *It's all selling, or trying to,* he thought; *or buying.*

And then belonging.

"Akeem promised you an explanation," the scientist said, shifting his fleshless flanks as if settling in for an extensive talk but not especially agreeing with the necessity of it. "So let me tell you that I was reluctant to mix magick with science, at first. I didn't know a thing about the so-called 'ancient arts,' still don't, for that matter." He and Dominique smiled at each other. "Then I saw with my own eyes the evidence of what magick can accomplish—even without the assistance of science." Kiper's gaze met Wes's. "So did you, out by the cemetery. That great damned bird with the white wings."

"But your . . . acceptance . . . of me began before then," Dominique said quite softly.

"It did," Kiper agreed, bobbing his head. But he hadn't removed his gaze from Wes's eyes. "When I discovered that Akeem here is almost seventy years old."

All the phone room people turned to stare at Dominique in amazement. The dignified, youthful head moved in a confirming nod.

"Now it's time for me to fill you in, in layman's terms," Albert remarked, "on my end of the sustained youth experiment. And a good place to start is with the conviction we both have that aging is . . . well . . . disgusting."

"Disgusting?" Clem Sparrow repeated with a scowl.

"Sorry if the word offends you." Kiper laughed thinly. "Admittedly, none of you is ready for the grave. But nature says that unless we die young, we all must go through it—and you people are much closer to it than Akeem and I am, thanks to his work and mine."

"Fuck you jokers," Brick growled. "Maybe you got lucky with some youth serum or monkey glands, but you're still however old your bodies are . . . for the time you've been alive."

"Admirably said," Dominique commented, lifting a brow. "In point of sheer fact, however—you're wrong."

"Here's the thing," Albert Kiper began again, crossing his abbreviated legs at the knee. "Some scientists proposed that the effect of the disease known as diabetes—the way it impacts the tissues and organs—is akin to speeding up the aging process. Untreated, that is." His upper lip curled in revulsion. "Untreated, the condition is a lot like the problems of the elderly but they occur earlier. So other scientists began looking into age impairment in relation to sugar glucose and proteins; enzymes that won't do their job properly; and reactions that wind up creating unwelcome connections with other protein molecules."

"Glad you're puttin' all this in layman's terms," Wes murmured. Brick, he noticed, wore the expression of a middle-aged schoolboy asked to stay after class.

"Yes, yes, of course," Dominique said with a chuckle. "Let us not lose sight, Albert, of the fact that these good people have not enjoyed the advantages of procedures that reduce or utilize the pigments and collagen in a more timely fashion than nature provides. Or your investigation into mammalian nucleic acids and the salutory results." His voice purred indulgently, almost affectionately. "They're doing the best they can."

"I'll just be forty this year!" Wes objected. But his tone of voice was far milder than his emotions at this instant.

"I've seen your kind before." Clemon rose, moved tentatively in Akeem Dominique's direction. Afoot, he was scantly taller. But while he sounded under control and again took his seat behind his desk, Clem was furious. "All the education in the world won't change what you are; time you faced that. Time you helped your people, 'stead of chasing them out of town!"

"Ah?" Dominique became impassive, facially. "You, Mr. Sparrow, have benefited our race by virtue of the ennobling vocation you pursue from this room?"

"I didn't use some kind of backwoods voodoo to scare the Boggs family half to death," Clem said levelly. His own sizable hands were fisted.

"Gentlemen," Albert interrupted, flushing, "the human species reaches its prime and starts to decline well before the fortieth birthday." He ran his small hand through his mass of dark hair, turned anxiously to the doctor. "I told you their glucose build-up was too advanced. Even if they have the IQ to handle it, they can't—"

"Your opinion was duly noted." Dominique closed his eyes. "Nevertheless, every opportunity should be accorded those who—"

"I don't like being treated as if I were an idiot, either," Cheryl Conrad interrupted—"or becoming senile!"

Inwardly, Wes shook his head, wishing she hadn't broken the big man's track of thought. Well, it was clear enough now that Frick and Frack were going to threaten them unless they volunteered their entire, collective support. Maybe with the marchers he sensed were drawing nearer. And since none of them would go along with anything based on murder, they'd have to make a move before long.

And sizing Dr. Dominique up, Wes all but despaired. Seventy years old or not, the man was a movable mountain who could probably handle everybody in the room.

"We prob'ly are too ignorant to get what you're saying about the scientific crapola," Wes said quietly. "But since you asked the doctor into your little experiment, I guess I'm smart enough t'see you needed help. From a foreigner, right—a witch doctor?" Wes saw the decided frown form on Albert's face and leaned forward, arms akimbo. "Maybe you could explain just one part of your meddlin'—like what happened to the folks in Walterville?"

"Very well, Mr. Teagle, I'll explain that tragedy to you." Kiper clearly looked annoyed; perhaps it was possible, Wes thought, to divide the two of them. "Then I shall let Akeem prove to you that he is infinitely more than a mere witch doctor." He jabbed an index finger at Wes, his anger showing. "Part of what's gone wrong is that on which you seem to place a high premium. Independence."

"How's that?" Wes asked, blinking his surprise.

"Consider the symptoms you have seen all over Stillwind Valley, if you're so intelligent, Teagle. You've seen enough of them."

"Albert," Dominique began, "I'm not certain—"

"Think of the short tempers, the irritability you've seen exhibited," Kiper went on. "The darkened tongues; the breaths that stink or smell like acetone; the restlessness." Kiper glared from Wes to the others, and back. "I made it damned near impossible for my people to eat or drink the wrong things, encouraged them to exercise, to lose weight.'' He was almost standing. ''Then *you* people begin subverting my schedule with your infantile needs and set an example of ignorant, willful, independent action that motivates them to go against the *best* scientific advice!''

''What the hell are you sayin'?'' Wes demanded.

''It was only *some* of them,'' Dominique interpolated soothingly. ''First the jogger, Appleton, then young Tedrick, Holroyd of course, Slaid at the cemetery—''

''It was *enough* of them!'' Kiper snapped. He whipped his hirsute head back to face Wes. ''Damn you, they didn't dare go off their diets! Not with Akeem's magick; not with the special insulin mix I devised to stabilize the aging process.''

Wes was openly, honestly horrified. ''Do you mean what I think you mean, man?''

Kiper nodded. ''Of course,'' he retorted. ''Their glucose and blood sugar levels had to be entirely modified; reregulated.'' He glanced at Dominique and finished it on a defensive note. ''Right from the outset it was necessary for everybody in Stillwind Valley to develop a particularly complex, violent form of diabetes.'' He sank back against the couch, folding his arms. ''But now that they've become a mob—I don't know what in Jesus' name to *do* about it!''

26

When he finally found her, he hadn't expended much time but he had used a psychic energy—and resorted to the kind of memory search not even a computer could match—that was profound. Insofar as time is concerned, beings in heaven and in hell come to know it as the complex rotundity of cosmic Play-Doh it is; they experience it pleasantly or miserably, but always with a clearer understanding of its infinitely adaptive nature.

Time, for what was left of Kenny Higgins, was simultaneously suspended and vexingly eternal. No longer fish nor fowl, he waded in it to his constantly mobile hips like a man going upstream in a rushing current of molasses, and it clung to him as if intending to eat through his reanimated calves and thighs like lava. Yet the pain he felt was restricted to his psyche, his residual spirit—

And was as nothing when he saw—dimly, at first; uncomprehendingly, only at first—what had been done to her.

Wafted from side to side by the dark and spurious lifeforce thrust upon him, condemned for no crime at all to a perpetual solitary waltz on the brink of forever, Kenny wept within, and he managed a moan . . . a sound that was perfect in its awfulness, like the recaptured, last breaths of all those fallen in war, like the wail of unjustly cursed things summoned from places in which they'd found no rest.

Then he attempted that one feat he could try to achieve—awkwardly, spastically, valiantly and lovingly. The loneliest creature upon Earth, Kenny strove to do for Angelane O'Brien's poor crumbling corpse what had been done for, or to, his own.

Jerking ceaselessly but kneeling, clumsily throwing out his long, bloodless arms in order to lower his painted face, Kenny kissed Angelane.

A stirring—not inside the brain or the body of the woman he had loved, for Angelane's mind and spirit had long since succeeded in flight, but stirrings of forgotten things . . . and those that have never been known to any man without love. Things that were, at once, present with Kenny, and not present. Forces, entities of a kind, convoluted circumstances with the viewless intricacy of molecular structure . . . possibly the unknowable heart of time . . . stirred.

Incapable of knowing that, or much at all, seeing just the jumbled tumble of events in their own dead lives and that motionless face he'd kissed to no apparant avail, the dancer retrieved the cap that had fallen from his head and snapped to his cold and restless feet, then spun, jerkily, to depart.

To make sure the enactment of this choreography of corruption was completed.

* * *

"Perhaps I do know what's to be done about them," said Dominique, in dulcet tones. He rose. "Perhaps—as it's ever been true with all *shamans*, sorcerers, men of magick—I have held something in reserve."

"What are you talking about?" Kiper asked. He looked up at the immense man dwarfing him and everything else in the room. "You sound almost as if you'd expected the town to react this way!"

"You could accept, Albert, only that magick of mine which I could prove to you," the doctor pointed out. "Yet there is magick that *I* can believe, or rely upon, until I have done it."

"Don't follow you," Kiper admitted, listening intently.

"Astrology, alchemy and magick were humankind's first efforts directed toward seeking the order—and the *secrets* of order, of purpose—which even you scientists prefer to imagine in a world of general chaos. So it is that the Pedi tribe in South Africa cured their people, through ritual and repetition, with a mold much like penicillin . . . long before your more, um, *civilized* tribes." Dominique's large eyes sparkled. "But like science, magick depends upon experimentating. Testing. The jogger who never rests, Albert; you see him as a worthy, early failure of your own experiments. *I* see him as a man I have not permitted to die . . ."

"Beg pardon?" Wes asked.

"The control of one's involuntary functions—breathing, metabolism, pulse rate and so forth—was an achievement centuries ago; a familiar feat in yoga . . . and also in certain African tribes. In Tibet, Alexandra David-Neel observed *lung-gom*, the product of an arduous training method involving almost four years of special breathing exercises . . . and total seclusion. Mastered, *lung-gom* enables the Tibetan to traverse incredible distances on foot—in effect, to alter the physical limitations of their environment." He turned to his scientific partner. "In roughly a day and a half, the master of the Tibetan art averages some ten miles an hour—and travels more than three hundred miles without rest or sleep."

"But . . . why?" Kiper demanded. He didn't flinch when Cheryl shot daggers in his direction. "I don't want to sound coldhearted, but why keep that jogger alive, Akeem?"

Dr. Dominique paused; sighed. "Apart from answers that would be obvious to the more elemental members of my tribe hundreds of years ago, my reply is linked to how you have misjudged me, Albert. From the start." What might have been anger but was probably resentment flashed in the deep, dark eyes. He'd donned, for that evening, a summer suit of immaculate white, phenomenally tailored to fit his impressive form. Even the shirt and tie were snowy, even the wing-tipped shoes; at times shifting light patterns cast from the nearby window made him seem all head and hands, and they appeared to move disembodiedly.

"For now," he told Kiper politely, sadly, "let it stand that I wished the people of this town to experience and thus subscribe to the supernatural . . . for my own, good reasons."

Brick and Clem Sparrow looked without expression to each other. Passing between them, however, was a swarming mass of mutual, alarming concern, a shared realization that Akeem Dominique was steadily taking charge—and that Albert Kiper could well be afraid of what happened when Dominique was done.

"Albert is not in error, factually, about the

growth of the older population," said the giant, linking his enormous hands at the small of his back and seeming on the verge of pacing. "There are ten million *more* people over sixty-five today than existed in nineteen sixty-five." A not quite readable grin. "More of those people vote than any other group; consider the power, and the power *potential,* inherent in such facts." Half-turning, he regarded Wes again. "The reason—and this information may well be news to Professor Kiper, as well—is this: Energy sites are *shifting.* All over the world."

"Energy sites? Are you referring to that old business about *ley lines*?" Albert demanded, trying to throttle the incredulity rising with his words. "Lines no one can see in the ground under ancient religious landmarks, yet they're somehow linked?"

"More than that," Dominique sighed, "but yes, subterranean power pools where more enlightened people built those edifices and monuments that were intended to last . . . and venerate the planet that sustains us, gives us all the powers we possess." He looked toward Clem and Brick. "As my fathers before me, I have studied many cultures, many times in history, and ley lines are known—by many names—everywhere on earth. Even today, in China, wise and wealthy men would never construct a building without the guidance of the *Feng Shui,* a psychic who provides counsel about the location, suitable interiors, even the furnishings of major structures."

"What does this Feng Shui man do?" asked the absorbed Clem.

"Something essential, Mr. Sparrow. He locates the *Ch'i,* the energy flow influencing every aspect of a living creature's life"—Akeem gestured toward Albert, smiling rather playfully—"whether he's aware of it or not. Stonehenge is the famous example of the monuments, mounts and menhirs raised to propitiate and not antagonize this planet. But think too of the megaliths in South Wales, Carnac and Avebury, the Celtic Merry Maidens, the pyramids! Think of Glastonbury Tor, the Sphinx—*all* constructed where *Feng Shui* commanded. The *face* of China is landscaped by it, down to artificial hills on which whole cities are erected!"

"What does this . . . flow, this *Ch'i* . . . do?" Wes inquired.

Dominique beamed down upon the bespectacled phone man. "Why, sir, it regenerates when it is honored, earnestly and sincerely. It *revitalizes* us!"

"That big bird with the white wings," Wes began, catching his breath before plunging into deep waters. "That was a product of ley lines—of *Ch'i*?"

"Only indirectly," Dominique answered, looking keenly at Wes. "I said that I employed the magick of many ages and cultures, and the *bruxsa* was Portuguese. I conjured and modified it in order to prove my skills to Albert." He tilted his huge head, almost mockingly. "In its original form, the night-bird was also known as a *xorguina* when it attacked adult prey. I chose to summon its racial memory, somewhat altered, by virtue of what science itself has learned about . . . hallucinations."

"You *are* a surprising man, Akeem," Kiper said sourly, sinking down on the couch and pouting. "Science, eh?" he grumbled.

"Precisely that!" the doctor protested without ire. He looked at the others. "We mammals become hallucinatory when something shortcircuits our sensory apparatus. You see, we acquire data by means of light, smell, and sound borne to our central nervous systems. Now: when that information is diverted—as with those sounds that are mistaken, due to the absorption of drugs and chemicals, by *other* senses—wrong parts of our brains are stimulated and we may believe anything. Anything whatsoever!"

"And somebody else can make that happen, control and direct it?" asked Wes. Dominique nodded and went on looking at him as if expecting a further reaction. "I've got it! The racket of that *rock music* all the time," he said, staggered by the insight. The big man's smile spread, encouragingly. "So you wanted it played by everybody all the time as—"

"As the suitable psychological backdrop for Albert's physiological modifications in the residents," Dominique finished, chuckling along with Wes, "and my own introduction of hallucinations! Capitol, Mr. Teagle . . . excellent!"

"Pretty smart, Wes," Brick complimented him.

Kiper shook his head at the standing jolly giant. "I'd never quite understood why you insisted on that constant clatter," he confessed.

"No doubt," Clem told the doctor with dripping sarcasm, "the professor imagined that you just had to hear jungle drums—and rock music was the closest you could get to that in Stillwind Valley!"

Akeem laughed with open delight. "Perhaps so, Mr. Sparrow," he cried, clapping Clem on the shoulder so heavily he almost drove him to the phone room floor. "Perhaps so!"

Sumbitch, it's startin' to seem like old home week, Wes reflected, arduously keeping his grin in place. *Brick thinks I'm smart 'cause I figured this gee-dee witch doctor dreamed up somethin' to scare Ocie t'death!*

Wes hadn't forgotten, this time, the fate of those who could never share such mad hilarity. He also hadn't lost sight of the way they were all being buddy-buddy—when Dominique had used *mind control* on the whole town! Were folks always willing to laugh and party so long as *they* got off the hook?

Outside the building, though he appeared the only one who heard them, a mob was gathering, whispering hoarsely. A mob that had killed a—

"Now to finish relating my story," Dominique said, rubbing his wide, pale palms together with zest. He dropped with remarkable litheness to the edge of the couch, next to Albert, and nudged the little scientist to be sure he knew that he was wanted. Kiper's entire body swayed from the impact. "Many reliable sources around the world have informed me that the energy flow of the ley lines, the *Ch'i*, is shifting. It departed the pyramids hundreds of years ago; it has now left Stonehenge . . . England, the Scandinavian nations . . . most of Europe." He sat up straight, eyes blazing. "The pathways of occult yore are altering, and they are accessible to those people who wish to take charge, who desire to continue life in fine health." He smiled modestly. "Now, you see, it has departed Africa—only after it revitalized my fathers and my father's fathers!"

So you followed *the lines,* Wes thought; *now we know that much about* your *motivation!*

"That doesn't sound so bad," Brick acknowledged. He crossed his legs, got comfortable; relaxed. "How long could a guy like me live if I was part of the program?"

"A sensible query," the doctor praised him, "but you are overlooking the fine point—that you won't *age!* Neither Professor Kiper nor I is a minute older than when we arrived in Stillwind Valley." He leaned forward, became almost boyish of manner. "And thanks to the brilliant scientific contributions of Kiper Research—neither Albert nor I expect to age for at least *one hundred years!*"

"A hundred?" Cheryl, astonished, intrigued despite herself, gaped at the two men on the couch. "You're offering us immortality?"

"Come, let us not be greedy!" Dominique smiled hugely, excitedly, and it was wonderfully contagious. "We offer you a mere hundred years . . . without becoming older!"

"Yeah, let's not be greedy." Wes, speaking very, very carefully. Wondering if he was sealing his death warrant. "Let's talk about the statue you donated, Akeem, all right? Just for a minute?"

"What about the Jagannath?" The giant's smile shrank.

"Suppose you tell us," Wes said shortly. His own smile was stuck in place, like that of his deceased friend Kenny. "Just why was that old hunk of wood so important to your success and Albert's, here, when y'had the shifting ley lines and all?"

A prolonged, suspenseful, psychically agonizing period of time passed while Wes wondered if he had gone too far. Dominique could swat him like a mosquito on his buttock, a gnat on his incredible biceps. And while it was true that the doctor looked no older than his middle years even without the now familiar, ingratiating beam of a smile, Akeem had become so oppressively grim that his ruggedly handsome, black features appeared to have been carved from a substance similar to that of his long-ago-plundered statue.

"You are the only human being," he told Wes distinctly, in syllables that were sharp and frightening all the more because he was accentless and did not raise his voice, "I shall ever meet who is capable of *questioning* the gift of a long and happy existence! What kind of man are you? Because I cannot, this minute, be sure whether I am obliged to admire you above all men, or to condemn you as a hopeless inbecile."

"I am pretty good," Wes conceded. "Y'see, aside from those folks I'd have to climb all over to take your gift, I guess I'm not positive that 'long' and 'happy' mean just the same thing—or even that they ever met each other!" He scratched the back of his head, thoughtfully, looked apologetic. "T'tell you the pure truth, Doc, there's also the fact I kinda liked bein' a boy, and a teenager, then a horny young dude; and all. So, while I may not be singin' any hymns t'life the way those really scared-shitless folks do, especially when they want you to donate some money or somethin', I s'pose I sort of look forward to seein' what old age is gonna be like too."

"You look forward," Kiper muttered in disgust, "to *that?*"

Wes shrugged. "Sure. I never saw nothin' more beautiful than my grandma. Or how nice she and grandpa was, together. Bravest sight in my life was grandma when her time came." He hesitated, looked away. "Said she was goin' home, and I believed her."

"Doctor," Cheryl reminded the big man quietly, almost primly, "he asked about the Jagannath. Why was it Mr. Kiper needed it?" Barely unasked was the question of why Dominique had needed Kiper, or vice versa.

Dominique drew in a slow, contemplative breath. "The pyramids, the acropolis, Glastonbury Tor, primitive cave drawings—all the rest—can't be budged from where they are. There is one monument, to our Earth, a single creation that has absorbed the reverent prayers of hundreds of thousands, which is capable of movement." A pause. "Of transport." Ponderously, Akeem turned in a slow circle to include Kiper in his remarks. "*Only* the Jagannah could keep pace with the shifting energy flow . . . because its wheels may be returned to it." Hovering above Wes, Dominique appeared truly menacing for the first time. "Do you, Mr. Teagle, begin to understand?"

"Yessir, I think I do." Wes sighed as he nodded. Now he felt Clem's and Brick's steady eyes centered questioningly, almost resentfully, upon him. Even Cheryl, he knew, probably doubted his judgment that second when sharing the beliefs and ambitions of the much-lauded soul-doctor and the businesslike scientist might permit them not only to live, but to live for another century.

But they had to be reminded, the surviving head of the Wesken Company figured it, just the way most salespeople needed periodically to be reminded, that there were no "giveaways" anywhere, never had been. That very little, indeed, was ever an "extra added bonus" or a "three-for-two day." That nothing whatever was free, not ultimately even the air they all breathed. Because, sooner or later, they had to pay for everything they'd scribbled down on their personal order sheets, and the final bottomline was always the biggest one there was.

"Y'know, Akeem," he said, glancing at Kiper to make sure he was included in his remarks, "sometimes when you're tryin' hard t'get a point over on a customer, it's all in the words you use. Or *don't* use. I'm not positive Albert, there, knows that the Sanskrit meaning of your ole statue's name is juggernaut, and I'm pretty sure these other folks don't remember what poor Cliff told me before that crazy Holroyd got him."

Each of them stared at Wes, silently. For the first time, it seemed to him, they were all aware of the fact that a mob was forming outside the apartment building.

But maybe none of them understood that the best of mobs required just a well-directed word or two to set it off—none, of course, except the good doctor. "Among a lotta things the office dictionary said a juggernaut is," added Wes, slowly standing, "is an irresistible force. Maybe even a mob of people out to *kill* other people."

Albert Kiper's fretful face developed an onslaught of sudden fear. Like Wes, Clem was on his feet; he rushed to the window to stare out at the living, breathing juggernaut and Clem's action—whether he was seen by the townsfolk or not—appeared to magnify their angry sounds. Akeem Dominique stood, too, facing Wes squarely. It was, Wes realized, bracing himself, like a man balanced on a high ledge peering down at tiny people on a distant street.

Or more, maybe, like a taloned, furious, and deadly night-bird.

27

Dr. Dominique did not utter a further word for several more contemplative and, for Wes, suspenseful breaths.

Eventually, at last, he straightened to his full height and, even more slowly, the corners of his wide mouth turned up. "Well, well, well," Dominique said good-humoredly, drawling the word out with each repitition. "Can it be that I was correct about your native if uncultivated intelligence?"

More relieved than he seemed, Wes glanced around the room, grinning like a boy who had done something clever but precocious for a family audience. "Maybe. And it could be that you and Albert have underestimated all of us. Just a mite." Still afoot, Wes slipped his fingertips into his hip pockets and turned toward the puzzled scientist, acutely aware that the phone people were still the farthest thing from scot-free.

And that even if Dr. Dominique held the upper hand in his collaboration with Albert Kiper—even if Akeem himself proved to be the one who'd created the mob that was massing outside the entrance to the apartment building—there was no reason for being sure he could disband them with a simple command.

"Maybe the weirdo undertaker of yours and a few others got a little bit too close to the weed or the wine, Albert," Wes said, as if cheering Kiper up. "You just forgot they were only human. Seems like scientific people do that a lot." Staring straight up, Wes gave the black mountain a wink of bold audacity. "Just the way it 'pears religious folks do, too, sometimes. You just didn't figure on your partner being entirely his own man."

A noise outside—a member of the mob maybe, hurling something against the building—deflected Kiper's irritation. "Is this yokel telling it the way it is, Akeem?" He shifted on the couch, looked aggrieved and put-upon. Wes also thought he was uneasy, if not more than that, because of the crowd's proximity. "I approached you in good faith, remember, gave you an opportunity to be accepted in a rather different kind of community. Shared an experiment with you, right down the line—and it ought to mean a fortune to each of us." Kiper's lower lip trembled. "Now, it appears that you've been less than open and aboveboard with me."

"Come, Albert," Dominique smiled beguilingly. "You begin to blather like a silly old woman. Discussions of honor . . . of word keeping . . . are simply too ludicrous for my tastes under these conditions." Still relaxed, his huge arms folded across his fullback's chest, the doctor was clearly amused as well. "I mentioned that we've never shared the same interests. Fortunes of the variety to which you refer are the targets of small men, men devoid of imagination." Wes, to his surprise, received an audacious wink from Dominique. "None of which means we shouldn't work together—or that we cannot continue to do so, when everything . . . as you put it . . . is open and aboveboard."

Kiper looked definitely relieved by that reassurance. But he couldn't resist adding, "What can be more important than earning a fortune? It's the well-deserved and honest payment for months of work—and a scientific procedure affording mankind a chance at a hundred more healthy years of life!"

"At the cost of many other lives," Cheryl Conrad said before Dominique could counter.

"Everybody who came to this damned town signed legal releases," Kiper retorted promptly, snipping off each word.

"*We* didn't," Clem Sparrow put in, bristling. He had continued to stand after Wes and Dominique rose, and looked, to Wes, near the outer limits of his customarily abundant patience. "Nobody told us nothin' or asked us to sign a fucking thing until we'd started being killed, and that statue was unveiled."

Kiper replied with alacrity. "But that is exactly why we wanted to have this meeting, to put all our cards on the table this evening and—"

"*Nor,*" Brick broke in, virtually quivering with indignation, "did Cliff Macy or Ocie Teagle, Lucia Mahorn or Purvis Richwine, have a chance to say yea or nay!"

"—or Angelane O'Brien, or Kenny Higgins," Cheryl added swiftly with a half glance in Wes's direction.

"Please, my friends, please." Dr. Dominique's laugh was short, ameliorating. "I've received no word about anything unpleasant happening to

Mr. Richwine. We thought he was a fine, bright, healthy young man."

"He phoned," Wes grunted pointedly. "From Walterville."

Very little about the gang of human beings thronging outside the Blackwood Apartment building would have looked, to a passerby with keen vision and alert intellect, remotely normal. Although they wore clothing, their garb was whatever they had chanced to wear at the moment a signal to march reached them. Some combinations of costume, given the behind-closed-doors idiosyncrasies of most women and men, were outlandish and others might have proved to be embarrassing to the people—

At another time when they understood, exactly, what they were doing.

This evening . . . *now* . . . they had almost no idea except when additional prearranged signals went off in their controlled minds and they moved as one, relentlessly, toward the next, the ensuing, massacre.

Stumbling over the corpse of their scout, Holroyd, before reaching the apartment building, no member of the mob had felt frightened, outraged, or disposed to disperse justice; neither justice nor vengeance had anything to do with their nocturnal plans.

They merely tore the undertaker's suicidal body to ribbons, just as they did the corpse of Harlan Rowe when they arrived at the entranceway to the Blackwood.

The sensible move, after all—if it was ever sensible to kill, particularly for no better reason than one had been told to do so—might well have been entering the building the same way Wes Teagle had: by climbing over the newspaperman's remains and shoving the front door open.

In common with all mobs, however, this one lacked all independent will and was obliged to shuffle its collective feet, wait the appointed period of time, then do what it had been programmed to do.

A mob is much more like a computer than any single man.

Unimpatient but physically restive, they twitched, jerked, lurched for several feet in one direction and then pivoted to return to the departure point, whispered brainless things, jostled one another, wriggled and sat down and jumped up, chuckled at nothing and coughed, caught in a convulsion of bovine group cooperativeness that might be the death of them yet.

But there was nothing bovine about what they'd been programmed to do, and it was certainly meant to be the death of Wes Teagle and the so far surviving employees of the Wesken Company.

The earth moved, time clicked . . . said *Now!*

And the mob reacted, parts of it fanning out toward the rear of the apartment building. Not one of them recalled what they'd already done to a town approximately the same size, and none of them would remember what they were scheduled to do tonight.

Cows don't keep files. Computers remember only what they're supposed to recall.

"I did everything in my power," Kiper said defensively, "to provide healthy food and drink right here—and keep people out of Walterville!"

"As for Stancel Holroyd's insane attack upon your Mr. Macy," purred Dominique, "I have also said I did not hire nor seek to influence him." The doctor shrugged his mountain-range shoulders. "Truthfully, I do not mourn Cliff Macy's passing—"

"What'd you say?" Clem asked angrily.

"—Any more than I grieve for our impetuous undertaker. Mr. Macy would have posed some difficult theological differences of opinion." He glanced straight at Cheryl. "As for lovely Ms. Mahorn, madam, I remember reading that the lady took her own life just as Holroyd did."

"That was bullshit," Cheryl blurted, cheeks aflame. "Lucia wouldn't have taken her life."

"Perhaps we will never know for certain," Dominique said. "Sorrowfully, we are left with the coroner's death certificate, which officially reported suicide as the cause of her demise. As for your father, sir," the doctor told Wes, "he was old by most standards. Unwell, too, as you know."

"Doc," Wes said, "I saw his face. I really believe he was probably scared to death. By what he saw." He spoke as if reading from some official and detached form; without accusation. Yet he had to add, almost under his breath, "By that half make-believe gee-dee bird you dreamed up." Dominique's gaze was upon him and he worked to keep his voice level, unargumentative, devoid of aggressiveness. Yet he could not quite restrain an expression of sad, muted outrage. "That feathered thing from hell, or somewhere, killed a father I was finally beginning t'know after all these years."

"If your belief is accurate," the doctor said softly, somehow succeeding in creating doubt even while he seemed sincerely to project his personal regrets, "it is a pity." The solemn eyes sought out the scientist, and perhaps a scapegoat. "Can you explain that incident,

Albert? For that matter, would you wish to expound upon your prior comment—that Kiper Research's inquiries might 'afford' mankind the chance to live another hundred years?" His expression was subtly sarcastic. "I've always thought the operative word in your comments about our work was 'afford.' Given the money you hope to make, it might be a trifle broad . . . or generous."

He had never been part of the crowd, any crowd, even if he'd sometimes said he was, even if he'd been lonely much of his life—right up to the times when he had formed the two really meaningful relationships of that life.

He understood dimly but well enough that one of those vital relationships was severed, now, forever and, by the time he had boogied downtown and begun dancing jerkily from building to deserted building, Kenny understood that the other relationship was also at an end. Even if Wes, unlike Angelane, remained alive.

Because nobody formed relationships of meaning with a corpse, or kept them, and Kenny had a solid if difficult grasp on that, too, by now. The fact that he was a dead man who ought to be lying down somewhere, becoming nothing.

That wasn't the hardest thing he'd ever done because he'd done *that* at the instant he had accepted the fact that Angelane was never going to move, never sit up or walk or speak to or make love with him, ever again.

So he had one sort of unrequited love going, and now Kenny was going to opt for another: showing Wes he'd loved him and continued to do so, after his own new fashion, by protecting the little four-eyed *nebesh* and trying like hell to prevent Wes from joining him in zombieville.

At some plunging depth of Kenny's scarcely functioning mind, next to his fettered soul, he was happily if vaguely aware that keeping Wes from death was really one terrific thing to do.

The problem was how to protect his ol' mate, how to prevent him from being killed, too, and in trying to decide his own next step—a process intellectually not unlike sifting through an outhouse crapper filled with shit for a marble fallen from one's boyhood blue jeans. A potential solution occurred to Kenny suitably enough when, slipping around the mob of merely part-time zombies, he'd inadvertently tuned-in to the intentions of the man who revivified him: Dr. Dominique. Not much of it was clear, in Kenny's condition, but he had picked up the intelligence that everything was scheduled to come to a head in the Stillwind Valley town square.

So he'd arrived early, bobbing and jittering, foxtrotting and schottisching around behind trees and bushes in the park at the center of the town square, unaware of how grotesque or amusing his paroxysms could have appeared to a living man, aware at last of *why* he had to keep dancing—

And what would happen to him if, in some wonderful way, he could just *stop.*

. . . Kenny gazed for the first time at the ancient wooden statue. He didn't know that its wheels were usually removed or that it was sometimes towed in a mammoth wagon. He didn't know it was a focal point of bizarre faith, a god, or capable of inflicting hideous death on people.

He didn't know it even when the Jagannath's immobilized wooden eyes gazed back at Kenny Higgins . . .

Kiper opened his mouth as if he might speak

up, offer a true, complete statement. He thought better of it, settled for shaking his head.

"I have one additional question for you, Albert," Dominique pursued him. "You asked me what could conceivably be more important than a fortune, lots of good American money . . . and a long, healthy life?"

"I guess I did," Kiper said curtly.

"Well, *tell* him the answer, Mr. Teagle." Akeem stared directly at Wes. But instead of being challenging, he'd turned warm and welcoming again. Wes realized this was a test. "I believe you know the answer in your heart, your soul, your veins, Mr. Teagle—because you are all down-to-earth businessmen."

"Businesspeople." Cheryl spoke automatically, then blushed.

"Of course!" The giant bowed, gallantly, rephrased his remark. "I believe that *each* of you phone people knows the answer to Professor Kiper's question." A furry brow shot up. "Well, sir? Your reply?"

Wes sighed, glowered at his feet instead of at Dominique. For the first time in his life he despised mind games. His answer, however, might well buy them additional time, even get the doctor on their side. "Power," he said, shortly. "And influence. See, Albert, if y'got enough of them, you don't need dough." He fought to control a burgeoning feeling that he'd walked straight into an asylum for the criminally brilliant and was finally outmatched in using the spoken word to get his way, because reason appeared to have fled and appeals to human nature might be impossible in coping with these two men. But that wasn't the sum total of their peril because he'd detected sounds from the back of the building and was ready to swear the mob outside was, at least in part, the mob inside. That meant time was running out if they hoped to make it to the company car he'd left out front. He directed a humorless grin in Akeem Dominique's direction. "With enough power, Albert, you already have everything there is t'spend money on. How'm I doin', Doc?"

"Splendidly." Dropping his tree-trunk arms to his sides, Dominique at last peered toward the phone room door, unhurriedly; steps, even whispers, were audible now. Distant, disorganized but there. Wes wondered what the hell was taking them so long. The doctor tugged down his snowy white vest and spoke somewhat more hastily: "About Walterville and the ley lines of *Ch'i* shifting around the world," he said. "To establish harmony with them required a considerable outpouring of love, esteem—even reverence. Which is why I donated the Jagannath, erected it in the town square."

"I still don't follow you." Cheryl, standing now, slipped her hand into Wes's.

"He wouldn't have followed but your Mr. Macy *would* have understood," Dominique replied. "Ours has become an age of figureheads, you see. The Holy Roman Catholic Church saw it coming centuries ago and commissioned paintings and statues of their own portals to a better life. Most hypothetically civilized persons are no longer capable of developing the requisite faith for effective prayer; I suspect Macy's Christ may have existed because the ostensibly civilized people of two thousand years ago already lacked a visible and manifest focal point for their prayers." He sighed regretfully. "Ah, even the Almighty may have been too grand, too deficient in recognizable human characteristics, for limited but . . . civilized intellects."

"There were lots of reasons for Jesus to come, damn you," said Clem.

Dominique did not appear to hear. "I wished to try to inform and inspire, teach the well-educated residents of Stillwind Valley about complex truths"—he threw up his arms in a gesture of grandiose and charming helplessness—"but they did not possess the capacity for faith of my own, plain people. Yet I saw, at once, that combining a donation of high intrinsic value, my unique persona, and a selfish, *demonstrably* functioning belief system was the single, sensible step." Unexpectedly, he turned up his handsome face and laughed in theirs, in heaven's. "My concept was unbeatable! A results-oriented cult based on a science that supported it, the supernatural, and their own self-interest—all with numerous 'mystical' facts withheld, of course!"

"Are you saying," Kiper asked, ashen at the possibility, "that you withheld information from me, too?"

"Of *course* I am!" the doctor chortled. "Just as you withheld information from me, and we both withheld it from everyone else. It's *modern times*, Albert—we're all *civilized* here!"

Probably Mary Barbara would never understand or forgive what he had done to her that evening, but that was all right with Dean Stamper.

Because *he'd* enjoyed it enormously—the first decent sex he'd had in twenty years, if the adjective wasn't too, too much—and it had been for the amazon's own good.

It occurred to Stamper with such impact that he raised his stonelike brown eyes from their gaze on Mary Barbara's naked big body and perceived that he'd always thought that, after seducing a woman.

This time, however, this *one* time, it really had been for the woman's good as much as his own self-gratification; because mobs were volatile, unpredictable, like chemistry . . . like women . . . and if he hadn't elected to switch the pill she usually took for the pill he'd wanted her to take, Mary Barbara Bomwell would have been out there killing with the rest of them—

And when you added the clear intention of taking human lives to the risky business of trying to fit oneself into a mob, nearly anything could happen.

To the biochemist's surprise, he discovered something new on one cheek—his own cheek—and realized with pure amazement that it was a tear. A sentimental *tear!* Good God, how long had it been since anything like *that* happened?

"Answer," Dean Stamper's unconscious mind replied, accompanying its response with a flash on an internal computer screen: "Never!"

Shocked and dismayed but increasingly pleased, Stamper climbed off Mary Barbara and the bed, slipped his bare feet into a pair of comfortable old slippers, and padded his way into the front room of his flat. "I," he whispered, crossing to the drawn curtains and pulling them back to peer out, "I am in love."

He waited for cannons to go off and banners to wave but nothing much happened.

Except, that is to say, in Stamper's brain.

Along with another bright flash of realization that was very much unlike its predecessor and came from a part of his mind that wasn't remotely computerlike. The realization that he'd spared Mary Barbara from participation in the mob—*Despite the sex, I behaved in an exemplary, almost paternal fashion—how could I be expected to know she was technically a virgin?*—but that *he* was fully expected to join it, consciously, when it reached his flat. Merge with, accompany them, do whatever Albert and the good doctor told him to do.

Head slumped over his own sagging chest and stomach, Stamper stared bleakly out of his window and tried to figure out his options. One of them was returning to the bedroom and doing it to Mary Barbara one more time before she came to, but that didn't exactly harmonize with his romantic mood; later, perhaps.

And another option scared him half silly, just considering it.

It was so hard to be a good team player, a leader, a pillar of the community, and possess the heart of a boy.

"Remember any authority figure you wish, Albert—a father or grandfather . . . a minister, perhaps, from your boyhood . . . a professor at university. Each of them attempts to retain the keys to the kingdom, and saves the inmost key for himself! We dare not relinquish that final, precious scrap of information until the end of our own game!" His mood shifted, became conciliatory, earnest. "I did tell you, Albert, that my statue, the 'lord of the universe,' offered a locked door through which waited all that a man could ask. You chose to believe in those articles of faith to which you've always given your allegiance—money and health." His voice fell to a whisper. "But there was much *more.*"

Kiper's attention was his, totally. "How can that be? *Why* should that be?"

"The *Ch'i*, dear fellow!" Dominique raised one brow. "The energy pool has been relocated, directly *beneath* the statue!"

"I've served the Jagannath, Akeem," said Kiper, starting to sweat. "You know I have!"

"Not *sufficiently,*" Dominique replied. "Why, man, when it was paraded through the ancient town of Puri, in India, there were uncountable thousands of Hindu believers who hurled themselves beneath its wheels voluntarily, to be crushed—either because they were asked to or because they wished to do so! *That* is a faith, gentlemen, lady. *That* is a belief system—and it is one which rewards the customary sacrifices of human blood and human life in ineffably more enriching, fulfilling ways than the mere extension of good physical health and common human existence. But to function fully with modern science and with ley lines, it demanded not only respect, reverence, love and bloody sacrifice—it required violent death. Lives taken, *not* offered. Other *varieties* of sacrifice, as well."

"What was your great sacrifice?" Albert Kiper asked, sardonically.

"My manhood!" Dominique retorted immediately. He smiled. "I was voluntarily castrated, decades ago."

"My God, you're crazy!" Brick gasped.

"No, I am a genius," Akeem smiled. "Because I know people, I know myself, and I have perfect faith in magick . . . which I know—perfectly." His eyes were like lumps of identical, burning coal and the uncanny intelligence Wes and the others saw in them smouldered along with the resentment of abuse and maltreatment, the lack of forgiveness, and a warped, lopsided lust to stand head and shoulders above others in ways much more important than height. "I wish to share in, and become a part of, the power of the ages," Dominique rumbled. "Of *all* ages."

Cheryl, shocked but single-minded, said, "You did know, then, what was going to happen to Walterville?" A realization that men of genius and faith were capable of using evil but calling it by other names was new to her.

Dominique nodded his head, nothing more.

"But I had nothing to do with it!" declared Albert Kiper, on his feet. "I didn't personally kill anybody, order anybody's death!"

"Yet you enabled it all to occur," Dominique said, glancing toward his partner. "Worse, Albert, *you* did not care. I did. *You* did not give a damn." He walked slowly toward the door of the rec room. "I gave *many* damns." His voice was pitched at a whisper level and each of them heard him. "I had wanted to spare at least some persons in Walterville their involuntary sacrifice. But my friends, the complement of love and death . . . it may be the oldest union of them all—and the hardest to choose between, or identify."

At the door, even with the mob stumbling its way toward them, Dominique paused to look back at them in turn. "Time was, I desired to heal the halt, the lame. I am a physician. From such worthy motives, according to convention—with an informed brain and devoted effort—a person may secure prominence; leadership; self-respect." The doctor was wistful; unforgettably regretful. "You and others like you taught me I was wrong, Albert, and I shall return that dubious favor today. When those who throng these halls arrive—*eventually*—at the town square, the life energies they have absorbed will be deposited—will merge with the *Ch'i* that flows beneath the site. You shall have everything you have sought.

"So shall I, at great cost," he continued, rolling his head until his strange but sensitive eyes could locate Wes. "What, then, of you and your friends, Mr. Teagle?" The accentless voice sounded weary and apologetic, but his threat was not otherwise clarified, or vitiated. "After the juggernaut has revived the Jagannath's glory, and mine, will you have what you wish? Are you to enjoy longevity . . . and freedom?"

Heart pounding wildly, Wes, for one flash, did not know how to reply.

Then he did. "We don't do things like that here," he said quietly, and squeezed Cheryl's hand. "Meaning a decision like that is not mine to make; not alone." Wes glanced questioningly past Cheryl at Darrell Brickowski, Clemon Sparrow, then back into Cheryl's adored face. "How do you vote, Wesken Company?"

With a noise midway between a furious growl and a wail of terror, Clem dove past Wes—at waist level—and hit Dominique with a perfect flying tackle.

28

Wes simply stared, motionless, at the frozen tableau—Clemon Sparrow stabbed into the midsection of the giant, Dominique, like an arrow. A part of Wes's helpless astonishment was based upon the sudden introduction of sharp, actual physical violence. Men were always growling, "I'm gonna kill your ass" or "Watchit, sucker, you're gonna get it" and muttering an assortment of other threats that generally came to nothing; it'd often reminded the more intellectual Wes of two pet dogs stiff-leggedly circling one another and wondering when their masters would separate them. One glimpse of somebody who was on drugs and losing it, of televised men-at-war or highly skilled prize fighters battling with the blood dripping down the lines of their jaws, tended to make it clear that direct, frontal violence—unlike cowardly sneak attacks on old ladies and unprotected store owners—required a very different sort of courage, another kind of mind-set entirely.

And fights to the death happened on midnight

streets, or at somebody else's place—not in a business office or middle-class apartment building. There was an unwritten law about things such as that.

But Clem had understandably been spoiling to get at Akeem Dominique for days, weeks; that was crystal clear to Wes now, belatedly. His friend's bold, brave dive at the much larger man should've been expected.

What wasn't predictable at all was the way Clem seemed, for a suspenseful and awful instant, to be literally stuck against the doctor—stuck *in* him—a harpoon plunged into the vast belly of a great whale, an unvanquishable two-legged Moby Dick. Wes merely gawked at them with Cheryl wringing his hand. Nothing, it seemed for a timeless moment, had happened or would happen.

Then Akeem Dominique began going over backward, slowly but steadily, like an old skyscraper coming down in time-lapse photography; the balance he'd striven to retain with his extraordinary concentrative powers lost . . . and both men went sprawling to the phone room floor with a sickening, awesome thud. Tackled at exactly the second when he hadn't expected it—and Wes doubted the doctor had ever imagined such rude handling as this lay within the realm of possibility—the gigantic Akeem had landed on his back and was vulnerable to punches that Clem Sparrow rained on his unguarded face and stomach as if a storm had burst above Dominique, and beached him.

Shouting as if an inner dam had burst and he was releasing the frustrations of a lifetime, Darrell Brickowski sped past Wes and Cheryl and, before Albert Kiper could do more than raise a mildly protesting palm, struck the little scientist with his own good hand. Amazingly, Kiper took the punch without going down, without even flinching; more surprisingly, he pawed out with his own fist, awkwardly swinging his arm—and Brick, ducking beneath the blow as if he did this kind of thing all the time, slammed the elbow of his bad arm against the point of Albert's chin.

—The phone room door creaked, swung open, almost as if it hadn't been touched. A powerful scent of *perfumery* pervaded the doorway, and Cheryl, smelling it first, yanked at Wes, turned him around.

Prichard Arnt, the oily, grinning operator of the video store that had rented Kenny Higgins the "movie" that in many ways had begun all this, had become the first member of the mob to reach the phone room.

But it was a new, a different Arnt, Wes realized at once. The phony smile of welcoming amiability had been replaced by a vacuous idiot's smirk containing only a detached fascination for killing, and following orders; the Pierre Cardin that Arnt wore had odiously merged with a stink that reminded Wes of flop sweat.

So Wes threw the first punch he could remember throwing since his boyhood, putting everything into it he had. It was a Supermanish, comic book blow any amateur boxer would have slipped, easily; but Prichard Arnt was a man momentarily possessed, not an athlete. The punch landed, he sagged to the floor as if the air had fled from a balloon, and Wes ventured a quick, cautious glance down the corridor outside the phone room.

He had just enough time to see that the way was clear to the front of the building—the mob had been directed to try a surprise invasion of the place, from the rear parking lot—and to recognize the druggist, Noxie Coomer, and the nameless, omnipresent jogger.

Then Cheryl was again yanking his arm. "Come *on!*" she hissed in his ear, tugging him after her.

Bewildered by what he had seen and what he himself had just done, Wes merely nodded, mentally, then allowed himself to be half-dragged, half-propelled down the hallway toward the entranceway. He glanced around, hearing mumbled shouts, unintelligible curses and taunts; rushing from the rear entrance, the juggernaut was following them, but stumblingly awkwardly, like the undead in an old Romero movie.

"Clem," Wes gasped as they reached the front door. Pieces of Harlan Rowe were strewn there like bones tossed out of a Kentucky Fried Chicken container. "And Brick . . . dammit, Cheryl, we—"

"Come *on*—get in the *car*!" she told him, giving him a shove that drove him toward the curb. "Wes, you *must!*"

The anguish of ambivalence washed over him where he stood on the lane, midway between the Blackwood and the old Caddy, anguish, and the abrupt, disappointing awareness that Cheryl Conrad wanted him to get them away from there—that the tall, athletic blonde he'd fallen in love with so suddenly, so recently, was terrified for herself.

But she was a woman, Clem and Brick were men, she was within her rights to expect this of him and, pierced by disillusionment and a reality he did not with to confront—yet another obtrusive fact—he nodded and jumped into the Caddy's driver's seat while Cheryl hurriedly climbed in on the passenger's side, locking the door after her.

Wes turned the key in the ignition, then listened as the old engine groaned and refused to function. *My God,* he thought, catching out of the corner of one eye a glimpse of the tireless, silent jogger and the others flooding from the front door of the apartment building. It was night now, some of the day's heavy humidity had let up, and Wes was drenched with sweat, awash in terror. The juggernaut had discovered them and was lumbering toward the car, down the walkway, gibbering like idiots. He turned the key and slammed down on the accelerator. Nothing.

"Wes," Cheryl whispered, choked the word out, seeing the two Tedricks starting to drool as they canted toward the Caddy like crazymen who thought they were climbing a hill; and Wes tried it again, turned, stomped—

And the motor groaned, turned over, smoothed out.

And the younger, Indiana All-Star Tedrick—what remained of him—smashed his clenched fist against Cheryl's window. She saw the jagged crack take shape like a lightning bolt, sensed the glass start to cave in, toward her, like yielding human skin, observed a ball of blood like a tropical sun rising and realized it as the teenager's wrecked fist—*his shooting hand,* something inside Cheryl wailed in sympathy. She saw the bloody sun begin to rise again, shrunk toward Wes because she knew it would go through this time and that force behind poor Jay-Jay's control would cause the ruined fingers to open and close, one last time, on a shoulder, a breast—

Then the company car was shooting away from

the curb like Fourth of July sky rockets—

And Wes, incredibly, was slamming on the brakes mere yards from the mindless mob, leaving the motor running but turning toward her, more incredibly pressing his left hand against the door release on the driver's side, preparing to *get out* . . .

"I can't, honey," Wes said in that earnest damned boyish way of his, "I just can't!"

"You can't *what*?" she demanded, turning her head and staring out the rear window, seeing the denizens of Stillwind Valley sweeping down upon them like a Hoosier tornado.

"I *can't* just go to Indi'nap'lis and leave the boys behind," Wes said, pleading with her. "Kenny and me, we got 'em into this gee-dee nightmare. I got to *help*!"

Cheryl's nails dug into his shoulders, clung to them when he muttered something about her taking the wheel and began to open the door. "*Listen* to me, damn you, Wes Teagle," she shouted, hanging on with all her might. "*Not Indy!* I don't want to abandon Clem and Brick, I'm not trying to *escape!* I want you to *go to the town square!*"

"What?" He glanced back, startled.

"We can't leave this place like it is," Cheryl said. Now he saw how calm, how cool, she was. The woman sitting beside him was the fine athlete who might have played pro, who sank clutch free throws, took timely, last-second shots with crowds of people only marginally different than that which pursued them screaming for her to miss, to fail. "You and I can't handle all those looney-tunes and neither can Clem or Brick." She squeezed his forearm, told him with her eyes what he knew was surely the truth about their friends, except he hadn't had the guts to face it. "But we can't let the doctor and Kiper win without a fight—without doing *something* before they can get to the Jagannath."

"Well, what?" he asked again, racing the motor with one foot, keeping it going.

Cheryl saw how close the mob was, then faced the street before them, tuned the opposition out. "I'm not certain it will work," she said quietly, sounding nearly relaxed. "But I have an idea." She turned her face, brightly, to Wes. "You wanta get this ol' boat goin', pal?" she inquired.

"Well . . . why not?" Wes retorted. All but gaily, he squeezed her thigh above a bare knee, dropped the transmission into drive, hit the accelerator and laughed. The worn Caddy tires squealed in the dumb faces of the approaching mob. "Shee-it, Cheryl—let's give 'er a try!"

I don't like doing this, I don't like it, don't like it, at all, Brick swore to his unconscious mind, banging Kiper's head again, against the leg of the closest Wesken Company desk. He had long since lost his presence of mind, his glasses, his long-standing reluctance even to attempt using his bad hand, the fingers of which were locked tightly—along with those of Brick's other hand—round Albert Kiper's neck. He knew, dimly, that he was crying like a baby, that tears were streaming down his cheeks and he'd partly peed himself, and was pretty sure Albert was already dead. *I don't,* Brick thought, *I—*

He rose gradually toward the ceiling of the phone room as if he had been levitated; he watched what began to happen to him, and around him, with a peculiar disaffection that was almost like reading the daily newspaper as his grip on the scientist's throat was broken and he saw that it was a huge black mountain that was lifting him away from gravity and thrusting him overhead as if he were a child. He perceived with detachment that the moveable cliff was Dr. A. Dominique, that his handsome face wasn't handsome any more but badly bloodied; it looked as if some determined and intrepid climber had striven to scale the mountain and repeatedly gouged it with pitons and spikes. He couldn't even have been sure it was Dr. Dominique except that he didn't know any other black man—white, either, now that he realized it—who was so goddamn fucking big.

At just about shoulder level of the solemn, silent, blood-pouring good doctor, Brick also perceived that the black man he had worked with was on his hands and knees by the window. Actually, Brick saw, still floating upward from the floor, Clem Sparrow had one knee and one hand on the floor and the others were coming out of his body at different angles than before. The rather broad back was to Brick—and Dominique—and much of the face, which was motionless but otherwise unmarked, was also facing Brick and the mountain. He noticed tiny white objects that he took for a moment as small pencils; the sort golfers kept score with. Several of them lay on the floor at a point that would have been beneath's Clem's chin, if Clem's chin wasn't forced around in their direction. They weren't pencils, though. They were pieces of bone that had broken off and fallen away when ol' Clem's scrapping body had been twisted into its horrible new arrangement. They'd just popped off, like popcorn in a hot pan.

Jesus! Brick thought, colliding against the ceiling for the first time. It jarred the hell out of him, brought him to a complete awareness of what was occurring . . . and he knew that was why he hadn't struck the ceiling harder than he had when he peered down into Akeem Dominique's swollen eyes. One was already closed, reminding Brick that the man was human, propelling him to action—to a passionate, energetic squirming meant to free him from the mountain's grasp.

He didn't budge a fraction of an inch, didn't loosen the doctor's hold at any point of his body. "Awww, *Jesus!*" Brick said aloud.

Now that I have your attention, said the mountain's mind, almost smilingly, with enormous clarity, in Darrell Brickowski's mind. . .

The powerful arms supporting him as if he'd been an infant tensed, then drove him at the ceiling full force, evenly, making sure the resultant pain was proportionately spread from head to toe.

"Oh, Jesus . . . ?" gasped Brick, turning it to prayer.

And his next overhead body slam against the ceiling shattered most of the bones he had.

And the last slam fractured the rest of them.

Falling sensation, almost like drifting, leafy and free, a fleeting interruption of the exquisite consuming avaricious agony—

And nothing much, really, at the point of landing impact, apart from the initial stages of agonized dying.

. . . The last thing Brick saw, before he was gone, was the last thing Ocie Teagle had seen.

It went through the Wesken Company window as if the window hadn't been there, and didn't even break the glass before it was gone, too.

But not as permanently.

It got darker at just about the time Wes whipped around a corner and aimed the Caddy toward the town square. A light might have been switched, power thrown off, somewhere. Wes hadn't turned on the car lights until then and, when he did, it was like watching something soupy drip down the insides of a clotted saucepan.

"You think he knows?" Wes wondered aloud.

Cheryl didn't answer at once. She was thinking. "I think he knows just about everything there is to know," she said finally, "except what folks like us are made of."

He nodded, drove silently for a few moments. Then he opened his mouth as if to speak.

"What?" Cheryl asked, seeing him through the darkness of the Cadillac interior.

"Nothin'." He saw something a block ahead of the car, and it was moving.

"What is it?" she insisted, fumbling for his right hand.

"I was goin' t'ask you if you thought Clem and Brick were dead yet," Wes answered her, hoarsely.

Then the straining car lights were on the *something* he had seen and Wes's buttocks raised part way from the driver's seat as he craned his neck to be sure his vision wasn't playing tricks with him.

Purvis Richwine, waving casually, stood in the middle of the street. He had a tight little familiar smile.

Wes braked at once, hard, turned his head to stare back at his youngest salesperson, felt the company car draaaaagggg to a shuddering stop, catercornered in the road. Purvis had whirled, was jogging after them, still waving, still smiling.

And he ran effortlessly, noiselessly, his feet barely touching the street. "*Yo, Wes,*" called Purvis's voice, and Wes put it on instant replay, thinking fast and knowing even before he'd looked at Cheryl that he'd heard it only in his mind. *Yo, Wes,* called the voice, while the smiling face got nearer, and bigger, and paler; *Yoooooo, Wesssssss,* like wind howling in cliffs above a deserted seashore; *YYyyyooooooo . . .*

"Sonsa*bitches!*" Wes swore, mad now, unnerved, sending the old Caddy forward. "I knew they'd never let him leave Walterville—I *knew* it!"

"Who, Wes?" Cheryl inquired, turning him cold; colder. "Why did you stop that time?" She put both hands on his forearm and his flesh goose-bumped, spasmed beneath her fond touch. "Honey, you're starting to frighten me."

His eyelids soared; he laughed his astonishment. "That's just one more thing that I would've thought was impossible!"

"Wes! *Stop!*" Cheryl cried, pointing. A whiteness grew at the edge of the road, rounded, took on detail. She stared at him, realizing he wasn't braking. "Stop, Wes—*it's Lucia!*"

He swiveled his gaze to the right but did not move his head.

There, picked up by the flickering car lights, it was—or seemed to be—Lucia Mahorn, just the way Cheryl had said. Of course. He almost laughed. Lovely, naked for him, looking utterly desirable and healthy except where her own car had run over her neck and killed her; they'd been too gee-dee logical about that! That, and the fact that he and Cheryl had both been to the funeral of the woman with the forlorn expression, gorgeous body, and broken neck, but Dominique hadn't known that.

So Wes trod on the accelerator and watched the shade of Lucia turn sadly to him and then, in the rearview mirror, to melting uremic shadow.

And he tuned Cheryl out, left her to figure out what had just happened and concentrated ardently on blanking his own brain out except for a razor-sharp focus on the town square and whatever idea Cheryl had concocted to *stop* this awful insanity. A few seconds later he heard her whimper, and sigh, and knew Cheryl had understood why he'd kept going; he sensed her heart ache and begin to pound with a mixture of fury and terror, the way his was . . .

And when both of them saw ole Ocie Teagle himself in the center of the road with a display case in one hand and his thumb lifted to them, as if good-humoredly pretending to be hitching a ride, Wes got the company car up to almost sixty, shut his eyes tight, and drove *through* his father as if he wasn't there.

Which he wasn't.

*"Sons*abitches," Wes mumbled, tears in his eyes turning hot—"Sonsa*bitches!"*

As if Akeem Dominique or Albert Kiper hadn't liked being called names, the old Caddy died. Like that; just like that. Only blocks from the town square, now, but dead as either a doornail or any of the Wesken phone people the sons of bitches had seen fit to sacrifice. He tried, twice, to start the car, then acknowledged its passing, threw his door wide, and jumped out into the darkness of Stillwind Valley. "That's it," he groaned, hands on hips and taking a few steps before pausing, kicking at pieces of concrete. "Want to just lie down here and wait for them t'catch up, or d'you prefer to jog back up the road and *meet* 'em?"

She slammed her door closed behind her, marched toward him . . . blond and fair and, in all senses of the word, enlightening. She snapped, "Unlock the trunk."

"Huh?"

Cheryl took out her fright and frustrations on the rear end of the Wesken Company car with the point of one shoe. The heel was already gone, anyway. "Just unlock the trunk, Weston!"

He did as he was told, shaking his head, muttering, "I don't want t'hide in any damn trunk!"

"We aren't going to hide anywhere," Cheryl promised him, softly, leaning past Wes to grope inside the darkness.

Before she came out again, Wes heard the sounds of the juggernaut, knew for a fact that the apparitions they'd seen would have proved incapable of harming them and that they'd been sent by Akeem Dominique or Albert Kiper merely to detain them.

. . . To enable the mindless, other-disciplined, greedy townspeople to begin catching up. Waves of rock music got Chery's attention, too.

"C'mon!" she whispered urgently, and was off down the street in the direction of the square—and the Jagannath—with whatever she'd wanted to get from the trunk in her arms.

Wes paused, trying to comprehend her mercurial chain of thought. Then he rushed back to the car, on her side, opened the door and lugged the weighty Eveready flashlight out of the glove compartment. Immediately, turning, he stumbled over something in the weedy blackness at the side of the road and almost fell. Spooked, he jabbed the flashlight beam at it fast, holding his breath.

Cheryl had slipped out of both shoes—good and bad—before tearing off, bravely barefoot, down the darkened sidewalk.

Hoosier hoop stars, Wes reflected, were by far the best. "I ever tell ya about seein' Steve Alford when he was a high-school junior?" He yelled it, but not too loudly. He was grinning as he pounded after Cheryl. "I'd sure like t'see you and ol' Steve shoot a round of horse."

Her darting figure was almost indiscernible, but her cocky tones returned to him, clear as a bell. "*He* wouldn't," she answered.

He went on smiling until he'd sprinted harder than he had in years just to catch up; then the ordeal of keeping pace began. "Y'want t'tell me now what your idea is?"

"Not really," she said shortly. A flash of white teeth, another withering but good-humored aside. "You'll find it easier to keep up if you don't talk so much."

Wes thought about that. He was silent while they were forced off the sidewalk by tree branches that surely predated the Boggs' family's residence in Stillwind Valley. Then, he gasped: "Why doncha want t'tell me your plan yet?"

She offered him a swift, scant glance. "Because I'm not sure it's worth diddily," she replied candidly. They ran, side by side, temporarily out-distancing the crashing rock noises, without comment. Two blocks, then a third, melted into the deepening night. "Even if you don't know what the idea is," she said, "you got any better ones? —'Cause we're nearly there and this is no time to be bashful!"

Sparked by affection, he almost threw out an arm for a last hug but realized it would probably make him pitch forward on his face. "Nope." Wes was breathing hard now. A shrug and a helpless grin. "Not really. Ain't that somethin'?"

But as they reached an intersection and spurted to the other side, they passed beneath a streetlight and Wes saw that what she'd taken from the Caddy trunk was his two-gallon drum of emergency gasoline.

Then Cheryl remembered a shortcut and, in the lead, she led Wes across the side street. Decades in the past, apparently, a couple of buildings from the turn of the century had been torn down; nothing had ever been erected to replace them, and the abbreviated stretch of pavement was deserted tonight—just as Cheryl had hoped. Empty lots, though, were overgrown with weeds that rustled like slim sentinels as they raced past, and their staccato heartbeats seemed accentuated. Wes felt he was sprinting among the shadows of a long dead planet, destined at any instant to topple off the edge and drift forever among the stars, hand in hand.

When they'd covered the width of the side street and emerged just twelve or fifteen yards south of the town square Wes and Cheryl found they were actually beyond the site of the small park and were able to approach it along a natural lane created by two sparse rows of older, fully vacated structures. Had anything living lurked ahead of them, they'd have seen it coming and could have sped around, or into, one of the abandoned buildings.

Nothing was, however. Nothing they could see, at any rate.

Cheryl slowed to a quick walk, grasped Wes's hand firmly. "C'mon," she said once more. "I want to see that thing in the park, up close."

"Okay," Wes replied agreeably, dutifully trailing after her. "But if you've seen one Jagannath, folks say, you've seen 'em all!"

The two-gallon can rattling against one leg, Cheryl hurried around the foundation on which the statue stood. "I'm sure you already figured out part of my notion," she remarked, stopping and putting the drum down at her feet. "Before I explain the rest of it, I want to get a good look at something like this, with nobody doing a PR job."

"I don't follow you," he said. They faced the wooden statue together and he watched Cheryl begin to study the motionless, solemn face.

Her glance his way was sharp. "Men; you all have your damn icons. From religious objects to sales cases and banners, but women long for living things to care about; a home; genuine progress." She stared back up, trying to get her thoughts in words. "You're all so fast to sacrifice everything—yourselves, the women you love, little children . . . for signs, badges, scepters—*symbols*—a few acres of earth—and principles nobody even understands twenty-five years later!" She brushed back a slack, sweat-dampened lock of fair hair. "Why, Wes . . . why?"

He frowned, considered answering her with an easy quip but realized she needed more than that. And deep inside him a feeling he would have denied another night surfaced, and he did not wish to make light of it.

"Maybe guys don't believe in the same stuff." He gazed into the strange, unreadable features of the Jagannath. "Maybe we should but we can't. Maybe we know a plot of earth is what we'll wind up with, regardless, so we try t'make the stuff that happens before that time . . . special." He swallowed, went with the flow. "Crosses, flags, a machine or a sample case or the name of what we do best—we b'lieve in 'em because it's not human just t'accept a hole in the ground . . . and 'cause wives and kids change. We try a lot t'believe in stuff that won't."

Above the wooden icon, subtle yet distinct sounds—they were like blinds on a window, sharply released—disturbed the moment. Wes and Cheryl gasped, saw that the steeped shadows overhead were filling out, solidifying . . . hovering, then descending, gracefully.

The majestic night-bird came from a sky of nowhere to perch in dead silence upon the smooth, ball-like skull of the statue. Pure white wings seeming to blanket Stillwind Valley with snow closed like a blindfold over the statue's sightless eyes—

And the curvate, sinuously muscled form of the *bruxsa* landed on the raised platform like a lowered coffin, beside the Jagannath's anthropomorphic feet. Enshrouded by night shadow, the creature began straightening and, when finally it peered at Wes and Cheryl, Akeem Dominique stood where the night-bird had been; his smile possessed the unmistakable dignity of a hangman or electrocutioner.

"I knew," the doctor said, his handsome features as unmarked as the past or future, "I absolutely *knew* you were a believer at heart, Mr. Teagle."

It had drawn within blocks of the town square when the mob, the juggernaut, saw a man step aristocratically into the street before them and lift his hand.

"Stop! That's far enough."

It did not recognize him. It made no effort to do so.

"You know who I am," Dean K. Stamper said distinctly, most authoritatively. "You possess, each of you people, the ability to recover your wits, now—to perceive what is happening." For the first time, enunciating the last word, Stamper's voice and upraised palm wavered. His marbled eyes rolled from familiar face to face and he backed up; one pace. So hot, tonight, so humid, and he sensed his manner was not as commanding as it customarily was. "*Halt,*" he said, louder. "You may disperse, return to your homes or to the laboratory."

Then it recognized him, dimly, but did not care. It advanced.

"That's all for this evening," Stamper continued, shouting. Abruptly, not knowing he meant to do it, he danced two, three steps toward the sidewalk. He suspected then it was not going to stop or veer from him, and he wondered if perhaps he should fall into step with it, then if Mary Barbara Bomwell had awakened and was watching his commendable effort from the bedroom window. The latter possibility rendered the former unthinkable. "Right, that's it," he addressed the closest clump of marchers. He'd spoken as offhandedly as he was able yet edged further toward the curb. "I-It's all over, p-people."

But *it* was not people. So it advanced, and swerved, to be sure to include he who was supposed to be with them. It chased him back out in the street. It heard him speaking, again, but it had turned up the volume on its tape recorders, drowning out his imperious accents any way it could. It had its orders; they weren't going where they were going for him.

Again it followed him, up on the sidewalk and a yard, pursued him there awhile, drawing nearer all the while because he was not in full retreat and therefore wasn't running from *it* as much as circling, trying to curtail it. He'd have reminded it of a sheepdog, if it had still been *they*.

It caught up, eventually, with Dean K. Stamper.

Mary Barbara Bomwell wasn't watching from the window and didn't see, because his rapacious attack had killed her.

It marched over his body after it had knocked him down by simply walking ceaselessly straight ahead; it swept smartly in a complete circle and, lacking the precision of a Rose Bowl parade but not devotion to the parade route, marched over Dean Stamper until his body at last became an *it*, too.

Then it left *it* lying against a curb like old horse manure and proceeded, its steaming music rising into the sticky spring sky around Stillwind Valley like audible smoke until it blotted out the senses totally, and night itself.

"Where's old Albert?" Wes asked. He hoped he might create an inference that would elicit information about the others; Clem and Brick.

"Gone to glory ahead of us, alas," Dominique rumbled. "No longer obliged to forage for it." He included Cheryl in his mocking glance. He added, obliquely, "There will be many new faces in Heaven this night."

Distantly, borne to them on a slight breeze, heavy and clanging imitations of music groped their ears. Akeem was first to hear it, and while his full-lipped, curling smile was no different than before at a casual glance, it emitted the menace of a single-minded man who has seen his sole offer rejected and intends now to proceed to other business.

Cheryl sensed what was happening before Wes, throwing her arms out from her sides, seeking balance. He had braced himself for a direct physical attack, clutching his hefty flashlight in both hands and watching the doctor intently.

But the single movement Dominique made with his masssive body was folding his arms across his deep chest; then he nodded toward the ground before the platform. "I cannot bear moralists or fools, and I shall *not* suffer them." His thick-set neck straightened; his black eyes blazed. "Two additional units of life energy will not be wasted."

The rumble of Akeem Dominique's voice became the rumble of the planet under their feet. Cheryl, slipping, fell heavily to the ground; because Wes had grabbed for her hand, to steady her, he fell too.

Earthquake! he thought, and heard Cheryl groan with pain.

When he attempted to get to his knees and help, groped for Cheryl, he felt the earth ripple beneath him as if turning to ocean waves. Then, it buckled—puckered as if something in the earth wished to kiss him—and he toppled on his side, stunningly. There—at the same second Cheryl detected it—he saw the subsequent horror:

A *fissure*, growing. While each of them gaped at it from opposite sides, the jagged tear in the earth's crusty skin ran like horizontal blood; it covered inches in seconds, until it was too great a gulf for Wes to reach Cheryl with his outflung arm.

And with each word uttered by the doctor the fissure widened, and the ground tremored.

"I was prepared to share with all of you the incredible benefits, the progress for humankind, which I achieved by cooperating with that stultifying and doctrinate ass, Albert Kiper—by tolerating his blanket intolerance, his circumscribed imagination," the giant thundered. "But you were all myopic . . . stunted!"

Wes tried to rise, fell back. Behind him, he saw when he slipped, there was a blur of motion in the park. He wondered how far the quake extended, if the doctor meant to rip up the trees by their roots; if the bodies sleeping in the cemetery had turned over.

"Now you'll experience the variety of powers . . . the throbbing heart of Earth . . . learn at last to worship the one dynasty that endures: that of the faithful man's dominion over nature." Half turning, putting out his arms, Dominique embraced the ancient statue. Even then, while he did not yell, his voice might have poured out of the yawning fissures in the earth. "All the underlying forces are shifting, my friends. Marvel at them while yet you may!"

Up on one knee, wiggling his arms in his effort to rise and vault the dilating ravine to Cheryl's side, Wes glanced back at the doctor and at the wooden revenant. . . .

And what he saw was so shocking the sight almost thrust him back to the palpitating ground.

Staring directly at the head of the icon, Wes believed that it had *moved.*

Suddenly—as if deciding to consume him—the zigzagging earthen tear fanned out, made him somersault away to escape its hungry maw—

And from the copse of trees on his side of the crack a long shadow fell, the tall and slender familiar body of Kenny Higgens seemingly dragged forward by it. For an instant, a flash, he peered steadily at Wes, clearly recognized him. It was a peculiarly touching yet uncanny stare with undercurrents of poignant meaning, the stare of someone bewildered trapped in a bicameral existence on the boundary between fantasy and reality, heaven and hell—someone for whom belief itself no longer held significance or value.

Wes wasn't sure whether two of Kenny's fingers touched his sallow temple in his blithe salute of old, or if the oscillating *rolang* that advanced with no further pause toward the towering figures on the platform had merely wished to straighten a cap it had already lost for good.

But when Dr. Dominique caught a glimpse of the reedy being reeling his way, as if macabrely entranced by melody—grimly motivated to mock-frolic by the strains of music only it heard—he turned his concentration darkly upon Kenny—

And the earth ceased moving, the quake was over. At once, most of the gashes clotted, closed; two that were left could have been the result of terror, or momentarily misplaced faith.

Just then Cheryl heard more modern, electronic sounds and, hauling herself to her feet on sheer guts, she glanced wildly around for the two-gallon can. She'd dropped it when the vibrations began beneath their feet and the chance that its contents had already spilled had disturbed her more than the pain in her ankle and calf.

When she spotted and snatched it up Cheryl saw that the doctor had taken two steps away from the icon in order to confront—*My God—what's wrong with him?*—Kenny Higgins. Wes, nearest his old friend, was half hopping after him, so Cheryl, gritting her teeth, promptly veered in the direction of the Jagannath. She'd crept within a few yards of it when, despite its absence of wheels and the indisputable fact that it had never known life of a variety known to Cheryl Conrad—despite all reason except that invented or devised by Akeem Dominique—the Jagannath *spun* toward Kenny and Wes—

And took two ponderous *steps* in the wake of its protector and manipulator.

Wes's legs seemed to take root; each of them began to shake, and he kept from running only because of the way his girl—his woman—was courageously limping after the icon. It hadn't seen her, Wes thought, or didn't fear her. *BBbbrrtt*, and the damned thing was abreast of Dominique, but not yet to the platform's edge. *BBBrrrtttTT* and it was stepping off, drawing closer to the undulating Kenny Higgins—who cut, abruptly, toward the doctor. Then Cheryl was *right behind* the statue, lifting the two-gallon drum above her head—and, stretching as high up the thing as she could, splashing . . . *emptying* . . . the gasoline on its legs and feet.

"Honey," Wes shouted, then, starting forward in terror for her—*"Look out!"*

Just as the marching, living juggernaut paraded into the park at the midpoint of the town square Wes saw the enormous head of the Jagannath begin *turning* . . . creakingly, like chalk scratching a blackboard . . . on its titanic shoulders. With the threnodic deathsong of the self-damned as accompaniment, the carved eyelids cracked open for the first time in centuries, and it stared curiously down at Cheryl Conrad with wooden pupils imbedded in wooden sockets—the life energy of innumerable human sacrifices glittering from them like horrified guests at a holocaust.

When the moving monument began attempting to rip its arms free from its wooden sides with sounds like boulders falling from mountain cliffs Wes darted around Kenny as well as the freshly enthralled and admiring Dominique to assist Cheryl, fumbling in his shirt pocket as he ran. He had a glimpse of Kenny at the microsecond he reached the doctor, whose own head was turned in admiration to the lurching Jagannath—

And to see Kenny's floundering arms go round

the hips of the immense Dominique in a bizarre and desperate hug.

Then Wes was dropping to his knees at the feet of the revivified lord of the universe with his Djeep lighter cupped in his shaky palm. Biting his tongue, holding his breath, he had time to flick it once . . . saw it catch . . . watched the responsive flame—

As it licked the great icon's toes, humbly, and subtly initiated its destruction.

That moment was the first they'd heard the voice of the Jagannath, or suspected it had one. It might have been the shrill voice of the human past. Even the doctor, grappling with Kenny, was astonished, but that could have been a grimace of abject chagrin because of how the inhuman and strident sibilation ran the gamuts of outrage, agony, and the scale . . . how Akeem emphathized at first with the alternating shrieks and booms of anguish . . . or how he loathed the fact that the Jagannath's ferocious bellow of pain ended in a gurgling squeal of tintinnabulation, like fairies weeping.

After helping Cheryl away from the burning statue, Wes was amazed to see the flames ascending the length of the Jagannath as if elevated, skirting its exterior with vivid crimsons and yellow-oranges, then burning into the interior of the icon as if propelled, willfully boring to some invisible nucleus, or heart, in a fiery frenzy that seemed liberating.

Just at the point Cheryl perceived that the marchers had halted their advance to stare . . . realized that each of their musical machines had ceased functioning when the smouldering statue mooed its misery . . . she was horrified to see Kenny plunge forward with a rigid strength she had never imagined he possessed, his skinny arms stubbornly entwined around the enormous Dr. Dominique—

And she pressed her face against Wes Teagle's neck when both Kenny Higgins and Dominique crashed into the Jagannath's pillar of flames.

From the marchers—the temporary residents of Stillwind Valley—a single, collected gasp rose to the skies along with a billowy burst of smoke. Cheryl opened her eyes and stared at them, wonderingly. Each young man, each young woman, somehow appeared to change; for another instant she could not detect the difference, the nature of the change, except that they were beginning to look more normal, more like people Cheryl had known, and the cunning and malice were leaving their faces in exchange for the sort of bewilderment Kenny Higgins had shown in his own.

Then she *did* comprehend what was happening to them when the jogger they had noticed on their first day in town, clad as always in his athletic uniform, shivered as if he'd become cold, and stopped jogging. As Cheryl stared at him, his legs turned pale, spare; older. Realizing she was looking at him, the man blinked at her in confusion yet managed a tentative expression of curiosity, and welcome.

Wes, however, had continued to face forward despite the tears coursing down his cheeks. Maybe he was the only one of them to see it that way, but he had the impression, somehow, that he was watching a single, inanimate object smoke, and burn, that two had been one all along and that, at the end, there certainly hadn't been three. Many things surprised or perplexed him at that point, none of them terrifying now, only a couple enough that he'd be able to discuss them, later, with Cheryl. The central things were that he was looking with tears in his eyes at an old, smouldering stake that possessed no sign of life . . . and that somebody he'd liked, very much, was on his way to a new and better existence.

"G'd'y, mate," Wes said aloud, softly, holding tight to the rest of his own life. "I know Angelane's waitin'. Y'can't talk me out of it."

Then he turned to face the mob, the juggernaut, and found that he and the too-tall blonde he'd come to love were alone in the park . . . the last of the townsfolk and possibly the only permanent residents of Stillwind Valley.

"We can never completely immerse ourselves in the crowd because we *do* have an internal point of view and can never really escape it through ideological reductions that leave out the personal . . ."

—Katherine Ramsland, Ph.D.
The Psychology of Horror and Fantasy